Enjoy the journey.

Treachery

Book 3 in The Orphan Train Saga

Written by Sherry A. Burton

Treachery, The Orphan Train Saga Book 3 © Copyright 2019

by Sherry A. Burton

ISBN: 978-1-951386-03-0

Published by Dorry Press

Edited and Formatted by BZHercules.com

Cover by Laura J. Prevost
www.laurajprevostbookcovers.myportfolio.com

For more information on the author and her works, please see www.SherryABurton.com

To my husband, aka Prince Charming, research assistant, travel partner and self-appointed "roadie," thank you for all you do to make my life easier.

Table of Contents

Chapter One

Much to her mother's dismay, Cindy spent the better part of the morning shopping online for school supplies for her classroom. The money for the supplies came from her own pocket. While the school had a budget for supplies, it was never enough. Like so many of her peers, she dug into her pocket with little to no complaint. Cindy loved her job and the work that went into planning for a successful year with her students, and sometimes that success meant going over the budget allotted to her by the school.

Cindy knew her mother was not upset at her spending; she was upset that she'd been made to wait to continue their summer reading. They'd powered through two of the children's stories thus far, and Linda was anxious to delve into the past of Anastasia, the child whose journals were next in line to read.

Cindy was just as anxious to see where the story led; however, from what they'd read about her in the previous journals, she knew Anastasia's story would be one full of turmoil. Not that the others weren't, but it was obvious that something had happened to the girl to turn her bitter. Knowing this, she'd insisted on waiting until they could give the journals their full attention and that wasn't going to happen until she'd ordered the extra supplies for the approaching school year. She'd left Linda to the task of copying the journals while she did what many teachers did on their summer break: work without pay to spend money that was never going to be recouped.

She smiled, knowing the latter to be untrue. While she

could not recoup the money in cash, she would see it within the eyes of each child whenever she handed them a new pencil, a pad of paper, or supplies for them to make a treasured art project. Then the money would be repaid tenfold. At least that was what she told herself each time she pressed the charge button. In reality, most children never knew of or acknowledged her contribution. Wasn't that the way for all moms whose selfless acts ensured their children's lives were made just a bit more tolerable? And wasn't it she who was the mom to these children for at least seven hours a day for the majority of the year? Cindy laughed and closed her laptop. "Going to pull your arm out of joint if you keep patting yourself on the back there, Cindy."

"Did you say something?" Linda called from the other room.

Cindy leaned back in the computer chair. "No, I was just giving myself credit for buying all the school supplies."

"Ha, Lord knows someone has to; you do a lot for those kids," Linda said, joining her in the office.

"I'm not the only one, Mom; most teachers I know do the same thing. Heck, you did the same thing when you were a receptionist at the real estate office. How many times did you take everyone coffee, bake cookies and brownies, and all the other not-so-little things you did to make people happy? I guess we all do it in some form or another. A mechanic who furnishes his own tools, a hairdresser who brings her own products, the visiting nurse who goes above and beyond to see their patient is happy."

Linda laughed. "Yes, but nursing pays more."

"It does, but they're still spending their own money," Cindy replied. She watched as Linda stifled a yawn. "Want to take a nap before we start reading?"

Linda looked conflicted. "No, I'll just grab a cup of

coffee. I think I'll be good once we begin. You want a cup?"

While she wished Linda would have agreed to a nap, she knew she'd be pushing it if she insisted. "Sure, I'll take a cup along with whatever is in the oven. It smells terrific."

Linda's face brightened. "I used the last of the blueberries to make a cobbler."

"I thought we were watching our weight?" Cindy said with a sigh. Not that Linda had anything to watch. It was she who'd packed on extra pounds since her mother had moved in.

"We agreed to eat healthier," Linda corrected. "Blueberries are brain food. I don't know how it gets any healthier than that."

Cindy stared at her mom. "Maybe eating them on their own without three sticks of butter and seven cups of sugar."

Linda's eyes grew wide. "Remind me never to eat your blueberry cobbler."

"You get the cobbler; I'll pour the coffee," Cindy said, following Linda into the kitchen. She opened the cabinet and smiled, reaching for two of the china cups she'd rescued from Grandma Mildred's storage shed. "Let's sit at the table."

Linda saw the delicate cups and switched out the Corelle plates for the good china, scooping a large spoonful of cobbler onto each plate. "Just like regular ladies."

"Pinkies up," Cindy said, lifting her cup.

Linda's brow wrinkled. "I think that's only for tea."

Cindy studied her pinky finger. "Are you sure?"

"I'm not sure about anything these days," her mother said, lifting her pinky to match Cindy's. The smile left Linda's face. "I have to admit, I'm nervous about the next set of journals."

Cindy lowered her cup. "You sure you want to read them?"

Linda stopped chewing mid-bite. "What do you think?"

"Just making sure. Oh, and I think I'd like to go to Frankenmuth later in the week. You know, Christmas in July." Cindy neglected to add that her father's birthday was on Thursday and she was using the excursion to keep her mother distracted. Linda had perked up so much since beginning the journals, the last thing Cindy wanted was to see her mother regress.

Linda laughed. "It's Frankenmuth. It's always Christmas."

"Yes, but they have their Christmas-in-July sales, and I think it would be nice to get away for the afternoon."

"I'll go if you promise we can stop at Zehender's for chicken."

"Mom, do you realize we spend most of our waking moments discussing food?"

"Isn't it great?" Linda said, taking another bite of cobbler.

Cindy finished and collected the delicate plates, rinsing them and setting them in the sink for handwashing later. The copied journals were in two piles on the living room coffee table. They'd taken to making duplicate copies to preserve the original writings. As with the previous journals, it was apparent these journals had been cleaned, with most of the slang and all profanity removed. Unfortunately, they had yet to discover the identity of the cleaner. *Just another one of life's mysteries, perhaps*, Cindy thought as she removed the cover sheet from each pile and handed one to her mother. Taking a breath, they began to read.

When I was first asked to write a journal, I didn't think I would have anything worth saying. Who'd want to read something from the likes of me? I promised I would try and that I would be truthful. I found the latter to be most difficult, as the truth has a way of escaping me. Still, I wanted my story to be

4

accurate and knew no one would read my words until after all breath had left my body, so I agreed to lay the words down on paper. If you see water marks within my words, never fear; I've shed many a tear in recounting my past. I'm not saying that to gain your pity; I am merely telling you some things in my past are not remembered without sorrow.

I am not a Christian woman, nor have I ever claimed to be. If that statement gives you pause, I ask you to remember the times in which I have lived and read my words before casting judgment upon my character. If you've never gone to bed hungry, fell victim to a wicked man's lust, or never had your newborn child torn from your arms because you had nothing of value to offer it, then I say you are not fit to stand in judgment of me.

I was nearly ten when the man who married my mother entered my room and exposed himself to me. Terrified, I pulled the covers over my head. When I grew brave enough to look again, the man was gone. His early forays into my room were much the same: he'd enter, I would hide under the blankets, and within moments, he'd be gone. At first, I kept the man's indiscretions to myself, fearing my mother would be angry. One morning, I approached my mother, telling of the man's visit. Instead of taking me into her arms and comforting me, her eyes narrowed, and she slapped me across the face for telling lies. Later that day while with my mother in the market, I watched in stunned silence as she spent some of the food money Father had given her on a wedge of wood. I remember it clearly as she haggled over that wedge for several minutes. I couldn't understand at the time why it was so important for her to purchase that worthless piece of wood. Once home from the market, she put away the market purchases and then motioned for me to follow as she led me to my bedroom. Taking the wedge, she showed me how to jam it under the door to prevent anyone from coming into my bedroom without my permission. That was the only present I received on my tenth birthday. In truth, it may have been the best gift I ever received. I cherished it even more, as I knew how much it cost my mother. Not so much in terms of monetary means, but in that the man knew it was she who prevented him from reaching me. She who paid the physical price for keeping him away. The beatings he gave her grew worse. The screams that leaked from the walls of their bedroom tore at my heart. More than once, I woke to the sounds of the man jiggling the doorknob, followed by the tormented screams from my mother's room. I knew I had the power to relieve her pain if only I had the courage to open my door. I did not. And so her screams continued. Daughters should not be held responsible for their mothers' tears, yet the guilt resides in me to this very day.

If what you have read thus far did not scare you away, then I guess you are capable of hearing what else I have to say. My birth name is Anastasia Charlotte Millett. This is my story.

Cindy stared at the page for several moments, wishing she could find Anastasia's mother and thank her for the sacrifice she made in protecting her daughter. Cindy's stomach clenched as the guilt gnawed at her. Just moments earlier, she was comparing herself to mothers because she had reached into her pocket and doled out dollars she'd never miss to help children succeed. That was not being a mom; that was doing her job. She was a teacher. While she considered herself a very good one, she'd yet to be put in a situation where she would have to choose her own safety over that of a child. As much as she considered the children she taught to be her own, never actually having one of her own, she could not truly comprehend the selflessness it took to be a mom. For the first time in all her years, she felt she was missing something important. She worked to mask her sudden feeling of maternal inadequacy before at last turning to Linda to gauge her reaction. While her mother's face remained stoic, her eyes held unshed tears.

Cindy handed her a tissue. "This is going to be a tough one."

"Looks to be," Linda said, dabbing at her eyes.

"Mom, are you sure you don't want to take a break? Not forever; just a few days."

"No, I'm okay knowing whatever I read happened years ago. To be honest, I figured this would be part of her story. When we read Tobias' story, the girl seemed to know too much for a ten-year-old."

"I felt the same way. I'm not sure how old she was when she wrote the journals, but she sounds angry."

"Yes, but something had to have happened to make her leave her brothers."

Cindy nodded to the stack of journals. "Only one way to find out. Remember, if you want to stop or take a break, just let me know."

Linda's eyes sparkled. "I can see why your students think so highly of you. You care."

Cindy looked at Linda anew, wondering what sacrifices her mom had made to ensure she had a good life. While she couldn't think of any at the moment, she knew they were there, of that she had no doubt. "That's because I had you to teach me. If I haven't told you enough, I love you, Mom. Thanks for making sure I grew up protected and loved."

Linda dabbed at her eyes once more. "I didn't have a choice; it's what moms do."

Cindy wanted to argue that point, to tell Linda she knew plenty of moms who failed when it came to their children, but she didn't. Instead, she picked up a stack of papers and handed them to her mother. "Remember, whatever we read happened a lifetime ago."

Chapter Two

August, 1908

Anastasia followed behind her momma as she walked through the daily market. Wagons lined both sides of the street with vendors selling, meats, cheese, fruits, vegetables, and just about anything else a person could need. The vendors called to them as they passed, each shouting to be heard over the person next to them.

"Hey, pretty lady, could I interest you in some silk to make yourself a new dress?" one man asked, holding out a lovely purple fabric that shimmered in the sunlight.

Her mother looked longingly at the fabric but continued without stopping.

"How about a new pair of shoes for the little girl? I have a few used pairs in the back of the cart if you'd prefer," the man said when Sharon waved him off.

Anastasia heard a commotion and looked to see a young shoeless boy close to her age running down the street with a hand full of stringed sausages. A black and white dog ran alongside the boy, his pink tongue hanging from the side of his mouth, obviously enjoying the game. Anastasia stopped to watch and was nearly mowed down by a policeman who followed close behind, blowing a whistle and commanding the boy to stop.

Paying him no heed, the boy skirted around another man, who reached to catch him, then ducked into an alleyway, both he and the dog disappearing from sight. Realizing her mother had moved on without her, Anastasia hurried to catch up.

She loved market days, as her momma was always happy when away from the apartment house. Her momma turned and smiled at her. A breeze caught Sharon's hat, and Anastasia ran, chasing after it. Collecting the hat, she returned it to her mother, pleased to have rescued it before the wind carried it away. Momma pushed her long black hair from her face and smiled. The smile faded as she placed a hand at the bruise just below her right eye. A bruise Papa had given her mother for not moving fast enough when clearing the supper dishes, saying, *You're my wife, Sharon; wives do as they are told*. Anastasia narrowed her eyes. She was mad at her papa.

Her mother bent and placed a finger on the tip of Anastasia's nose and smiled once more. Sharon was beautiful, with thick eyelashes blinking over dark brown eyes. "Remember, Anna, only happy thoughts on market days. When we leave the apartment house, we are as free as the wind."

Anastasia didn't know what that meant, but she mimicked her mother's smile anyway.

Her momma straightened and began walking once more, her long brown dress flowing with the movement. Anastasia wondered what her mother would look like in the shiny purple fabric the man had offered, something she found difficult to do since she'd never seen her mother in anything but the dark brown dress she was currently wearing. A dress whose style and color matched the one Anastasia had on. They each had three dresses, all exactly the same. The one they had on, put on clean just this morning, one on the line just outside the fire escape, drying in the morning sun, and the other hanging in the closet, ready to be worn the next day. Each day, after her father left for work, she would help her mother wash the clothes they'd worn the previous day. Then they would hang them to dry on a line stretched between the buildings, making sure to pull them in through the window long before Papa returned home from work. While Papa liked having clean clothes, he did not like to see the family's dirty laundry hung out for all to see. Therefore, she and Momma would wear their Saturday dresses again on Sunday, meaning they had double the laundry to hang come Monday morning.

Anastasia's mother carried a large brown basket looped over the crook of her arm and hummed as she picked out vegetables from the farmer's cart, handing the cart owner several coins in return. Approaching the fish cart, she pointed towards a large silver-colored fish with fixed black eyes.

"Is that fish fresh?" Sharon inquired.

The man placed his palms together and his eyes seemed to disappear as his bald head bobbed up and down. "Much fresh, delivered just this morning."

"I'll take one," Sharon said, handing him a coin.

He pulled the fish from the bed of ice and wrapped it in clean paper, tying it with a piece of brown twine before handing it to her mother.

She thanked the man then motioned for Anastasia to follow. "I think I'll get a few apples and make a pie for supper."

This made Anastasia happy, as she enjoyed talking to the apple man—a man with smiling eyes and silver sprinkled in his hair who seemed to think everything was funny. He also appeared to like when she and her mother visited, as his face lit up whenever he saw them. Today as they approached, the man didn't seem happy to see her mother, as he stopped smiling as soon as he saw her face. Sharon lifted a hand to her cheek and shook her head. The man looked past them, as if seeing something that wasn't there, something he did not wish to see.

After a moment, the tension left his face, and he smiled at Anastasia. "I swear you look more like your mother every time I see you. Tell me, how is my beautiful little girl today?"

Her mother didn't seem to like his comment, so Anastasia ignored it, instead eyeing the mound of apples in his cart. "Can I try?"

"Sure you can. Just remember the rules," he said, and waved a hand towards the cart.

Every market day for as long as she could remember, the apple man had allowed her to pull an apple from the pile. It had become a game of sorts. If she managed to pull the apple from the cart without making the other apples fall, he allowed her to take it home at no charge. After several failed attempts, and leaving empty-handed, she'd became quite adept at pulling an apple free without so much as a shift from the pile. The apple man would then make a big deal of how he'd lost a penny today, further insisting she'd robbed him of his hard-earned money. Of course, the apple never made it home, as she'd have it eaten long before they reached the stairs to their apartment house.

She walked around the apple cart twice before deciding which apple she wanted. Holding her breath, she slid her tiny fingers into the pile and gently pulled the apple free, smiling a triumphant smile when the others remained in place. "I did it!"

"You sure did." The apple man returned her smile and handed her another apple. "Give this one to my horse. Make sure to keep your fingers out of her mouth this time."

Anastasia took the apple to the front of the cart and giggled as the horse lipped the apple from her hand. When she returned, her mother and the apple man were talking in agitated whispers. The conversation halted as she approached. Sharon's face reddened as she neared.

"Tell Mr. Castiglione thank you for the apple, Anna."

Anastasia did as told, though she wasn't sure why she should thank the man when she'd won the apple fair and square. She waited until they were away from the cart before she spoke.

"Are you mad at the apple man, Momma?"

Her mother paused and turned towards her. "Of course not. What makes you think that?"

"You were yelling at him," Anastasia said, and took a bite of apple.

"We were not yelling. Yelling means everyone can hear you."

Anastasia swallowed. "You mean like Papa does?"

"Did you hear what we were saying?" Sharon asked, ignoring her comment.

"No."

"Then we were not yelling. I was merely telling Mr. Castiglione he should not have let you take the apple to the horse. Remember that time she tried to bite your finger?"

They were walking again. Anastasia decided not to push the issue, as her mother might not let her visit the apple man again.

***

The door opened, and Papa strolled in, a tall, broad shouldered man, with neatly combed hair and eyes so dark, one could almost see their reflection, if they dared stare into them long enough. Except for dark stubble over his face and chin, he looked much the same as when he'd left earlier that morning. He worked at the shipping docks supervising a group of men. With the exception of smelling of sweat, he came home clean most days. His gaze stilled upon Momma, who left the stove she'd been standing in front of and hurried to the door to take his lunch pail. He brushed the hair from her face and kissed her cheek. While her back was to her, Anastasia knew he was kissing the angry bruise he'd left there the evening prior.

"I'm sorry," his words came out on a whisper.

"I know," Sharon answered just as quietly.

Anastasia stood by the table, waiting for her father to acknowledge her. At almost four, she'd already learned what was expected of her when her father returned home from work.

"Anna, come give your papa a hug," he said, reaching a hand to beckon her closer.

She hurried to where he stood and squirmed as his stubble scratched at her cheek. "It hurts, Papa."

He released his hold and went to the cabinet, pulling out both a bottle and glass. As he moved towards the table and poured his first drink, she could see the fear in her mother's eyes. As she did every day, Anastasia silently wished he would stop after just one glass, while he was still happy. It was during the next glass when his mood would turn anything but agreeable. Sometimes she wished he wouldn't come home, as before his arrival, she and her mother would laugh and sing. Then as time for her papa's return drew near, Momma would change. Papa would cross the threshold in good spirits, and soon spirits of the liquid kind would squelch the happiness. Even though daylight was still streaming through the windows, darkness would settle over the apartment. Long before the supper dishes were returned to the cabinet, her mother would shed her first tears of the day.

Anastasia sat in the corner of the room watching her parents, knowing it wouldn't be long before the liquid monster once again took hold of her papa. Sharon stood at the stove stirring the contents of a large pot. The fish, cleaned and scaled, simmered in the heavy black skillet on the front left burner. It smelled good, and Anastasia hoped they would be able to finish the meal before Papa grew too angry. Papa tilted the glass, finishing the contents, and reached for the bottle. She held her breath when Momma dimmed the flame under the skillet, pulled up a chair, and covered the glass with the palm of her hand as she joined Papa at the table.

Papa's eyes narrowed, and he released the bottle. "You got something to say, woman?"

"I'm with child," Sharon blurted.

Anastasia wasn't sure what that meant, but it must have been a good thing because her father left the bottle on the table and pulled Sharon into his arms, kissing her. When they finally pulled apart, he placed his hand on Sharon's stomach and asked her if she were sure.

"I am. He kicked me today."

Anastasia was shocked her mother dared tell such a lie. She'd been with her all day and hadn't seen anyone kick her. She almost said as much but reconsidered, seeing how happy they both seemed. Papa looked in her direction, and for a moment, Anastasia thought he'd heard what she'd been thinking. She let out her breath when he directed his attention back to Sharon.

"Are you sure it is a boy?" His voice sounded eager.

"Well, I can't be certain, but it feels the same, so I think it may be. He can use the extra room," she said hesitantly.

Some of the people within their building lived two and three families deep. Anastasia and her family lived comfortably in their apartment and still had a bedroom they were not using. The room was originally used for her younger brother, but he'd gone to a place called heaven last year to live with Grandpa.

"You'll buy a new crib and some fabric to make my son new curtains for his room." Her father's eyes twinkled.

To her surprise, he pulled his wallet from his trousers and handed her momma some paper money before returning the bottle to the cabinet. Mama smiled a real smile. It had been ages since Momma had smiled when Papa returned home from work. If Anastasia had known being kicked was such a good thing, she would've done it to her mother ages ago.

Chapter Three

Anastasia sat in the rocking chair holding Ezra while her mother napped in the other room. The clock on the mantel began to chime. She spread her fingers, closing one with each chime as her momma had taught her. When at last the clock grew silent, she still had one finger extended. She rose from the chair, hiked Ezra onto her hip, and walked to her parents' bedroom. Pushing open the door, she made her way to the edge of the bed. "Momma? My fingers tell me it's time to wake you."

Instantly awake, Sharon rose, hurried to press the wrinkles from the bed, and took the baby from her. Anna ran to the kitchen sink and held a washcloth under the faucet until the water grew warm. Wringing the water from the rag, she returned to the room just as her mother unfastened the metal pins that held Ezra's diaper in place. She placed both pins between her teeth, something she did each time she changed the baby.

Anastasia had asked about it the first time Sharon placed them into her mouth. Her mother had stopped what she was doing, pulled the pins from her mouth, and told her a story about Zachariah. Sharon told of pushing the pins into the mattress while she changed the boy's diaper. He'd grabbed one and stuck his tiny hand before she could stop him. She told of crying along with him as she kissed the trickle of blood from his hand. From that moment on, she'd taken to sticking the pins in her mouth, well out of reach of curious fingers.

Anastasia handed her mother the washcloth, waited for

her to finish wiping the urine from Ezra's bottom, then took it to the water closet, placing it in a covered pail.

Sharon came out of the bedroom, sat in the rocker, and placed Ezra to her breast. "Anna, take the potatoes to the sink and wash the dirt off them."

Anastasia ran to the kitchen, delighted to be involved with the cooking. Gathering the potatoes, she carefully washed them and placed them on the counter. Momma had bought a jar of strawberry jam at the market from the woman who sold preserves. Wanting to be of further help, Anastasia moved the stool over to the counter so she could reach the jar, hoping to place it on the table to use on the bread Momma had kneaded earlier and placed under the towel to rise. She'd just grabbed the jar and stepped one foot off the stool, when the stool tilted, sending both her and the jar to the floor. The jar hit first, pieces of glass flying in all directions. As she toppled to the floor, her face connected with a large chunk of glass, cutting through the length of her small cheek.

Sharon was beside her in an instant. For a moment, Anastasia couldn't tell who was screaming louder she, her mother, or Ezra, who'd been stripped of his mother's breast and dumped into the playpen without warning. Sharon carried her into the hallway, pleading for someone to help. The door across the hall opened and a rail thin woman stuck her head into the hall. Though they'd passed in the hallway many times, she didn't know the woman's name. Her mother often referred to the woman as trash and grew angry each time the woman left her door open. Papa didn't seem to mind. Maybe that was because the woman often sat on a chair just inside the door with her dress hiked up to her thighs in an effort to stay cool.

"It's my daughter, she's bleeding badly," Sharon wailed.

Acting swiftly, the women handed her baby off to an

older lady who'd followed her into the hall then pulled Anastasia from her mother's arms. Pain seared through Anastasia's face with each step as the woman rushed down the flight of stairs and pushed through the door to the first floor. Instead of taking a left and heading outside, the woman turned right and headed down the long hallway, where she finally stopped. Juggling Anastasia to gain a free hand, she pounded on the closed door. Anastasia could feel the woman's heart beating against her uninjured cheek as the woman struggled to catch her breath. The door opened and Anastasia found herself staring into the bosom of a heavily made-up woman with brilliant red hair.

"Mrs. Johnston, I didn't know where else to take her," the woman holding her said between breaths.

Mrs. Johnston moved aside and pointed towards a chair in the kitchen. "Set her down near the table while I get my sewing basket. Take care not to get blood on the rug or I'll have a devil of a time getting it out. Come in," the woman called. Seconds later, the door opened and the elderly woman entered holding the baby. Sharon stepped around her with Ezra, who suckled his mother's breast between heavy sobs.

"Are you a doctor?" Sharon asked, watching as Mrs. Johnston went to work cleaning the jelly from the wound.

Mrs. Johnston, a shapely woman with kind eyes and mostly steady fingers, shook her head. "No, but if you choose to wait for one, the child might bleed to death. Your choice, but if it were me, I'd leave me to it."

Indecision played at her mother's face. Finally, she nodded her approval.

Mrs. Johnston's hand neared and Anastasia screamed and pushed the woman's hand away just as the needle pierced her cheek.

Mrs. Johnston swept the table clean with her arm and

nodded towards the older woman. "Hand that baby off and come help your daughter hold the girl."

Ezra scowled at the baby as his mother took it into her free arm.

It took both women to hold her still as Mrs. Johnston rinsed the wound with whiskey then, dousing the sewing needle with the same, sewed twenty-six stitches into her cheek with a needle and thread she'd been using for quilting just moments before.

"That'll do it," Mrs. Johnston announced at last.

Anastasia's sobs decreased as the hands holding her let go. The two women collected the baby and left without as much as a word in her direction.

Mrs. Johnston checked her handiwork, then turned her attention to Anastasia's mother. "The whiskey's not pleasant, but it helps clean the wound."

At hearing that, new tears spilled down Anastasia's cheek. She tugged at Mrs. Johnston's dress. "Does that mean I will be mean like Papa?"

"ANASTASIA, mind your words!" Sharon gasped.

Mrs. Johnston smiled. "You'll still be the sweet little girl you always were."

Since it was the first time they'd met, Anastasia was curious how the woman knew anything about her. "Papa will be mad at me for ruining his supper. I broke the jam; now we'll have nothing to put on the bread."

Sharon glanced at the clock and turned pale. "It doesn't matter. I don't have time to cook the bread or anything else before your papa gets home. We must go. What do I owe you?"

The woman shook her head. "I'm not a doctor; you owe me nothing."

"My husband won't be happy if I accept your services without paying." Sharon wrung her hands as she looked at the clock once more. "Please, I must give you something."

The woman studied her mother for a moment, looked at Anastasia's cheek one final time, and turned back to Sharon. "You can give me the bread you made. I have some honey with which to eat it. I'll give you some to put on the girl's face. She'll have a scar, but the honey will help keep the wound from getting with fever. It does that, and you'll have a devil of a time."

Sharon blinked back tears. "I'll settle the children and bring the bread dough down. I'm sorry; I didn't have time to bake it."

"You'll do nothing of the sort. Give me a moment, and I'll follow you upstairs."

They waited while the woman placed a small amount of honey in a cup. Taking the butter knife, she placed a thick layer of honey over the cut and then handed the cup to Anastasia to carry. Next, she placed a lid on the pot simmering on the stove, and to their surprise, she gripped the handles with hot pads and motioned them towards the door.

"We can't take your supper." Sharon's voice trembled as she spoke.

"You can, and you will. My guess is you have nothing you can fix that will be ready in time. And, if supper is not ready when your man comes home, things will not be pleasant for you," Mrs. Johnston said firmly.

Sharon nodded and lowered her eyes.

Mrs. Johnston laid a hand on her mother's arm. "Once upon a time, there was a Mr. Johnston."

Sharon smiled a slight smile. "How can I ever thank you?"

"No need. I'll sit with the children while you get yourself cleaned up. Your man sees all that blood on you, and he's likely to topple over."

Once upstairs, Mrs. Johnston shooed Sharon from the room to clean herself up. Anastasia was left to tend to Ezra while the woman stooped to her knees, cleaned up the jam and glass then scrubbed the blood from the floor. The borrowed dinner warmed on the stove, and everything was back as it should be when Papa returned home from work. Mrs. Johnston had left only moments before, most likely passing Anastasia's papa on the stairs.

Anastasia stayed on the sofa watching as he handed his lunch pail to her mother and sought out Ezra, hoisting him in the air and speaking in excited tones. Ezra jabbered with delight and giggled happily when Papa gently rubbed the baby's foot over the stubble on his face. She wondered for the hundredth time if her Papa had ever been that excited to see her after a long day at work. Something told her the answer was no.

Papa returned Ezra to the basket where he'd been playing, then paused as if mildly surprised to see her sitting on the sofa instead of standing stoically waiting for him to greet her.

"Anna, come give your Papa a hug," he said gruffly.

She scooted from the sofa and hurried to greet him, the cut on her cheek throbbing with each step. His brow creased as his gaze rested on her wound. She cast a glance to her mother, who was wiping her hands on the crisp white apron she wore over the clean dress she'd changed into.

Papa placed a finger under her chin, tilting her face to examine the cut. "What happened?"

Momma stepped up beside him and looked Anastasia in the eye. "I'm afraid it's all my fault. Ezra woke while I was starting supper. He's teething, as you know, and crying so fitfully that Anna could not soothe him. I tried to hurry so that I could tend to him, and in the process, knocked over an empty jar I'd neglected to put away after supper last night. Poor Anna placed the baby in the basket and hurried to help, when she lost her balance and fell upon a piece of broken glass."

"Is that what happened, girl?" Papa asked, meeting her stare.

Not at all. At least that was what she wanted to say. Instead, she shook her head, agreeing with her mother's lie.

Her father leveled his gaze on her. "You wouldn't lie to me, would you, girl?"

"No, Papa. It happened just as Momma said," Anastasia said, holding his gaze. As he withdrew his finger, she realized not only was it the first lie she'd ever spoken, her mother had given her permission to tell it. She wasn't sure why her mother had taken the blame, at least not at that moment in time.

"Supper's ready," Sharon said, moving back to the kitchen and lifting the cover to her large cast iron pot. *Nothing left to chance,* she'd said when she transferred the chicken and dumplings to one of her own, sending Mrs. Johnston home with the original pot.

Papa walked to the counter, removed the bottle, and poured himself a glass of dark tea-colored liquid. Momma was in the process of scooping the chicken and dumplings into bowls and hesitated when Papa took the bottle to the table. He hadn't had more than a single glass since before Ezra was born.

Papa sat at the table and took a sip from the glass. "Did the doctor say the girl would have a scar?"

"He said maybe, but he placed the stitches so that at least it would be a straight scar," Momma said, placing a bowl in front of him and shooting Anastasia a look that told her not to contradict her.

"How much did that cost me?" he asked and took another drink.

"Only a loaf of bread," Sharon said, moving to the stove to fill up another bowl. "It worked out so well. I don't know what I was thinking making the bread in the first place on account it would've been too much what with the dumplings and all."

Her father drained the contents of the glass and poured another. "So if not for the girl getting hurt due to your clumsiness, we would have wasted a full loaf of bread. Not to mention the time it took you to make it. Time that could have been put to other use."

Anastasia started trembling. Though it had been a while since she'd heard it, she knew her father's tone preceded her mother's tears. She had to find a way to distract Papa. Ezra made a noise, drawing her attention. *The baby!* Papa was always happy when he played with Ezra. Especially when they took him for a walk. Papa would puff his chest whenever anyone stopped to take a peek inside the pram. Especially if the onlooker marveled at how much the baby looked like him. *Of course he does*, Papa would boast after the person was out of earshot. *The boy has my name. Why shouldn't he have my fine looks as well?* Anastasia ran over to where Ezra lay cooing in the basket, scooped him into her arms, and took him to her papa.

"The doctor told Momma Ezra needs to go for more walks, Papa," she said, offering the baby to him.

Papa took Ezra in his arms, his face showing more concern for the baby than it had when seeing the fresh wound upon her cheek. "Woman, is something wrong with the boy?"

Her mother lowered the ladle and forced a smile. "The baby is fine. While the doctor was sewing Anna's cheek, I asked about his crying. He mentioned a book he'd read called *The Care and Feeding of Children*, which states babies are healthier when they get fresh air. Not to worry; he did not charge me extra."

Anastasia knew of the book of which her mother spoke. It was hidden under the stack of cloth her mother used to diaper

Ezra. Only, the doctor had not mentioned the book. Her mother had purchased it with money Papa had given her for food. Always able to seek out a bargain, her mother was able to save a few coins each week by buying food that was not as fresh as some would like, except for fish, which her momma insisted on buying fresh. Her mother knew her way around food, so Papa was never the wiser. Her momma had a sock hidden under her mattress where she kept the extra coins. She'd made Anastasia promise never to tell Papa about the money, which she said she was keeping for a rainy day. Once, her momma used some of the money to buy a book and read it aloud to Anastasia. A couple of days later, she finished the book and placed it under the towel in her market basket. The next day, she and her mother stopped at the book man's cart and, to her surprise, her mother handed him the book. At first, he'd refused to take the book, saying he'd sold it to her fair and square. Her momma smiled at the man, blinking her long eyelashes and touching him on the arm with her slender fingers. She'd passed her tongue over her lips and told him she didn't want any money. She told him he was free to sell the book to someone else to double his money. The man had looked at her as if he didn't believe her, then asked why she would allow him to sell a book she had paid a whole penny for. She told him she only wished to have another book in return. After that, her mother would find a book she wished to read and return it for another whenever she finished with it. The book man didn't seem to mind, as he smiled at Momma whenever he saw her.

One day last week, her mother had picked a new book to read and was just leaving when she picked up another book. The book man told her she had to choose because he couldn't allow her to have two. To Anastasia's surprise, her mother had removed another shiny penny from her coin purse and paid the man for the second book. The book man had taken the penny with the understanding she would not be allowed to return the book for another. Her mother agreed, something Anastasia found fascinating because it wasn't even raining. She read aloud from the book, and Anastasia hung on every word. Because unlike some of the books her mother would read, this one she understood. This book told Anastasia and her mother how to properly care for her little brother.

Her papa held Ezra in one arm and poured the contents of his glass back into the bottle with the other. Anastasia snuck a glance at her mother and was met with a smile. She tried to return the smile but stopped when doing so proved too painful.

Chapter Four

Cindy held the door for her mother as they left the medical care facility. "Uncle Frank looked good today."

Linda stood on the passenger side, looking over the roof of the car. "He did. Did you see the look he gave when you told him we're reading his mother's journals? It sure looked as if he wanted to speak."

Of course she'd noticed her uncle's reaction. She'd purposely told him in hopes it would evoke a response. It had, but not the one she'd hoped for. Oh, what she'd give for just one more lucid conversation with the man. "He did seem as though he had an opinion about it. Do you think he'll ever come around?"

Linda sighed and ran a hand through her short grey hair. "He might. He's had clear moments. Just none since we discovered the journals. I wonder if it would help if we read some of them to him."

Cindy put the key fob into the ignition and turned towards her mom. "You don't think he's ever read them?"

"I don't know; he never mentioned them. Then again, I don't believe I ever heard him speak of his mother."

Cindy used the dashboard camera to back out of the parking space. "Maybe he didn't remember her. Still, if he'd expressed interest in the woman, you'd think Grandma Mildred or Grampa Howard would have let him read the journals."

"Unless there's something in there they didn't want him to see," Linda replied. "Maybe we should finish reading them before we mention them again."

"I think maybe you're right; it's obvious from reading Tobias' journals that Anastasia took a turn to the dark side. Maybe Howard and Mildred were protecting him," Cindy said as she pulled into the garage and turned off the ignition.

"The man served during World War II, and yet they didn't think he could handle reading his own mother's journals? What could be so bad they didn't think he could handle it?" Linda asked.

"Only one way to find out," Cindy said, leading the way to the living room where the journals awaited their return. Settling in, they each picked up a stack of papers and began to read.

***

Momma enjoyed a newfound peace after Ezra was born. If Papa seemed ready to reach for another glass, either Anastasia or her mother would take Ezra to him. Ezra was unaware of his ability to calm Papa; he just liked the attention. One day, Papa came home dirty and said something about a power struggle at the docks. Anastasia had never seen him dirty and wasn't sure what to say, so she said nothing. He moved straight to the cabinet and grabbed a glass, filled it with brown liquid from the bottle, drank it down, and poured a second on the way to the table. Anastasia took Ezra to him, and for the first time, Papa yelled at her to take him away. Ezra cried and reached for papa, but Papa had already emptied the glass once more. Papa was never happy once he'd started into the second glass.

Since Ezra had lost his touch, her mother had to find another way to calm him. Anytime Papa grew angry, she'd paste a smile on her face and kiss him until his anger diminished. Anastasia could tell her smile was not real, but he didn't appear to notice. If he did, he didn't seem to care. Anastasia watched the way her mother was with him, fascinated at how she could change his mood with a simple kiss. Anastasia often wondered why her mother wanted to kiss him when he did things behind closed doors to make her scream. She even went so far as to ask her once. Her mother looked her in the eye and said she belonged to him and had to do whatever he said. Anastasia asked her what made her belong to him. She said it was that way when women got married. She told her it was the job of the wife to do what her husband said.

A couple of years after giving birth to Ezra, her mother became pregnant once more. At first, Papa was happy, but then her momma stopped kissing him. She stopped singing to Ezra, so Anastasia would sing and comfort him when he cried. That pregnancy was hard on her mother; she was ill throughout most of it. The pregnancy took its toll on more than just Anastasia's momma.

***

November, 1909

Anastasia rubbed the cloth against the washboard, determined to get the brown stain out of the white cotton diaper. Her small hands had scabs from where the skin had come in contact with the washboard. Dunking the diaper, she reached for the soap, drawing it the length of the stain then returning the fabric to the washboard and scrubbing once more. She dunked the diaper into the water and held it up to inspect the progress. Smiling, she dunked the cloth into the clean rinse water. She lifted the cloth with a large wooden stick, as the water was much too hot to touch. Using the stick, she pushed the diaper against the wringer and turned the handle until the cloth caught between the rollers. Sharon was able to feed clothes through the rollers by hand, but she'd showed Anastasia how to use the stick after she'd gotten a finger caught in the vise.

Anastasia went to the sofa where her mother slept. Sharon's face was pale against the dark circles that lined her eyes. For a moment, she considered letting her sleep, but her mother had made her promise not to try to hang the laundry by herself. She placed a water-pruned hand on her shoulder. "Momma, the wash is ready to go on the line."

Sharon opened her eyes, placing a hand to her mouth. "Where is Ezra?"

Anastasia bit her lip. "He's in the playpen. He wouldn't stay away, and I was afraid he'd get burned by the water."

"You did good." Sharon sat up, grabbed the bucket from the floor, and threw up. Taking the bucket with her, she rose and slowly walked to the open window. "Bring me the basket, Anna."

Anastasia took hold of the heavy basket with two hands, dragging it to the window where her mother stood. One by one, she handed her the clothes and watched as her mother placed the item on the line and pushed a clothespin on top. Anna loved watching the process, as the wooden pins reminded her of dolls without arms, using stiff, straight legs to hold the clothing and linens in place. As a spot on the line became full, Sharon would pull on a second line attached to the building across the alleyway, which would send the clothes soaring high above the alley below. The level of sun and wind determined how long it would take the laundry to dry. Today, there was a good mixture of both. Sharon stopped to use the bucket three additional times during the course of hanging the laundry.

"Did the baby get his breakfast?" Sharon asked, settling onto the sofa.

"I cooked us both some eggs just like you showed me," Anastasia said, neglecting to tell her she'd had trouble cracking the eggs and had to dig the shell out with a spoon.

"You are going to be a wonderful mother someday, Anna," Sharon said and placed her hand upon the long-healed scar upon her cheek. "You'll have to go to the market alone today. When it is time, I'll help you with supper."

"Alright, Momma," Anastasia said, nodding her head. Her mother's words didn't come as a surprise. Sharon had been ill since before her stomach started growing big. She knew most of the vendors at the market, and nearly all inquired about her mother whenever she stopped. Along with the household chores, her mother was teaching her to cook. Sitting on the chair with the bucket nearby, Sharon would tell her exactly how to prepare the food. The only thing Anastasia couldn't do was lift the skillet or bring the pans in and out of the oven. The cast iron proved too heavy for a girl of her size. Her papa never truly knew how sick Sharon was, as she and her mother would listen for the doorknob to jiggle and trade places before her father made his way inside the apartment.

"Run and grab me my coin purse," Sharon said, hoisting Ezra onto her lap.

Anastasia did as told and handed the small purse to her mother.

"Go to the cart where they sell meat and tell them you need a chicken. Don't go to the man's cart; you want the lady with the white hair. She'll cut the chicken into pieces if you give her an extra penny. When you're finished, go to the vegetable wagon and get four potatoes and two, no three, handfuls of fresh green beans. I'll not be able to make the bread today, so you'll have to buy a loaf. Don't let them sell you any day-old bread; your papa doesn't like stale bread." She returned the coin purse to Anastasia. "Remember how I showed you how to tell the coins apart. Make them give you a price before you show them the money; you've been shopping with me enough to know how much things should cost. Keep a hand on the purse, and don't let anyone take it from you. Straight to the market and straight home. Understand?"

"Yes, Momma, straight there and straight home," Anastasia promised.

She hurried down the steps, out the door, and turned left towards the market, making sure to keep a hand on Sharon's coin purse. Running, she made it to the market in half the time it usually took trailing behind her mother when she pushed Ezra's carriage. She passed the first two meat carts and went to the one with the lady with the white hair as her mother had instructed. The woman sat on a stool beside her cart, bent plucking feathers from a freshly killed hen. Her hair was tucked into the bonnet tied securely to her head, but Anastasia knew this was the woman her mother wanted her to visit. The woman looked up, spit some tobacco juice onto the ground and smiled a yellow-toothed smile.

"Good afternoon, Miss Anna. How is your mother today?"

Anastasia frowned. "She's quite ill yet today. She says the baby is taking all her strength. He must be an ornery one, seeing how sick she is and all."

The woman shook her head. "I don't think your momma be having a boy a'tall. Wee bairn's got to be a lass. Girl babies are a lot more rambunctious afore they are born. Not to worry, the bairn will settle down afore long. They always do. What can I get you today?"

"A chicken, please. Momma asked if you'd cut it for her."

"It'll be another penny. You want to come help me pluck some of these chickens, and I'll cut the hen at no extra cost," the woman said with a nod to a crateful of live hens under the wagon.

Anastasia looked at the crate and shook her head. "That looks like it would take all day. I have to get back to my momma."

"Would ye help me pluck if your momma wasn't ill?" the woman asked pointedly.

Anastasia looked at the brown hens then at the balding hen upon the woman's lap. "No, I don't think I would."

The woman chuckled and sat the half-plucked chicken aside, wiping her hands on her apron. "You'd better marry yourself a fine man, little girl. One that can afford to let you purchase chickens already plucked."

"COME BACK HERE, YOU LITTLE THIEVES!"

Anastasia turned to see a group of boys running past. Barefoot and wearing rags, the boys laughed as they stayed well ahead of the man chasing them.

"Don't you look at them that way, Miss Anna," the woman with the white hair said, pulling her attention away from the boys. "Those Street Arabs are nothing but trouble. The cities are full of them. Rotten orphans are no better than a pack of dogs roaming the streets and stealing good people blind. At least it's legal to shoot the dogs. You meet up with them, don't you give them the time of day. They're nothing more than filthy animals without the fur upon their backs. That's not the kind of boy a girl such as yourself needs to trouble yourself with. No, you need a learned boy who will grow up to be just like your papa."

Anastasia swallowed. She had no desire to find herself a boy, and if she did, she would much prefer to have a boy who laughed and smiled. She'd made up her mind long ago she would never marry anyone like her papa.

"You got more shopping to do?" the woman asked, gaining her attention once again.

"Yes, ma'am," she said, shaking her head.

"You go get the rest of your list, and I'll have the chicken cut up when you're finished," the woman said, shooing her away.

Anastasia was still thinking of the group of boys when she reached the vegetable cart.

"What'll it be today, Miss?" The man tipped his hat, showing dark hair that stopped halfway across his head.

"I need four potatoes and three handfuls of green beans," Anastasia replied.

The man returned his worn hat to his head. "Three handfuls, huh. Would that be your hand or my hand?"

Anastasia considered his words. "Momma didn't say."

The man scratched at his chin. "How about we do two of mine and one of yours."

It sounded fine to her. "Okay."

She watched as he grabbed two handfuls of green beans from the basket and placed them in the bowl to weigh. He tilted the basket and allowed her to grab a handful then lowered the bowl so she could add her beans. He weighed the beans then removed the bowl from the metal scale. She handed him one of the cloths from her mother's market basket, and he poured the beans onto the cloth, scrunched his eyebrows then added another handful of beans.

"Anything else?"

She shook her head.

"That will be six cents."

She opened the coin purse and poured some coins into her hands.

"One brown and one of the silver ones. No, the smaller one," he said when she picked up the wrong coin.

She handed him the coins in exchange for the cloth full of beans, which he'd tied in place with a piece of twine. She then held up the basket as he placed the potatoes inside.

"You tell your mother I asked about her," he said, placing the final potato.

"I will," she said and hurried on her way. She waited in line at the bread cart, anxiously listening as the lady in front of the line chatted with the bread lady about the weather. The lady in front of her joined in the conversation, and the man standing beside her laughed at something she said. The ladies appeared to be enjoying their conversation. She wondered if her mother would be pleased if she were the one standing behind them. Something told her she would not. While her mother smiled sometimes, she didn't laugh. Not like the ladies in front of her anyway. Papa would not be happy if he were here. He'd say the women should be working, not gabbing. She remembered her conversation with the lady with the white hair and how she'd said Anastasia should marry a man like her father. She studied the man in front of her with his tattered clothes and mussed-up hair, admiring the way his eyes twinkled when he looked at the woman he was with. She thought about the group of boys she'd seen earlier, racing through the streets without a care, the bottoms of their bare feet black as the dirt upon the street. She thought of her mother, whose smile left the moment the doorknob jiggled, announcing her papa's return. Sharon was always trying to please her papa, and all he did was make her cry. Anastasia grew angry; she was not eager to please her papa.

"Why so serious?"

Anastasia felt her face flush. In her musing, she hadn't realized the people in front of her had left. She stepped forward, looking the woman directly in the eye. "I'd like a loaf of day-old bread, please."

Chapter Five

April 26, 1910

Anastasia held her chalk tight as it glided around the slate board. Lowering the chalk, she smiled. She'd written her name, at least the shortened version. Anna, as her parents called her. Though she never objected verbally, it was not the name she favored. She preferred the longer version, the one her parents called her when she did something they didn't approve of. She preferred it so much that hearing it sometimes lessened the harshness of the way they said it. She looked at the small chalkboard, reading her name once more; only this time, the writing did not produce a smile. Her teacher, Mrs. Ellis, had taught her the letters needed to write her name, and though Anastasia had asked many times for help writing her full name, Mrs. Ellis refused to take the time to help her, insisting that if she did, every child in the class would want to do the same. She further stated that some of the names were so long, the letters needed would not fit upon the small slate. To help lessen her disappointment, Mrs. Ellis promised that in time Anastasia would be able to write anything she wished.

She searched the room, hoping to gain her teacher's attention, frowning when she saw the woman bent over a desk helping another child. Anastasia glared at the girl, a freckle-faced blonde-haired girl who always seemed to need Mrs. Ellis' help in performing even the simplest of tasks. It was that way with most of the children. Though she was the youngest in the group, many in the class seemed like babies to her. Some of the girls needed help with the simplest of tasks such as buttoning their coats and fastening a shoe buckle. Alphonso needed help to blow his nose, and he was a boy.

Just the other day, one of the girls dripped jam on her dress while eating lunch and the whole class stared in stunned silence when Anastasia jumped from her desk and ran to the water bucket to get water to remove the jam, further telling the girl it was important to get as much of the stain out before the jam had a chance to dry. She'd gone on to tell the girl to make sure she put the washing powder directly onto the stain before scrubbing the dress. It had shocked Anastasia to learn that with a few exceptions of some of the older classmates, she was the only one who not only knew how to wash clothes but did so on a daily basis. She'd been carrying her mother's workload so long, it had not occurred to her she was doing things most other six-year-olds weren't.

It wasn't until a month ago that her mother felt well enough to take over some of the household chores, thus allowing her to begin school. Still, Anastasia brought her mother's basket to school on market days. While most of the children hurried straight home, she rushed to the market to gather the things her mother made her memorize before leaving the apartment. Grownups went to the market, not children. Scowling, she placed her index finger onto the slate, then pressing firmly, she moved it across the board, sending the letters' dusty remains to the floor. She was tired of being called Anna; she was not a baby. If she was going to do grown-up things, she would insist Mrs. Ellis teach her how to write her grown-up name.

She raised her hand, determined to get the teacher's attention.

Mrs. Ellis stood and walked in her direction, her long burgundy skirt skimming the wood floors as she approached. A lock of brown hair escaped from the bun pinned to the back of her head. She frowned, pulled a hairpin free, and used it to tuck the errant strand back into place. As she viewed the blank slate on Anastasia's desk, the frown returned. "Why aren't you practicing your name, Anna?"

"I want to write my proper name," Anastasia said, lifting her chin. "Anna is a baby name. I wish to write my given name."

"I'm sorry, Anna, there are just so many children. I simply haven't the time." Mrs. Ellis pulled out her brass pocket watch and sighed. Returning the watch to her pocket, she clapped her hands to gain the students' attention. "Children, put your slates away and gather your pails. It's time for the afternoon meal. If any of you forgot to bring lunch, there are apples and oranges in the basket on my desk."

Disappointed, Anastasia raised the top of her desk, placed her slate board inside, then walked to the back of the room to retrieve her lunch pail.

As she returned to her desk, she saw Frieda, the girl who sat next to her, returning with an orange. Frieda was one of her only friends. Freda spoke with a stutter, but Anastasia didn't mind. She liked her because the girl always told stories of her sister working at the Triangle Factory. Frieda would wrinkle her nose when she spoke of the long hours and things her sister had told her. Things like sneaking a kiss from a boy who worked in the elevator. While Anastasia wasn't interested in the kissing part, she'd often dreamed of things she could buy with the money she made. Frieda's sister made fifteen whole dollars a week. Sure the girl complained about how hard she worked, but Anastasia was used to working hard and she didn't get paid anything. Anastasia opened the lid on her pail and pulled out a fried chicken leg wrapped in a cloth. She took a bite and slid a glance at Frieda. As she chewed, she watched Frieda, who was a good head taller than her, struggle to peel the orange. Frieda's dark hair fell in front of her eyes as she tried to dig her fingernails into the outer skin. She repeated the process several times before finally biting into the bitter rind. Frieda scrunched her face, and Anastasia laughed. Her laughter was short lived when tears trickled from the girl's eyes.

Sighing, Anastasia took the knife from her lunch pail walked to Frieda's desk. Snatching up the orange, she cut it in half, handing it to her as she'd done for Ezra so many times. She wiped the blade of the knife on her napkin and returned it to her pail as Frieda blinked away her tears.

"Y-you have a knife," she said, staring at the pail.

Anastasia shrugged. "So."

"You used it and didn't even cut your ff-finger off."

Anastasia didn't know what the fuss was all about; she'd been using a knife for years. She'd used a larger knife than the one in her pail the previous afternoon when her momma had finally had enough time to show her how to properly cut up a chicken. By knowing how to cut the chicken into proper pieces, they could save a whole penny on market days.

She cleaned away the last of the fried chicken with her teeth and wrapped the bone in the cloth, returning both to the pail before removing a second cloth. She pulled back the edges of the cloth and smiled at the small wedge of apple pie. Peeling the cloth away, she tried to ignore Frieda's hungry sighs. She slid another glance towards Frieda, who'd finished the orange and was eagerly eyeing her slice of pie.

Anastasia looked at the pastry, debating. It was the last slice from a pie she'd made under her mother's supervision two days prior. Made with apples she'd purchased from the apple man after saving a few pennies by buying slightly withered greens. She had used the same knife in her pail, cutting and peeling the apples herself. Sharon often said a woman needed to know how to make choices. You can buy fresh produce or do you save a couple of pennies by buying items that needed a little more work. Mother always chose the latter, telling her a penny saved is a penny earned. The earned penny was always their secret, as Papa would have insisted upon its return.

She pictured her papa and wondered what he'd say if she told him she'd forgotten her lunch. *He wouldn't be happy.* He'd tell her that Sharon had more important things to do than remind her to take her lunch pail. If she'd left it at home, her Papa would tell her she deserved to go hungry, knowing the hunger would go a long way to see she didn't forget it again. Making her decision, Anastasia picked up the pie, eating the entire slice without a moment's hesitation. Sure she could've shared, but that wouldn't have taught the girl anything.

***

Anastasia dallied around the busy market in no hurry to get home. She knew Sharon was expecting her to help watch Ezra while she finished her chores, but she'd come up with a small lie about helping her teacher, which she would tell to explain why she'd been late. She'd told the same lie a few days ago, and her momma had surprised her by accepting it as the truth. In fact, she'd done much as she was doing now, walking about looking into the wagons pretending she could purchase anything she wished. She'd never lied to her mother before and something about doing so without getting caught excited her. She held her head high as she walked through the market with Sharon's basket in hand, pretending she was a grand lady without a care in the world. She stopped at the silk wagon and studied the bolts of fine fabric, wondering how she would look in a dress made from all the bright colors. In the front of the wagon stood a temporary structure made of wood with bins of precut fabric in colors so bright, she'd have a hard time deciding which color she actually should choose. She looked at the plain brown dress she had on and sighed. She didn't realize she'd reached out to touch one as blue as a clear summer sky until a rough hand slapped her fingers away.

"Keep your grubby hands off unless you have money in your pocket!" Dressed in black trousers with matching suspenders draped over a white shirt, the man's tone was as rough as his hands.

Rubbing the sting from her hand, she narrowed her eyes at him. "My hands are not grubby."

"Yeah, well, unless you have money to pay, I'll not have you touching anything," the man replied gruffly.

Anastasia was just about to walk away when she noticed a young boy standing just at the head of the wagon. Filthy and dressed in rags, she recognized him as the boy who'd stolen the sausages the day she'd come to market with her mother. She looked for the black and white dog and saw him crouched near the rear of the wagon. The boy caught her attention, pointed at the fabric, and placed his finger to his lips. As he tiptoed towards the end of the wagon, he motioned for her to keep the man's attention.

"Oh, but I do have money," she said a little too loudly.

The man's face scrunched. "You show me the money, and I'll let you take a look."

"Oh, but I don't want to look at just any old fabric. I wish to see the one that matches the sky," she said when the boy reached for the wrong piece.

"All the same to me. Show me the money, and you can look at whatever you please."

She pulled out Sharon's coin purse and made a show of opening it as the boy tucked the sky blue fabric in the waistband of his filthy pants and slowly slinked away.

Seeing the money, the man moved aside to allow her to see.

She looked over the cart and frowned. "Oh my, I guess I was mistaken. I thought for sure there was a blue piece."

The man searched the pile, looking just as confused. "I'm sure it was here a moment ago."

"A shame. I had my heart set on the piece. It would have perfectly matched my dear mother's eyes." A lie, as Sharon's eyes were the same rich brown as her own.

"Surely you can find something else to suit your mother?" Much to her delight, the man's gruff tone had changed to one of urgent pleading.

She dropped the coin she'd been holding back into the coin purse and pulled her shoulders straight as she'd seen her mother do when she had to walk away from something she could not afford. *Do not let them see your defeat,* Sharon would say once they were out of earshot. "No, that will be all for today. I shall come back tomorrow to see if you have the color I am searching for."

She walked away, smiling, knowing the man was watching her. She'd barely made it out of view before the boy approached, dog at his side. He smiled, showing several missing teeth, brushed the mop of dirty brown hair from his eyes, and pulled the soft blue fabric from his waist.

She reached for it, and he pulled it away.

"Not so fast."

"What do you mean not so fast?"

"What you going to give me for it?"

She paused, staring at him in disbelief. "Why should I give you anything? You didn't pay for it. Besides, you wouldn't even have it if I didn't help."

"Says who?"

"Says me," she said and reached for it once more.

"Yeah, it's mine now. If ya want it, you're gonna have to pay."

"I'm not going to pay you for something you stole. Besides, this is not my money; it belongs to my mother. She's ill and gives me money to do the shopping for her."

"So tell her you lost the money."

Her eyes went wide. "Never!"

"Then tell her I took it," he said, eyeing the pocket where she'd placed the coin purse.

"Don't you dare!"

She doubled her fists, and the boy laughed.

"What's it matter to you? That's not even your money."

"It is too my money. I promised my momma I would look after it. That makes it mine. Besides, if I don't have money, I can't buy food, and if I can't buy food, there will be no supper." She looked at him, willing him to understand.

Instead, he laughed. "I go to bed hungry most nights."

She did not doubt his claim, but going to bed hungry wasn't her biggest concern. "I don't mind going to bed hungry, but if there is no supper, my papa will do bad things to my momma."

The boy sighed. "Don't start blubbering; I'm not going to take your money."

She narrowed her eyes. "I don't blubber."

"Course you do. All girls do. At least, most of them."

"Not me."

He studied her for a second. "I'll trade ya the fabric for a kiss."

She wrinkled her nose.

"Aw, don't go looking so disgusted. I was just foolin' with you anyhow."

"Then I can have the fabric?" she said, smiling.

"Sure," he said with a smirk. "Just as soon as you have

something to trade."

Chapter Six

April 28, 1910

Anastasia hurried from the classroom and raced down the stairs and through the ivy-covered gates, anxious to get to the market. She had her mother's basket draped over the crook of her arm, only today she was not dawdling, as Sharon hadn't looked well when she'd left the house. Anastasia had offered to stay home, but Sharon had insisted she go, saying Papa wouldn't approve of her missing school. She'd gone but promised her mother she wouldn't be late. She ran all the way to the market skirting around people, often taking to the streets and darting out of the way of buggies and motorcars. She headed straight to the silk wagon, careful not to catch the attention of the man who owned the cart. She'd promised to return and didn't have time to pretend to look through the fabric he'd brought that day. She stood several carts over searching for the boy, sighing her disappointment when he didn't show himself.

She remembered the day she'd seen him running the streets trailing a string full of sausages, and made her way to the sausage cart. While there were plenty of people around the cart, none were the boy she was seeking, nor the dog he traveled with.

Remembering her promise to her mother, she hurried to the meat wagon. A dark-skinned boy near her age stood in front of the wagon shooing away flies with a large palm leaf. A robust man in an apron smiled when she approached.

"Afternoon, Miss Anna. How is your mother this fine day?" he asked when she neared.

"Not well. I promised I'd hurry. I'm to bring home a roast."

The man bent over the edge and plucked a roast from the ice-filled bed. The roast looked small against the man's pudgy hand.

"That one looks a bit small; we'll need extra for Papa and my lunch tomorrow."

The man nodded and traded the roast with a larger one. She waited until he wrapped and tied it then held out her hand to show several coins. The man took two and handed her the roast in return. Leaving there, she headed for the vegetable cart and picked out four potatoes and a tied bunch of carrots with dark leafy greens on the end. She looked at the sky, trying to judge the time as she'd often seen Sharon do, to no avail. Her stomach grumbled, and she decided to take the time to visit the apple cart, knowing if she could pull an apple free, she'd have something to keep her belly happy until supper time.

Mr. Castiglione was busy talking to a lady but nodded toward the wagon as she approached. He'd done this before, and she knew it to mean *go ahead and give it a try*. She walked to the other side of the wagon, found one to her liking, and carefully pulled it free. She thought to have a word with the man, but he was still talking to the woman and had several others waiting. Taking the apple, she started for home. She'd barely left Market Street when the boy she'd been looking for appeared. A second later, the dog joined them.

"You're pretty good at that," he said, falling into step beside her.

She slid a glance in his direction. "Good at what?"

"Stealing apples. Though I don't know why you stopped at just one."

"Oh, that. I only needed one." She thought about telling him it was part of a game she'd played with the apple man but didn't. He seemed impressed, and truthfully, she enjoyed his admiration. She bit into the apple, and the boy licked his lips.

"That sure does look like a mighty fine apple."

She made a show of taking another bite, keeping her lips parted slightly so the juice ran the length of her arm.

"I sure would like to have a bite of that apple."

She stopped, making sure to keep the apple where he could see it. "I'll let you have the whole apple if you want."

His eyes went wide. "Really?"

"Sure."

He reached for the apple, and she pulled it away, keeping it just out of his reach. "What'll you trade me for it?'

***

Anastasia walked the whole way home with the material draped over her purchases where she could see the shiny cloth. She stopped at the base of the stairs and folded the blue silk, tucking it securely under the cloth in the base of the basket. She let her fingers linger a moment, enjoying the feel of the silky blue material between her fingers. She'd have to find someplace to hide it until she could think of a story to tell her mother. She'd considered telling her the truth but knew Sharon would not approve of her hanging around with one of the street kids.

The stairwell was stuffy and smelled of unwashed bodies, even though she was the only one currently using the stairs. The windows in the stairwell were often kept closed, and with nowhere for the odor to go, it festered. She hurried up the steps two at a time and pulled the door open to the second floor. The air here was somewhat better, as some of the residents chose to keep their apartment doors open, allowing for a small breeze when the wind was agreeable. Her parents preferred to keep their door not only closed but locked as well. Several people milled about the hallway, and as expected, several of the doors stood wide open. What she didn't expect was to see Ezra wander out of the open door across the hall. She knew the apartment, as it belonged to the woman who'd carried her down the stairs when she slashed her cheek. Though the woman had helped to get her care, they'd never spoken. Sharon and Papa kept to themselves, so seeing Ezra coming from the unit was highly unusual. She knew something was wrong the moment she saw him. She called his name, and he ran towards her on clumsy feet, smiling through dry-eyed sobs. His face was covered with dust except for thin streaks where tears had left trails along his cheeks.

Holding firmly to the basket, she lowered to comfort him. "There, there, Ezra. What are you doing out in the hallway?"

"He's been out here all afternoon."

Anastasia looked up to see the woman who'd carried her down the stairs. She wore an ill-fitting stained dress and was standing in the doorway of the apartment Ezra had just exited. Looking past the doorway, she could see clothes, blankets, and other items littering the floor. "Where's my mother? Why was he in your apartment?"

The woman shrugged. "I guess your marm got tired of dealing with him and sent him out in the hallway so she could get some rest. He's been wandering the hallway for hours; I got tired of hearing him cry. I didn't have anything fit to feed him, so I gave him my breast. My little one was finished and there was plenty to share."

Anastasia's mouth went dry. Sharon would not be happy to hear Ezra had suckled from the woman's breast. Then again, she'd never have sent Ezra out into the hallway. *Unless*…She grabbed his hand and led him to the apartment door, surprised to find it ajar. There was a chair beside the door, which Ezra must have used to open the chain. She pushed the door open, searched the room, but saw nothing amiss. She could feel her heart beating in her chest as she set the basket on the counter. She'd just opened her mouth to call for her mother, when she heard Sharon's cries. She scooped Ezra into her arms and hurried to her mother's room, only to find it empty.

"Momma?"

"Anastasia!"

Something's wrong. It had to be; she'd used the name reserved for anger or disappointment. Only this time the name, seemed to be used in fear. Anastasia placed Ezra in the playpen and ran to the counter to retrieve an end of bread to pacify him. She approached the water closet, cautiously pushing the door open. Her momma was hunkered in the corner of the small room, eyes wide, arms stretched out to her side. One hand gripped the counter, the other splayed against the wall as if trying to claw her way out. Dressed only in a thin night gown that was pulled to her knees, she sat in a squatting position, below her a pool of pinkish liquid.

"Momma?" Her words came out in a whisper.

"Anna, the baby. It's too early!" Sharon had barely gotten the words out when her back arched, and she screamed once more.

Anastasia raced from the room, out of the apartment, and down the steps without a thought to the smell. She pushed through the first-floor landing, running straight for Mrs. Johnston's door, ramming it with her fists.

"Lord almighty, girl, you nearly sent me to my grave with all that ruckus," the woman said when she answered. She was dressed in a low-cut purple dress that would have made her father look twice.

"You must come. My momma, she needs a doctor," Anastasia blurted, staring breathlessly at the woman's bosom.

The woman laughed. "Not to worry, child, you'll get yours soon enough."

"You must come. Momma needs a doctor. It's the baby; it's too early," Anastasia repeated, pulling at her arm.

"Aye, you're the girl with the sliced cheek. You've healed quite nicely," Mrs. Johnston said, following her up the stairs. "You know, I'm not really a doctor."

Anastasia didn't care at the moment; the woman was an adult and knew something about healing. "You know about babies?"

Mrs. Johnston chuckled. "I've helped deliver more than my share."

"Then you'll do," Anastasia said, pulling her forward.

Ezra was in the process of climbing out of the playpen when they entered. Upon seeing them, he pulled his foot inside and began to cry.

The woman patted Anastasia's hand. "Do you know your way around the stove?"

"Yes, ma'am."

"Good, start me a large pot of water to boil, and I'll go check on your mother."

"She's in the water closet," Anastasia said when Mrs. Johnston started for the bedroom.

Anastasia pushed a chair next to the stove then went to the cabinet. Using both hands, she tugged the largest pot from the shelf. Trying several times to lift it, she'd get it halfway before dropping it to the floor. As she was trying for the third time, Sharon screamed, giving her the needed encouragement to lift the heavy pot onto the chair. On the next scream, she managed to hoist it to the stove. Standing on the chair, she took a match from the steel holder on the wall and struck the head along the side of the holder as she'd watched Sharon do. The match lit and she turned on the gas, holding the match under the burner until the flame caught. Using a different chair, she transferred water from the sink using the container normally reserved for milk. She had the container under the spigot filling it for the final time, heard a noise, and turned to see Ezra climbing onto the chair she'd placed beside the stove. She grabbed him just as he was reaching for the flame.

"Must be good," she said, lifting him from the chair. Ezra kicked and screamed and started climbing from the playpen the second she placed him inside. Sighing, she hoisted him from the crib and took him back to the kitchen with her. She placed him in the chair and tied him in place with her mother's apron. He tried to move and began to scream when he couldn't get free.

"How's the water coming?" Mrs. Johnston asked, entering the room.

Anastasia turned, surprised to see her covered in the same pink fluid that she'd seen on the floor.

"It's a messy process. I'm afraid I'll have the devil of a time getting this dress cleaned," she said, approaching the stove. "Hearing that boy cry is upsetting your momma. Run downstairs and fetch up a chicken leg from the icebox on my counter. My sewing basket is on the chair in the front room. Bring it to me. Don't bother with the quilt I'm making. Just set it aside."

Anastasia raced down the stairs and entered Mrs. Johnston's apartment through the unlocked door. She closed the door behind her, happy for a brief reprieve from Sharon's screams. The apartment proved to be similar to the one she lived in except it only had one bedroom. She peeked inside and gasped. The room was papered with large colorful flowers and crowded with furniture so large, she wondered how it all fit within the small space. Bright pillows rested on top of the bed in a multitude of shapes and sizes. She plucked one from the bed, brushing her hand across the silky fabric then lifted it to her face, closing her eyes as it touched her skin. She thought of the blue fabric she'd brought home and wondered if she could use it to make a silk pillow of her own. Not likely, for then she'd have to tell her momma how she'd come to have it. If she told, then Sharon would not only know her to be a thief but would know it was the fabric that had caused her to be late. She tossed the pillow onto the bed and ran from the room.

By the time she returned with the chicken leg and sewing basket, Mrs. Johnston had lit the oven and placed the roast inside. Anastasia looked towards the market basket. *Empty.* Her heart raced as she looked around the room, wondering where the fabric had gone. Not seeing it, she narrowed her eyes at Mrs. Johnston.

The woman grabbed a potholder, lifted the pot from the stove with ease, and smiled at Anastasia.

"Give the chicken to the boy and ready those potatoes and carrots. Let me know when you're done and I'll put them in with the roast," she said and left the room, pot in hand.

Anastasia busied herself peeling the potatoes and carrots as Mrs. Johnston instructed when the clock began to chime. As she always did, she used her fingers to count the chimes. To her surprise, she used all the fingers on one hand. It wouldn't be long before Papa came home, and dinner was nowhere near to being ready. She checked on Ezra then went to tell her mother that her papa would soon be home. She pushed the bathroom door open, surprised when Sharon was not there. She went to her parent's bedroom door and listened.

"Come in, girl," Mrs. Johnston called from the other side of the closed door.

Anastasia pushed the door open and stared at the

woman, wondering how she'd known she was there. "Momma? The clock used all my fingers. Papa will be home soon."

Sweat beaded Sharon's forehead, and she blew out a breath as her face turned red. She gripped the side of the bed and groaned.

Mrs. Johnston moved beside Sharon and rubbed the center of her back. "Your papa is going to have to wait; your momma is busy having a baby."

Anastasia knew her papa. While he'd been happy to hear about Sharon's pregnancy, her mother had been so ill, all he did was yell. Sometimes, such as last night, he'd close their bedroom door, and soon after, her mother would scream. She looked at Mrs. Johnston, willing her to understand. "But Papa will be mad supper isn't ready."

Sharon loosened the grip on the sheets and lay back. Mrs. Johnston placed a washcloth on her forehead and whispered something Anastasia couldn't hear before turning and walking her out of the room. They passed by the water closet where the mess still remained on the floor. Anastasia moved to clean it, but Mrs. Johnston kept an arm around her as they walked to the kitchen. Ezra looked up when he saw them then went back to work on what remained of the chicken. Mrs. Johnston went to the oven and lifted the lid on the roasting pan, adding the vegetables Anastasia had prepared. The woman replaced the lid, stood, and placed a finger under Anastasia's chin, looking her in the eye. "Don't you worry about your papa. He won't be bothering your momma tonight."

But I am worried. "But…"

"No buts." Mrs. Johnston released her when her mother cried out from the other room.

***

Anastasia heard the doorknob rattle and jumped from the sofa where she'd been sitting, singing softly to Ezra.

"Where's your mother?" her father asked the moment he entered.

"She's in the bedroom," Anastasia said with a glance over her shoulder.

His face grew red. "She'd better not be sleeping."

"Oh no, Papa, she's having the baby. Mrs. Johnston is with her now."

"It's too early." He looked past her towards the bedroom but made no move to go to Sharon.

"It is. I came home from school, and there was a terrible mess in the water closet, so I ran and got Mrs. Johnston. She's a doctor." Anastasia added the last part to pacify him but refrained from saying she'd found Ezra outside of the apartment, knowing her father wouldn't be pleased.

Sharon screamed, and her father's face went pale. His hands trembled as he placed his lunch pail on the counter.

"Where are you going, Papa?" she asked when he turned back towards the door he'd just entered.

"This is no place for a man," he said, gripping the doorknob.

"But what about supper?"

"It'll keep," he said and left without another word.

Chapter Seven

"Papa's gone," Anastasia said when Mrs. Johnston came into the kitchen area. "I told him about the mess in the water closet, and he heard Momma scream and left. He didn't look so good."

Mrs. Johnston smiled. "Fill that bucket with soapy water and clean the water closet."

Hadn't the woman told her to leave it? "But you said…"

The woman waved her off. "The mess served its purpose. Clean it up before it starts to draw flies."

Anastasia pushed a chair to the sink, filling the bucket, watching as the washing powder began to form sudsy bubbles. Usually, she relished playing in the soapy sludge, but not today. Today, the bubbles reminded her of the mess at hand. She closed her eyes, picturing her mother hunkered and crying in the water closet, and guilt washed over her anew. She opened her eyes, saw the suds, and began to cry. How long had Sharon suffered while waiting for her to come home? A long time, according to the woman who'd taken pity on Ezra. She remembered her brother's sobs and sank deeper into her guilt. She turned off the faucet and wiped her eyes before turning to face Mrs. Johnston.

"Will Momma be okay?" She wanted to add to the question and ask where the pretty blue fabric had gone but decided against it. She knew where it had gone. No matter. Maybe it was best Mrs. Johnston took it. Now she wouldn't have it to remind her of her wrongs.

"Your mother's having a rough go of it, and the baby's facing the wrong direction. It's small, so that should help, but coming out feet first is dangerous for both mom and babe." Mrs. Johnston looked over her shoulder when Sharon's scream pierced the air. She nodded towards Ezra. "Take the boy to the apartment across the hall. Tell her I told you so and do not take no for an answer. Be quick about it. I'll need your help when the baby comes. It shouldn't be much longer now."

***

Anastasia watched as her newborn brother suckled Sharon's breast. He was incredibly small, but Mrs. Johnston and Sharon both seemed pleased when after several attempts he'd latched on to Sharon's breast, eager to eat his first meal. Sharon's face scrunched and Anastasia dared a glance to where Mrs. Johnston stood bent over the bed, sewing stitches into her mother from the place the baby had just pushed his way into the world.

He'd come out feet first, kicking in the beginning, then his little body had turned blue. Mrs. Johnston said something about a cord around his neck and told Sharon to stop pushing. Seconds later, Mrs. Johnston told Sharon to push really hard. She did, and her brother came out slippery and lifeless. Anastasia was scared. Not because the baby wasn't crying, but because her mother was. Tears raced down Sharon's face as she cried and begged to see the baby. Mrs. Johnston didn't pay her any mind. She was too busy rubbing the baby and telling him to breathe. The woman had said some words she'd only heard her papa use, and in the end, the baby took his first breath. Sharon had collapsed onto her pillow in grateful sobs; her crying ebbed as the infant's screams filled the air.

Anastasia walked to the head of the bed where Sharon

lay propped upon the flattened pillows. Dark circles tugged at the skin under her eyes, and when she lifted her gaze, red brimmed her eyelids. She looked as tired as Anastasia had ever seen her, but when she looked at Anastasia, she somehow managed a smile. The baby squeaked, and her mother patted him lightly on his bottom. The shift fell from her shoulder, leaving plenty of room for the naked infant to suckle unobstructed. The baby's mouth stilled, and Sharon gently lifted him, moving him to the other breast. She slid a finger along his cheek to guide him on to the nipple. A fleeting moment of jealousy caught Anastasia off guard. She couldn't decide who she envied more: Sharon for having a baby to hold in her arms or the child within her mother's embrace. It had been ages since she'd felt those arms for more than a moment's hug.

"What shall you name him?" Anastasia asked, pushing her jealousy aside.

Sharon lifted her gaze. "That's not for me to say."

"Why not? He's your baby."

"I gave birth to him, but your papa is the man of the house. It is he who will give him his name as he gave both you and Ezra yours."

"But you made him in your belly. He belongs to you," Anastasia countered.

"It's just the way things are," Sharon said softly.

Anastasia put her hands on her hips and narrowed her eyes. "When I grow up, I'm going to name my own baby."

Sharon smiled once more. "Well, thankfully, that will not happen for many years."

"And I'm only going to kiss my husband if he's nice to me." She regretted her words the instant she saw the smile disappear from her mother's lips. "I'm sorry, Momma."

The smile returned. "There's no need to be sorry. I hope

you get everything you wish for."

Mrs. Johnston lowered the sheet and stood. "The child is very astute."

"Too much so sometimes," Sharon replied.

Mrs. Johnston washed her hands in the pan that had held the boiling water, which had long since cooled. "Though he was small, the baby did some damage. You need to refrain from relations until you are fully healed. Don't let your man pressure you into anything before your body is ready. Blame it on the baby. The boy is extremely fragile. Keep him near you and do not allow him to cry too long. He is weak and will need his energy to nurse."

Sharon switched the baby to the other breast. "You know a lot about babies."

The woman nodded. "I gave birth to three and helped with so many more. It seems like someone's always giving birth. No wonder there are so many children running the streets these days. Not many around here can afford to feed the ones they've got, much less the new ones that come along. Why, just the other day, I was asked to take a baby to the church and leave it on the chapel doorstep."

Anastasia wondered which church she was speaking of and further wondered if the baby was still there. She wouldn't mind having a baby of her own to care for.

Sharon pulled the infant closer. "I can't imagine having to give my baby away."

Mrs. Johnston paused, looking from Anastasia to Sharon. "Sometimes, mothers have to do what is best for the child. The mother I speak of already had eleven children, all skin and bones, and all living in a two-bedroom tenement. You are very fortunate in some ways, not so much in others."

"Momma?" Anastasia said, wrinkling her brow. "How many fingers is eleven?"

"Two hands plus one more finger," Sharon answered and grinned when Anastasia tried to figure out how to add an extra finger.

"Child, you should go and fetch your brother. We've been imposing on your neighbor for much too long."

Guilt pulled at the pit of Anastasia's stomach. Not only had she let her mom down by dawdling, she'd been so caught up in the birth of her new brother and counting fingers that she'd completely forgotten about the brother she already had. She hurried from the room, eager to collect Ezra and bring him to see their new brother.

***

Ezra's breathing softened, showing he'd finally fallen asleep. Anastasia pushed off the low bed and tiptoed from the room. The living space was dark except for a small lamp in the corner of the room. Mrs. Johnston had left, and her father had yet to return home, leaving the apartment eerily quiet. She crossed the room quickly and stuck her head into her parents' room.

"Come in, Anna," Sharon said upon seeing her.

"Ezra's asleep and Papa hasn't returned." She spoke softly so as not to disturb the sleeping baby who'd yet to be named.

"Come sit by me," Sharon said, patting the bed beside her.

She hurried onto the bed, eager to be next to her mother and get a closer look at the baby.

Sharon lifted the baby to her shoulder and softly patted his back. A few moments later, the baby made a small sound. "Do you want to hold him?"

"Oh, yes. Very much so," she said, and trembled slightly

when Sharon transferred him to her arms. Clean and wrapped in a thin blanket, he fit in her arms as if he belonged. From the extra padding on his bottom, she could tell he was wearing one of the soft cotton diapers she'd helped her mother make from fabric bought at the market the last time they went shopping together. He opened an eye and tried to focus, then shut it once more. His skin was blotchy red and left darker splotches when she touched him. His nose twitched. Except for the dark fuzz on top his head, he reminded her of a newborn mouse squirming in a nest, red and devoid of hair. The baby's face scrunched and he wriggled in her arms.

Please don't cry or Momma will take you away.

As if hearing her request, his face softened and he stilled once more. "He's so little."

"He is," Sharon agreed. "He'll need a lot of tending to so that he can grow big and strong."

"I'll help you take care of him," Anastasia said without looking.

"Anna, I have something to ask of you. It'll be our secret and something you must not tell Papa."

It must be extremely important if she didn't want Papa to know. She raised her head and looked at her mother.

"I need to get my strength up, and I cannot do so while nursing the baby and chasing after Ezra. I'll need you to stay home from school and help me. You'll need to do the daily chores and help look after Ezra like you did when the baby made me ill. Will you do that for me?"

Anastasia swallowed. She didn't want to tell her mother no, but she was afraid of what her papa would say. "What will I tell Papa when he asks me what I learned in school that day?"

"I will teach you your lessons while the children sleep. Then if he asks, you can tell him what you learned."

Anastasia sighed. "Okay, Momma."

Sharon frowned. "I'm sorry. I know how much you enjoy school."

I don't, not really anyway. "I don't mind."

Her mother reached and lifted Anastasia's chin. "Your face tells me different."

"It's just that Mrs. Ellis told me she would teach me to write my name."

Sharon's frown deepened. "But you know how to write your name, Anna. I've watched you do it."

Anastasia shrugged. "Anna is a baby name. I wish to write my proper name. Only, Mrs. Ellis is too busy to teach me."

Her mother's face brightened. "Did you know I was a teacher before I married your papa?"

"Really!?" Anastasia said so loudly, the baby's eyes fluttered.

"Indeed. I was fourteen when I took the test that allowed me to teach."

"Why are you not a teacher anymore?"

Sharon sighed. "Because I married your papa."

"Mrs. Ellis is married, and she teaches." She knew it to be true, as the woman was always speaking of something her husband had either said or did.

"Yes, but your father wishes for me not to work."

Not for the first time Anastasia found her answer difficult to accept. "Were you happy when you were a teacher?"

Sharon stared at her for a moment before answering. "Yes, teaching made me very happy."

I don't understand. "Papa doesn't make you happy. He makes you cry."

"It wasn't always like that. There was a time when he made me happy and I him."

"If you're my teacher, will that make you happy?"

"Yes, Anna, it will make me very happy. But remember,

we cannot tell your father. Not ever."

"I wish Papa would never come home."

"Oh, Anastasia, you must never say that. We need your papa. He works hard to make sure we have a roof over our head and food in our belly. So many people do not have that these days. Don't ever wish that away."

Anastasia held her ground. "But if Papa were not here, you could be a teacher again. Then you'd be happy."

"A teacher's pay would not be enough to keep us in this apartment alone. We'd have to rent out some of the rooms, and things would be much worse than they are now. I know you don't understand, but it's how things are done. Women stay home with their families, and men work to give them a home."

Anastasia narrowed her eyes. "When I get bigger, I'm going to work and keep all my money for myself. Then I can be happy all the time."

Sharon cast a glance towards the window as if looking for an escape. "And just where will you work, my daughter?"

She shrugged her shoulders. Maybe I will work at the Triangle Shirtwaist Factory. One of the girls in my class said her sister works there and she's going to work there when she gets older. She says her sister gets fifteen whole dollars a week."

The baby started to cry, and her mother took him and placed him at her breast. "She told you this, did she?"

"She did. She said she'll be going to work there soon herself." Anastasia purposely left out the other things Frieda had told her, knowing her mother wouldn't approve.

"You mustn't get caught up in the glamour, Anna. Those factories are not nice places to work. The people in them work very long hours for their money. I guess they should be grateful to have the job. There are so few to be had, especially for girls. You make sure to remember that when you sit down to eat your supper each night. Your papa may have his faults, but he's a good provider. Trust me when I say we could be a lot worse off."

Worse than hearing your screams and listening to you cry? "I don't like it when Papa makes you cry."

Sharon closed her eyes. The next time she spoke, her words were barely a whisper. "Neither do I."

***

It was the following evening when her father finally returned home. The way he casually entered the house as if coming home from a day's work bemused Anastasia. Unshaven and smelly, it was apparent he'd slept in his clothes. Anastasia stood at the stove carefully reheating the roast, which was mostly untouched from the evening prior. Sharon had showed her how to make a brown gravy from flour and pan drippings, which Anastasia then ladled over the roast to help keep it from growing dry.

Her father looked past her, saw her mother sitting on the sofa with the baby, and let out a breath. He walked to where they were sitting and stood without speaking.

"You have a son," Sharon said, turning the infant where he could see. "He seems to be healthy."

"He's eating, then?" her father asked.

"My milk's not in yet, but he's latching on," Sharon replied. "He's small, so he will need a strong name."

Her father considered this for a moment. "Alright."

"Maybe Momma can name the baby?" Anastasia said from the kitchen.

Her father glared in her direction. "Mind your place, girl."

"I'm not 'girl.' I'm Anastasia," she said, meeting his

stare. She was angry at him for leaving her mother when he knew she was in distress. And she was mad that Sharon would not be allowed to name the baby that had caused her so much pain. "Momma should be allowed to name the baby. He hurt her really bad. Mrs. Johnston had to use the needle and sew her up, there was blood and everything. I know; I had to wash it out of the sheets."

She watched as the color drained from her father's face. She'd seen that look before many times just before her mother lowered her head into a bucket. While she cringed every time Sharon retched, thinking her father was about to do the same emboldened her.

"It took me a lot of scrubbing and I did a good job, but you can still see the stain. I wouldn't look under the covers if I were you," she warned.

"Anastasia, that is quite enough," Sharon chided.

Anastasia turned so neither could see the smirk spreading across her face. "I cleaned the water closet too. It sure was a slippery mess. Boy, Papa, you don't look so good."

She'd barely gotten the words out when her father raced towards her and grabbed the cleaning bucket. Leaning forward, he spilled the contents of his stomach.

She smiled and looked to her mother, who to her surprise, was just as pale. The woman narrowed her eyes in warning and shook her head.

Bravado spent, Anastasia rushed to the water closet to retrieve a cloth for her father's face. When she returned, Papa was gone.

"You are playing a dangerous game, Anastasia," Sharon said when she turned.

Anastasia shrugged her shoulders. "He's gone and he didn't get a chance to make you cry."

Sharon's face softened. When she spoke, her words

were barely audible. "It's only temporary, Anna. You mustn't fuel the fire."

Chapter Eight

Sometime during the night, Anastasia woke to the squeak of her bedroom door. Opening her eyes, she saw her papa's silhouette in standing in the door frame. She closed her eyes, hoping he didn't realize he'd woken her. Even though she hadn't dared peek, she knew when he moved to the side of her bed, as she could smell the liquor that seeped from his pores and mingled with day-old sweat. He rarely came into her room, and his presence scared her. She remembered how she'd acted towards him earlier and wondered if he'd come to punish her for making him get sick. She listened for the sound of his belt being pulled from his waistband. The sound never came. She trembled when he sat on the edge of her bed.

"Anna, are you awake?" His words came out in a drunken slur.

Her heart raced, but she refused to open her eyes. *Surely he wouldn't beat her if he thought she were sleeping.*

He pushed off the bed, and she willed herself not to move. A moment later, she heard the click of her bedroom door. *He's gone.*

She slipped from bed and tiptoed across the room, opening the door as quietly as possible. She watched him walk to his bedroom, where he pushed open the door and looked in on Sharon. *Maybe he's hungry. He left without having his supper. Maybe that's why he wanted to know if I were awake. Maybe I should ask him before he wakes up Momma.* She opened her mouth to do just that when he turned and staggered his way to the sofa. He swayed in place for several seconds then stretched out without removing his clothes. By the time she summoned the courage and made her way to the sofa, meaning to ask if he'd had any supper, his breathing showed he was already asleep.

She went to her parents' room, entering without a sound. A low lamp was burning on the dresser, illuminating the room in a soft glow. She entered and stood beside the bed for a moment, watching her mother sleep. She looked peaceful with the baby nestled in the crook of her arm. The baby's eyes remained closed, but on occasion, his lips pursed as if sucking on something she couldn't see. She worried Sharon would roll over onto him in the middle of the night and reached to move him to the dresser drawer that had been cleared for his bed. She stopped when her mother opened her eyes.

"What is it, Anna?" she asked, her voice husky with sleep.

"You were sleeping so soundly; I thought you might roll over on the baby. I was going to put him in his bed."

Sharon yawned. "Leave him for now. It has been a while since he last nursed. He should be waking soon to eat. Why are you not asleep?"

"Papa came home." She thought about telling her mother he'd come into her room, but something told her that Sharon would not be happy with that news.

"He came home? Where is he?" She was fully awake now.

"He's on the sofa. I thought to ask him if he wanted his supper, but he was already sleeping. He didn't remove his clothes, and he smells mighty bad of the drink and other things."

"Go back to your room, Anna. And you must be quiet so as not to wake your papa," Sharon said firmly.

"Yes, Momma." She left the room but decided to check

on Ezra before returning to bed. She found him curled into a ball sleeping on the floor at the base of his bed. *He must have fallen out.* She struggled to lift him back into his bed. Difficult to do, as his body hung like a heavy wet mop. As she dumped him onto the bed, his eyes fluttered, and he mumbled something she didn't understand. She sat beside him and rubbed his back until she was certain he was sleeping. She thought about staying with him, but knowing how he tossed and turned, knew she'd sleep better in her own bed. Closing the door, she returned to her room and quickly fell asleep.

She woke to the sound of the baby crying. Her door was still closed, and it frightened her she could hear him so clearly. Remembering Mrs. Johnston's warning about not letting him cry, she hurried to get dressed, eager to see what the problem was. She opened her door and glanced towards Ezra's bedroom. The door was open, showing the room to be empty. A quick sweep of the living space produced neither Ezra nor her father. She hurried to her parents' room to find Ezra on the bed, crouched on chubby legs, staring up wide-eyed at his mother, who was trying unsuccessfully to get the baby to stop wailing. For a moment, she wasn't sure who was crying harder, the infant or her mother. Though, unlike Sharon, the baby's eyes produced no tears. His little fingers splayed out from his tiny hands, arms outstretched and flailing as his angry wails filled the room.

"The baby's crying, Momma," Anastasia said, stating the obvious.

"Baby crying," Ezra repeated from his perch upon the bed.

Sharon looked down through tear-filled eyes. "My milk has not come in yet."

"But he was eating just yesterday," Anastasia countered.

"That was the early milk; it's not enough. Run

downstairs and ask Mrs. Johnston what will help my milk to flow," Sharon said and turned her attention to the baby without waiting for a reply.

Anastasia was halfway down the stairs when she saw Mrs. Johnston coming up the stairwell, wearing a crisply ironed yellow print dress. Her silky red hair was pulled back with a matching bow. She had a large covered basket draped over her arm and looked as if she didn't have a care in the world. Anastasia felt her shoulders relax. She'd never been so happy to see anyone in her life.

The woman smiled a wrinkled smile. "Young lady, from the look on your face, I'd say you were just coming to find me."

"My momma sent me," Anastasia said, turning and falling into step beside her. "The baby is crying something fierce. Momma said her milk isn't coming in. Momma's scared. I can tell, because she's crying as hard as the baby. Papa's not home. He came home last night, but he was gone when I woke. He smelled real bad."

Mrs. Johnston laughed. "Do you have any more news for me?"

Anastasia thought about telling the woman about her papa coming into her room but decided against it. Instead, she shook her head.

The woman tapped the basket she was carrying. "I brought something that will help with your momma's milk."

Anastasia stopped and stared at the woman. "How'd you know?"

Mrs. Johnston continued climbing the stairs, and Anastasia hurried to catch up. "The baby was early. Besides, when you've been around babies as long as I have, you just get a feel for these things. Nothing to worry about unless the milk never comes. It shouldn't be that way for your momma, but it happens sometimes."

Anastasia felt her stomach tighten. "What will we do if the milk doesn't come in?"

When they got to the second floor, the woman headed to the apartment across the hall. As usual, the door was partially open.

Anastasia sighed her frustration when Mrs. Johnston knocked on the door. *Hadn't she told them they should not allow the baby to cry?* She hurried to catch up with the woman, tugging on the length of her dress.

"No, Mrs. Johnston, you're at the wrong apartment," she said anxiously.

The woman opened the door, and Anastasia reluctantly followed her inside. As was the case the previous times she saw inside the room, the apartment was a mess of clothes and trash and smelled nearly as bad as the hallway from where they'd just come. The woman who'd carried her down the steps came out of the bedroom, her full attention on the baby that was straddling her left hip. She looked up, saw them standing in the living room, and her eyes narrowed.

Mrs. Johnston looked around the filthy room and shook her head. "Just look at this mess. Don't you know this is how disease starts? Come on, Caroline; you know as well as I that little one on your hip needs a clean place to crawl."

Though the baby had been changed, the woman was wearing the same tattered dress Anastasia had seen her wearing the previous day. She waved her hand at Mrs. Johnston. "You don't have no right coming in here and telling me what to do. I didn't invite you in."

Mrs. Johnston stood her ground. "The blazes I don't. You got bugs crawling up your walls. I live in this building too. It's bad enough we have to deal with rodents, now we have to fend off the bugs as well. Hand that child to the girl. I need you to come across the hall with me."

"I ain't lost nothing across the hall," the woman shot back.

"Didn't say you did. But there's a baby over there that will die if he doesn't get something to eat."

Caroline dared a glance towards the door. "And that's my problem, why?"

"The baby needs a wet nurse."

Caroline looked to the door again. "I hear people pay for that."

Mrs. Johnston took a step closer towards her. "Just get your sorry self across the hall, woman."

Caroline grumbled something under her breath and handed her son to Anastasia, who placed the child on her hip the way his mother had and followed the two women across the hall. The second they opened the door, they could hear the baby's cries. Mrs. Johnston took a jar from the basket then placed the basket on the low table in the living room. She motioned for them to follow and led the procession to the bedroom, where Anastasia's mother was still frantically trying to get the baby to nurse. Anastasia took the child she was holding and moved to the corner, staying quiet so as not to be sent from the room.

Caroline approached Sharon and reached for the baby. Mrs. Johnston put up her hand to stop her. "Go to the water closet and wash. Make sure to scrub your breasts."

The two women stared at each other for several moments before Caroline finally turned and walked away.

"What is she doing here?" Sharon asked when Caroline was out of earshot.

"I brought her to feed the baby."

Sharon's eyes grew wide and she pulled the screaming infant tighter to her chest. "She'll do no such thing."

"Then it's likely your child will die," Mrs. Johnston said, holding her ground.

"But he's my baby," Sharon said on a sob.

Mrs. Johnston handed the jar to Anastasia's mother. "Drink this. It will help your milk to come in. Until then, Caroline's milk will help keep the baby alive."

Sharon removed the lid, sniffed, and wrinkled her nose. "What's in it?"

"Milk with a bit of garlic. My mother used it and her mother before her. I'll bring you some up each day until your breasts are full."

"It's awful," Sharon replied after tasting.

"You can always wait and see if your milk will come in on its own. I'm sure Caroline won't mind nursing the baby until it does," Mrs. Johnston said, reaching for the jar.

Anastasia was mesmerized by the way Mrs. Johnston handled the situation. Especially the way she took charge when the room was spinning out of control. Caroline didn't want to feed the baby any more than Sharon wanted her to, but Sharon didn't know it, and in the end, Sharon drank the contents of the jar, holding it high and making sure she got the last drop.

Caroline came out of the water closet smelling of Sharon's perfume. If her mother noticed, she didn't mention it. She simply handed the baby to her and turned away as Caroline placed the baby to her breast. Instantly, the crying ceased as the baby suckled hungrily at the milk-filled breast.

"He's so little," Caroline said, watching him eat. "Does he have a name yet?"

"Tobias," Sharon said without turning. "Tobias Alphers Millett."

Anastasia blinked her surprise. *Papa must have named him before he left for work.* She wanted to ask if that were the case, but Sharon didn't seem to be in the mood for answering questions.

"I've never held such a little one before. He seems strong, though. Just look at him suckle." Caroline's voice was softer now.

"He was born before his time. Your milk will help him survive until his mother's milk comes in," Mrs. Johnston replied, then turned to Anastasia's mother. "Make sure to offer him your breast often. The stimulation will help. Try not to get upset if he doesn't eat. Doing so is good for neither you nor the baby."

Sharon nodded but refrained from turning.

Mrs. Johnston placed a hand on her shoulder. "Have you or the children eaten breakfast yet?"

"No." The words came out on a whisper of guilt.

"Go to the kitchen and find them something to eat. I'll see to things here." Mrs. Johnston looked in Anastasia's direction. "Take the boys and go with your mother."

She wanted to resist, but the woman's tone left no room for argument. She admired that about the woman. When she spoke, people did what she said. As Anastasia neared the door, she looked over her shoulder, meeting Mrs. Johnston's eye. She liked the way the woman seemed to know what people were thinking before they even spoke. It was in that moment Anastasia knew she was looking at the person she herself would be someday.

Mrs. Johnston smiled as if knowing her inner thoughts. "Anastasia, I made you a pillow for your bed. You'll find it in the basket in the other room. There was enough left over for a pretty bow for your hair. I'm sure you'll recognize the fabric."

***

"Mrs. Johnston is right. Anastasia is very astute," Cindy

said, finishing the first stack of papers. "Somehow I feel as if the woman was grooming her for something."

"She was a quick study, that's for sure. No wonder she has an attitude. Just like her brother, she had a pretty heavy load on her shoulders," Linda said, lowering her stack of papers. "I do worry about the untolds."

"You mean her father? I agree. What do you think about Sharon?"

"I think she is a product of the times. Too scared to say boo without her husband's permission. Women did not have identities. I remember seeing letters from my mother that were signed 'Mrs. Jonathon Wilkins.' For the longest time, they were thought of as no more than property. An unruly wife was a reflection of her husband and the men were allowed to discipline their wives, expected to even. Men didn't get in trouble if they beat their wives, unless maybe the beatings went too far."

"And you wonder why I've never married," Cindy said with a huff.

"Times have changed and you know it. You've never married because you don't socialize. When was the last time you went out?"

"Speaking of going out, I think tomorrow will be a good day to go to Frankenmuth," Cindy said, hoping to change the subject.

"I guess I could do with a bit of retail therapy." Linda pushed off the couch. "I'm going to go find us something for supper. "Oh, and you can wipe that smile from your face. I saw what you did there, trying to change the subject."

"I love you, Mom." Cindy snickered.

"I love you too. Even if you are an old spinster," Linda said and left the room.

Cindy remained seated long after Linda left the room,

thinking about the pages she'd just read. She wondered at the schoolteacher Mrs. Ellis and how difficult her job must have been. The classroom would have been filled with children, most of whom would have spoken little to no English. How frustrated she must have been not to be able to help with such a simple request of teaching a child their proper name. She thought of her own students and wondered if there were things they'd like to be taught she hadn't had time to teach. If anything, reading the journals was giving her insight to how things used to be and reminding her not to take her position for granted.

She wondered at Anastasia's mother and how she'd been made to give up teaching because her husband wanted her to stay home. Though she had no suitors at present, would she be willing to give up everything for a man? Why should she? Linda was right; times had changed and so had the thinking. One thing was for sure, if a man ever laid a hand on her, it would be the last time he'd hit a woman. Her or anyone else.

Chapter Nine

Cindy walked through the aisle looking at the dazzling ornaments. They'd taken a break from the journals and spent the morning walking through the shops in Frankenmuth, known as Michigan's Christmas town. Now they were in Bronner's Christmas Wonderland, the world's largest Christmas store, enjoying Christmas in July. Cindy picked up a light blue ornament in the shape of baby booties. The top of the booties had white lettering that read *Baby's First Christmas*. Below it, a blank surface was intentionally pressed flat, ready to be personalized. She looked around in search of Linda and sighed when she didn't see her. *Good grief, you're acting like a child afraid of being caught.* Still, she didn't want to have to explain. At least not until she had something to show for her actions. Clutching the ornament, she hurried to the personalization station and filled out the paperwork, all the while expecting Linda to come up behind her and chide her for the silliness of her actions.

The woman behind the counter looked to be double her age. Wearing a red and white frilly apron, bright red lipstick, and an even brighter smile, she could have passed for Mrs. Claus, save the absence of snow white hair. She took the ornament and looked over the paper Cindy had given her. She read the name and smiled. "I call mine Pig."

Puzzled, Cindy wrinkled her brow. "Excuse me?"

"My grandson, he has the cutest little pudgy nose, so I call him Pig. He's my first. How many grandchildren do you have?" the woman asked, looking at her expectantly.

Cindy had a sudden desire to look in the mirror. *Do I really look that old?* She pulled herself taller and brushed her hair behind her ears. "This is for a friend. I don't have any grandchildren. Or children to give them to me."

The woman blushed. "Oh, I'm sorry."

The way she said it gave Cindy the impression she'd apologized for Cindy's lack of family, not the presumption she'd made. Cindy read the name on the woman's nametag— Linda—and sighed. *Maybe it comes with the name.*

Linda Claus walked to the back counter and handed the ornament to another worker, then returned to the counter and handed Cindy a claim ticket. "You caught us in a sweet spot. We're not that busy, so it'll only be a few moments."

Cindy thanked her, took the ticket, and returned to her shopping. She'd accumulated several ornaments and a new piece for her Christmas Village by the time her mother joined her, dropping an armload of ornaments into Cindy's cart.

"What?" Linda asked when Cindy frowned.

Cindy pointed to the ornaments. "Are you paying for those or am I?"

"They're for your tree," Linda said with a shrug.

"Mom, we only have a three-foot tree. I don't have room for all those ornaments. Besides, I have all the ones we found in Grandma Mildred's storage shed that we still have to figure out what to do with."

Linda's face scrunched for a moment then gave way to a huge smile. "You're right; we need a bigger tree. Good thing we came to Frankenmuth early. If we'd waited for the holidays, they'd probably be sold out."

Cindy watched in stunned disbelief as Linda took a right and made a beeline to the back of the building where the Christmas trees were on display. For a seventy-five-year-old lady, the woman was surprisingly spry.

"Why don't we just purchase one that's fully decorated," Cindy fussed when she finally caught up with Linda.

Linda's eyes glazed over as if considering the possibility. "That's not a bad idea."

"I was being facetious," Cindy groaned.

"Pity, I saw a white tree gloriously decorated with brilliant blue ornaments," Linda replied.

Cindy knew exactly the one she was speaking of; she'd stopped to admire it as well. But some things did not fit within a teacher's budget. Things like the ten-foot spruce Linda was currently staring at. "Rein it in, Mom. That tree won't even fit in the house."

"It would if we cut the top off," Linda said, taking another lap around the huge tree.

Cindy bit her lip. "Or we could look at a smaller tree."

"What's the fun in that?" Linda said with a sigh.

"The fun is not paying for something we don't need. Like a ten-foot tree."

"Fine, we'll get a seven foot," Linda grumbled.

Cindy moved past her to look at the trees in the next row. "Six foot will be fine."

For a moment, it looked as if Linda were going to stamp her foot. Cindy sent her a look she normally reserved for an unruly child in her classroom. The funniest part was that it was the same look her mother had often used on her. To her surprise, Linda gave in and walked to the area that held the six-foot trees.

"This one looks real," she said, pointing at a lighted tree with snow-covered pinecones.

"Real expensive. Take it down a notch. This is Michigan. We get plenty of snow, and we can do without the pinecones."

Linda pointed to a tree Cindy herself had been admiring. "I like that one."

Cindy checked the price tag and let out a breath. "So do I."

"I'll get a salesperson before you change your mind," Linda said, heading off before Cindy could argue.

As Cindy waited, she looked through the basket to see what had captured Linda's eye. As she dug through the treasures, she smiled. There in the center of the cart was the same ornament she'd chosen. She picked it up, wondering if Linda would choose to personalize it with Tobias, or Mouse, which was what she'd chosen. Funny they'd both been drawn to the same ornament for the same reason. *I guess we're more alike than I realize.*

"Aw, you found the blue bootie," Linda said, coming up beside her.

"I did," Cindy said, suddenly feeling extra close to the woman.

"I got a pink one too. Who's to say if my future grandchild will be a boy or girl," Linda said, breaking the moment.

***

"Something wrong with your chicken?" Linda asked.

Cindy looked to see her mother staring at her. "What?"

"You're picking at your chicken; I was wondering if there was something wrong with it."

"No, I love Zehnder's chicken. I was just thinking of the journals. Of Tobias and Anastasia's mom's predicament, to be exact." Cindy tilted her head. "Mom, did Dad ever raise a hand to you?"

Linda pointed her fork at her. "You know better than to

ask that. And today of all days."

She'd been purposely avoiding mentioning her father's birthday to prevent upsetting Linda. "I know what day it is. I didn't mean to upset you. It seemed like you two had the perfect marriage, but as we've seen from reading the journals, no one knows what goes on behind closed doors."

Linda set her fork down and wiped her mouth with the linen napkin. "Your father never laid a hand on me. He knew I'd never tolerate it, but that wasn't the reason. Your father was not a violent man."

Cindy sighed. "I didn't think so, but I wanted to know for sure."

Linda took a bite of mashed potatoes and pointed her fork once more. "I had a friend in one of those relationships. They got married, had a couple of kids, and he started his crap right after that. My friend's mother was long dead, so she did the only thing she could think of. She went to his mother and told her of her son's actions."

"What'd she say?" Cindy asked.

"His mother told my friend not to spread lies. Told her if she ever said anything to anyone, they'd see to it she was declared unfit and take the children from her. Even worse, his sister was there and sided with the man and his mother."

"Wow, what'd she do?"

"Had no choice. At least in her mind."

"Did things ever get better?"

"No. You know what they say about a leopard changing its spots. I tried to get her to leave. She did once, but he wooed her back. It was good for a while, but I knew when it started again. She didn't say much to me, as she knew I'd have a thing or two to say about how he was treating her. But it was there. I could see it in her eyes. Stayed with the man for sixty years putting up with his crap. Didn't get out of the relationship until she died."

"That's too bad."

"It was. She was different when she was away from him. Happier. I often wondered how much she would have blossomed if she hadn't stayed. You know, I harp about you getting married, but I'd rather see you die a spinster than get caught up in a relationship like that."

Cindy smiled. "Thanks, Mom."

"Yep, thankfully, nowadays, a girl doesn't have to be married to have kids," Linda said, digging the last of the buttered egg noodles out of the bowl.

***

Anastasia walked through the market gathering the things on her mother's shopping list. She'd just finished collecting the last thing on her list when she saw the boy who'd given her the silk fabric. He wore the same rags she'd seen him in previously and looked as if he hadn't had a bath in weeks. He stood next to a cheese cart looking longingly at a large wedge of cheese. He looked up, saw her, and smiled. Forgetting the cheese, he rushed to where she stood. A few seconds later, the dog joined them.

"What's in the basket?" He started to lift the cloth that covered her wares when she slapped his hand away. "Hey, what'd you do that for?"

"For one thing, your hands are grubby. For another, what I have is none of your business."

He grinned. "I bet you stole them. That's why you don't want me to see."

She pulled her chin up. "I did nothing of the sort. My mother gave me the money so I could buy the things on my list."

"Why?"

The question was so simple, she didn't understand it. "What do you mean 'why'?'

"I saw you take the apple. The pile didn't even move. Why not take what you want instead of turning over your hard-earned money?"

She thought about telling him it'd taken ages to learn to pick an apple from the cart without disrupting the others. Pride kept her from doing so. "It's not my money; it's my momma's."

He shrugged. "Well, where'd she get it from?"

"Why, from Papa, of course."

"And where'd your papa get it from?"

"He earned it."

"There you go. So if your papa worked so hard to get it, why just give it away?"

"I didn't give it away; I used it to buy the things my momma asked me to bring. Besides, Papa's a proud man. He'd be angry if I didn't spend the money wisely." Not that he knew it was she spending it. Neither she nor her mother had ever divulged the fact it was Anastasia who'd done the shopping for the past year. She smiled, knowing her papa still thought of her as a baby.

"What's so funny?"

"Papa doesn't know I'm here. He thinks my momma does all the shopping. Wouldn't he be surprised?"

"See then, he won't even know."

"But Momma would. She doesn't like people who steal." She wanted to say that included him but decided against it.

"So don't tell her."

Anastasia wrinkled her nose in frustration. "She'll know when she looks in her coin purse."

"Not if you take the money out before you return it," the boy said with a grin. "Think of how rich you'd be if you kept all that money for yourself."

Anastasia felt her eyes grow wide. "I couldn't take money from my own momma."

"What about your pop? You said yourself it isn't your momma's money," the boy pressed.

He's right. She thought about the items on her list and wondered how hard it would be to get them without being caught.

"See, you're thinking about it. Just think of all the things you could buy if you had money."

She considered this for a moment, then frowned. "I cannot buy anything. My momma would see it and then she'd know."

"Where did you tell her the fabric came from?"

She hadn't. Mrs. Johnston had taken it before she'd had a chance. She reached a hand to the bow she wore in her hair. "She doesn't know about it."

"There you go. Just make sure whatever you buy is small so you can hide it. If your mom ever finds it, just tell her I gave it to you."

Anastasia remembered the look on Sharon's face when she'd seen the boy running through the streets. *She would not like that. Maybe I could just keep the money. I could put it in a sock, like Momma does, and keep it for a rainy day.* "Maybe I could take a few things next time and save the money."

He tilted his head to look at her. "What's the fun in that?"

"I don't know, but I could hide money better than hiding things, so I think maybe that's what I'm going to do."

He didn't look impressed with her decision. "If you're going to do that, you might as well get a job."

"I'm not old enough to get a job. But I will when I get older. I'm going to make my own money, and nobody can tell me what to use it for."

"My friend James has a job. He has to give all his money to his momma. That's 'cause his pop likes to pick up the bottle. His momma would kick his pop out, 'cept she likes he keeps putting babies in her belly."

Anastasia stared at him. "How's he do that?"

He shrugged. "Don't know, but that's what my friend says."

Anastasia decided not to believe this. Tobias was her mother's baby; she'd seen him come into the world. Her father had left before the baby was born and had played absolutely no part in it.

"I'd work at one of these carts that sells food so I never have to go hungry. What kind of job would you do?" the boy asked, bringing her out of her musings.

"I think I'd like to work at the Triangle Factory. I heard a girl say her sister gets paid fifteen whole dollars a week to work there."

The boy whistled through what few teeth he had. "Wow. Fifteen dollars. Maybe I should get a job there too."

"You can't work there; it's a sewing factory. Only girls work there and it's real hard work."

He considered this for a moment. "Yeah, well, I wouldn't want to work there no how 'cause they don't have food and I want a job where I can eat."

Eating made her think of dinner and dinner made her think of the shopping she still had to do. "I must be on my way. Momma is home with both babies and needs my help."

"That's okay; I got some shopping to do myself."

"You got money?"

He grinned. "Girl, ain't you learned nothing 'bout me? I don't need money."

Something about what he'd just said bothered her. She

thought about it a moment and realized he'd called her "girl." Her papa was the only one that ever did that. She didn't like it then, and she didn't care for it now. "My name's Anastasia."

He nodded his head. "Suits you. They call me Runt."

"What kind of name's that?"

"The only kind I got," he said, narrowing his eyes.

"What's it mean?"

"Means I'm small."

"You're bigger than me," she offered.

"That's 'cause I'm older than you. I'm small compared to most."

"Do you like the name?"

"It's the only one I got," he repeated." He looked at the cheese cart and smiled. "Time for me to go. Guy's got a crowd."

She grabbed his arm. "Aren't you afraid you'll be caught?"

"Not likely. It's the best time to get what you want. The guy'll be too busy helping the paying customer to see you lift something. Watch the customers, though. They see you take something, and they'll rat you out. Make sure you have a plan."

"What kind of plan?"

"A plan of where to run if you get caught," he said with a wink.

She stood at the edge of the road watching as Runt made his way to the edge of the cheese cart. Pretending to look in the other direction, he waited until the man turned his back to place a hunk of cheese in a cloth then made his move, pocketing a huge slice of cheese and disappearing into the crowd.

Chapter Ten

Anastasia stood at the edge of the wagon, trying to gather her nerve. She'd come for garlic, bunches of which hung from the canopy close enough to grab if only she could summon the courage to do so. She smiled at the man behind the cart and moved to the front, pretending to inspect the vegetables. Though vendors were understandably wary of street children who often stole from the carts, she'd purchased from him dozens of times, so her presence didn't appear to alarm him.

The man limped closer and smiled a yellowed smile. "What'll it be today, Little Miss?"

"A couple of handfuls of those green beans," Anastasia said, pointing to the far side of the cart.

As the man busied himself gathering the beans, Anastasia moved back to where she'd previously stood. Keeping a watch on the man, she casually plucked a bunch of garlic and swiftly placed it under the towel that hid the contents of her market basket. She pulled Sharon's coin purse from her waistband and paid for the beans with trembling fingers. Collecting her purchase, she walked away from the cart, fully expecting to be called back and pronounced a thief. She'd gone ten steps before chancing a look over her shoulder. She relaxed upon seeing the vegetable man busily chatting with a woman who'd moved into her place.

She lifted the towel and stared at her ill-gotten gain. Runt was right; it'd been so easy. She moved to the bread cart and waited for the man to become engaged in conversation before palming a whole loaf of fresh bread, slipping it under the towel unnoticed. She moved through the market claiming each item on her list, marveling at how easy it was to procure everything her mother had sent her for. For everything she purchased, she had at least one additional item to show for her efforts. When at last her basket was full, her coin purse, normally empty, had a handful of coins remaining. Emboldened by her success, she surveyed the market, wondering what else she could pilfer.

The wind shifted, and the smell of cinnamon invaded her nostrils. She'd smelled the nuts each time she walked through the market. Until today, she'd never thought to be able to obtain something so frivolous. She turned and headed toward the source of the smell. Two carts up, a man wearing a wide-brimmed straw hat stood watch over a large metal bowl that rested on a grate over a low burning fire. Inside the bowl were fistfuls of nuts, which he stirred with a large metal spoon. Every few moments, the man would stop and pull his hand through the air, bringing it to his nostrils as if testing the doneness via smell. When satisfied, he scooped spoonfuls of nuts into several small bags. Once full, he'd hand the bags to his helper, a boy in his early teens with short curly brown hair. Unlike most boys who roamed the streets, this boy was clean and reasonably well dressed. The boy slid a glance in her direction before placing the nuts in a basket at the end of the wagon.

Anastasia moved closer, pretending to watch. The moment he turned to retrieve another, she snatched a bag of nuts, quickly placing them under the towel in her basket.

"I saw that!" the man roasting nuts shouted when she went to move away.

Anastasia froze, wondering about her next move. Should she stay and offer to pay for the stolen nuts or bolt and hope she could outrun the man the way she'd seen Runt do on several occasions. No, it wouldn't be the man who ran after her, but the boy, who was more than a foot taller than she. *I'll never outrun him.* Not wishing to break the eggs that lay loose within her basket, she sighed and reached for her change purse.

"Ha! I knew it. I saw the way you were drooling over the smell. I thought to myself, that girl is going to buy herself some roasted nuts."

Anastasia breathed a sigh of relief. *He didn't see me.* She smiled and pulled the coin purse from her waistband. Opening it, she peered inside, her smile disappearing. Summoning the saddest look she could manage, she looked up. "I'm afraid I don't have the money to purchase anything extra today."

The man looked toward the boy, who was studying her with a look she couldn't determine. "What do you say to that, Fern?"

The boy licked his lips and smiled. "I say she's pretty enough. Except for that scar on the side of her face, she'll do, I guess."

Do for what? And what does being pretty have to do with anything? Her question was answered when the boy next spoke.

"I'd say if she were to give me a kiss, I'd be willing to give her a few roasted nuts."

A kiss? Is the boy daft? Still, if I do as he says, I can have even more. Besides it's only a kiss. Momma kisses Papa all the time. Especially when she wants him not to be mad. She shrugged her acceptance.

The boy licked his lips again. He crooked a finger to draw her near then placed the finger to his cheek. She moved forward to place the kiss on his cheek, and the boy surprised her by turning his head at the last moment, kissing her directly on the lips. She pulled back, wrinkling her nose, and he laughed.

He licked the kiss from his lips. "What's the matter? Ain't you never been kissed before?"

Only by Papa and Momma. "Sure I have, plenty of times."

"Well then, don't look like you didn't like it. I've kissed plenty of girls, and they all like it just fine. Hey, how old are you anyway?"

She pulled her chin up and squared her shoulders. "My momma says menfolk ought not ask those things."

"Yeah, well I don't think I liked the kiss enough to trade."

She narrowed her eyes at him and pointed into the crowded street. "If you don't give me the nuts, I'll tell that policeman over there that you stole a kiss from me."

The boy looked to see where she was pointing. "I don't see no policeman."

"Well, he's there. Give me the nuts or I'll scream."

The man lifted the hat from his head, wiped the sweat from his scalp, and laughed. "Better do as she says, boy. The girl earned them fair and square."

The boy sighed and picked up a small bag. He dumped some of the nuts into his hand before handing her the half-filled bag. "The kiss was half good, therefore you get half a bag of nuts."

Anastasia smiled her sweetest smile and turned, knowing she'd gotten the better part of the deal. Not only had she gotten her first kiss, but she'd also gotten away with a bag and a half of freshly roasted nuts and still had a handful of coins in her coin purse.

She was still smiling when Runt stepped in front of her. Hands on his waist, his nostrils flared as he stared through narrowed eyes.

She'd seen that look one too many times, mostly before

her papa reprimanded her for something that displeased him. He brought his hand up, and she took a step backward before realizing the hand was not aimed at her but a fly that buzzed around Runt's face.

"Why'd you have to go and kiss the guy?" he asked heatedly.

She felt her face turn red. "What's it to you who I kiss?"

"Ain't nothing to me. Just wondered why you done it."

"He said if I give him a kiss, he'd give me some roasted nuts. It was only a kiss. I'd kiss him again too," she said, dropping one of the salty treats into her mouth. "What's it to you who I kiss?"

Runt glared at her. "That boy's not anything special, and yet he's always kissing girls. I tried to trade you a kiss for the blue cloth, and you wrinkled your nose."

She laughed. "Oh, that."

His breathing intensified. "What do you mean, oh that?"

"I'd have kissed you if the cloth was yours to give."

"Course it was mine to give. I stole it, didn't I?"

"Yes, so it wasn't worth a kiss. It's not as if you paid money for it."

He scratched the top of his head. "You aren't making a lick of sense."

She brushed at a fly that was buzzing around her basket. "I've got to get this meat home before it spoils. Want to walk with me?"

He cocked his head to the side. "Now why would I want to do that?"

She pulled back the cloth to show the second bag of nuts. "I can't take these home. Nor can I eat them all by myself. If I did, I wouldn't have room for my supper."

The scowl left his face as he fell into step beside her. "I just don't understand girls."

She smiled and poured some nuts into his hand. "Mrs. Johnston says men aren't supposed to understand girls. You know all there is to know about a girl and the magic is gone."

"You know how to make magic?" he asked, holding out his hand for more nuts.

"I don't think so, but if Mrs. Johnston says it, then it has to be true," Anastasia said, handing him the bag.

***

"That girl's going down a wicked highway," Linda said, setting the papers aside and shaking her head.

"Maybe it is the only way she's able to survive," Cindy said, rolling her neck to relieve the tension. "Besides, if she has to learn from someone, Mrs. Johnston seems to be a pretty good teacher."

"Are you serious? I get the impression she's been around the block a time or two." Linda shook her head. "You're seriously going to sit there and tell me you'd want that woman teaching your child?"

"I don't have a child." She regretted her words the moment she said them. She pressed on anyway, "But if I were living in that era under those circumstances, then probably I would. Better she gets her education from a woman who's been 'educated' than the boy who wants to educate her. Seriously, he licks his lips one more time and…"

"You know, your great-great grandmother did that," Linda said, cutting her off.

"Ophelia licked her lips?" Cindy asked, surprised that Linda hadn't jumped on the lack of grandchildren comment.

"No, well, I guess she could have. But I know she was a wet nurse."

"Really? How'd I not know that?"

Linda shrugged. "Guess it never came up in conversation."

"Ophelia passed long before you were born. How'd you find out?"

"It's in the family history if you ever bother to read it. Wet nursing was fairly common in the nineteenth century. The royal families pretty much started it because they wanted larger families. They would hire a wet nurse to care for the newborns so the women would not have to wait until they finished nursing to become pregnant."

Cindy slid a glance sideways. "Are you trying to tell me that my great-great grandmother nursed a royal baby?"

"Of course not. I doubt her experience was anything as exciting as that. But you see, people kept up with the royals and it was thought if it was good enough for them, it must be the right thing to do. The wealthy often looked to the royal family as an example and set about hiring wet nurses for their own children."

Cindy was intrigued. "So what, they just approached a random person with an infant and handed over their baby?"

Linda leaned back on the couch and propped her legs on the table. "It was much more precise than that. In those days, it was thought things could be passed through the breast milk."

"Things can," Cindy agreed. At least, that was what she'd heard.

"Yes, but not personality traits," Linda replied. "A woman with questionable character or a hot temper wouldn't have been allowed to wet nurse."

"Seriously?"

"Yep, it wasn't uncommon for the wet nurse to undergo a background check. Not like the ones we have these days, mind you, but they were vetted pretty well before being hired."

Cindy thought back to the journal she'd just read,

"Something tells me the neighbor across the hall wouldn't get a passing grade."

"I'm pretty sure she'd get rejected before she even applied," Linda agreed.

"So how'd you learn so much about breastfeeding anyway?"

"I was curious, especially after reading Ophelia's history. I found the subject fascinating and wanted to have all the information possible for my FG."

"FG?"

"Future Grandchild," Linda said with a grin.

Chapter Eleven

March 3, 1911

Anastasia ran her brush through the length of her hair and studied her reflection in the mirror. Though the scar remained, the angry redness had dimmed. She brushed her hair so that the heavy strands covered the scar.

The door clicked open, and Sharon entered, Tobias on her hip. He smiled when he saw her, then hurriedly closed his mouth around his thumb. Sharon lowered him to the floor and took the brush, brushing through the strands and pulling them tight against her scalp, twisting the length into a tight knot at the base of her head.

"I wanted to leave it down," Anastasia said, pulling at the knot.

Sharon sighed. "Anna, why do you insist on hiding your beautiful face?"

"I don't want my friends to make jokes about my scar."

"Tsk, it's so much better now. I hardly even notice it anymore," Sharon countered.

"That's because you see me every day. I haven't seen my friends in the year since Tobias was born."

At hearing his name, Tobias clasped on to Anastasia's skirt, pulling himself up. He stretched an arm and whined, "Momma."

It was not the first time he'd called her that. When they were alone, she often encouraged it. She bent, lifted him into her arms, and smiled at him.

"Momma," he said as his tiny fingers patted her face.

A frown flitted across Sharon's lips. She stepped forward, collecting Tobias in her arms. Tobias whimpered and stretched his hands towards Anastasia. Sharon shifted him to the opposite hip and took a step back, ignoring his demands. "Anna, I'm sorry it has been so difficult for you. You've played mother to the boys for so long, they think of you as their momma. I've asked things of you a mother should not ask of a child so young. You've been my angel. You know that, don't you? I couldn't have regained my strength had it not been for you."

"I didn't mind, Mother. You've taught me so much," Anastasia said with a smile. While helping her mother had proved difficult, Sharon had kept her promise to act as Anastasia's teacher. They'd been able to work the lessons into the household chores. Counting was the easiest to learn, as Anastasia would count the number of times she ran the soap over the wash. Each dunk into the rinse water got counted, as did the number of churns through the wringer. She counted each potato along with the number of times she sliced off a piece of the peel. She could count higher when she peeled the skin, as they had to be peeled thin so as not to waste the meat of the potato. Anastasia had learned not only to write her own name, but the name of everyone in her family as well. "I'm sure I'll know more than most of my class."

Sharon's eyes moistened. "And I so enjoyed having you here. Teaching you has brought me joy."

"Momma, you're crying. I don't have to go to school. I can stay here and help. I won't miss school at all." They'd had the same conversation the evening before, but Sharon hadn't wavered. Her papa's job at the dock was in jeopardy, something about younger workers being brought in for half the pay. She didn't know what all the fuss was about, as she'd seen inside her papa's wallet. She'd gladly work for half of that.

"Even still, I do wish you could have stayed in school with your friends," Sharon said softly.

She almost told her mother she had no friends, then thought of Frieda, the girl who sat next to her, and wondered about what new stories she'd have to share. She thought of her teacher and lifted her chin. "If I'd stayed in school, I would not yet know how to write my proper name."

"I'm sure your teacher does the best she can." Sharon paused as she shifted Tobias once more. "Anna, I want you to promise me that if you don't understand something you're taught or if you wish to learn more than what the teacher is telling, that you'll come to me so I can help you understand. Will you do that for me?"

"Do you wish for me to wait until Papa isn't around?"

"Yes, Anna, I think that would be best. And, Anna, leave the market basket with me today."

"But, Momma, I always do the shopping," Anastasia argued.

"Not anymore. Besides, your father is worried about money. He didn't give me as much as he normally does, so I need to go so I can pick things to save money."

Anastasia's heart sank. She'd gotten so adept at stealing that she always managed to get the best quality and had several handfuls of coins hidden in the bottom drawer of her dresser. Unlike her mother, she was not saving the money for a rainy day. She was saving so she could leave. However, she had no intention of going alone; she planned to take her brothers with her. Her mother could stay with Papa if that was what wives were supposed to do, but she was going to see that the boys got out. She'd been too greedy. It hadn't occurred to her to return some of the coins to her mother. Maybe if she had, she would be allowed to continue. "I can do better, Momma."

"You did fine, Anna. I'm not doing this to punish you. It's time for you to act like a little girl. Besides, it looks like a nice day. I want to take the boys out to get some fresh air."

"I could take them," Anastasia offered. She'd taken Ezra before; taking Tobias as well shouldn't be too difficult. She'd have to get used to handling them both outside the house anyway. Besides, the baby might make for a good distraction.

"That's enough, Anastasia." Sharon's tone left no room for further discussion.

"Yes, Momma," Anastasia said, trying to hide her disappointment.

***

Anastasia walked into the classroom as if she'd never missed a day. She scanned the room and frowned when she saw the seat beside Frieda occupied by a girl with long blonde hair. She thought of Mrs. Johnston and wondered what she'd do in this situation. *"Don't take no for an answer, child,"* the woman had told her on more than one occasion. *"You don't ask a person to do something you tell them. Just make sure you tell them in a way that leaves little room for further discussion."* Channeling the woman, she walked to the desk and narrowed her eyes. "You're in my seat. Get out."

The girl blinked her confusion. "This is my seat."

"It was mine first. Move!" She might have said that a bit louder than was necessary, as the whole room looked in her direction. She glanced towards Mrs. Ellis, who stood at the front of the room leaning over the desk of another student. The teacher looked to see what the commotion was about, then lowered her head without comment. Anastasia smiled and turned her attention back to the girl. "Scram."

The girl sighed. Picking up her books, she stuck her

tongue out at Anastasia as she left. Anastasia ignored the childish action as she slipped into the still-warm seat.

"Gyda isn't s-so bad," Frieda commented. She'd locked her gaze on Anastasia's face but refrained from asking questions about the scar. "Where've you b-been?"

"I've been helping my mother. She was awfully ill and needed my help with my brother and the baby. There are just so many more chores now. She's better, so I had to come back to school before my papa found out."

"I th-thought maybe you'd died."

Her comment didn't come as a surprise, as people—children included—were always dying of something. "No. I'm still alive. Haven't had so much as a cold."

"But something did h-happen to you," Frieda said, eyeing the scar once more.

Anastasia pulled her hair to cover the scar with her hand.

Frieda shook her head. "Don't hide it. I think it will help you."

"How can something this ugly help me?"

"It looks…it looks plumb fr-fright-frightening." Frieda must have been nervous, as her stutter grew worse.

Anastasia traced the scar with her index finger. "Why is that good?"

"It m-made Gyda m-m-move."

Anastasia wasn't convinced the scar had anything to do with the acquisition of the seat, but then again, maybe it did.

"How'd you get it? W-w-was it your papa?"

"No, I was clumsy is all." She was growing weary of all the questions and decided to change the subject. "Is your sister still working at the Triangle Factory?"

"Oh, yes. I will be joining her soon. Wuh-one of the girls is going to have a b-b-baby, so they'll need a girl to replace her. My sister told them about me, only she l-lied and t-told me to say I'm fourteen," Frieda said, speaking clearer. "I don't look fourteen, but my sister said she knew how to make the man agree. There's another girl leaving, s-so there will be another spot. Her family is going west to find a new home away from the city."

Frieda kept speaking, but Anastasia barely paid attention. She'd keyed on the upcoming opening and wanted to hear more about that. If she got a job, then she could make some real money. Even if she gave some to her parents, she would still be able to put a good amount away. Surely a few weeks of real paper money would be enough to take the boys away from her papa's anger. She could handle the beatings, but Ezra was getting older, and Papa didn't seem to like him anymore. Truthfully, Papa didn't seem to like any of them anymore. It didn't help that he smelled of liquor when he walked into the house each evening. She'd seen the way he looked at the baby. She'd never seen him hold him. Thinking of the way Tobias reached for her and called her "Momma" made her even more determined. "I wish to work there as well."

Frieda shook her head. "I don't know you don't look fourteen. Are you sure? They make you work really hard. My sister comes home tired."

"Well, you'll be working there, and you don't look fourteen either. You can't even use a knife."

"Oh, sh-sure I can. My mother showed me last year after I needed your help with my orange. Even s-s-so, they don't use knives there. They use scissors and sew."

As luck would have it, Mrs. Johnston had gifted her with her own needle and thread, which she'd been using to darn her family's socks. "I can sew."

"What will your parents say?"

"Why, just this morning, Momma was saying how Papa is concerned about the money. I won't tell them. Not until after

I get the money, and then they'll have to allow me to stay." In her mind, she was already thinking of how she could hold back some of the money she earned.

Frieda's face brightened. "Then I'll have my sister tell them of you as well."

"Tell her to tell them I work real hard."

"Y-yes, I will."

"Frieda?"

"Yes?"

"Tell her to tell them my name is Anastasia. It sounds older than Anna."

***

Anastasia rushed home as soon as the teacher dismissed them, only instead of heading upstairs, proceeded to Mrs. Johnston's door and knocked three times in quick succession.

"What is it, Anastasia?" the woman asked, opening the door.

"I need to talk to you," Anastasia said, stepping inside.

"Talk? The way you pounded on the door, I thought for sure someone was dying. What's gotten you in such a state?"

"I'm getting a job." The words came out in a breathless rush. "Frieda, she's my friend, says they will hire me if I tell them I'm fourteen. She says I must work very hard."

Mrs. Johnston laughed. "This is something to be happy about?"

"Well, sure it is. They'll pay me fifteen dollars a week."

Mrs. Johnston walked to the kitchen area and turned on the water. She let it run for a moment before holding a glass underneath. She turned off the flow and handed the glass to her. Anastasia took several gulps before returning the glass.

"You know you don't look close to fourteen years old,"

98

Mrs. Johnston said, lowering the glass into the sink.

"How are they to know if I say it's so? Frieda said she can make the guy think we are fourteen. Besides, they won't mind after they see how hard I can work."

Mrs. Johnston sighed. "You're probably right on that one. Just where is this job anyway?"

"The Triangle Factory. Frieda's sister works there. Frieda's going to work there too."

Mrs. Johnston's eyebrows arched. "I've heard of that place. They don't treat their girls very well. And that fifteen dollars may be a stretch."

"They'll pay me. I'll see to that. Besides, it'll be better than going to school every day. I spent the whole day in class and didn't learn nothing. Mrs. Ellis is always helping the kids that just came from the boats. If I need to learn something, my momma can teach me."

"Do you really think your momma and papa are going to agree to you working all day?"

"I do. At least once they see the money I bring home. Papa isn't giving Momma the money he used to. He's keeping it and spending it on the drink. They don't think I know, but I do."

Mrs. Johnston's jaw twitched. "Just how do you plan on keeping it a secret until you get paid?"

Anastasia blew out a sigh. "That's why I came here. You always know the right thing to say so people listen. I need you to tell me what to say."

Mrs. Johnston laughed. "So you've been taking notes, have you?"

Anastasia wanted to tell her that she'd been doing so since the first day she'd met the woman and that she'd even used her words today. Something told her Mrs. Johnston would not like that she'd forced Gyda to move from her seat. Instead, she simply nodded her head.

"Run on upstairs to your momma and let me do some thinking about it."

"Okay, but don't think too long. I only got a couple of weeks."

There were several boys playing marbles in the hallway. Anastasia darted around them and hurried up the stairs, knowing her mother would be getting worried that she hadn't returned home right after school. *I'll tell her Mrs. Ellis needed my help with the children from the boat.* She'd used that excuse before, and it always worked. She reached for the doorknob and stepped inside the apartment. The second she entered, she knew something was terribly wrong. Sharon was standing in the middle of the living room, face ashen. Tobias was inside the playpen holding on to the sides, screaming to be released. Ezra held on to his mother's leg, sobbing.

"Why are you crying, Momma?"

Before Sharon could answer, a shadow fell over her. Anastasia turned and saw the fury in her father's eyes.

"Where've you been, Anna?"

"I've been at school. I had to help Mrs. Ellis with the—" His hand struck her face before she could finish.

"I was at the window when you came into the building. Now tell me the truth, girl. Where've you been?"

She clenched her jaw against the pain, her mind whirling, trying to decide what to say. She didn't want to tell him she'd visited Mrs. Johnston. For some reason, he didn't think too highly of the woman, and she didn't want him to forbid her from visiting.

"Tell me!" he growled.

She thought of the boys she'd passed when leaving Mrs. Johnston's. "I stopped to play a game with some boys in the hall."

His hand came down once more, sending her into the door she'd just entered. He whirled on Sharon. "Is this what goes on while I am at work? My daughter playing the harlot with scum?"

"Papa, I wasn't—"

"Silence!" He took a step forward, and her mother moved in between them.

"She's learned her lesson." Sharon's voice trembled as she spoke. She held a glass of amber liquid. Where it had materialized from, Anastasia did not know.

Her father reached for the glass, and Sharon moved it just out of reach.

"Anastasia, take the children into the hall," she said without looking. Her mother had used her full name, which meant she was not to argue.

Sobbing, Anastasia walked to the playpen, withdrew Tobias, and held her hand for Ezra to grasp. She held her breath until she got the boys into the hallway, letting it out as she closed the door. She slid down the wall and pulled the boys towards her as their mother's screams filled her ears. It wasn't the first time nor would it be the last.

Several people walked past. It seemed there was always someone out in the hallway. No one ever asked why they were not inside the apartment. Anastasia guessed if she could hear her mother's screams, so could they, yet no one seemed inclined to interfere. She'd once seen a man beat his mule because the mule wouldn't listen. When she asked her momma why no one stopped him, Sharon said it was because the mule was his property. Anastasia guessed the same was true for wives.

Chapter Twelve

Saturday, March 25, 1911

Anastasia arrived at the meeting place just as Frieda and her sister, Helka, a girl ten years older and three heads taller, rounded the corner.

"Come," the older girl said without stopping. "I shall tell you what must be done as we go."

Anastasia pulled her coat tighter against the chill of the morning and fell into step behind the sisters. The city was bustling with workers heading to work, herself being one of them. It was to be her first day at the Triangle Shirtwaist Factory, and she couldn't wait to get started. She'd covered by telling her mother she'd gotten a job helping her teacher clean the classroom while the children weren't in school. Sharon had hesitated at first, then Anastasia told her she would be bringing home one whole dollar. Sharon had relented when Anastasia promised to give it to her mother to use for food. If what Frieda said was true, she would be able to pocket the same amount for herself. She looked to the sky like she'd seen Sharon do so many times before. *It must be true, it simply must.*

Helka led them into the street, and the girls dodged just in time to keep from getting trampled by a horse and carriage. The girl waited for them to catch up, then began speaking. "I lied and told Mr. Withers you are each my sisters. You are twins, and both just turned fourteen. I told him you were early babies and are small for your age. You are only to speak in whispers and only to each other, as I told him you do not speak much English. Mr. Withers likes to hire girls who cannot tell people about the conditions in which we work. Mr. Withers is tough, but he likes me. He'll leave you alone as long as you're doing your job."

Anastasia listened intently, marveling at the girl's knowledge of the job and also the way she walked with grace and determination. Something about the girl's willowy form and carefree attitude reminded her of her mother. No, that wasn't true. Sharon hadn't seemed that happy since she'd become pregnant with Ezra. And she hadn't sung since before becoming pregnant with Tobias; a pity, since Sharon's voice was so pleasing to the ear. Sadness tugged at Anastasia's heart, and she realized she missed the mother she once knew. *How can you miss someone who's still here?* She didn't know the answer to that, but it was true all the same.

A motorcar blew its horn, startling the girls. Helka waved the driver off, yelling something in a language Anastasia didn't understand. The man yelled back, and Helka tossed her head back and laughed. Anastasia hadn't a clue about what was said, but she took an instant liking to Helka and the way she didn't seem bothered by things that would have caused a meeker woman to shrivel.

"You are on trial today to see if you can keep up," Helka continued. "If you do a good job, they will keep you on and bring you back on Monday. If not, they will pay you for the day and tell you not to return. Either way, you will get paid for today. It's Saturday and we always get paid on Saturdays."

"W-w-what if I do not get to come back?" Frieda asked.

Helka stopped and placed her hands on her sister's shoulders. "Fear not, little one. You'll do just fine. Just stay close to me and do what I tell you."

Frieda nodded, and they began walking once more. At the corner of Washington Place and Green Street, they came to a stop in line behind a group of girls waiting to enter the Asch Building.

"Remember, no talking," Helka said when the line began moving. The line moved inside the building, and the group made its way onto the elevators a dozen at a time, sometimes more if the girls were small. Even crammed full, it took several trips to disperse the line.

Anastasia had only been on an elevator a handful of times but knew the compartment shouldn't be crammed so full. While the hallways were spacious, the same could not be said for the inside of the elevator. At least not when packed full of teenage girls. The attendant slid the cage door shut and the elevator rumbled to a start, jerking and groaning its discontent as it crept its way upward. By the time it reached the eighth floor, Anastasia's heart was racing. Most of the girls got off, but Helka held back, motioning for Anastasia and Frieda to do the same. Anastasia sighed when the doors closed once more. A short ride later, the three of them exited on the ninth floor while the rest of the girls continued to the next floor.

Helka led them down a short corridor and into a room with large windows with several handfuls of people sitting behind cluttered desks. A tall, sad-faced man in a dark suit leaned against a wooden desk near the far window. He held a stack of papers and didn't appear happy with what they said. He looked up when they entered, saw Helka, and the sadness left his face. As his gaze traveled to Anastasia and Frieda, the smile evaporated. Helka extended a hand, telling the girls to wait as she continued to where the man stood. Though Anastasia could not hear, she could tell the man was not happy. She watched with rapt attention as Helka took the man's hand and placed it to her bosom. He must have liked the feel of Helka's dress because the smile returned. Helka leaned in and whispered something in the man's ear. The man pushed off the desk and walked into the other room. Helka followed, stopping to motion for the girls to wait once more before stepping inside the room and closing the door behind her.

Frieda's lips trembled, but she didn't utter a sound. Anastasia held her breath, waiting for screams that never materialized. When at last Helka returned, her eyes were bright, and a smile stretched the width of her now rosy cheeks. Except for a few wrinkles in her skirt, she looked just as poised as she had when leading them along the busy streets. Anastasia wanted to ask what the man had said to her to make her so happy, but remembered Helka's warning not to speak and remained silent.

"Mr. Withers is allowing you both to stay," Helka whispered as she approached. "Come along, and I'll take you to the sewing room."

"M-mother will not b-be pleased what y-you did," Frieda said once they were in the hallway.

"What'd she do?" Anastasia asked.

"K-k-kissed the m-man," Frieda said over her shoulder.

Helka laughed a hearty laugh. "A simple kiss would not have let you stay. Now hush, before someone hears you."

The elevator was empty, save for the attendant, a teenage boy. The boy wore an attendant's uniform, which consisted of a black shirt and matching trousers. Unlike many boys his age, he appeared well-groomed with the exception of two cigarettes tucked behind his right ear. As they entered the elevator, he brushed several fingers across Helka's arm. Turning, he pulled the gate across the opening and pushed the button to the eighth floor. He lowered the lever, and the box crept into motion, inching its way along the outer brick casing. As the elevator descended, the boy turned and spoke directly to Helka. Though Anastasia couldn't understand what he said, Helka laughed and leaned into him as he spoke.

Anastasia dared a glance at Frieda, who was staring

straight ahead, the expression on her face showing she not only understood but disapproved.

The elevator dinged their arrival, and the boy lifted the lever to cease the movement. The box jarred to a stop, and he pulled the cage aside, releasing the gate to allow them to exit. Helka hesitated at the opening, and the boy gifted her with one of the cigarettes. Helka tucked it into the front of her dress, bent and kissed the boy on his cheek, and laughed when his hand brushed brazenly across her backside.

"You too will learn to use your gifts in return for favors," Helka said upon seeing Frieda's disapproval.

Anastasia wondered what gifts then remembered many times seeing Sharon act the same way around her papa. Suddenly, she understood. She wondered if there were a time when Sharon enjoyed her father's company the same way Helka seemed to enjoy the attentions of these young men, then remembered her mother's screams. *Probably not.*

A heavyset man with caterpillar-like eyebrows stood in front of the door to the sewing room. Unlike the men she'd seen before, this man didn't seem pleased to see Helka.

Helka didn't seem to like him either, as for the first time since meeting her in the street, the girl's shoulders sagged, and her cheerful demeanor vanished.

"You're late," he said gruffly. There was an unpleasant odor about the man, and when he spoke, saliva pooled in the side of his cheek.

"I was taking the new workers to see Mr. Withers."

He lowered his gaze to Anastasia and Frieda and shook his head. "Those girls' feet will never be able to reach the pedals. How do you expect them to work the machines?"

Helka spoke but avoided looking the man in the eye. "I've seen smaller girls at the sewing machines."

"Yeah, well, there are only two machines left. One of

them will have to go up to the tenth floor. They can at least stand at the tables and cut the fabric. Who will it be?"

Helka kneeled in front of her and lowered her voice. "I'm sorry, Anastasia. I promised my mother I would look after my sister. When the day is over, meet me near the front door, and I will see you home. Understand?"

For the first time since she'd left the house, Anastasia was afraid. Only the thought of money to be earned gave her the courage to nod her head.

"Remember, you are not supposed to know English. Just watch and do as you are shown. Cutting fabric is easy; you simply follow the line. Listen to me; this man is a pig. If he takes you anyplace but the elevator, scream and run for all you are worth." Helka stood and waited for the man to unlock the door. He pushed the door open, waited for Helka and Frieda to step inside, then locked it behind them.

Motioning for her to follow, he walked to the elevator and addressed the boy. "Take this one to the tenth floor."

As soon as the elevator began to move, the boy turned in her direction. Something about the way he looked at her made her nervous. Maybe it was just because of what Helka had said, or maybe it was because the boy now regarded her with the same lopsided smile he'd aimed at Helka after she'd kissed him on the cheek. He took a step forward and laughed when she stepped back. The smile evaporated, and he took another step. She remembered a conversation she'd had with Mrs. Johnston one day when she'd gotten brave enough to tell the woman of the boy she'd kissed in the market place. Mrs. Johnston had bristled, but her anger was geared at the boy instead of Anastasia. She'd told her sometimes boys and men did things to women without their permission. She'd spent the rest of the afternoon showing Anastasia ways to protect herself. She'd told Anastasia that when she went out, she always traveled with a brick in her purse in case she had to use the purse as a weapon. She had neither purse nor brick, so she had to use the other trick Mrs. Johnston had told her.

The boy took another step, and Anastasia swung her leg forward, kicking him directly between his legs. Instantly, his mouth dropped open, eyes bugging wide, and he fell to his knees moaning his discomfort. He attempted to speak, but his words came out in a squeak of air.

Seeing the floor come into view, Anastasia raced to the panel and pulled the handle down. She'd stopped the box a bit too early and the floor was about a foot higher than the bottom of the elevator door. She pulled open the cage, climbed out of the box, and left without so much as a backwards glance.

***

Anastasia flexed her fingers to relieve a cramp then lifted the scissors once more, cutting through the fabric. Helka was right; the work wasn't difficult, just tedious. She'd been at the task for nearly eight hours with only a few short breaks to run to the water closet. Her stomach grumbled, reminding her for the hundredth time she hadn't thought to bring a lunch. She would remember to bring one on Monday. She smiled. Though her fingers ached, she'd overheard the shift manager tell the man at the door she'd done a fine job and to make sure to hand her a note with her day's pay telling her she should come back. According to the girl next to her, who'd overheard the same conversation and spoke to her in broken English, she was lucky to be getting her pay that day, as most girls had to work a whole week to get paid on Saturday. Anastasia had merely nodded at the girl, not letting on she'd not only heard but understood the same conversation. It seemed she was not the only one that spoke English. She wondered how many others were staying silent just to keep their job. Not that she was interested in finding out; she wasn't about to do anything to lose the job now that she had it. She finished her cut and looked at the clock. If she hurried, she would have just enough time to cut one last shirt. As her scissors made the first cut, shrill screams filled the air. She spun around, scissors in hand, ready to use them against her attacker. Only the screams were not aimed at her. One of the girls had left to go to the water closet, and on her return, had smelled smoke.

Girls flooded their way to the door, pushing towards their escape. In their panic, they'd managed to forget the doors opened inward. After several moments of confusion, some of the boys that worked on the cutting floor managed to clear the way for the doors to open. As the doors were pulled inward, smoke filled the room, stinging Anastasia's eyes. Blinking through tears, she followed the crowd to the elevator, anxiously waiting her turn as people pushed their way inside. She'd just moved to join them when, to her horror, the boy pulled the gate closed. Though the box was already filled beyond capacity, those standing beside her pleaded for him to open the doors. Smoke was wafting up from the elevator shaft, and those inside the small box screamed for him to hurry. If the boy noticed the panic around him, he did not show it; he was too busy peering at Anastasia, gloating his control. He winked as he pulled the lever to allow the cage to lower. For a moment, Anastasia regretted kicking him. If she hadn't, maybe he'd have made room for her to step inside. The moment of regret ended when the rope that held the cage snapped, drifting downward. Panic-filled screams filtered up through the opening, followed by a boom that shook the ground beneath her. A cloud of smoke bellowed from the opening, then all was quiet, except for the sobs of those who'd witnessed the ordeal.

Anastasia didn't have time for her shock to register

before someone took hold of her arm, pulling her towards the stairs. The girl's lips were pressed together as she looked at Anastasia without blinking. "Must go!"

Anastasia did not recognize her, but since the girl seemed to know where she was going, she was happy to follow, as were others stranded on the tenth floor. The group headed towards the Washington Place Stairway, and someone screamed to get their attention.

"No, not that door; it is always locked! Must use the Green Street stairway!"

At hearing this, the procession turned and ran in the opposite direction. While the door proved unlocked, smoke and flames prevented them from heading down.

"What about fire escape?" someone offered.

"No, it gone. I see from window, the people..." a woman said in broken English and began to cry.

Tears sprang from Anastasia's eyes anew. She was going to die, and her parents would never know why she didn't come home. More than that, her brothers would think she'd abandoned them. The girl who'd been leading the way turned and headed up the stairway. Without asking why, everyone followed. Anastasia sucked in the crisp, biting air in greedy gulps that stung her smoke-filled lungs. She heard screams, went to the edge of the roof, and looked over the side, watching in silent horror as people leaped from the flame-filled windows below. Not wishing to see them land, she turned her head. What she saw next terrified her even more. Several girls were walking across a small plank that had been placed between the buildings. Without stopping to debate the logic of her actions, she stepped onto the board. As she neared the other side, she heard a snap, felt the board give, and jumped.

Chapter Thirteen

Anastasia hit the roof with a thud, her knees scraping against the hard surface, ripping her dress. Her ankle twisted at an odd angle as her body tumbled to a stop. Someone landed next to her, crying out in pain as she landed. Anastasia sat for a moment, taking inventory of her aches. She was sore, her ankle throbbed, but she'd survived the leap. Rising, she gingerly hobbled to the edge. Her breath caught as she watched a girl leap from the Asch Building, only to plummet downwards between the buildings. She closed her eyes, refusing to allow her gaze to follow the girl. Another girl stood at the edge of the roof, refusing to jump. Anastasia wondered if she'd have been able to screw up the courage if she'd taken time to consider her actions.

She heard a commotion and turned to see men with ladders coming from the covered roof opening. *If only the girl would have waited a few moments longer.*

Tears stung her eyes, her knees were raw and bleeding, but she'd survived. She walked to the opening, and slowly and painfully, began to descend the stairs. A few times, she bent her injured leg behind her and used the handrail to lower to the next step. While fairly sure the building had an elevator, she wasn't ready to risk a ride. *I may never be ready again.*

By the time she exited the building, the fire was under control, but the chaos was far from over. Lifeless bodies lay in heaps from where they'd fallen or jumped to avoid the flames. While some were covered, others remained untouched for all to see. She dared a look, thinking to recognize the girl she'd seen fall, although there was nothing left to recognize. When someone shouted for her to keep moving, she limped away without hesitation. A man in a white suit approached, camera in hand, asking if she'd pose for a photo. She declined, saying she had no desire to recall this day. He persisted and she thought about kicking him, then remembered where that had gotten her and simply turned and stumbled away. She took several steps before realizing if she hadn't kicked the boy, he might have allowed her on the ill-fated elevator. Her body trembled, her mouth watered, and for a moment, she thought she would be sick. She stared, mouth gaping as she watched streams of water attempt to reach the upper floors of the Asch Building. On any other day, the sight of the horse-drawn fire engines stationed at the base of the Asch Building would be fascinating; horses glistening from sweat, the firemen shouting orders as water rained down upon them. At the moment, she hadn't the strength to care. A group of police officers stood guard in an attempt to keep gawkers at bay. Why people wished to see the carnage was beyond her.

She turned away from the horrific scene and saw a group of girls standing in a circle, arms linked in solidarity. Though she couldn't see their faces, she knew they too had survived the horror. Gritting her teeth against the pain, she crossed the street and made her way towards the girls. As she neared, moans of bewilderment, pain, and gut-wrenching loss greeted her. She considered running the other direction but didn't think her injured leg would take her very far, so she continued towards the group. She'd seen photos of the Civil War in magazines her papa sometimes brought home. The group of soot-smeared girls, with burns, cuts, and bruises, reminded her of the men in some of those photos. Some of the girls were crying because they'd been burned or injured.

Anastasia cried simply because she didn't know what else to do.

Her tears had long turned to dry sobs when she first heard her name. At first, she didn't recognize the husky voice of the caller. She turned, tears returning as she saw Helka and Frieda hurrying towards her hand in hand. She stumbled her way towards them, falling into their embrace.

"I th-th-thought y-y-you were dead," Frieda sobbed.

I almost was. "And I you," Anastasia said, wiping her nose on the back of her sleeve. "How did you get out?"

"W-w-we t—" A coughing fit interrupted her answer.

"We took the elevator," Helka replied, finishing her sister's sentence. A frown flitted across her face. "I sent him back for you. Someone said the elevator had collapsed. That's why we thought you were dead."

"The elevator came, but the boy would not allow me to get on. If I had—" This time, it was she who couldn't finish.

"Are you hurt badly?" Helka's voice was full of concern.

While she ached all over, she didn't think it was anything to be concerned about. "Not as bad as others."

"I w-want t-t-to go home."

"So do I," Anastasia agreed.

Helka's eyebrows knitted together. "Are you sure you're okay to walk?"

No, I can't possibly walk another step. She shook her head.

It was dark and well past suppertime by the time they arrived at Anastasia's apartment building. The girls had walked her all the way to the door, allowing her to lean on them for support, only leaving after they saw her safely inside the building. She paused at the base of the stairs, then turned and stumbled her way to Mrs. Johnston's door instead. Using what little strength she had to knock, she turned and slid down the door. Closing her eyes, she waited for her knock to be answered.

***

Anastasia opened her eyes, surprised to find herself lying on Mrs. Johnston's sofa. She heard soft snores and peeked over the side. She saw Mrs. Johnston sleeping on a heap of quilts beside her.

Anastasia pulled her blanket aside. When she moved, her body resisted, causing her to moan her discomfort.

Mrs. Johnston was instantly awake. "Where do you think you're going?"

"Momma will be worried." For the first time, Anastasia realized her voice sounded as raspy as Helka's. It dawned on her she had not gotten paid for her day's work. She'd thought to use it to soothe her papa's temper. She swallowed at the thought of getting beaten. *I can't take anymore.* She twisted the blanket in her fingers. "Papa will be angry."

"Why don't you tell me what happened?" Mrs. Johnston's face was full of concern.

Tears streamed down Anastasia's face as she related the events of the day. She didn't have to tell where she'd been, as the woman had helped her with the lie she'd told her mother. She shared her joy at finding out they wanted to keep her on at the factory and how she'd used the woman's teachings to put the elevator attendant in his place. She told of how angry he'd been and his refusal to allow her to escape with some of the others. Of being angry herself and wishing him ill and of the guilt she'd felt when the ropes holding the elevator gave way. She told of the locked doors and how she and the others had made their way up to the roof. Of running across the roof without thinking, and injuring herself when she landed on the other side. She paused, then told how helpless she'd felt watching the girl leap from the building and disappear. When she'd finished, it was hard to tell which of them was crying the most.

"It was all so very awful. I worked so hard and don't even have a penny to show for it." Only she didn't want a penny; she wanted the two dollars and fifty cents she'd expected to bring home at the end of the day. It was fifteen minutes before quitting time. Fifteen minutes and yet she'd come home empty-handed.

Anastasia let out a deep sigh. "Momma is expecting that money, at least a part of it."

Mrs. Johnston pushed off the floor and wiped the tears from her eyes with her fingers. She was halfway across the room when she spoke. "How much is your mother expecting?"

"I told her I would bring her a whole dollar," Anastasia sniffed.

"A whole dollar it is," the woman repeated and pulled a crisp dollar bill from her purse.

Anastasia kicked off the blankets, surprised to see her ankle wrapped with white cloth. She lowered her foot to the floor, then deciding it would hold, proceeded with her full weight, limping to where the woman stood. "I can't take your money."

"Good, because I'm not giving it to you. I'm giving it to your mother. Don't you go arguing with me, because I do intend to have you work it off."

"What'll you have me do?"

"I guess I haven't given it much thought, but have no fear, I'll be fair." The woman picked up a piece of paper and laid it across a dinner plate. Next, she reached into the matchbox, plucked out a matchstick, and struck it against the side of the box, catching the match with the first strike. The tip flared then settled into a low flame. Satisfied, Mrs. Johnston lowered the flame to the paper. The second the flame took hold, she waved the match to extinguish the flame.

Anastasia blinked her surprise as the woman picked up the dollar and held it close to the burning paper. A second later, she wet her fingertips using them to cease the fire. She sat the charred bill on the table and watched as the paper burned itself out, leaving nothing but a pile of black ash on the plate. Wetting her finger once more, she collected some of the ash, pressing it firmly into the bill. Looking it over, the woman smiled a wide smile and handed the bill to Anastasia.

"But why?" Anastasia asked, looking at the now filthy bill in disgust.

"Ain't no one going to believe a bill's going to go through what you went through and still look and smell brand new. You take a look at the dollar in your hand. It looks like it's had the devil himself chasing it. Smells like it too! Pretty darn good work if I do say so myself. "

Anastasia had to admit it did look pretty bad. Almost as bad as the girls who'd been standing in the street. "You sure are smart for a lady."

"For a lady? Now what in blue blazes is that supposed to mean?"

"Papa says women aren't smart. That's why he wouldn't allow Momma to keep working after they got married. That and he told her he's the man of the house and it's the man's job to bring home the money. Momma told me Papa almost didn't marry her on account she was a school teacher and people might think she was smarter than him. He made her promise to quit her job and not tell anyone she used to teach. Momma told me so."

"Did he now?" A strange smile played at the woman's lips. "What else did your momma say about your papa?"

Anastasia shrugged her shoulders. "Just that girls are not supposed to work. He said if Momma worked, people might not think Papa was man enough to provide for his family. She said Papa is a very prideful man…at least when he's not full of the drink."

The smile spread wider. "Anastasia, I think it's time we go let your momma and papa know just what you've been up to."

***

The door was open when they reached the apartment. The sight alarmed Anastasia, since the last time she'd found the door ajar, she'd also found her mother in a pool of blood-tinged liquid. She gulped the bile that threatened. "I'm scared."

"It's all right, girl. Your papa's not going to hurt you."

But what if he has hurt Momma instead? She kept her thoughts to herself as she pushed the door open and hobbled her way inside the dark room. Sharon was upon her in an instant, gathering her in her arms and giving thanks for her safe return.

"Where've you been, Anna? I've been so very worried. I had your papa go to the school to look for you. He couldn't get in because the doors were locked up tight."

Anastasia swallowed. "I wasn't at the school, Momma."

Sharon's hand came down hard upon her face. The impact caught her off guard, knocking her off balance. She stumbled, landing on an already bruised knee. Mrs. Johnston was by her side in an instant, gathering her into welcoming arms.

"Turn the light on, woman," Mrs. Johnston said through gritted teeth.

Sharon hurried across the room, doing as the woman commanded. The second there was enough light to see, Sharon took in the bruises, scrapes, and bandages. Her hands flew to her face. "Anastasia! What on earth happened to you?"

"She was trying to tell you before you knocked her on her backside. I can tell you one thing: the girl's been knocked around enough today. Is your man about?" Mrs. Johnston asked, looking towards the bedroom.

Sharon slid a glance in the same direction and nodded.

"Then you best go get him so she don't have to keep repeating herself." Though Sharon hesitated, the woman's tone left no room for argument. In the end, she did as told.

Sharon returned and took a seat on the sofa without comment. A moment later, her papa came into the room, blinking sleepily in the glare of the light. Though his gaze traveled over his daughter, he made no move to approach. He narrowed his eyes at Mrs. Johnston. "What's going on in here?"

"If we can all have a seat, Anastasia will tell you herself."

"Don't you tell me what to do in my own house," her father bellowed.

"You wake those young'uns and ain't no one going to get any sleep afterwards," Mrs. Johnston warned. "Now, do you want to hear or not?"

Her father's jaw tightened as he took a seat on the sofa next to Sharon. Mrs. Johnston nodded, and Anastasia began. She told them a similar story as the one she'd told Mrs. Johnston, only this time, she left out the fact that it was she who'd showed her how to protect herself from the boy in the elevator. When she finished, she opened her hand and held out the fire-scorched bill. Lowering her eyes, she continued with the words Mrs. Johnston had coaxed her to say. "I was only trying to help. I know how difficult it's been for Momma, with her not having enough money for the market and all."

Her father started to open his mouth, when Mrs.

Johnston cut him off.

"This girl's been through a lot today. Nothing's broke, but it'll take a while for her to heal. She'll be needing her sleep. Run along to bed now, Anastasia."

"She'll do no—"

Mrs. Johnston raised a hand to silence him. "Go along now, Anastasia."

Anastasia did as told, only when she got to her room, she left the door slightly ajar and stood listening at the door.

"If you lay a hand on the girl, I'll make it known that you're not capable of providing for your family. I'll put posters up at the dock if I have to. I'll tell everyone that your only daughter nearly got killed because her no good papa couldn't provide enough for his family and sent his baby girl out to work."

When her father didn't respond, Anastasia turned the doorknob, easing the door shut with nary a sound. She made her way to the bed, falling asleep the moment her head hit the pillow Mrs. Johnston had sewed for her. Neither of her parents ever mentioned the events of that day. Even the newspapers denied anyone under the age of fourteen worked in the factory. Then they wouldn't know, as she'd lied about her age.

***

Cindy closed the journal, hugging it to her chest. She waited for Linda to finish reading before she spoke. "Can you imagine living through that kind of ordeal without grief counseling?"

Linda shook her head. "I guess we're starting to see how she got her edge."

"Maybe, but Tobias seemed to think she was sweet before she disappeared." Cindy checked her phone to check the time. Nearly eleven, much too late to dive into the next journal. She bit her lip, wondering when she'd gotten too old to stay awake past eleven. "So, are you feeling any differently about the Johnston woman?"

Linda sighed. "Maybe. But if she's so good, why doesn't she take Anastasia in? You read Tobias' journals. His sister didn't go downstairs to live with the neighbor. She flat-out disappears."

Cindy considered this for a moment. "You know, we can debate this all night or we can get some sleep and get an early start on the next journal. Which will it be?"

"Third option; we keep reading," Linda offered, stifling a yawn.

"I vote no. Let's call it a night and start fresh in the morning."

Linda yawned once more. "First one awake makes coffee."

The women stood, and Cindy embraced Linda. "In case I don't tell you enough, I love you."

"You don't, and neither do I. Luckily, there's still time to correct that. Sometimes people don't get that chance."

Cindy wondered if her mother was speaking from experience. Before she could ask, Linda yawned. Cindy kissed the top of her head. "Come on, Mom. I'll put you to bed."

Chapter Fourteen

A young girl stood on the rooftop of the next building calling her name, waving and begging her to jump before it was too late. Flames licked at her heels and Cindy found it nearly impossible to breathe. Gathering her courage, she ran, jumping from the building as the flames grabbed hold of her dress. Though she could see the roof on the other side, she knew she'd misjudged the distance. The fear in the girl's eyes matched her own as she plummeted downwards between the tall buildings. She reached out in a desperate attempt to grab hold of something that would break her fall. Her final thoughts were of her mother, wondering what Linda would do without her there looking after her. "Momma!"

Cindy woke with a start, her chest pounding as she realized she was safe in her own bed. *It was only a dream.* She looked over at the clock and groaned when the clock flipped over to 4:42. She lay there for several minutes trying to go back to sleep, but her mind was already retracing the events in the dream, meshing the dream with the journal she'd read before going to bed. She dressed and quietly made her way to the office, closing the door so as not to wake her mom. She signed into her computer and waited for it to come to life. Bringing up the search engine, she typed in "Triangle Factory." To her surprise, the computer filled in the rest. She clicked on one of many links and began to read.

The door clicked open and Linda came in wielding two cups in her right hand. "I thought we agreed the first one up was going to make coffee," she said, handing Cindy one of the cups.

"I've just been up a moment," Cindy said, taking a sip.

Linda cocked her head and looked over her glasses at her. "I've had my shower, made coffee, and have oatmeal ready on the stove."

Cindy glanced at her computer screen, surprised to see it was a little after seven. "Sorry, Mom. I didn't realize it had gotten so late."

Linda laughed. "Seven isn't late. What's got you so enthralled?"

Cindy sat her cup on the desk, clicked onto the Wikipedia page discussing the fire, and turned the computer screen around so Linda could see. "I was reading about the fire. It says here the Triangle Shirtwaist Factory fire was the deadliest industrial disaster in the history of the city and one of the deadliest in U.S. history. The article says over 146 people died and that many jumped to their deaths in an attempt to avoid the flames. It even talks about the elevator failing. Apparently, the company was notorious for hiring immigrant girls fourteen and older that couldn't speak English."

"Or, in some cases, girls who said they were fourteen," Linda mused.

"If Anastasia is to be believed, yes. Just reading the events gave me the chills," Cindy said, rubbing her arms, and went on to tell Linda of the nightmare she'd had. "I think I called for you out loud. I'm surprised I didn't wake you."

"Had my fan going and didn't hear a thing. Did they say what caused the fire?"

"Several theories, but nothing definitive. One article suggested that the owners had set the fire because the factory was in danger of going under. The Fire Marshal said it was probably due to one of the workers throwing a cigarette butt into a bin of rags."

Linda's eyes went wide. "Do you think Helka started it?"

"Helka? What makes you think that?"

"She flirted with the boy in the elevator. He gave her a cigarette, remember?"

"I'd forgotten about that. Still, I doubt Helka was the only girl who smoked."

"Who's to say it was a girl? She got her smokes from the boy," Linda said.

"Another of life's mysteries, the answer to which we'll never know." Cindy stood, stretched, and picked up her coffee cup. "How about we have some oatmeal and see what other mysteries we can uncover?"

"Works for me," Linda said, leading the way.

***

February 21, 1914

Anastasia watched as her mother's bruised arms struggled to lift the heavy window nearest the clothesline. She wanted to help, but Sharon had warned her to stay back, grimacing against the biting wind as she finally succeeded in pulling the window free. Shivering, Sharon stepped one foot onto the fire escape and held out a hand, which Anastasia filled with one of her father's shirts. Placing it on the line, she pushed the clothespin securely onto the line to hold the shirt tight against the blowing wind and snow. She pulled the line, freeing up another space, then held out her hand, which Anastasia filled with another shirt.

"It's going to be a race to see if the wind will be able to dry the clothes before the chill freezes the garments on the line. I don't know why your father is so dead set against us drying them inside when the weather is bad." Sharon shouted to be heard over the wind. While Sharon had taken to spot-cleaning the rest of the family's clothing during the bitter winter months, she always took time to thoroughly clean her father's clothes.

Anastasia didn't answer, knowing if she did, Sharon would realize she'd spoken out of turn.

"Dress the boys warm, Anna. They're likely to catch their death of cold if you don't," Sharon said, pulling the window closed.

"I can go to the market, Momma. There's no need to drag the boys outside today."

An indecisive frown fleeted across Sharon's face. "You don't mind going alone?"

"I can manage," Anastasia said, trying not to show too much enthusiasm and knowing one wrong word would change Sharon's mind.

"The market list is on the counter. Don't forget the basket. My coin purse is inside," Sharon said with a sigh.

The moment Anastasia lifted the basket from the counter, both boys raced to her side.

"We're coming too," Ezra said, lifting his coat from the chair.

Tobias, the quieter of the two boys, ran to the closet, opened the door, and jumped in an attempt to get his coat.

"No, Ezra, you're going to stay here and help Momma keep up with your brother. It's much too cold to go outside today." She leaned down and whispered in his ear, "If you do as I say, I'll bring you each a special treat."

Ezra narrowed his eyes. "What kind of treat?"

"Shh, I'll bring you both a juicy piece of toffee. Just remember, you mustn't tell Momma," Anastasia said, removing his coat. "If you do, Momma will not allow you to have it."

Ezra considered this a moment before finally nodding his agreement. "Tobias is gonna cry."

Anastasia walked to the closet and kneeled beside her youngest brother. "Tobias, I need you to stay here and watch your brother. Can you do that for me?"

Tobias tilted his head in his brother's direction. "What's he gonna do?"

She bit her lip to keep from smiling. "Ezra will tell you he's watching you, but he's the one who needs watching. Momma is busy hanging the wash and you just never know what kind of trouble Ezra will get into. If you see him doing anything wrong, you're to tell Momma at once. Understand?"

Tobias nodded his head once more.

"Good, and if you do a good job, I'll bring you both a piece of candy. Just remember, you mustn't tell Momma."

Anastasia pulled on her coat and plucked the basket from the counter, leaving without a backward glance. It wasn't the first time she'd had to bribe her way out of the house alone. If either of the boys had put up a fuss, Sharon would have insisted she take one of them along. Funny, the older she got, the less Sharon seemed to trust her to go out on her own. Maybe her mother was afraid she wouldn't return. Though she'd given leaving plenty of thought, she'd never shared those thoughts with Sharon. She'd shared them with Mrs. Johnston a time or two, but she was fairly certain the woman hadn't betrayed her confidence. Reaching the bottom of the steps, she pushed open the door to the first-floor hallway. Once there, she decided to see if Mrs. Johnston needed anything from the market. She knocked on the woman's door, but the knock went unanswered. She knocked several more times to no avail. *She must be out visiting today.*

Anastasia pulled her hat onto her head, walked to the outer door, and braced herself for winter's chill. Her breath caught the moment she opened the door. For a moment, she thought about returning to the apartment for a wrap to place around her neck. *Momma won't let me go if I do.* Pulling her coat closer, she leaned into the wind and pulled her hat lower to help shield her face.

The weather proved to be no match for hungry shoppers. Scores of people littered the street, bartering and bickering over prices. It'd been that way of late with more and more people coming in from the boats, something her papa grumbled about each night after he came home from work. She didn't mind the throngs of people in the marketplace; it helped her procure the items on Sharon's shopping list without getting caught.

Her father, on the other hand, was bitter there were so many people coming to the city in search of jobs. These people were willing to do the same work for less money. He'd lost his supervisor job on the dock over a year prior and was himself forced to replace a man he'd once supervised. With the decrease in both power and wages, he'd become exceedingly difficult to live with.

Gone were the days of stopping him after one glass; most nights, he'd finish a bottle and dive headlong into the next. For some reason, he always seemed angry with Anastasia and was quick to remind her he was the man of the house. Sharon tried to buffer his anger, though she was no match for his evil temper. In return, Sharon had become a shell of the woman she'd once been. Unable to escape their father's wrath, the boys quickly learned to keep a low profile whenever Papa was in the house. It angered her to see little Tobias huddled behind the sofa, shaking as her father boomed his displeasure over the least little infraction.

One of these days, I'll take him away.

Sadly, she no longer felt that way about Ezra. The boy had reached an age where he'd started questioning everything she said. Tobias still hung on her every word and on occasion still referred to her as "Momma." Anastasia thought about the boy each time she pilfered an item from her shopping list. It eased her guilt knowing he was the reason behind her thievery.

She looked at the last item on the list and smiled. It had been ages since she'd visited the apple man, and she'd purposely saved his cart for last. If she'd had to pay for the rest of the items, she would have had to steal more than one apple from him, something she didn't want to do. He'd been so nice to her over the years. It just didn't seem right stealing from the man.

He saw her approaching, and his face lit up. "Good day to you, Miss Anna. How's my girl on this fine morning?"

She looked towards the sky, saw the low, dark clouds, and grimaced. "It's freezing, and the snow bites the face. How can you say it is a fine morning?"

"Aww, but you are looking at the world all wrong. Any morning you wake to see the light of day is a fine morning indeed. You should count your blessings each day the Lord puts a smile on that pretty little face of yours."

Her hand instantly traced the scar on her cheek. *Did he really think she was pretty?*

"How's your mother faring these days? She doesn't come around here so much anymore."

It was true Sharon hadn't fixed anything with apples in much too long. She thought about telling him the truth but decided against it. Sharon wouldn't approve of her telling that Papa had beaten her again. "I guess Momma has not been of a mind to fix any apple pies of late. Mr. Castiglione, how come you always call me your girl?"

The smile left his eyes as he looked off into the distance. "I promised your momma I wouldn't tell you this, but you're older now and have the right to know. I was sweet on your momma and her on me. We were mighty close. Mighty close indeed. We were to be married, but before that happened, Albert came along and promised her the world. I was but a poor boy whose parents owned a small apple orchard, living just outside the city. Albert, he was a dreamer, a smooth talker who filled her head with tales of city life, and next thing I knew, she'd married him. I don't think she told him about you. Things seemed to be going well at first; then I began to notice the bruises. We'd see each other from time to time and she'd tell me stories of how she'd fallen, but being a country boy doesn't make me stupid. I knew what was going on. I tried to get her to leave him. I told her I'd accept her, even though she'd lain with another man. I told her I would accept you as well because I knew you to be in her belly before she'd married the man. I told your momma I knew you to be mine. But your momma was raised to stay with her husband, so she thinks she owes him something. I know I'd like to give him what he's owed."

Anastasia didn't understand. Mr. Castiglione said she was his and momma kept saying Ezra and Tobias belonged to her papa. They'd all come from her momma's belly, so in her opinion, they all belonged to her mother. Still, she didn't mind the apple man saying he was her papa. She liked him much more than she liked her other papa. "What do you owe him?"

An odd look crossed the man's face as if he hadn't realized he'd spoken the words out loud. A blush crept over his cheeks and made its way to his exposed ears. "Sorry, Anna, I guess I've forgotten my place. My mind isn't what it used to be. Got kicked by a mule a time or two. I ain't got no reason to speak ill of your Pop. No reason at all."

"You ain't said nothing that wasn't true. Papa's not nice to Momma." *He's not nice to me either.*

"You tell that momma of yours that I said my offer still stands." His nostrils flared as he spoke.

"What offer?"

"Never you mind. You just tell her what I said." His

frown deepened. "I should be ashamed of myself keeping you out so long on such a cold day. What can I get for you?"

She wanted to remind him that he'd said it was a fine day, but the smile had left his face. "Four apples. Momma is going to make an apple crumb cake."

"Four, huh, and what color would she like?"

"Red, please," Anastasia said, holding her basket for him to fill.

He placed double the amount into the basket and smiled. "Don't you go and eat all those before you get home. See to it them brothers of yours get one too. That'll be one shiny penny."

She knew the price should be more but didn't question him on it. He rarely charged her full price when she was alone. "I will."

"Did you forget something?" he asked when she turned to leave.

Grinning, she walked to the edge of the cart, looked the pile over, and plucked an apple free without disturbing the rest.

"You've come a long way since you started, Miss Anna," he said, clapping his hands together in approval.

"I sure have, Mr. Castiglione," she said, thinking of the other items she'd taken that afternoon. She took a few steps and stopped, turning to face him once again. "Mr. Castiglione?"

"Yes, Anna?"

"I'm glad you're my papa."

He opened his mouth as if to say something and then closed his eyes briefly. When he opened them, she saw a touch of sadness. "As am I, Ms. Anna. As am I."

Anastasia sucked in her breath as an icy stream of air whipped between the buildings. Shivering, she pulled her coat tighter against the chill. Though the sun was high in the sky, it did nothing to stave off the bitter wind that carried flakes of snow, which circled her head in angry whispers. Hunkering against the assault, she lowered her head and slushed her way towards home. She'd just left the market when she caught movement out of the corner of her eye. She threw her hands up to cover herself as she ducked out of the way. As she did, several of the apples fell to the ground at her feet.

"Jiminy Cricket, you'd think I was going to clobber you or something," Runt said, rescuing the apples and falling into step beside her.

I sure did. She took a breath to settle herself. "You just caught me off guard is all."

He gave her one of the apples and smiled when she rejected the other, placing it into his coat pocket for later. "You ever think of leaving?"

All the time. "Where would I go?"

He waved his hands wide. "Why, into the streets, of course."

She wanted to more than anything. She'd seen plenty of other children living on the streets, and they seemed to be faring well enough. They'd had the same conversation many times over the years. Runt was always trying to get her to run away with him. She'd considered it a time or two, but the thought of leaving Tobias kept her returning home. She stopped and placed her hands on her hips. "Now why would I want to go and do a dumb thing like that?"

"Cause it's only going to get worse."

He'd said that before, and he'd been right. *I want to go. I really do.* "I can't leave my brother."

"When it gets too bad, you'll leave."

She noticed he'd said "when" not "if." "What makes you so sure?"

He smiled. "Kids like us have a choice."

Before she could ask what he meant by that, he turned,

walking in the opposite direction. A shrill whistle pierced the air. She watched as the black and white dog rounded a building and raced to Runt's side. Anastasia took a step towards them, wishing to be as free as they both seemed to be. A horse and buggy passed between them. When the road cleared, both Runt and the dog were gone.

Chapter Fifteen

March 5, 1914

Anastasia sat on the floor reading to her brothers. She kept her voice in low whispers both to hold her brother's attention and so that they had to be quiet in order to hear the story. Sharon's breath hummed along in soft gentle snores, letting her know her mother had finally drifted off to sleep, a good thing as Sharon had not looked well of late. It was past time to wake her, but since dinner was in the oven, a few moments longer wouldn't hurt.

She had a natural knack of inflecting emotion where needed to further bring the story to life, which meant the boys were always begging her to read to them from one of several books they had in the apartment. As she read, she enjoyed the comfort and warmth as the boys snuggled next to her. Sometimes as she read, she imagined them in a different place, all alone with nary a care in the world. A place where no one lost their temper, bellies were always full, and papas loved their children like papas were supposed to do.

She heard the click of the door and closed her eyes, knowing there was no time to wake her mother. She looked up in time to see the anger in her father's face as he saw Sharon sleeping on the sofa.

"Woman!" he bellowed loudly enough to be heard clear down to the first floor.

Sharon opened her eyes and looked at Anastasia accusingly.

Anastasia blinked back tears as her papa slammed his lunch pail onto the counter.

Anastasia felt the boys tremble and pulled them in close, realizing her mother was not the only one she'd let down. *I'm sorry.*

Her father stormed to the window and opened it with ease. Reaching for the clothesline, he began pulling it across, breaking the wooden pins as he snatched the clothes from the line and tossed them onto the floor.

Sharon was off the sofa in a flash, gathering the garments and placing them into the basket.

"What kind of woman did I marry?" her father fumed as he continued to strip the line free of clothes. "Sleeping while your undergarments hang from the line for all to see."

While her father knew Sharon and every other woman in the building hung the wash on the lines stretched between the windows, he expected the clothes to be removed before the men in the building began making their way home. Many times he'd arrived home, walked to the window, and shared his displeasure at seeing the other tenants' undergarments dancing in the wind like girls in a chorus line, adding that no respectable woman would keep their clothes on the line for all the letches' eyes to see. Only women hoping to gain attention from men other than their husbands would be so bold.

"Go," Anastasia whispered and watched as both boys scooted across the floor, huddling under the kitchen table.

"Husband, we've been married long enough for you to see this thing would not begin to cover me. It belongs to your daughter. I've not shamed you in any way," Sharon said, plucking the brassiere from his hand. "The girl's growing up, not that you've ever paid her any mind."

Anastasia trembled as her father looked in her direction. *But he has.*

She watched in silent horror as he went to the cabinet and removed the bottle, knowing it wouldn't be long before his anger deepened. Further, she realized this tirade could have been prevented had she simply done as her mother had asked.

***

Angry shouts jarred her awake. Anastasia flung the blankets aside and tiptoed to her bedroom door. She eased the door open and crossed through the living space, pausing at her parents' door to listen.

"I can't feed the family on this." Sharon's voice sounded desperate.

"You'll do what you can. It's all I have to give you."

"You give me less and less each day. There's barely enough food for the children or me. You do not notice, as you'd rather drink your supper."

"You're a woman. You'll find something to cook that fills their stomachs."

"I've tried, but the money just isn't enough. Maybe if you would stop spending all the money on your drinking, your wife would have—"

Sharon never got to finish the sentence. Though she couldn't see, Anastasia knew her papa's hand had silenced her mother's words.

"Wife?!" The words came out on a laugh. "Wives tend to their husband's needs. You are nothing but a housemaid, and if today is an example, you're not much good at that either."

"You know I am unable because of the baby." Sharon's words came out as a sob.

Baby? Tobias is four. Surely she's not speaking of him. Is it possible mother has another baby in her belly? Of course it is. That would explain how sickly she's been of late. Why didn't she tell me?

"A baby does not cause such problems. You've had plenty of children before and always managed to keep the house in order and fulfill your wifely duties. Why, that girl of yours does more around the house than you do."

"Anna is your daughter." Sharon's voice sounded even more desperate than before.

"Your lies don't make it true. You said she came early, but she looks nothing like me. None of the children do."

"The boys look like both of us," Sharon argued.

"And the girl?"

"Doesn't."

"Because I'm not her father."

"You were here when she was born. That makes you her father."

"Wrong. Fathers love their children. The girl's never been more than a reminder to me."

"She looks just like the girl I once was." Sharon's words were cold. "As I remember, you liked that girl well enough."

"I see her and I see your sin. We both know Castiglione is her father. If I see you near the man again…"

Anastasia looked at the door in disbelief. *It was true!* The man on the other side of the door, the man she loathed was not her father?

Heavy footsteps startled her out of her musings. She darted across the room, slipping inside her room and quietly closing the door behind her. She stood pressed flat against the door, heart pounding, praying she hadn't been seen. The footsteps came closer, and she raced across the room, sliding under the covers and pulling them up over her head. The steps stopped beside her door. She swallowed, knowing she'd forgotten to lock the door. It was a habit she'd gotten into after waking to find her papa standing over her that night. The doorknob jiggled once more. She heard a click and listened as he walked to the side of the bed and paused. She thought of pulling the covers down to ask him what he wanted. Instead, she remained perfectly still. He was quiet so long, she thought he'd left. Only the sound of his breathing assured her he was still there. Moments later, he sighed his disgust, and a moment after that, he left the room. She heard him moving about the living area until he finally left the apartment, slamming the door behind him. Lowering the covers, she listened. When she'd made certain all was quiet, she scrambled from her bed and locked her bedroom door.

***

March 6, 1914

Anastasia opened her eyes, wondering what had woken her. A second passed before she realized there'd been a knock at her bedroom door. For a second, she thought her papa had returned, but then she heard her mother's voice telling her to unlock the door. She smiled, remembering today was her birthday. *Momma must be wishing to tell me happy birthday.* She kicked off the blankets and rushed from the bed to unlock the door.

"What are you doing in here?" Sharon asked, looking past her into the room.

"I was sleeping," Anastasia replied, hiding her disappointment.

Her mother pointed to the door. "Why was the door locked?"

"Because I was sleeping."

"Why do you feel the need to lock your bedroom door unless you are doing something you should not be doing?" Sharon stepped inside the room and looked around. "Unless you are hiding something you do not wish me to find."

Anastasia felt her jaw twitch. It was not like her mother to accuse her of such things. *Has she found my sock full of money? Maybe she has and is waiting for me to confess.* "I'm not hiding anything, Momma."

"Then I will ask you again, why was your door locked?"

"I locked it when Papa left my room."

Sharon's eyes grew wide. "When was your papa in your room?"

"Last night."

Sharon looked her up and down. When she spoke, her words held an edge. "What did he do?"

"He stood by my bed like he always does."

Her mother's jaw clenched as her nostrils flared. "I hate you!"

She felt the sting from Sharon's hand before she'd even realized she'd been slapped. She placed a hand on her cheek to soothe the fire from the impact as tears spilled from her eyes. Though the sting of her mother's hand hurt, the words she'd said hurt worse.

"He's not even my papa!" Anastasia shouted to cover the pain.

Sharon's face went white. "Who told you that?"

"Mr. Castiglione did and then I heard you and Papa arguing. Mr. Castiglione's my real papa, isn't he? He told me I was in your belly before you even met Papa. He told me he wanted to marry you, but you wanted more than he could give. Are you happy with your choice? Mr. Castiglione doesn't have much, but he's never raised a hand to you. He wouldn't either. I know he wouldn't." Her brain was telling her to stop, but her heart willed her to continue. She'd never borne witness to her mother's anger, and for her to have said those words hurt more than any beating her father had ever given her. At least she'd come to expect that.

"You could've been happy, Momma. We all could have been happy. It's not too late. Tell Papa the truth. If you don't, I will."

Sharon raised her hand once more, but this time, Anastasia saw it coming and ducked out of the way, and her mother crumpled to the floor in hysterical sobs. Ezra and Tobias had been watching the exchange and raced to their mother's side, prodding and asking if she was okay.

Anastasia's heart ached with indecision. Finally, she turned and walked to the chair beside her bed. She pulled on her dress and stockings then pulled on her boots, crossing the eyelets and tying the strings in place.

"Anastasia." The word came out in a sob.

She paused, waiting for Sharon to continue.

When Sharon spoke, her fear was palatable. "If you tell your papa what you told me, he will kill us all."

Gathering her coat, she pushed past Sharon and left the apartment without a word.

***

She stood in front of Mrs. Johnston's apartment, wondering how she'd arrived at the woman's door. She wiped her eyes, sucked in a breath to steady herself, and rapped on the woman's door.

Seconds later, the door was opened by a boy no older than Ezra who studied her with unblinking eyes.

"Where's Mrs. Johnston?" Anastasia asked, pushing her way into the room. The moment she entered, fear crept over her. For a second, she thought she'd entered the wrong apartment, as she recognized nothing.

"MOMMA!" the boy shouted, face full of fear.

"What tis it, boy?" a woman, presumably his mother, asked, coming into the room. She was young, carried an infant in her arms, and stopped when she saw Anastasia. "What are you doing in here?"

I could ask you the same thing. "I'm looking for Mrs. Johnston."

"Nobody here by that name," the woman replied.

Anastasia felt the panic rise. "Mrs. Johnston, the woman that lives here."

"No, we live here," the woman countered.

"We live here," the boy repeated and sidled close to his mother.

Tears streamed down Anastasia's face as she slowly backed from the apartment. She walked across the hall and knocked on the door, trembling as she waited. It didn't take long until the door opened a crack and a woman with white hair peeked through the opening. Seeing Anastasia, the door opened wider. Anastasia didn't know the woman's name, but they'd passed each other in the hall often enough that she knew the woman was missing most of her teeth.

"Where's Mrs. Johnston?" Anastasia blubbered the moment the door opened.

The woman's jaw flattened as she shook her head. "She's gone. Died about a week ago. Least that's when I found her. I got worried as I hadn't seen her. So I went in to check on her and found her in her bedroom. I thought she was sleeping, as her face looked so peaceful, that red hair of hers spread out all over those shiny pillows. That woman sure did like the sparkles. I called her name, but she didn't move. That's when I realized she was dead. Doctor said it was probably her heart, said he'd been treating her with the tonic. I guess if a person has to go, that's the way to do it. Just close your eyes and never wake up. They cleaned out her apartment the day I found her.

A new family moved in the day after that."

Anastasia found it hard to catch her breath. She remembered the day she'd knocked, and Mrs. Johnston didn't answer, and wondered if she'd been dead.

"You don't look so good, girl. Come in here for a moment and collect yourself."

Anastasia followed the woman inside, feeling as if her knees would buckle with each step.

"Have a seat. I'll get you a cup of tea."

Anastasia did as she was told and the woman busied herself filling the kettle. As her tears subsided, she realized much of the items in the room, including the chair she was presently sitting in, had once belonged to Mrs. Johnston.

"This is Mrs. Johnston's chair," Anastasia said when the woman brought the tea.

"It was. It's mine now," the woman said without apology.

"You stole from her?"

"No, I stole it from the landlord. Mrs. Johnston was already dead." The woman walked to the table and returned, handing Anastasia a red coin purse. Anastasia recognized it instantly as the one Mrs. Johnston had pulled the dollar bill from. Only, when it was in Mrs. Johnston's hands, the purse had been full of paper money.

Anastasia lifted her gaze and glared at the woman.

"It was empty when I found it," the woman said with a shrug.

"Just how'd you get into Mrs. Johnston's apartment?" Anastasia questioned.

"I picked the lock. I told you I hadn't seen her and was worried. I should have known something was amiss; the hall smelled worse than usual. You want that purse or not?"

I do. "Yes."

"I have some of the pillows from her bed if you'd like one of those too," the woman offered.

Anastasia remembered what the woman had said about the smell and shook her head.

"Suit yourself," the woman replied. "I'd offer you the mattress, but I had a bugger of a time getting the smell out, so I'm keeping that."

Once outside the apartment, Anastasia stuck the coin purse into her coat pocket. Now that the initial shock was over, her legs were no longer shaky. She stood in the hallway for several moments debating her next move before finally turning and heading up the stairs.

"You came back," Sharon's face showed no emotion as she entered.

"Mrs. Johnston is dead," Anastasia said by way of explanation.

"Oh," Sharon said from where she was sitting.

Anastasia waited for her to say more, but her mother remained silent. Odd how news of a person's demise could be absorbed by such a simple word.

Ezra and Tobias stood by the table wearing coats and boots. For the first time, Anastasia realized how their situation had changed. The boy's coats were riddled with holes, and Tobias' boots, which had once belonged to Ezra, had rips near the toes.

Anastasia thought about the money sock and considered retrieving it to give to her mother, but Sharon's words still hung between them, and she couldn't bring herself to chance hearing them again.

"Come along, Anastasia. The boys and I are heading to the market," Sharon said, rising from the chair.

Though she'd longed for the day when her mother would treat her as an adult, she took no joy in the way Sharon said her name. She didn't know it at the time, but her tenth birthday was a day that would change her life forever.

Chapter Sixteen

Anastasia stood, mouth agape, watching Sharon haggle over a wedge of wood. The small-framed man could tell how badly her mother wanted it, and he was holding firm, shaking his head at every offer Sharon threw out. She wasn't sure what her mother wanted the wood for, but it must be important if she was willing to use what little food money she had for the purchase. Anastasia almost told her she could get the wood for free but knew her mother would not approve of her stealing.

She looked at the dark clouds hovering overhead and tugged at Sharon's arm. "The skies are growing dark, Momma. Give me some money for the chicken, and I'll get it for you."

Sharon looked at the wedge of wood then lowered her eyes, looking at each child before finally handing Anastasia a few coins.

"Find the largest chicken this will buy. I'm afraid it will be all we have tonight," she said, handing over the empty basket.

Anastasia wanted to ask why the wood was more important than dinner, but she'd been taught never to question her parents in public. She turned to tell the boys they had to stay with their mother, but to her surprise, neither seemed inclined to go with her. For a moment, she felt slighted, then deduced it was probably much more entertaining to watch their mother argue with the man.

Anastasia stood near the meat wagon, watching as a robust woman in a heavy brown skirt, spectacles, and oversized hat chatted with the chicken woman while the woman pulled feathers from a freshly killed bird. While the chicken lady wasn't paying Anastasia any mind, the lady wearing the hat hadn't taken her eyes off of her. A shame, as she'd hoped to lift a second chicken from the ice bed without getting caught. She'd just about given up her quest to pilfer the second bird when the woman extended a finger and called Anastasia over.

"Yes, you. Come here, child," the woman beckoned when Anastasia looked around to make sure it was in fact she the woman was summoning.

Anastasia approached, sure she was going to be outed for stealing the first chicken, which she'd placed inside her basket just seconds before the woman arrived. To her surprise, the woman pointed to the limp birds lying breathlessly on the ice and instructed her to take one.

Anastasia reached for one of the birds, placed it into her basket, then reached into her pocket with a sigh. She'd hoped to be able to get both birds without paying.

"Leave your money. That is, if you even have any," the woman said.

Something about the woman's tone caused Anastasia to bristle. Sure she was a thief, but that didn't mean she liked being treated like one. She lifted her chin and pulled the coins from her pocket. "I've got money."

"Fair enough," the woman said in return. She handed the chicken lady several coins and turned back to Anastasia. "Now put them away."

Anastasia did as told.

"What's your name, girl?"

Anastasia debated giving her a fake name, then decided against it. "Anastasia."

"Walk with me, Anastasia," the woman said and left without waiting for a reply.

Anastasia glanced to where Sharon was still standing then fell into step beside the woman.

"I saw you steal the chicken," the lady said when they were out of danger of being overheard.

Anastasia came to a stop. "I didn't steal it. You told me to take it. Besides, you paid for it, so it's not stealing."

"I'm not speaking about the one I told you to take. I'm talking about the one I saw you place in the basket as I arrived."

So she had seen her. "Then why didn't you say anything?"

"Because I didn't wish to see you thrown into jail," the woman replied. "Have you ever been to jail?"

"Of course not. I'm too good to get caught."

The woman lifted her eyebrows. "And yet, here we are having this discussion."

The woman had a point. "I was in a hurry is all."

"It doesn't matter what the excuse; getting caught is getting caught. Do you know what happens to little girls like you in jail?"

"No."

"Bad things. Very bad things. If you are lucky, they only cut off your hand. Or maybe they'll give you a new scar to match the one you already have on your pretty little face."

Instantly, Anastasia's hand went to her face, tracing the length of the scar. *Did she just say I'm pretty?* "How is having a hand cut off lucky?"

"Because there are much worse things that can happen to a girl," the woman said firmly. "Why do you need two?"

"What?"

"Chickens. You could have stopped at one, but you were after a second. Why do you need two?"

Anastasia slid a glance to Sharon's market basket. "Because my mother needs them for our dinner."

The woman paused. "Your mother?"

"Yes."

"And she asked you to steal them for her?"

"No, she gave me coins," Anastasia said, lowering her eyes.

"So why not use the coins?"

So I could keep the money. "Because there isn't enough. The boys are hungry, and now Momma's going to have another baby. If you're not going to turn me in, then why all the questions?"

The woman's brow furrowed. "I wasn't going to turn you in because I thought you were homeless. I was going to give you another option."

Anastasia swallowed. *Did that mean the woman had changed her mind about turning her in?* "What kind of option?"

"It doesn't matter now. You aren't homeless."

"Please don't turn me in. I can pay for the chickens," Anastasia said, digging for the coins.

"Give the money back to your mother, Anastasia. She needs it more than either of us do," the woman said softly.

Anastasia merely nodded and turned to go.

"Where'd you get the bruises?" Again, the woman's tone was soft.

Anastasia knew she was speaking of the bruises on her face, as her coat covered the rest. She shrugged. "From the gettin' place."

"The world can be a cruel place. If you ever find yourself on the streets, look me up. I'll do what I can to help you," the woman said, handing her a folded piece of paper.

"Ma'am?" Anastasia said, pushing the paper into the pocket of her coat without reading it. "Do I remind you of your daughter?"

The woman smiled. "I don't have any children,

Anastasia."

"Then why would you want to help me?"

Her question produced another smile. "Maybe that's the reason; because I never had any children of my own.

"Anastasia?"

Anastasia turned at the sound of her mother's voice.

"I've been looking for you. I thought you were going to get the chicken."

"I did, Momma. I got two." Anastasia was going to add the lady had paid for them, but when she looked, the woman was gone.

"Two?' Sharon gasped. "Anastasia, you know we can't afford two."

"It's okay, Momma. I found a ten cent piece in the dirt and used it to buy the chickens. See, I still have the money you gave me," she said, handing her the coins.

For a moment, she thought her mother was going to cry. As the tears pooled in her eyes, she blinked and turned away.

"Where are we going, Momma?" Ezra asked.

"It looks as if we have enough left to buy carrots and potatoes for our dinner. Maybe even a little rice to make a nice chicken rice soup for tomorrow." Sharon sniffed.

***

Anastasia peeled the final potato and placed it in the simmering pot with the others.

She wiped her hands on the apron and looked across the room where her mother was sitting, quietly reading to Ezra and Tobias. The boys looked up when she neared, but neither smiled. It had been like that from the moment they'd heard her and Sharon fighting. They'd taken sides, and she was not the chosen one. She smiled at Tobias and was met by a blank stare.

It was the first time he'd chosen Sharon over her, and her mother reveled in the victory, kissing the top of his head.

Anastasia felt her lips twitch and turned to hide her sorrow. She knew she should be happy for her mother, but the sense of loss was too much to bear on top of the other events of the day. She'd yet to cry over Mrs. Johnston, pushing the woman's memory aside each time the tears threatened. She did the same with this new loss and busied herself tidying her room, not that there was much to do. It was a small room with nothing more than a small metal frame bed and a tall chest of drawers, of which she held claim to one drawer. The rest held what few extra linens the family owned.

"Your papa will be home soon," Sharon said, entering the room.

"My papa is selling apples," Anastasia countered.

"This is for you," Sharon said, ignoring the comment and handing her the wedge of wood she'd haggled over.

Anastasia turned the wood over in her hand several times, at a loss as to why Sharon had thought it so important. "What is it for?"

Sharon glanced towards the door. "You are to put it under the door each night."

An image of being locked in the cutting room in the Triangle Factory sprang to mind, causing a moment of panic. "Momma, please don't make me block my door."

"Don't you sass me, girl. I realize I have not been firm enough with you in the past, but I am the woman of the house, and as such, I expect you to do as I say."

"But, Momma, I'll be good. I promise. Please don't make me do this."

Ignoring her pleas, Sharon took the wedge from her hand and showed Anastasia how to place it beneath her bedroom door. Removing the wedge, she placed it into her hand once more. "Make sure it's jammed tight. You are not to open the door until you see daylight coming through your window. Do you understand?"

Too upset to answer without crying, Anastasia merely nodded. Though the woman had not raised her hand, she was still delivering pain. First, she'd recaptured Tobias' love and now this. Her mother was well aware of the fact Tobias sometimes crawled into bed with Anastasia whenever he awoke from a bad dream. Or whenever he grew frightened by his mother's screams.

Sharon left without another word, leaving Anastasia standing in the middle of the room with the object in her hand. She glared at the wedge of wood, so simple in design, yet to her, it was yet another barrier between her and her family.

***

Anastasia lay wide-eyed in the dark, fear keeping the sleep at bay. Her stomach ached as she recalled the events of the day in dry-eyed sorrow. She'd crossed into her tenth year, and yet no one in the family wished her as much as a happy birthday. She understood the boys not saying anything as they were too young to know without being told. But her mother and Albert—as she now thought of the man—had treated her no differently. No, that was not true; after the events this morning, Sharon now treated her as if she were a stranger, speaking to her only when necessary. Anastasia placed her palm to her cheek, remembering the shock she'd felt when her mother's hand connected with her face. And those vile words. Was it true? Could a mother truly hate their child? From the look on Sharon's face at the time, she believed the answer to be yes.

What did I do to make you hate me, Momma? Maybe Mrs. Johnston can help. She stopped mid-thought as she realized Mrs. Johnston would never be able to help her again. And just like that, the flood gate that had been blocking the tears lifted. Salty tears spilled from her eyes, running freely into the depths of her ears, her breaths coming in stomach-wrenching sobs until at long last she'd cried herself to sleep.

She woke sometime later to the sound of someone twisting her doorknob.

Tobias. He must have had another bad dream.

Tossing the covers aside, she ran to her door, thinking to let him in. Just as she reached for the wedge of wood, she remembered Sharon's words. *Do not remove the wedge until you see sunlight coming in through the window.* She hesitated, peeking at the window in an attempt to judge the time. *It's still dark. Momma will be angry. She's already angry*, she thought and reached for the wood once more.

"Anna, open the door." Albert's words slurred as he spoke.

She fell backward with a soft thud and scrambled to the opposite side of the room, back against the wall, waiting.

Albert's voice became more insistent as his fists hammered relentlessly against the door. She could hear Tobias' cries in the adjacent room and placed her hand to the wall, silently willing him to remain in his room. Moments passed, then finally, the pounding and shouting stopped. She sighed as she heard a door slam. On the other side of the thin wall, she could hear Ezra quietly comforting his brother. Her heart broke anew as she realized she was not needed anymore.

Sharon's screams broke through the silence. Picking herself up off the floor, she crawled back into bed and pulled the quilt over her head in an attempt at silencing her mother's screams.

It was quiet in the house when at last she woke. Sunlight poured in through her window as she dressed and placed her hand on the doorknob, attempting unsuccessfully to open her bedroom door. She tried once more. The handle turned, but she couldn't get the door to open. She looked down and realized the wedge of wood was still planted securely underneath, keeping it from opening.

That's why Albert couldn't get in.

Her breathing increased as she realized her mother's sacrifice. The wedge of wood was not to distance her from the family. It was to protect her from things she could not control.

She still loves me.

Anastasia removed the wedge, eager to find Sharon and tell her she finally understood.

"Momma…" Anastasia stopped when she saw the fresh bruises covering Sharon's face and arms. "Why do you allow him to hurt you like that?"

"I'm his wife."

"But it's not right. He shouldn't be allowed to beat you."

"I know it is hard for you to understand, but when a woman gets married, she must abide by her husband's rules."

"So that means you have to kiss him when you don't want to?"

Sharon closed her eyes briefly. "It means I have to do many things I do not wish."

"I'm never going to get married," Anastasia promised.

"Go to school, Anastasia," Sharon said, turning away.

"But I…"

Her mother put up a hand. "Just go."

***

Cindy flipped the page, expecting there to be more.

"Are you looking for this?" Linda asked, holding up a sheet of paper. "I had two of them. Yours must have gotten added to my stack by mistake."

Cindy took the paper and read the last paragraph. *Neither Momma nor I ever mentioned what happened with Albert, but after my tenth birthday, he started looking at me differently. Sometimes he would simply jiggle the knob. Sometimes he would pound on the door and demand I let him come in. I never did.*

Cindy placed the paper on the finished pile and turned to Linda. "Why the change?"

Linda's eyebrows went up. "You didn't figure it out?"

"Figure what out?"

"Her mom feels guilty."

"What does she have to feel guilty about? She gave her the wedge of wood to keep the man out."

Linda smiled. "Yes, but it was Mom who brought attention to the fact that Anastasia was maturing."

"When?"

"When she laughed at her husband for thinking it was her bra. The man was a letch before, but that woman basically pointed out there was another female in the house."

"So instead of pulling her closer, she started pushing her away? It doesn't make sense. Maybe she was beginning to think Anastasia was a threat. She couldn't live up to her wifely duties, and Anastasia's running around playing surrogate mom to her sons. Add to that dad giving the girl the eye. Maybe Mom got jealous."

"He's not her father," Linda interjected.

"Even more of a reason to feel threatened," Cindy argued. "But then, why not just kick her out of the house?"

Linda leaned over and placed her hand on top of Cindy's. "Because above all else, she's still the girl's mother."

"I guess we know why the Johnston lady didn't take her in."

"I admit I had her pegged wrong," Linda agreed.

"I feel bad for Anastasia. She's certainly headed down a rabbit hole," Cindy said, rubbing at her temples. She found herself wishing she had a time machine so she could reach through the journals and pull Anastasia and her brothers to safety. "What these children had to endure."

"It wasn't easy for their parents either," Linda said softly.

"But why not just take the children and leave?" Cindy countered.

"And go where? The woman barely had enough money for food. There were no homeless shelters, and it was long before the social service program."

Cindy knew Linda's points were valid, but that didn't make it any better. "She could have run away with the apple man."

"You make it sound so easy," Linda snapped. "Sitting here, making judgments on other people's relationships when you're afraid even to give one a try."

The shock of the words was like a slap in the face. For a moment, she thought of Anastasia when Sharon had told her she hated her. "Whoa, where's that coming from?"

"I'm just telling you that it's always easy to see an answer to someone's relationship problem when you're not the one going through it. People think they know what's best for you, and maybe some of them do, but they don't see your inner turmoil. Yes, there are days when you want to leave. There are days when you would like nothing more than to kill the man, but then there are days when the onion gets peeled back, and you see the man you married. The one that told you he couldn't live without you. The one that placed a ring on your finger and promised he would love you forever. The one that pleads for forgiveness when they realize what they've done. They don't see the look in their eyes when you tell them it's over and you are leaving."

As Cindy listened to Linda's words, she realized her mother's voice was trembling. Chills ran the length of her arm when she realized Linda was not speaking about the woman in the journals or her friend from long ago. "Mom, you're speaking from experience, aren't you?"

Linda blinked, and tears welled in her eyes. When she spoke, the word came out on a whisper. "Yes."

Chapter Seventeen

Cindy stood at the window, staring out into the yard. "I can't believe you never told me you were married before."

"Cindy, we've been through this. I was only married to the man for a minute. It doesn't count."

Cindy laughed. "Seven months is more than a minute."

"Not when you get to be my age. We'd have gotten an annulment, but the judge wouldn't grant it. Apparently, abuse was not considered grounds for annulment, at least not in Kentucky."

"But why didn't you tell me? We've been going through these journals for months, uncovering secrets, some of which we'll never know the answers. Can you imagine if I would have found this out after you were dead? Then you'd have just been one more person that lied to me."

"I didn't lie."

"The heck you didn't. I've asked you many times if you are keeping any secrets I should know about."

"There's your answer right there. You had no reason to know about this," Linda replied.

"I'm your daughter. I deserve to know everything about you. Even your dirty little secrets."

"I've got the hemorrhoids," Linda said with a grin. "Doesn't get much dirtier than that."

Cindy turned from the window to stare at Linda. "Mom, I'm being serious."

"So am I. Those little buggers are no joke."

Cindy walked to the counter and picked up her keys.

Linda shot her a worried look. "Going somewhere?"

"To see Uncle Frank." Cindy knew she should ask her if she wanted to go, but she needed a little time to get past the hurt. Of course Linda wouldn't want to talk about something so painful, but that didn't make the fact that her mother had never trusted her with the information any easier to bear. She paused before closing the door. "I love you, Mom. I'll be back in a bit."

"Bring me back a salad burger," Linda called after her. "And one of those peachy drinks."

"Okay, Mom." Cindy sighed.

Cindy drove the short distance across town and waited to be buzzed into the facility. She waved at the girl at the front desk and headed down the hall to her uncle's room. He was sitting in his wheelchair near the window and looked up when she entered. He smiled. For a moment, she thought this might be the day he remembered her. "Hi, Frank, how are you doing today?"

"Bella, the love of my life. My forbidden wife," he said, reaching his hands towards her.

Wife? "Uncle Frank, who is Bella?"

The smile faded from his face, and his hands dropped to his lap. Just like that, he'd slipped back into the shell that was his home.

Cindy closed her eyes. *What's with all the dang secrets?* "Are you okay?"

Opening her eyes, she smiled at Melinda, the young aide who'd just entered the room. The girl's long, dark ponytail bounced merrily as she moved about the room tidying the space.

"It's been a long morning," Cindy said.

"I'll let you two visit a moment while I change Mr. Frank's bed."

Cindy moved from the bed and leaned against the

windowsill. She watched as Melinda moved through the room changing the linens and returning objects to their rightful place. For a moment, she found herself feeling somewhat envious of the girl's carefree energy.

Melinda finished with the bedding, washed her hands, and turned her attention to Frank. "How's Mr. Frank doing today?"

"He spoke for a moment, then shut down again. I'm surprised I got that much out of him."

"I'd say he's doing pretty amazing for a man his age. We don't get many residents that live to be a hundred. I'm sure he has a story to tell. Don't you, Frank?"

"Has he told you anything?" Cindy asked.

"Anything?" Melinda asked, removing a set of clean clothes from Frank's drawer.

"It's just that sometimes I wonder how much I really know about the man."

Melinda tilted her head. "He's your uncle, right?"

"He is, but every family has its secrets," Cindy said casually.

"I guess, if you say so." Melinda shrugged. "I'm going to give him a sponge bath. Are you staying or leaving?"

"I guess I'll go for now," Cindy said with a sigh.

***

Cindy pulled the brown carton out of the paper bag and handed it to Linda. "Just because you call it a salad burger doesn't make it so."

Linda opened the carton and pulled out the burger. "It has lettuce, cheese, pickles, onions, and sesame seeds. Sounds like a salad to me."

"Next you'll be trying to convince yourself that that

drink equals a serving of fruit."

"It's peach," Linda said and took a drink.

"Mom, I think you are becoming addicted to fast food."

Linda raised her eyebrows. "Says the girl with the fish sandwich and large order of fries."

"I'll have you know these are real potatoes." Cindy smiled when Linda didn't have a comeback. "Have you ever heard Uncle Frank mention anyone named Bella?"

"No. Who's that?"

Cindy picked up a fry and dunked it into ketchup. "I'm pretty sure she may have been his wife."

Linda nearly choked on the burger she was eating. "Wife? Frank had a wife he didn't tell us about? Who does that?"

Cindy raised her eyebrows at Linda. "Do you really want to have this conversation again, or do you want to finish our lunch and read some more of the journals?"

"If you're going to be grumpy, I'd rather read," Linda said and took a bite of her sandwich.

***

August, 1914

Anastasia sat on the stoop with her arms around her brothers, trying her best to quiet their cries. A difficult thing to do through tears of her own. Her father's tirades were growing increasingly brutal and she wasn't sure how much longer she'd be able to stay in the home.

"Does it hurt?" Tobias asked, touching one of the welts on her arm.

Of course it hurts. "Not too much."

"Father's mean. I hate him." Tobias sobbed, using the more formal moniker they sometimes used when they were upset with the man.

"Don't you say that," Ezra warned. "Papa will beat you if he hears."

Anastasia knew Ezra was right. Still, she had to force herself to agree. "Your brother's right, Tobias. You mustn't say things like that. Your papa would not be happy with you if he heard you saying that."

"I ain't scared of Father," Tobias said on a sob.

Anastasia smiled. "I know you're not, but all the same, don't say things that will make him mad."

"He's your papa too," Ezra reminded her.

No he's not. "I know," she said, humoring him. "How about we take a walk?"

"Papa will be mad," Ezra warned.

Anastasia dried her eyes with the hem of her skirt. "Papa's already mad."

They walked without direction, ending up in the market. While most of the vendors had left for the day, there were a few remaining, most crammed with late afternoon shoppers. She momentarily regretting having the boys in tow, as it would not be possible to steal without them seeing her. Especially Ezra. The boy was at an age where he didn't miss anything. Her stomach growled, reminding her she'd not gotten enough to eat for dinner, something that happened more and more often of late. Each night when she lay in bed listening to the rumble of her stomach, she dreamed of marching up to her mother and telling her she knew how to get food. Then she'd come to her senses, knowing Sharon would never condone stealing, which was also the reason she couldn't tell her of the money hidden in the bottom drawer of her dresser. They stopped at the corner drug store gawking at the jars filled with colorful candy.

Tobias pressed his forehead against the window and sighed. "I'm hungry."

Anastasia heard a whimper and turned. "Why, hello there."

At the greeting, the black and white dog that traveled with Runt twirled in a circle, wagging its tail. She placed a hand on the dog's head, ruffling its fur in greeting. While she didn't see Runt, she knew he must be near.

Tobias turned from the window, dropped to his knees, and squealed with delight when the dog lapped at his face.

Always a bit more reserved, Ezra watched from a distance.

Anastasia looked through the window and saw Runt casually approach the end of the counter. He had on a different set of clothes. Still ill-fitting and not new by any means, but they didn't appear as grubby as the ones he normally wore. He pretended to be looking at something on a higher shelf while his hands lifted the lid on one of the lower candy jars. He reached his hand into the jar, easily plucking a handful of lollypops and sliding them into his pocket. The clerk, busy talking to a well-dressed man at the other end of the counter, never looked in his direction. Probably because the man at the counter seemed irritated, waving his arms and pointing across the room. This proved a good distraction, as Runt was able to grab two additional handfuls and make a clean escape without being noticed. Runt had his cap pulled low and exited the building, turning without as much as a glance in their direction.

The dog whimpered its indecision then went back to smothering Tobias with eager kisses.

"Ezra, watch your brother for a moment," Anastasia said and hurried off after her friend. She saw him slip into the alley and ran to catch him. She stopped short when she saw him leaning against the building as if he'd been there the whole time.

"What's the hurry?" he spoke as if he'd expected her.

She looked over her shoulder, making sure they hadn't

been followed.

Runt's face turned red as he took in her bruises. "Did you run away?"

"No." The word came out on a whisper.

"You don't have to go back. You can stay with me."

She remembered her conversation with the woman in the hat. "I'm not going to live on the streets. It's not safe for girls."

He let out a laugh. "It's better than having your papa pound on you."

"I can't leave my brothers." She felt a tear and wiped it away with the back of her hand.

"You said yourself he doesn't pound on them as much." He reached into his pocket, pulled a lollypop free, and plopped it into his mouth. He reached for another, holding it for her to see. "Want one?"

Her mouth watered and she took a step closer.

"Not so fast," he said, pulling the candy just out of reach. "What'll you give me for it?"

She thought about the money in her sock drawer and frowned. If she was going to pay, she might as well go to the store and buy them herself. "What do you want for it?"

His face turned serious. "I want what I've always wanted."

"That's not fair."

He placed the lollypop in his mouth and withdrew it slowly. "Like it or not, it's the way things work. Better get used to it, kid."

She jutted her chin. "I'll kiss you for three lollypops."

"Three? Whatcha think? I'm made of lollypops?"

She pointed to his pocket. "You've got a bunch more. I saw you take them."

He pondered that for a moment. "Three lollypops, three

kisses."

She shook her head. "Three lollypops, two kisses."

"No deal," Runt said with a wave of the hand.

Anastasia lowered her eyes and licked her lips the way she'd seen Sharon do. "Okay, never you mind."

"Wait," Runt said when she turned to walk away. "Three lollypops, two kisses, but they'd better be good kisses."

"Of course they're good kisses. I'm a great kisser," she said, facing him once more.

"Oh yeah? Who've you kissed?"

"Lots of boys," she lied. She'd only kissed one boy, and Runt had witnessed the whole thing.

"On the lips," he said, pulling out two more lollypops.

"Deal," she said when her stomach growled once more.

Runt smiled a triumphant smile and pushed the suckers back into his pocket.

"Wait, why are you putting them away?"

"Cause I'm no sucker. No way am I going to let you grab them and run."

She had to give him credit; she'd planned on doing exactly that. He reached for her and she ducked out of the way. "What are you doing?"

He blinked his confusion. "You said we're going to kiss."

"That's right. A kiss on the lips. Hands will cost you another lollypop."

Runt frowned and shoved his hands into his pockets. "Two kisses, lips only."

Anastasia stepped closer, placed her lips on his, then pulled back to judge his expression. "What's the matter?"

He shrugged.

"You didn't like it?"

"I guess?"

She thought about it for a moment. "Give me one of the lollypops."

"Nope, you still owe me a kiss," he said, shaking his head.

"I'm not trying to cheat you. Just hand me one."

"Fine," he said, handing her a red one.

She licked the lollypop and then touched it to her lips, rolling it back and forth several times. Stepping closer, she kissed him once more. "Now lick your lips."

He did as instructed and a smile spread across his face.

She grinned when his face turned nearly as red as the lollypop. "Was that better?"

He nodded and shoved two more lollypops into her hand. The instant she looked away, he kissed her a third time, then tore off in the other direction. A second later, the black and white dog trotted past, catching up to Runt just as he turned the corner.

Before she could protest, Ezra appeared at her side.

"I'm telling Momma and Papa you kissed that boy," he threatened.

"You do and you'll not get a lollypop," Anastasia said, holding one in front of his face.

Ezra's eyes grew wide. "Where'd you get that?"

"I traded for it. You want it, you have to keep your mouth shut."

"Traded what?" he pressed.

Anastasia narrowed her eyes at him. "You want it or not?"

"Want what?" Tobias asked, joining them.

"One of these," Anastasia said, handing him a bright green lollypop.

"Hey," Ezra objected. "How come he gets one and he didn't see nothing?"

"You were going to get one too, but now you'll only get it if you promise not to tell," Anastasia replied.

"That's not fair."

"Like it or not, it's the way things work. Better get used to it, kid." she said, repeating what Runt had said.

Chapter Eighteen

Late September, 1914

Anastasia heard her mother's sobs and pushed open the door to her bedroom. "What is it, Momma? The baby?"

Sharon hurried to dry her eyes. "No, Anastasia, the baby is long gone."

"Gone where, Momma?"

"I've not the strength to explain such things," she said, shaking her head.

Was her mother ill? She seemed to be doing much better this time. "You're sick?"

"Sometimes a person can be sick up here," she said, tapping her head. She moved her hand to her chest. "And sometimes the sickness is in here."

"I don't understand, Momma."

"I know, girl. I hope you never do. Being a mother has brought me my biggest joy. Now it's bringing me my biggest heartache. What I'm about to say to you is something no mother should ever have to say to a child."

As Anastasia watched Sharon struggle with her words, she realized how gaunt the woman's face appeared. Her eyes had sunk into the recesses of her cheeks and were laced with dark circles. For the first time, Sharon looked old. *When had that happened?* "What's wrong, Momma?"

"Go on and get out of here, boy," Sharon fussed when Tobias wandered into the room.

Startled, he turned and rushed from the room.

Sharon's words frightened her even more than the hollowed look on her face. The woman had never so much as raised her voice to Tobias before.

"Let him be," she said when Anastasia turned to go check on her brother. She patted the bed beside her. "Sit."

Anastasia did as told.

"You must leave." Sharon's voice shook as she spoke.

She wasn't sure what she'd expected, but this wasn't it. "Leave? Where will I go?"

"There are plenty of children living on the streets. You'll do what you must to survive."

She'd thought of going, even dreamed of doing so, but she never imagined her mother turning her away. When she spoke, her words came out on a whisper. "Why?"

"I cannot afford to feed you. Your papa, Albert," she corrected, "does not give me enough. The boys are starving. We're all starving. It is the only way I know. I'm going to try to get Albert to take in a boarder, but if that doesn't work, you'll have to go."

Allow a stranger into our home? Albert would never agree to that. Anastasia searched her mind for another solution. She could offer up the sock money, but that was only a temporary solution. "I'll get a job."

"You saw what happened the last time. Albert will never allow it."

"I can steal. I'll bring you food and Albert will never know."

"No, Anastasia," Sharon said firmly. "They'd put you in prison, and my heart would not bear it."

"So you'll send me to the streets instead? And just what do you think I'll do there, Mother?" Anastasia said coldly.

"You'll do whatever it takes to survive. But you'll do it for yourself and not because I made you," Sharon replied.

"Maybe I can go and stay with my papa. My real papa," she clarified.

"No, it'll be the first place Albert looks for you. You can't stay around here. Do you not know what your… what Albert will do if he finds you? What he'd do to both of us if he were to find out I sent you away? You must go far away; it's the only way to keep us both safe."

"But what about Tobias and Ezra?" Anastasia asked on a sob. "I won't be here to protect them."

"I'll protect them."

Like you are protecting me? "How?"

"Anastasia, I give you my word. I'll protect those boys or die trying; it's what mothers do," Sharon said, wrapping her arms around her.

Anastasia wanted to pull away, but she needed the security only a mother's embrace could give. As tears streamed down her cheeks, she wondered what made some children worth fighting for and deemed others expendable.

***

Anastasia lay in bed listening to her mother and Albert shouting. While she couldn't decipher their words, she was certain the argument stemmed from money. One thing was for certain, she wasn't going to miss hearing their shouts. A door slammed in the distance. Her lip twitched. She knew what was coming next. The doorknob jiggled. Seconds passed, then the jiggle was followed by Albert's fists pounding relentlessly against her bedroom door.

Go away. Nobody wants you here. Maybe if you go away, I can stay. For a moment, she contemplated opening the door and telling him of her thoughts, but then the pounding stopped, and the house grew quiet once more.

"I'm not going to miss you," she whispered to the dark.

She thought about getting up and sneaking off into the night. But she could not bear the thought of leaving without saying one final goodbye to Ezra and Tobias. She thought about what her mother had said about protecting her brothers. *Why them and not me?* Instantly, the tears began to flow. She curled into a ball and drew her knees close. *Momma, what did I do to make you hate me so?*

Anastasia opened her eyes to sunlight filtering in through the sheer curtains that covered her window. On any other day, the sight of the sun would produce a smile, but today, she was in no mood for smiling. She wasn't sure when she'd fallen asleep, but when she had, her dreams were filled with shadowy figures trying to reach her in the dark, pounding on her door and screaming, telling her to leave. She rose from the bed, choked back tears as she opened the drawer, and pulled out the sock full of money. In the past, the weight of the sock had held a glimpse of possibility, a promise of a new life for her and her brothers. Today, the reality of her situation set in. She tossed the sock onto the bed and began to empty her dresser drawers, stacking the contents neatly on the bed next to the money. She went to the closet and pulled out her dress. She started to pull it over her head then changed her mind. She would not be washing yesterday's dress today, so she might as well wear it again and keep this one clean. She dumped the pillow out of the pillowcase and shoved her dress and undergarments inside. She took hold of the blue silk pillow Mrs. Johnston gave her and pulled it to her chest, wishing the woman were still alive. *She'd know what to do.* As she stood there hugging the pillow, she remembered the woman in the hat. She tossed the pillow onto the bed with the rest of her things then walked to her closet and pulled out her coat. She slipped her hand inside the pocket and removed the paper the woman had given her. Unfolding it, she read the words: *Ms. Anna L. Hill, Children's Aid Society,* and there was an address at the bottom. Anastasia wasn't sure what the Children's Aid Society was, but the woman had told her if she ever found herself on the street, she would do what she could to help. *Anna. She even has my name.* Surely that meant something. She considered the coat, wondering if she should take it with her. The September days had remained warm, so she returned the coat to the closet and tucked the note in the pocket of her dress.

She rummaged through her sewing basket and pulled out a long length of ribbon. She put the silk pillow and a change of clothes into the pillowcase, then lifted her dress. She placed the pillowcase against her waist. When it proved too bulky, she removed the silk pillow. Using the ribbon, she tied the pillowcase to her waist. Lowering her skirt, she took several steps to ensure the pillowcase would stay in place, smiling at her ingenuity. Anastasia picked up the money sock, debating at what to do with it. As she held the weighted mass in her hand, she thought of the drawn look on Sharon's face. She thought to remove a few pennies then remembered her mother's words. *We are all starving.* Sighing, she placed the sock under the silk pillow. Sharon knew how to stretch a penny; neither she nor the boys would have to go to bed hungry anytime soon.

She heard voices coming from the living space, removed the wedge of wood, and opened her bedroom door. A man she'd never seen before stood in the front room talking to her mother. Dressed in dark slacks and a white button-up shirt, he stood ramrod straight with his hands behind his back as if he were hiding something.

Ezra and Tobias stood by their mother's side, somberly staring up at the stranger. While her mother smiled, the woman's shoulders remained tense. She looked up when Anastasia opened her door and waved her hand to summon her closer.

"Anastasia, this is Mr. Bentley. He's come to see about the room we have for rent. Is it ready?" Sharon asked when she approached.

"Yes, Mother. There's even two drawers in which he can place his things, and a beautiful silk pillow for his head," Anastasia replied coldly.

"My husband is out getting the morning paper," she said, ignoring Anastasia's tone. "Would you care to see the room, Mr. Bentley?"

He nodded and extended his hand, showing he held nothing more than a brimmed hat.

"Of course we'll wash the linens, and you can have another drawer if you'd like."

The man shook his head as he looked about the room. He lowered himself to the bed and tested the firmness. He reached for the pillow and Anastasia held her breath. She hadn't planned on being in the apartment when the money sock was found. She breathed a sigh of relief when Bentley simply smoothed his hands over the pillow.

"I'm a simple man. Two drawers and one silk pillow will suffice," he said.

Anastasia blinked her surprise. *Did that mean she wouldn't have to leave?*

"Your rent will be a dollar fifty a week. Add another fifty cents if you wish to take meals with the family."

The hope she'd felt started to dwindle. Even if Albert agreed to let the man stay, he'd never allow him to take up a meal with them. Not that the man would want to on any account. Mealtime was nothing more than a shouting match between Sharon and Albert of late. Maybe that would change if the money brought in proved enough to buy food.

The man reached for his wallet, and the hope returned.

Anastasia heard the front door jingle and ran to see who was there. Fear crept over her when the door opened, and Albert entered.

"Oh no," Tobias exclaimed, then struggled when Ezra clamped his hand over his mouth.

"What's the matter? Does a man need permission to enter his own home?" Albert asked, seeing their faces.

"No, Papa," Anastasia said in reply. "It's just that…"

"Where's your mother?" Albert asked, cutting her off.

"She's in Anna's bedroom with the man," Tobias answered, pulling Ezra's hand away.

Albert's face turned bright red. He threw down his paper and stormed across the room, disappearing into Anastasia's room. He returned a second later, leading Mr. Bentley by the ear. He shoved the man out the door, tossing his hat into the hallway after him. If not for the seriousness of the situation, Anastasia would have laughed at the confused look on Mr. Bentley's face. She couldn't help but think that Mr. Bentley was lucky Albert had not yet settled into the bottle.

"Albert, you had no right!" Momma said, coming into the room. "That man was willing to pay two dollars to sleep in that room."

"I have every right," Albert growled as he bent to retrieve his newspaper. "This whole tenement is filled with roaches. People open their doors, let the roaches in, and pretty soon those roaches have other roaches. It's not long before a man cannot move in his own house because there are cockroaches living in every room. I've seen it before, and I'll not live like that."

"But, Papa, we don't have any bugs," Ezra said, looking around the room.

"I'm not talking about bugs, boy. I'm talking about people in the lowest form. The ones that come in from the boats and steal our jobs. You wouldn't believe the hordes of immigrants coming in through Ellis Island every single day. Waving flyers and jabbering in whatever language they speak. One doesn't have to know the language to know they think the land rush is still going on."

"Albert, don't talk to the children like that. Your family came over on the boats, as did mine. The only difference is our families entered through Castle Garden. There's nothing wrong with wanting a better life for your family. The problem comes when you're so stubborn that the ones you love have to suffer because of it."

Momma's sigh was not lost on any of them, including Albert.

Chapter Nineteen

Anastasia stood against the far side of the living area watching her mother and Albert argue. Sharon was in the kitchen desperately trying to fix breakfast for the family of five using just three eggs, a large potato, and two slices of bacon.

"I can't continue to feed the family on what you're giving me," Sharon said for the hundredth time. "The children are skin and bones. If we rent the room, there'll be enough money for food."

"I'll not have people thinking I cannot provide for my family," Albert fumed.

"You'd watch your children starve to death to save your foolish pride?" Sharon shot back.

"At least there'd be fewer mouths to feed," Albert said and turned his attention back to the newspaper he was reading.

Trembling with fury, Sharon reached for a glass of water and took a sip. Anastasia pushed off from the wall, thinking to help with breakfast. She froze in place as her mother flung the glass to the floor.

"Woman, are you so inept you cannot even hold a glass?" Albert said, unaware she'd broken the thing on purpose. "Now you'll have to use some of the food money to replace it."

"Maybe we should use some of the money you spend on liquor or cigarettes instead." Sharon's tone was cold.

Albert's smoking was new. Her mother had been furious when she'd discovered he'd taken up the habit, even more so when she found out he was spending a full nickel purchasing twenty cigarettes a day.

Albert hastily folded the paper, pushed from the sofa, and stormed into the kitchen area with fists clenched.

Anastasia started in their direction and Sharon shook her head, mouthing the word "go." Anastasia had been waiting for this moment, but now that it was here, she wondered if she could actually go. She looked at her mother, eyes pleading for her to reconsider. Instead, Sharon lowered her eyes. As her parents' argument intensified, Anastasia hurried to where Tobias sat cowered behind the chair and reached for his hand. She motioned for Ezra to follow and led the way to the front door.

She met Sharon's gaze just before pulling the door closed. She saw the fear in the woman's eyes and wondered if it was due to her husband being so near or because she saw that Anastasia was taking the boys with her. She drew in her breath and closed the door against her mother's screams. She turned her attention to the boys and brought a finger to her lips, warning them to be quiet, smiling when both boys nodded their agreement. She reached for Tobias' hand once more, sighing as he took it without question. She moved quickly, leading the way down the stairs and out the front of the building. She wasn't certain where they were going, just that they needed to get far away as quickly as possible.

Knowing they wouldn't get far on empty stomachs, she followed the familiar route and led them to the daily market. The market was in full swing, carts lining both sides of the streets and vendors shouting and hawking their wares. She felt a moment of regret at not having brought the sock full of money and full-blown panic when she realized she was the only one with an extra set of clothes. Breakfast, she could do something about; the rest she'd have to think on. Taking a calming breath, she plastered on a fake smile and addressed her bothers.

"What shall we have for breakfast?" she asked, kneeling in front of them.

"Apples," both brothers shouted at once.

She smiled and touched the side of each boy's face. Apples were easy. She pulled the ribbon from her hair, ran her fingers through the long, dark strands, and then replaced the fringed ribbon. "Apples it is. But I need you both to do something for me."

"What kind of something?" Ezra didn't seem pleased.

"What kind of something?" Tobias parroted.

Anastasia stood, searching from side to side. Finding what she was looking for, she smiled. "See those steps over there?"

"Yes." The boys nodded.

"I want both of you to go sit on the top step and wait for me to come for you." There would come a time when they'd realize how she scored their food, but not yet. Let them be innocent for a while longer.

"But what about our breakfast?" Tobias groaned.

"I'm going to get you the apples, but you need to wait here. Don't move until I come for you, promise?" *Please listen to me. I can't keep you safe if you won't listen.*

"Promise," Tobias said, nodding his head.

"You too," Anastasia said, looking at Ezra.

Ezra sighed. "Yes, I will stay."

Anastasia kissed them each on the cheek before leaving. *I'm your momma now. I'll take care of you and never let any harm come to either of you.* She was feeling pretty confident in her decision, smiling as she crossed the street. She saw a woman with two small children at her side moving through the market. The woman wore a lovely green gown and the boys were handsomely dressed in new clothing, complete with matching bowties. For a moment, she imagined it was she walking through the market as if she belonged, Ezra and Tobias by her side. She heard a commotion on the other side of the street and watched as two police officers dragged a young boy who looked to be no older than Ezra from the market kicking and screaming. She hurried to the apple cart and the apple man smiled at her. *Good morning, Papa.* She wished she could say the words aloud, but remembering her mother's warning, remained silent.

"I hope they string that child up by his heels," the elderly woman standing beside her said, bringing her out of her musings.

"What child?" Anastasia asked.

The woman blinked at her through thick-lensed glasses. "Why, that boy the police just took away. Didn't you see all the commotion?"

"I just came from over there." Anastasia stretched her finger to show where she'd come from and the woman looked.

"Well, the little thief came from that direction. You're not traveling with him, are you?" the woman accused.

"Oh, no, ma'am, I wouldn't hang around with thieves," Anastasia said, shaking her head.

"That's good, because that boy is probably going to be thrown in jail. It'll serve the little bugger right too. Stealing a bunch of scarves. What's a boy going to do with a scarf? They're doing that more and more, don't you know, locking them in jail. A good thing, as those little Street Arabs are just as bad as the cockroaches that roam our city."

Anastasia remembered what her father had said and wondered if the woman was speaking of people or actual bugs. The woman pointed in the opposite direction. As she did, Anastasia slipped three bright red apples into the pockets of her dress.

"The city is crawling with vermin, rats, roaches, and kids no one cares about," the woman said, continuing her rant.

"Some of them don't have a choice, as their parents are dead, but I saw a group of boys playing in the rain last week. I asked them why they weren't home and they told me they ran away. They said they'd been living on the streets for years. You're a child. Can you imagine just up and running away? Those boys should be home. They should be going to school and getting an education, not living on the streets like a pack of dogs. Mercy, even dogs know to get in out of the rain. Do you have a mother and father, girl?"

Anastasia slid a glance towards Mr. Castiglione. "I do."

"Good. You stay with them and listen to them, as they have your best interest at heart. Parents sometimes say things that don't make any sense, but in the end, a good parent would rather die than let any harm come to their children."

Anastasia remembered what her mother said about protecting the boys and a pang of sadness crept over her heart. Though their home was not the best, it was still a home. And they had a mother who was willing to give her life to protect them. All she had to offer was a life on the street with a strong chance of being thrown into jail. And even if she did all the stealing and managed to keep them out of it, then what would happen to them if she were caught? Who would look after them then? Anastasia managed to smile a weak smile at the woman before heading off in the direction she just saw them take the boy. She had to go, but she now knew taking the boys with her was no longer an option. She'd walked nearly a block when she realized she had not even told her brothers goodbye. Turning, she headed back to where she'd left them.

As she approached, she handed each boy an apple, sat beside them, and pulled one out for herself.

"You forgot to pay for the apples," Tobias chided.

Oh, how she wished he hadn't seen her take the apples. It would be the last thing he remembered about her. *Oh well, nothing to be done about it now.* "I couldn't pay. I had no money."

Tobias frowned. "Father will be mad."

Oh, he's going to be mad all right, as soon as he sees I'm gone. She turned to him, suddenly angry at having to pretend everything would be okay. She narrowed her eyes at him. "If you tell Father, I will never bring you with me again, do you understand?"

"But what if the apple man would've caught you?" Tobias asked.

She took another bite. "I know how to be careful. The man won't catch me."

"But what if he did catch you?" Tobias pestered.

She sighed. "Then I would give him something to keep him from being mad."

"What kind of something would you give?"

I would wrap my hands around his neck, kiss him on the cheek, and call him my papa. "I would give him something only girls have to give."

"What kind of something?" Tobias pestered.

"She would kiss him," Ezra said with a snicker.

Tobias wiped the juice from his chin and licked it from his grubby hand. "A kiss is better than money?"

"Sometimes it is." *Not really.* Anastasia took another bite of the apple and tossed the core onto the street. She struggled between the urge to go and the urge of spending just a bit more time with the boys. "What shall we do today?"

"You'll teach us how to steal apples," Ezra said, dropping his core off the side of the porch.

"I will do no such thing." Anastasia rose and started to leave the stoop.

Ezra caught hold of the hem of her dress to stop her. "But you will."

She slapped his hand. *Being a mom is tough.* "And why would I do that?"

Ezra rubbed at his hand. "Because if you don't, I will tell Father what you did, and he will beat you with the belt again."

Albert will never beat me again, but he may beat you if you tell. Her heart ached to shake him and tell him he was playing a dangerous game. A part of her felt guilty knowing she would not be there to protect him. *Maybe it wouldn't hurt to teach the boys how to pull apples from the cart. Papa, my real papa would never send my brothers to jail.* "Okay, I'll show you, but you'll need to do as I say. Understand?"

The boys nodded their agreement.

"First, you need to wait until there's someone else at the cart. That will keep the apple man busy. Then you step up as quietly as possible, so the apple man does not notice you. You'll take the apple and be gone before he even knows you're there."

"Quiet like a mouse?" Tobias asked.

Anastasia smiled, pleased he remembered the name she used to call him. "That's right, Tobias; I want you to be quiet as a mouse. Just remember, no squeaking. You're going to walk very softly, take the apple, and hurry along before anyone sees you. That goes for you too, Ezra. After you get the apple, hurry down the street that way. Circle behind the food carts and hurry back to this spot. Wait for me and then we'll all go home together. Understand?"

Ezra nodded, and Tobias did the same.

"I'll go first and talk to the apple man to distract him. Once he is talking to me, take your apples and do as I've told you."

Tobias' eyes grew wide. "What if the apple man sees me?"

"You're four years old. He will not see you unless you

forget to be quiet as a mouse. Remember, Tobias; you're a mouse and mice are very quiet."

"I'm a mouse," Tobias repeated.

"Okay, we'll all start walking together, and then I'll move ahead. Once I'm talking to the apple man, you do what I said. Ezra, you're older, and I expect you to watch over your brother." She tried her best to keep the emotion out of her voice. She was saying goodbye, but they wouldn't know it until it was too late.

"I will," Ezra promised.

"Do not let him out of your sight. If he gets in trouble, you come back and get him." Anastasia's voice was firm.

Doubt crossed Ezra's face. "Where will you be?"

"I'll be talking to the apple man. But if I'm delayed, I want you two to go back home. Do you remember how to get there?"

"Don't be stupid. I'm not a baby," Ezra bristled.

Anastasia stooped to look Ezra in the eye. It was all she could do not to cry. "I didn't say you were a baby. You are six years old and are a smart fellow. I want you to promise me that you'll see to it that your brother makes it home if I'm delayed. Can you do that for me, Ezra? Can you watch over your little brother when I'm not around to do it?"

Ezra shrugged and nodded his head. "Sure I can."

Anastasia stood and patted him on the head. "Good. Now follow me and do not take your apple until you see that I have the apple man's attention."

Anastasia held Tobias' hand until they neared the apple cart. She squeezed his hand for the last time before releasing it. By the time she'd reached the apple cart, her tears were falling like rain.

Castiglione frowned when he saw her tears.

"It's okay, Papa. I've come to say goodbye. My momma

can choose to stay if she wants, but I shall not stay another day."

Though his eyes looked worried, he smiled. "Did you tell your momma you're leaving?"

"She knows." Why she didn't tell him the truth she did not know. Maybe so he wouldn't think worse of the woman than he already did. As she spoke, she kept an eye on Tobias and Ezra, who'd moved closer to the cart.

"If it's not too much to ask, can you maybe allow my brothers to take an apple every now and again?" she asked.

"You know I wouldn't mind," he said and lifted a tear from her cheek. "You could come and live with me and my family."

His comment surprised her; she hadn't thought him to have a family. This cemented her decision not to go with him. If Albert hurt him, what would happen to his family? Before she could respond, Tobias pulled an apple from the bottom of the pile and apples spilled onto the ground. She smiled as Ezra grabbed hold of his arm and pulled him off in the opposite direction.

"Run, boys!" Her voice cracked as she sent them on their way.

Castiglione laughed and went to pick up the scattered apples. As he bent from sight, she blew each of them a kiss and turned, running in the opposite direction.

Chapter Twenty

Anastasia ran blindly through the vendor market, tears stinging her eyes. The pillowcase batted against her legs, slowing her progress. She ached to return to where she'd left her brothers, scoop them up, and take them home. She'd show her mother the sock full of money and beg her to allow her to stay just a little longer. *But what if one of the boys slips and tells Albert about the apples? No, it's too dangerous.*

"Hey, look where you're going, girl," someone yelled.

Anastasia felt a hand grip her arm and yank her to the side. As she fell backwards on her bottom, she realized she'd come close to being trampled by a horse and buggy. She turned to thank the person who'd pulled her from harm, surprised to see Runt standing over her looking perplexed.

"Girl, you trying to get yourself killed?" He reached a hand to help her up. "What's got into you anyway?"

She blew out a long breath and used the back of her hand to wipe her nose. "My momma made me leave."

He considered this for a moment. "For good or just for today?"

"For good."

Runt rocked back on his heels and blew out a long whistle. "I've heard of that happening with boys, but not so much with girls. Not that I know many girls, 'cept you."

"I don't know what I did to make her hate me so," Anastasia said and burst into a new set of tears.

"Well, didn't she tell you why you had to leave?" Runt

seemed unfazed by her tears.

"She said the boys are starving and there's not enough money to feed the family."

Runt shook his head. "Yeah, I've heard of that. My friends Sickly Joe and Piney got pushed out the same way. Sickly Joe got pushed out 'cause he's always sick. That's how he got his name. Piney's mom had a baby and she had to choose between him or the baby. Said she could keep the baby 'cause all it does is drink from her breast. Guess she ain't figuring on what she's going to do when the baby gets teeth. That babe's gonna want more than his mom's tit after that. What about your brothers? You think your momma's going to push them out too?"

"Oh no, they're too young," Anastasia said with a sob.

Runt laughed. "I've seen younger than that out here on the streets."

"Momma would never do that. She promised to protect Ezra and Tobias."

"Well, I guess you got to trust a promise," Runt said. He placed two fingers in his mouth and whistled. Seconds later, the dog raced to his side. "Have you eaten? We were just going to get breakfast. Then I can show you around the neighborhood."

"I had an apple." She thought about what her momma said about Albert coming to look for her. "Momma said I have to go far away. If Albert catches me, he'll be really mad at Momma and me."

A frown tugged at his mouth. "Where'll you go?"

She pulled the paper from her pocket and handed it to him.

"What's it say?" Runt asked, scratching his head.

"Can't you read?'

His frown deepened. "Not much in the way of schooling for kids like me."

Anastasia took the note and read it to him, then filled him on the lady who'd given it to her.

He took off his hat to swat at a fly. "Well, how's she going to help?"

"I don't know, but she told me she would," Anastasia said, pushing the note back inside her pocket.

"What if it's a trick? What if she just said that and the minute you tell her you're living on the streets, she throws you in jail?"

"She didn't look like she was lying."

"Maybe she's just good at it? Those do-gooders can be pretty tricky at times. Want to come with me and dog? The sausage man has fresh sausages on Saturday mornings."

Her stomach growled at the mention of the sausages. "I could eat."

Runt led the way to the meat wagon. Sure enough, there were ropes of fresh sausage links hanging all around the edge of the cart.

"You go on the other side, and I'll pick one from this side. Wait until his back is turned and we'll both grab a link and go," Runt instructed.

"I know how to get what I want," she said, narrowing her eyes.

"Yeah, but it's different now."

"Different how?"

"Because you're different now."

"How am I different?"

"Before, you took things cause you wanted to. Now you're going to be taking things cause you have to. If you were a boy, you maybe could get a job, but people don't hold much to hiring girls. Out here, if you don't beg or steal, you die of hunger. I've seen it. Kids come out here, and they're desperate. Hunger makes a person greedy. You get greedy. You get caught. Simple as that."

She thought about the boy she'd seen taken away for stealing scarves. "Like the boy earlier?"

He cocked his head to the side, his dimples disappearing. "You saw that, did ya? Mick was careless, not greedy."

"How can you say that? They caught him stealing scarves."

"Which is exactly my point. Mick wasn't stealing food."

She didn't realize living on the street was so complicated. "I don't understand."

"A person steals food; he's going to eat that food. A boy steals scarves, and it's not cold out, either he's snatching it for his sweetie or he's going to sell it to someone and pocket the money. Knowing Mick, he was going to pocket the coins to get him a room for the night. He doesn't like to sleep on the streets. It's too dangerous."

"Dangerous?" The word came out on a gulp.

"Why, sure; the gangs find you and they will pummel you. Hey, the man's got his back turned. Now's the time," Runt said, easing his way towards the other side of the wagon.

Anastasia stepped up beside the wagon. She was still processing Runt's words as she took hold of a sausage. In her distraction, she didn't realize the link she grabbed was part of a larger group. As she pulled, the line of sausages resisted. She'd just managed to get one free, when the man turned saw what she was doing and yelled for her to stop. She froze, link in hand. Returning to her senses, she took off running in the opposite direction, the pillowcase hindering her steps once more. As she ran, she heard Runt yelling, telling her she was headed in the wrong direction. She turned too late and ran smack dab into a police officer's arms.

"Ye made it too easy for me, girly." The officer grinned

and laughed a hearty laugh. "If you were all this easy to catch, we'd have the vermin off the streets in no time."

Anastasia struggled to get away, but his grip proved too strong. Resigning herself to going to jail, she stopped fighting. To her surprise, he loosened his grip, unfortunately for the officer, as an instant later, Runt steam-trained between them, knocking his arm free.

"Run!" the boy said without slowing down.

Anastasia lifted her skirt, yanked the pillowcase free, and ran as fast as her legs would carry her, chasing after Runt while Dog yipped happily at her side. She heard heavy breaths behind her; Dog dropped back, his happy tones turning to furious snarls. She caught up to Runt a block later. He led her into the ally, where they hid behind a stack of barrels while pausing to catch their breath.

"See what I mean," Runt said between breaths. "You get desperate, you get sloppy."

"Thank you for coming back for me."

"It wasn't nothing. You'd have done the same for me," he said.

Would I have? She wasn't sure that was true. She heard a noise and looked to see Dog standing behind her holding a sausage link in his mouth.

"He earned it; might as well leave him to it," Runt said, holding up a link with five plump sausages on it. He tore one off and handed it to her. "Let's move in case the beat cop's still looking for us."

"You going to want me to trade for that?"

"Nah, like I said before, things are different now."

***

Anastasia looked at her grubby hands and grimaced.

She'd never in all her years been so dirty. Her legs were just as grimy, her dress torn in multiple places. She didn't need a mirror to show her she looked as bad as the kids she and her mother used to turn their noses up at when they passed them on the streets. She'd fallen a long way in the week she'd been sleeping on the streets. Runt lay on the step below her, the dog on the step below him. They'd have to move soon. The city was waking, and the folks that lived in the building didn't take too kindly to finding children sleeping on their stoop. Runt had referred to their current sleeping arrangement as their summer home, saying they would find a nice steam grate to sleep on when the weather turned. It was too hot to sleep on them now, he'd explained, further saying they'd have to claim a spot soon before they were all taken. Anastasia pulled her legs to her chest and cried silent tears. Dog lifted his head, looked at her, then lowered his head on a whine.

She pulled the crinkled paper from her pocket and studied it as she had countless times before. Making her decision, she prodded Runt with the toe of her shoe.

"I'm leaving, Runt," she said once he woke. "I didn't want to go without telling you. I know you'd be worried if you didn't know what happened to me."

"You going to find the woman on the paper?" An easy guess, as she'd spoken of doing so often enough.

"She said she would help me. Maybe she'll help you too if you come with me."

He shook his head and ruffled up the fur on the dog's neck. "He's not mine, but I think maybe I belong to him. I like you good enough, but I'm not sure Dog can get along without me."

She'd never had a dog before, but she thought maybe she understood. Tobias wasn't hers either, but it sure hurt when she thought about not being with him.

"I'll walk with you, though. I've got nothing better to do today," he said, rising from the stoop.

She nodded. Some things didn't need an answer.

***

It was well after lunch when Anastasia entered the lobby of the Children's Aid Society. A kind-eyed man sitting behind a large wooden desk appraised her appearance as she approached. She handed the man the tattered note the woman in the market had given her.

"My name is Anastasia. The lady who gave me this said she can help me. She said she would take me far away from here." The last part was a lie, but Anastasia didn't think it could hurt trying.

"Did she now?" the man said, reading the note. "Gave this to you today, did she?"

"No, sir. It's been in my pocket for a bit." *At least that part was true.*

He looked up from the note and took in her appearance. "I'm afraid Miss Hill's not here right now."

Anastasia sighed and turned to leave.

"Now hold on there, Little Miss. I said she's not here. I didn't say she wasn't coming back. Have a seat in one of those chairs. She'll be along directly."

Anastasia walked to the other side of the room and sat in a comfortable chair. The moment she sat, she yawned her exhaustion.

"Anastasia?" A woman's voice pulled her from her sleep.

She opened her eyes, expecting to see the woman in the hat but was greeted by a tall, thin woman instead.

"I understand you're in need of a little help?" the woman

said softly.

Anastasia looked towards the door. "Where's Miss Hill?"

"She's away," the woman said.

"The man said she's coming back?"

The woman looked towards the desk, frowned at the man, then smiled at Anastasia. "She is, but not today."

The man had lied to her. *Runt was right; it is a trick.* She stood, prepared to run, when the lady spoke once more.

"Please don't go. Mr. Burgess said Miss Hill told you she would send you away. Did she mention the trains?"

This sounds promising.

"Yes, she told me she'd send me far away on a train." Another lie.

The woman pulled at the chain around her neck and looked at her timepiece. "I do wish she would have told us you were coming. We've not much time. Are you sure she told you to come today?"

Anastasia nodded.

"There are so many others. Maybe we should wait until we can speak to Miss Hill."

The thought of spending another night on the streets frightened her. She clutched the woman's hands and tilted her head so her scar was in full view. "Oh no, you must send me out. I've no parents to go home to. It's much too dangerous on the streets. Just look what has already happened to me. Miss Hill promised she'd take me away. It simply must be today."

The woman's face brightened as if coming to a decision. She traced a finger the length of Anastasia's scar. "Well, you can't go out like this. You'll never get adopted."

Anastasia felt her eyes grow wide. While she was happy to be leaving the city, she hadn't expected this. "Adopted?"

"If you're lucky. You're older, so you have a good

chance of at least being placed. Providing, of course, we can make you look presentable. You'll need a bath and a change of clothes, but I think we can get you ready in time. Care to give it a go?"

Anastasia wasn't sure what it meant to be placed, but she nodded her acceptance. The lady seemed to think it was a good thing, and at this point, she'd do just about anything for a bath and clean clothes.

Chapter Twenty-One

Draped in only a rough towel, Anastasia stood staring at the dirty ring she'd left in the bathtub. She wrinkled her nose, remembering how dirty the water had been, and vowed never to allow herself to get that dirty again. She heard footsteps and turned to see a young girl entering the bath area. The girl was maybe six or seven years older than her and walked with a noticeable limp. The girl approached and placed a stack of clothes on a nearby table. She pulled a brush from her apron and began brushing the tangles from Anastasia's hair.

Anastasia reached for the brush and the girl used it to slap her hand away. She glared at the girl and rubbed her knuckles to soothe the sting. "I'm perfectly capable of brushing my own hair."

"There's no time to dawdle. If I don't have you dressed and ready in time to be sent out, I will miss my meal."

Anastasia knew what it was like to miss a meal, so she gritted her teeth against the pulling. "You work here?"

"I don't get money, if that's what you are asking, but yes, I work here," the girl said, pulling the brush through her strands.

"Why work if you don't get paid?"

"Because there are other ways to get paid."

"I don't understand."

"I have food in my belly, a bed to sleep in, and I'm in charge of some of the girls. As long as I do what is asked of me, the house mistresses leave me be," the girl explained.

Anastasia considered this. "Maybe I could work here instead of going on the trains."

The girl laughed. "You are too young to have a job."

"I had a job before." *For a day anyway.*

"It doesn't matter. You'll be going out on the trains today. How'd you manage that anyway? There are kids that have been here for years, and they haven't gotten picked yet."

Anastasia detected a touch of sadness in the girl's voice. "Have you not been picked?"

The girl pulled her hair once more, lifting the length of the strands and pulling them into a high ponytail. "I went out a time or two. Never got picked, though. Girls like me don't get chosen, so I've stopped asking to go. I'd rather stay here. At least here, I'm not treated like I'm a cripple."

"Well, what's wrong with you?"

"I have a gimpy leg. It doesn't hurt, but it makes me walk funny. People are picky. They don't want kids who are sickly."

"You said it doesn't hurt."

"It doesn't. Never has, but they don't see that. They just see my limp and move on to the next kid."

Anastasia caressed the scar on her cheek, wondering if the people would see it as a sign of weakness.

"It's not so bad," the girl said, reading her thoughts. "You're pretty enough even with it. Maybe you can still find a husband someday."

Anastasia thought to tell the girl she would never find a husband because she didn't wish to ever get married, but the girl pushed away, breaking the mood.

She limped to the table and returned, shaking the wrinkles from a folded blue dress. It took Anastasia a moment to realize the dress was intended for her. She blinked her astonishment, as she'd never owned anything so lovely.

"All the children get a new set of clothes when they leave. It makes them look more presentable," she said, lowering the dress over Anastasia's head.

Anastasia turned so the girl could button the back and then stood in front of the large mirror admiring the tiny white flowers printed on the fabric. "It's beautiful. Do you think it will help me get adopted?"

"Make sure you smile when someone approaches. When you smile, your scar is barely noticeable," the girl offered.

The clock on the wall chimed, and the girl ran to gather the shoes and stockings off the counter, thrusting them at Anastasia in a panic. "Hurry, or you'll miss your ride and have to stay."

Stay? Was that an option? "What if I don't want to go?"

"Don't be silly; the kids in this place can't wait to get out."

"Not you," Anastasia reminded her.

The girl bit her lip. "If I'd have gotten picked, I would have gladly left this place."

***

Anastasia stood on the platform, taking in the enormous size of the train engine that sat idling alongside the track. Though she'd been excited at first seeing the train, reality had set in, and she knew the massive engine would soon whisk her away from everything she'd known. Everyone she knew. The thought of never seeing her brothers again had her teetering on the verge of tears. She studied the faces of the children alongside her, wondering if any of them had lied their way into their current predicament or if she were alone in her deceit.

The doors to the train car opened and the children began

making their way inside. Anastasia followed, knowing full well whatever happened from this point on was of her own doing. Well, maybe some of the blame could fall on Sharon, not that the woman would ever learn of her daughter's fate.

The inside of the train car was barren with simple wooden bench seating. Anastasia saw an open bench and quickly took a seat, sliding next to the window so she could see. It didn't take long for the cabin to fill, and before long, she'd gained two seatmates, fair-haired girls each a good head shorter than herself. It was obvious the girls knew each other as they chatted amongst themselves with ease. Within moments, the doors closed. A short time later, the train whistle blew and the train started inching its way out of the station, sending a wave of excitement throughout the train car. Sunlight filled the cabin as the train breached the station house and rumbled its way from the city. The buildings soon dissolved into a landscape of trees and hills. Anastasia took in the scenery with a mix of awe and fear. She'd never seen so many trees in one place and what structures they passed were small and few between, leaving her to wonder where everyone would sleep if there were no apartment buildings to hold them.

The train passed a farm with a red barn and a field full of cows. She craned her neck to be sure of what she'd seen; while she'd seen oxen in her picture books, never had she seen a black and white cow.

"Look at all those apples!" a child exclaimed, and all the children raced to the left side of the train, elbowing their way to the windows, eager to see.

Anastasia joined them and found herself wondering if this was the orchard of which Mr. Castiglione had spoken. Probably not, as it would make for a long ride into the city each day. As the orchard disappeared from sight, she felt a pang of sadness of yet another loss. She sniffed as the sadness overtook her.

"Are you all right?" the girl sitting closest to her asked.

"I'm fine," Anastasia said, wiping her eyes. The last thing she wanted was for the girl to think she was a baby.

The girl on the end tugged at the middle girl's arm. The girl turned to her, and the first girl whispered something in her ear. She nodded and faced Anastasia once more. "My sister wants to know if you are scared."

"I'm not scared," she snapped. "I have smoke in my eyes from the train."

The girl pulled away and whispered something to her sister. Had she have been there, Anastasia's mother would've insisted Anastasia apologize. *She sent me away. I don't have to apologize.* Leaning her head against the window, Anastasia watched as the strange new world passed on the other side of the glass.

Most of the children had never been out of the city before. Every few moments, something would catch a child's eye. They would squeal with delight, and the car would erupt in excited jabber. A stop to refill the water supply to the steam engine had all the children abuzz. Eager faces pressed against the cabin windows, protesting their disappointment at not being allowed off the train to watch. Their disappointment turned to joy as the placing agents took this opportunity to pass out snacks of wafers and cheese. As Anastasia munched on the offerings, she found herself wondering if she were the only one who didn't view this as a grand adventure.

As the train began rolling once more, the agents started dismissing the children to the water closet a seat full at a time. When their turn came, Anastasia followed the two girls through the aisle, swaying as they went. They slid open the door, staring in awe as they walked onto the platform that connected the two cars. Black smoky steam from the train whirled around them as they stepped inside the adjoining car. While the two girls kept their eyes forward as they'd been instructed, Anastasia found herself observing the occupants of the cabin. Men sitting ramrod straight reading newspapers so engrossed, they never looked in her direction. Others pushed back in their seat, hats draped low, presumably sleeping. Women sitting next to them would either look away when they saw the children approach or stare at them as if they were animals on display. She passed a family with a boy around her age. He was chatting easily with his father and the man seemed engrossed in what the boy had to say. A couple rows up sat a woman with a small girl sitting on her lap sucking at her thumb. The girl looked at her as she passed. Her eyes grew wide and a smile replaced the thumb. Anastasia returned the child's smile and the girl turned to bury her face in her mother's bosom.

Further up, two small boys sat on the floor near their mother's feet, quarreling over a ball attached to a string. The mother looked up from her sewing, hushed the boys, then returned to the project in hand. She was not mean in her corrections nor did the man sitting next to her seem upset by the boys' shenanigans.

Instantly, Anastasia's thoughts went to Tobias and Ezra. If she'd not left them, maybe they would be on this train too. She could picture them, noses pressed to the window, taking in the passing scenery. The three of them could maybe have gotten a new home with parents who would smile and allow them to just be children. As she caught up with the two girls, she wondered what kind of person she would be going home with and further wondered if maybe she would be able to convince her new family to send for her brothers. Surely her mother would allow them to come if she were to write and tell her how happy she was.

Providing I have a happy home of which to write about.

Reaching the water closet, her two seatmates went inside, closing the door behind them. A few moments later, the door opened. The girls giggled as she opened the door and peered inside.

"Where's the toilet?" Anastasia asked.

Another round of giggles as the girls both pointed to the hole in the floor. The talkative girl spoke up. "You have to squat over the hole."

"What if I fall?"

"That's what the handles are for. Make sure you scrunch your dress up in your lap so you don't pee on it," she said and slid a glance to the girl standing next to her.

Anastasia stood there for a moment watching the ground move beneath the hole in the floor, debating if she really had to go all that bad. Deciding she did, she stepped inside and closed the door behind her.

***

As the day wore on, the newness of the trip waned. They'd eaten an evening meal of cheese and biscuits and drank tea brought on board during one of the scheduled stops. While other passengers were free to come and go as they pleased, the group of children from the Children's Aid Society remained secluded within their cabin. During another stop, the children were each gifted with a bright red apple brought over in bushels from a local orchard. While the others seemed delighted with the treat, Anastasia saw it as yet another reminder of what she'd left behind. Sighing, she shoved it in her pocket for later.

The girl on the end whispered something to the middle girl, who turned to Anastasia and spoke. "My sister wants to know if you don't like apples."

"I like them well enough. I am saving it in case I get

hungry later," Anastasia said with a shrug. The fact that the girls were sisters cemented her guilt. Obviously, they would have allowed her to bring her brothers along.

"Are you always this sour?" the girl asked after conferring with her sister yet again.

"Why doesn't she talk for herself?" Anastasia asked, ignoring the comment.

"Sarah doesn't like talking to strangers, not since our mother and father died. Oh, she's Sarah, and I'm Beth. Our parents died, so we are going to find a new mother and father."

"My name is Anastasia. Papa drinks up all the money, and Momma couldn't afford to feed me and my brothers. They got to stay, but Momma made me leave." The girls merely nodded, leaving Anastasia to wonder if her story wasn't so uncommon after all.

As darkness seeped into the cabin, someone yawned. Within seconds, more sleepy yawns filled the air, and the children's chatter dwindled, the only sound that of the train rumbling along the rails. There were no lights in the train cabin, no candles to ward off fears of the unknown. Within the silence, a child began to sob. It wasn't long until others joined in the tearful chorus. Anastasia lay her head against the window and breathed an audible sigh. Somehow it helped to know she was not alone in her sorrow. As the children drifted off to sleep, the train continued to rumble its way across unseen territory, bringing with it desperate hopes of a new beginning.

Chapter Twenty-Two

"You're thinking you judged the girl wrong," Linda said when Cindy finished reading. "You're a pretty good mind reader," Cindy replied.

Linda shook her head. "Not really. It's the same thing I thought when I read that Anastasia's mother made her leave."

"I can't imagine how hard it was for the woman, having to choose between her children. I still don't understand why she didn't just send the husband packing instead. She could have taken in several renters and kept the children."

"You're a teacher; didn't you learn anything in school?" There was an edge to Linda's voice. "She couldn't just kick her husband out. He was the man. It was his house."

"Tenement building," Cindy corrected.

"He paid the bills," Linda said, ignoring her comment. "Did you know before the 1970s, a woman could not refuse to have sex with her husband? Heck, I couldn't even get a credit card in my name until after 1975."

"So what would have happened if she went to the police?"

"They probably would have laughed her out of the station house. Or worse."

Cindy laughed. "How worse?"

"They would've diagnosed her with hysteria and had her committed to the mental hospital."

"You're kidding, right?"

Linda frowned. "What exactly do you teach those kids

of yours?"

"New Math," Cindy said with a grin.

"I hope you'll start teaching the kids a bit of history. Maybe then they'll learn something useful."

Cindy thought about reminding Linda she had to follow the curriculum but knew that would start a whole different argument. Instead, she picked up the next stack of papers and handed a copy to her mother. "Let's see what's happening in 1914."

"History, that's what's happening," Linda grumbled, taking the papers.

***

Five days after they left New York, the train pulled into Union Station in St. Louis, Missouri. The children paraded through the enormous depot under the scrutiny of all who stopped to stare at the procession of children. They were then taken to a large church, where they washed their hands and faces and had a morning meal of hot oatmeal and bread with honey. The placing agents, Mr. and Mrs. Swan, who some of the children affectionately referred to as Grandma and Grandpa Swan, spoke with each child, helping to push away fears of what the day would hold. Though Anastasia had spoken with Mr. Swan several times on the trip, she didn't feel the need to refer to him as anything more than Mr. Swan. Sure he was nice, but she'd never had a grandpa, so why start now? The massive hub of the church was already filled with prospective parents when the children were led into the room and told to sit on the floor on the raised platform near the pulpit. While the children had been instructed not to speak unless spoken to, they instinctively sat shoulder to shoulder as if taking comfort in the touch of another who shared their plight.

Anastasia sat staring out at a church full of onlookers as Mr. Swan moved to the pulpit and spoke about the Placing Out Program. To her surprise, he told the congregation the program had been ongoing for sixty years, further telling that others had joined in the program, and to date, they'd already placed nearly two hundred thousand children with great success.

Having captured the crowd's attention, the short, dough-bellied man moved through the aisle of the church, telling about the children in his care. Every so often, he'd return to the pulpit to take a sip of water and pat at his brow with a handkerchief. Why he was sweating she hadn't a clue, as she thought it to be rather chilly in the large church.

"We have assembled a committee. I'm sure most of you who live in the area already know them and know they are well-liked and trusted in the community," Swan said, waving a hand at the men seated in the front row. He called each man by name. When he did, the man stood and gave a nod towards the congregation. "These men, these upstanding men, who are doctors, lawyers, bankers, and businessmen. These men who live and work in your community will oversee the applications. If you can find it in your heart to take one of my children, and they are each my children until they find a suitable home, then I ask you to raise your hand and my good wife will bring you an application to fill out. We'll need references, as we cannot allow these children to go to just any old home."

"What kind of references?" a man in the third row called out from his seat.

"Five people who know you well," Mr. Swan said, "I ask they be friends, not family. While I'm sure your wife will say you are a real stand-up man, we need the references to come from someone else."

"Why, I'm not sure if my wife would say that a'tall," the man countered, drawing several laughs from those around him. He waited for the laughter to die down before continuing. "Say I decide to take home a child. There are so many of them. How do I know which one I want? Maybe I'll like one better than the rest."

Anastasia watched as several in the crowd nodded their heads in agreement, and resisted the urge to cover the scar upon her face.

"The children will be speaking to you shortly. They'll each have a chance to tell you their name and a bit about themselves. Some of the children only speak the language of their country. If that is the case, we'd prefer to place them in homes where they can be understood. Please keep that in mind when you are choosing. As the children speak, they will give their name. If you see a child you would like to take home, write that child's name on your application," Mr. Swan said and pointed to the spot on the paper he was holding to show where the name should go.

"What if several of us want the same orphan?" a lady in a white dress shouted.

"My good lady, there are plenty of children to choose from and plenty more where these came from. Place the name on the paper, and if more than one person wants the same child, the committee members will make the final decision on where the child is placed."

"Well, how do they know whose home is the best?" she pressed.

One of the men on the committee stood and addressed the woman. "Mrs. Beal, you know who we are as much as we know you and most of the others in this room. Mr. Swan has spoken with us in length and told us what we should look for when deciding on a home. As you heard, Mr. Swan has been doing this for a number of years with a great deal of success. I assure you we take our duties seriously and promise to be most fair in our choosing."

The rest of the men nodded their agreement, and that seemed to appease the woman, as she took her seat and waved her hand for an application.

"Now, without further ado, we will hear from the children who've traveled such a long way to make your acquaintance," Mr. Swan said, wiping his brow once more.

One by one, the children rose from their places on the floor and stepped in front of the pulpit to address the crowd. As instructed, they told their full name—if they knew it—and a bit about themselves. Some of the children spoke with confidence; some had to be told to speak up so all could hear. To Anastasia's amazement, one of the girls sang a song. After that, the children sang, did a little dance, or spoke of their special talent, each intent on outdoing the child before them. As she watched, she realized she had no special talent. With the exception of the scar upon her face, she could offer nothing that would make her stand out from the others. As she sat contemplating what to do, both Sarah and Beth stood and walked to the front.

"I'm Beth, and this is my sister Sarah. If you are looking for two little girls, then we'd be happy to go home with you," Beth said, and Sarah nodded her head in agreement.

"I'll take the quiet one," a man in the back shouted. "My wife will get her to talk. God knows the woman hasn't shut up since we got hitched."

"She didn't shut up a'for that neither," the older man sitting beside him said with a laugh.

As the church erupted in laughter once more, the girls clung to one another, begging not to be separated. Mr. Swan stepped forward once more, asking if anyone was willing to take in both sisters. In the end, two families who lived on adjoining farms each agreed to take one of the girls. As the girls took their seats, Anastasia thought about Tobias and Ezra once more. It hadn't occurred to her that they wouldn't all be placed in the same home. At least by leaving them with their mother, the boys would remain together. She wanted to take comfort in that knowledge, but all it did was make her miss them even more. She was on the verge of tears, when Mr. Swan tapped her on the shoulder.

"Go up and tell them about yourself, Anna," he said softly.

Anna? Where'd that come from? She'd told him her name was Anastasia. Actually, she'd told him it was Anastasia Castiglione, knowing she would never again use Albert's name. Scrambling from the floor, she walked to the center of the room and stared out at the faces. "My name is Anastasia. I don't know if I can sing or dance, as I've never tried. I'm a good cook and know how to clean. I can do your shopping at the market and know how to save you a penny or two."

Anastasia watched in astonishment as six hands pushed their way into the air, waving for an application.

She swallowed before tucking her hair behind her ear and adding, "In case you can't see it, I've got a scar. It don't cause me no pain. I just want you to know before you waste your time fighting over me."

Her lips quivered as two of the hands lowered, then curved into a smile as three others replaced them. Filled with hope, she returned to her spot, waiting as the rest of the children addressed the congregation. It took several hours for each of the children to be introduced, which felt like an eternity to Anastasia. From the number of hands raised after she spoke, she felt certain she'd be going to a new home. The only question was which of the seven people she'd be going with. She didn't allow herself to look into the crowd, as she was afraid of being disappointed if she picked the wrong one. She knew when introducing herself, she'd opened herself to going to a home where she would be made to cook and clean. That was okay; she was used to hard work. As long as she didn't have to live on the street, she could handle anything. She cast a glance towards Sarah and Beth, grateful she'd already said her goodbyes to Tobias and Ezra, knowing she wouldn't be as calm if she had to worry about what homes were being picked for them as well.

The last boy finished speaking, and Mr. Swan moved to the center of the room once more. He smiled at the children before stepping up to the podium. "While the committee looks over the applications, Mrs. Swan and I will take the children to get an afternoon meal. We'll meet back here after lunch. At that time, those who are approved will be able to take your child home."

His words added further encouragement.

Home. Did she dare hope? *What if?* No, she wouldn't allow the what-ifs to take control. She'd know soon enough. For now, she'd just allow herself to hope.

Chapter Twenty-Three

The afternoon meal had been most enjoyable, a beef stew with hearty vegetables, thick gravy, and biscuits so fresh, they nearly fell apart when she took a bite. As if that hadn't been treat enough, the restaurant owner had brought out several trays of cookies, hot from the oven. Most of the children had never tasted frosted sugar cookies and made clear their appreciation. The owner was so delighted with their response, she sent each child away with a second cookie to enjoy at a later time. Some of the children decided that now was the time and their cookies never made it beyond the restaurant walls. Having become accustomed to not knowing when she would eat, Anastasia placed hers in her pocket for later. Stomach full and eager to see what the future had in store, she and the other children sat waiting to learn their fate.

The door opened, and Mr. Swan stepped inside. "Good news, children, you will all be getting new homes. The town's folk have been most generous and have agreed to accept each and every one of you. Follow me to the congregation room and we'll see about having you in your new homes by supper time. Remember, children, we must be on our best behavior."

The children fell into line, each ready to see who their new family would be. Though there were plenty of people sitting in the pews, the crowd was at least half its previous size. Anastasia looked about the room, wondering which of the strangers had chosen her. She didn't have to wait long, as her name was the first to be called. She stood and waited for her new family to step forward. Her stomach clenched when a lone hulk of a man stepped forward. The man was well over a foot taller than Mr. Swan, who himself was quite tall. Stern-faced, he nodded at Mr. Swan.

Mr. Swan placed his hand on Anastasia's shoulder. "Anastasia, this is Mr. Payne. He's been so kind as to offer you a home. He's brought with him letters of recommendation from his employer and people in his community."

She wasn't sure what she'd expected, but the giant of a man standing in front of her wasn't it. Mr. Swan had told the children they should be grateful for being picked, so she craned her neck and smiled at the man. "I thank you, sir."

"If it's settled, we'll be on our way, then. It's a long way to Poplar Bluff. I thank you, Mr. Swan, I'll have the girl here write ye a letter when she's good and settled."

Mr. Payne nodded to Anastasia.

"Come along, girl, before we miss our train."

Train? I thought Mr. Swan said we were all staying here.

Swallowing her fear, she turned and followed after the man. Not only was he incredibly tall, but he was rail thin. His wrinkled suit hung on his body like a pair of ill-fitting curtains trying unsuccessfully to dress a much larger window. She wondered of the last time he'd eaten and patted her pocket, grateful she'd had the presence of mind to save the cookie. His gait was long, and she found she nearly had to run to keep up with the man. He led the way through the city streets, dodging as he weaved his way between horse-drawn buggies and the occasional motorcar. By the time they reached the train station, her heart was beating in her chest.

Mr. Payne stopped at a deli and ordered two ham sandwiches with cheese.

"You want a pickle with that?" the man asked, pointing

to the large jar filled with giant pickles.

Payne cast a look at Anastasia, who nodded her head. "Better give me a couple of those coke colas as well."

The man behind the counter turned and busied himself digging pickles out of the large jar with a pair of extended tongs.

"Can you read?" Payne asked.

Anastasia nodded.

"See those doors over there? You run and use the bathroom before we get on the train. It'll be well past dark before we get to where we're going. Girl," he said as she turned. "You'll want the one marked Ladies. No dawdling now; we've a train to catch."

Anastasia hurried across the hall, did what she had to do, and returned just as the deli man was handing Mr. Payne a brown paper sack. Payne looked at her when she neared, and to her surprise, he smiled.

"You listen. That's good," he said and started walking without another word.

The train conductor greeted them, looked at the tickets Payne was holding, and led them to the front of the train.

Payne climbed onto the train car without bothering to check if she was following. Anastasia's breath caught as she climbed inside and saw the elaborately decorated train cabin. Dark wood, smooth and polished to a gleaming shine, lined the walls of the train car. Red velvet curtains draped the windows. Large oversized chairs covered in gold fabric faced one another on either side of the window. A small table sat just under the window, adorned with a matching tablecloth and crisply folded newspaper. This cabin was even nicer than the family car she'd walked through on the way to the water closet during her previous trip, both a far cry from the basic car she and the children had traveled in.

Payne checked his ticket and took a seat on the left side

of the train. He saw her hesitate and pointed to the chair opposite him. "You going to stand there with your mouth open all day?"

She hurried to be seated, smiling as she sank into the softness. She looked at her travel companion once more. "Are you rich, then?"

"I'm not."

"Well, then, how can you afford these seats?"

He studied her for a moment. "I'm not a small man; as such, sometimes one has to weigh the price of comfort."

"I do not mind riding in the other car if it would save you money," she offered.

"Stay where you are. You'll not be so inclined to give up what little luxuries I can afford when you see where I'm taking you."

She thought about asking him where they were going and then decided it didn't matter. She had a full belly and was comfortable. That was enough for now.

***

As darkness seeped in through the windows, the train attendant walked through the cabin lighting the oil lamps that lined the walls. As she watched the flames flicker behind the sconce, she remembered the tears shed in the darkness during her last trip. She wondered why they didn't have lamps in all the cabins and further wondered if the soft glow from the lamps would've kept the fears at bay.

"Are you wondering what you've gotten yourself into?" Mr. Payne asked, interrupting her thoughts.

"Oh no, sir. I was just wondering why all the cars do not have lamps. When we, the others and I, came, it was so dark and cold…" She stopped, not wishing to tell him about the tears.

A frown creased his face. "Are you cold now?"

Freezing. Though her dress was pretty, the thin fabric did little to thwart the chill from the train. "A little."

Mr. Payne waved his hand to get the attendant's attention. "A blanket for the girl, if you please."

"Yes, right away, sir," the attendant said and hurried from the cabin.

She wanted to like the man, but even Albert could be nice when they were around strangers. She'd hold off judgment for now. "My name is Anastasia."

"What?"

"You keep calling me 'girl.' I would prefer you to use my proper name."

Though he didn't respond, a smile played at his lips.

She studied him for a moment. "And what shall I call you? Papa? Father?"

The smile disappeared. "I reckon I'll have to think on that. Are you hungry, Anastasia?"

Actually, she was. "Yes, sir."

He reached into the bag and took out both sandwiches, handing her one and keeping the other for himself.

She unwrapped hers, lifted the bread, and wrinkled her nose.

His brows knitted together. "You don't like ham?"

"I do, but the yellow stuff looks like something from my brother's diaper."

"It's called mustard." He pulled back the paper, lifted the bread, and sighed before placing the uneaten sandwich on the table. "You have a family? I thought you children were all orphans."

She searched her mind, wondering at how much to tell, then decided the man deserved to know the truth. Well, most of it anyway. "I had a family, but my papa liked to drink away all the money. Momma could not afford to feed me and my brothers, so she made me leave."

"That must have been a hard thing for your mother to do," he said softly.

She considered asking him if he'd be willing to adopt her brothers as well. Then again, he hadn't said he was going to adopt her, so she decided to wait. "Do you drink, Mr. Payne?"

"No. I used to, but don't have time for such things anymore," he said, alleviating her fears.

"Do you have a family?"

"I do. I have a wife and a son."

"No daughters?"

Payne's jaw clenched. "Not anymore."

"But you used to. What happened to her?"

"She, my wife, and son were in a buggy accident. My wife and son survived. My daughter, Emily, did not." He looked out the window, staring into the darkness, the pain in his voice evident as he spoke.

"So you picked me to replace your daughter?"

"NO!"

She jumped in her seat, ready to duck from the coming blow. The blow never materialized, and her flinch went unnoticed.

Payne turned from the window, looked around the cabin, and lowered his voice. "I'm sorry. I didn't mean to yell. I'll be honest with you. It was not my decision to bring you home. It was my wife who heard about the train bringing you children and asked that I come and see about bringing one home."

"Did she ask you to bring a girl?"

Payne merely nodded.

Her heart clenched at his words. While she hadn't fully expected to be placed in a perfect home, she'd allowed herself to hope. "So you don't want me?"

He looked at his hands and sighed. "Not in the way you're hoping. I'll never get over Emily's death and wouldn't wish to try. I can never be your father, but I'll do right by you, just as I told the gentlemen on the committee."

"So why'd you pick me?" she asked, trying to keep her disappointment from showing.

"I needed someone to look after my wife while my son and I are at work," he said softly.

She thought about her mother when she was sick with the baby. "Is your wife ill, Mr. Payne?"

He looked off into the distance. "Some would say so."

"There were lots of kids on the train. Why'd you pick me?" she pressed.

His face took on an odd expression as if he were seeing something that wasn't there. "Because scars don't bother me none."

She traced her scar with her fingertips.

He reached over and pushed her hand away from her face.

She looked at him in question.

"You don't let that scar bother you none. You hold your head up high and be proud of that scar, little lady; it shows you're a survivor. If a person can't see you for who you are inside, they don't deserve the time of day. Someone has a problem with the way your face looks, that's their problem not yours. You hear me?" His words were firm as he looked her in the eyes.

She nodded her head.

Payne's eyes grew misty and he turned back towards the window without another word.

She finished her sandwich in silence and ate the pickle as she mulled over what he'd just said. She had so much more she wanted to ask the man, but she'd seen that look before. It was the same look Sharon got when she'd asked too many questions. It wasn't long before Payne's head dropped forward, showing he'd nodded off to sleep. Anastasia took the paper from her sandwich and wrapped it around his, hoping the double wrapping would help keep it fresh. She pulled the cookie from her pocket, unwrapped it, and broke it into two pieces. She re-wrapped the second half and placed it on the table next to Payne's uneaten sandwich. Just because he didn't want to be her father didn't mean she couldn't be nice to him.

Chapter Twenty-Four

The train horn announced their arrival in Poplar Bluff just before seven. Payne, not a man who wasted time, collected his hat and stood. "Come along, Anastasia; we'll need to hurry if we're going to get to the store before it closes."

Anastasia looked to the table, surprised to see both the sandwich and cookie gone, the wrappers folded to precision, letting her know she'd fallen asleep. She clambered to her feet and followed the man from the train and into the depot. After witnessing the size of the train stations in both New York and St. Louis, she was surprised to see the small two-story train depot that supported Poplar Bluff. They hurried through the building and out the front door, which faced a hill, and followed a crowd of travelers to a grand double-sided staircase that met in the middle and continued up the hill. Most of the travelers took the left stairway; Payne hurried to the other side and took the stairs two at a time, reaching the center landing well ahead of the people they'd been following. Anastasia rushed to keep up as Payne ascended the main set of stairs. When they reached the top, she saw it led to a street lined with larger buildings. While not nearly as tall as those in New York City, the buildings were still substantial.

"I'm sorry, sir," the salesman said as Payne approached a building called Hecht & Sons. "We're just in the process of closing."

"Won't be but a few moments. The girl here just arrived in town and is in need of a few things to help settle her in,"

Payne insisted. He bent to keep from hitting his head and pushed his way inside the building.

The man opened his mouth to object, and Payne pulled himself to his full height. The salesman looked to the clock on the wall then begrudgingly nodded his head in agreement. Turning his attention to Payne, he smiled a weak smile. "Just a few things?"

Payne pulled a slip of paper from his pocket. "Three dresses, a few undergarments, and three pair of stockings will suffice. Oh, and we'd better add a proper coat; winter is almost upon us."

Instantly, Anastasia regretted her decision to leave her coat in the apartment.

"Will she be needing boots, then?" the man asked, trying to be helpful.

"No, just what I asked for will be fine."

"Mr. Payne, I really don't need all those things. I can wash out my dress each day," Anastasia offered.

"Sina—that's my wife—told me what to be getting for you. I'll do best to abide by her wishes," Payne said, leaving no room for argument. In the end, they left with every item on the list and an assortment of calico print fabric that had been marked down since each cutting was at the end of the bolt.

As they exited the store, the church bell rang its greeting. Payne tucked the bag under his arm and took his steps in long strides. Once again, Anastasia found herself nearly running behind the tall man as they made their way to the livery stable. The stable was dark when they approached.

"Helloo," Payne called as they neared.

Within seconds, a light drifted into view. The lantern lowered, showing the whitest eyes Anastasia had ever seen. She blinked twice before realizing the eyes were attached to the darkest skinned man she'd ever laid eyes on. Sure she'd seen colored men sitting on the corner shining shoes. Darkies, she'd heard them called. There were other terms, none of which seemed to please the men. Still, this man was even darker than any of the men she'd seen.

"Evening, Mr. Payne. I saddled your'n horse the moment I heard the train a-whistling." The man grinned a white-toothed grin. "Took real good care of her while you were gone, yes sir. Got along real good, she and I. Treated her like she was my very own. I'll just be get'n her for ya."

"Thank you, Buckley," Payne said, handing the man several coins.

Anastasia watched in stunned silence as the man named Buckley returned with the largest horse she'd ever seen, a sturdy brown mare with white on her muzzle. Payne tied the store packages to the saddle before taking the reins and climbing up on the horse. While Payne's size intimidated her before, the sight of him sitting on the big mare was terrifying. If he hadn't been nice to her thus far, she would have run off into the darkness.

She waited to see if Buckley was going to bring out another horse and found herself almost relieved when he did not. Almost, as that meant she was now going to have to run alongside the big horse. She looked out into the darkness and wondered how far she would get until they left her behind gasping for air.

Payne reached a hand to help her up. She wanted to object and tell him she'd never actually ridden a horse before, but the thought of running alongside the horse and getting lost in the dark outweighed her fear. She placed her hand in his and allowed herself to be pulled onto the back of the horse. Payne made a sound, and the horse started moving, Anastasia wrapped her arms around his waist and felt him stiffen.

"You were nice to that man," she said after he relaxed

once more. "Most people are not so nice to them."

"Them?"

"Darkies."

"You'll do best to call him by his proper name and talk to him the way you would any other man. You treat a man the way you want to be treated," Payne said over his shoulder.

"What about the man in the store? He wanted to go home," Anastasia objected.

"You don't miss much, do you, girl?" Payne said. "That was different."

She thought about reminding him to call her by her proper name but decided against it. "How was it different?"

"Did you hear the church bells ringing as we left the store?"

"I did."

"The store closes at seven. We arrived with minutes to spare. The salesman was trying to close up early. That's why he didn't put up a fight. What's so funny?" he asked when Anastasia laughed.

"I thought he stayed because he was scared of you."

"Why would he be scared?"

"Because you are so big."

He was quiet for a moment. "Do I scare you?"

"No." It was a lie, but if he noticed, he didn't say. "Mr. Payne?"

"Yes, girl?"

"How do you see in the dark?"

"I don't."

"Well, what if we get lost?"

"We won't."

She sighed. "How can you be sure?"

"This horse has taken me home in the rain, snow, and everything in between. She isn't going to let a little darkness slow her down." He reached and patted the horse on the neck. "Ain't that right, Gloria?"

Upon hearing her name, the horse snorted and picked up her step. Anastasia grabbed on to Payne's shirt to keep from slipping off the horse's back.

"You okay back there, girl?"

"Yes, sir. I've just never been on a horse before."

"You mean you've never been on a horse this big before."

"No, sir. I mean not at all."

"Well, how do you get to where you're going?"

"I walk. I took the trolley once, but mostly, I walk."

"How'd you go to the store to get your supplies?"

"My what?"

"Your flour, beans, oats, and such? You said you know how to shop."

"Oh, that. We didn't go to the store. We bought everything at the market. Momma was sick a lot, so I went most every day. The market was only a couple of blocks from where we lived. I'd bring back a freshly plucked chicken or a ham. Sometimes I'd buy fish fresh from the ice bed and loaves of baked bread. Though mostly Momma preferred to make her own bread. She taught me how. They have wagons in the street filled with everything we needed. Men would drive their wagons to the market each day. I'd bring home everything for the day's meal in my momma's market basket. How far is the market from your apartment?"

This time, it was Payne who snorted, though she couldn't figure out what she'd said to evoke the response. She was getting ready to ask, when the horse nickered and picked up speed.

"What is it?" she whispered.

"She knows were almost home. Hold on," Payne said,

sitting forward as the horse took the steep incline.

She wrapped her arms tighter and leaned forward to keep from slipping off the rear of the horse. As the horse breached the top of the hill, Anastasia was surprised to see lights coming from the windows of a small house. As they got closer, the horse whinnied their arrival. The whinny was answered by several others in the distance. The door to the house swung open, and a young boy raced out.

"Pa's home!" he shouted to someone inside. Lantern in hand, the boy raced to where they'd stopped. Holding the lantern higher, he stared up at them, mouth agape. Closing his mouth, he looked over his shoulder and yelled once more. "He's done brung home a girl."

"Mind your manners, Caleb," Payne fussed. He reached around, grabbed Anastasia by the arm, and lowered her to the ground.

Once on the ground, she realized the boy wasn't as young as she'd thought. Though it was too dark to tell for sure, he looked to be several years older than she, or maybe it was only the shadow from the lantern.

Payne slid off the horse and handed him the reins. He then moved to the saddle and pulled down the package that held the items he'd purchased at the store. "Caleb, take Gloria to the barn. Rub the sweat off and make sure to put a blanket on her back so she doesn't catch a chill."

"Yes, sir." Though the boy sounded disappointed, he didn't argue. He held the lantern in front to illuminate the way as he led the big mare to the barn.

"Isn't he scared of the horse?" she asked, watching him go.

"He's been around them long enough to respect them," Payne said by way of an answer. "Come along now; my wife'll be wanting to meet you."

Anastasia followed as the man led the way to the house. Unlike before, he didn't appear to be in much of a hurry. Once on the porch, he hesitated before finally stepping inside. He crossed the room and disappeared into a hallway. He hadn't told her to follow, so she stood in the doorway taking in the brightly lit room. So bright, it took her a moment to realize there were nearly a dozen lanterns sitting about the room providing the light. She wondered if the electricity had gone out and further wondered why they needed so many lanterns to illuminate the space.

Payne returned to the room dragging a chair. He turned and she realized he wasn't actually dragging the thing as much as pulling it atop a large set of wheels. A woman sat in the chair and it took Anastasia a moment to realize she was missing her right leg. Not wishing to stare, Anastasia lifted her gaze once more, her breath catching as she saw the scar. Unlike her own scar, this one was long and jagged and stretched the length of the woman's face.

"Oh, Charles, I can see you didn't warn the girl about me." The woman's voice was strong, considering how frail she looked.

Payne bent and kissed her on top of her head. "Now, Sina, you know that's a lie. I told Anastasia all about you. I just forgot to tell her how beautiful you are."

"Anastasia. Such a lovely name." The woman's hand touched the jagged scar on her face and smiled. "I see we have something in common."

Chapter Twenty-Five

Anastasia woke, looked around the sun-filled room, and sighed. *So it wasn't a dream.* She was no longer living on the streets. She had a real home. She rose from the bed and pulled the quilt up to the matching pillow. She turned towards the window and stared. She'd never had curtains that matched her quilt before. She pulled the curtain back and blinked her surprise at the large red barn. It had been so dark, she hadn't noticed it last night. Something near the barn moved, and she pressed her nose to the window to see. *Chickens!* Lots of them, milling about pecking at the ground. She'd seen live chickens before, but they'd been in wooden crates near the chicken lady in the city. Never had she seen them roaming free and pecking at the ground. She watched them for several moments until her bladder told her she needed to find the water closet. She looked at her discarded dress she'd worn during her trip and wrinkled her nose. She walked to the closet and pulled one of the dresses Mr. Payne had purchased for her from the hanger. She slipped it over her head and stood in front of the dresser mirror. She'd never had a mirror in her room before. Mr. Payne had said he wasn't rich, but she thought maybe he was. She slipped on her shoes and went in search of the water closet. There were several doors in the hallway, but she wasn't sure which was the water closet, so she passed without opening them.

"You're awake," Mrs. Sina said when she entered the living room. "I was going to give you a few more minutes, then wake you myself."

Anastasia felt her face flush. "I'm sorry, did I sleep too long?"

"No, not today. But I'll have you up earlier from now on. Charles said you can cook. Is that right?"

"Yes, ma'am."

"Good, we'll be needing to start us some breakfast. Charles and Caleb already ate some salted pork and are on their way to the factory. From now on, you'll be the one fixing a proper breakfast." Her eyes got teary. "God knows they deserve it after all they've done for me."

Anastasia wanted to ask what they'd done for her, but she had more pressing matters to attend. "Ma'am? Can you please tell me which door is the water closet?"

Mrs. Sina's eyes grew wide. "You mean to tell me you haven't used it since you've been here?"

"No, ma'am. I used it in town while at the store. I really need to find it now, though," she said, glancing toward the hallway.

"It seems there are many things Mr. Payne has neglected to tell you. We are but simple folks. I'm afraid we don't have a water closet. We have an outhouse." She pointed towards the kitchen. "Use the back door. It's closer."

Anastasia hurried through the kitchen and out the back door. She looked for another house but didn't see one. All she saw was a tall wooden box with a roof. Desperate, she walked towards the structure. If it was a house, it was a small one, but it had a door, so she decided to open it. Her breath caught as she did, the odor telling her she'd found what she was looking for. She stepped inside, looked for the light switch, but found none. Desperate, she closed the door and took a seat. As she emptied her bladder, she realized, with several exceptions, this was little different than the privy on the train. It was still a piece of wood with a hole cut for the purpose. The only difference was the outhouse wasn't moving. It was all here, and it smelled really bad. There was a small half-moon on the door, which allowed light to flow in. There were also streams of light coming in through various gaps in the wood. She finished her business and looked over her shoulder for the chain pull and found none. She stood, took a quick peek inside the hole, and wrinkled her nose. She unlatched the door and pushed her way outside, thankful for the fresh air.

She rubbed her arms against the morning chill as she stood soaking in the bright sunshine. The wind picked up, and she watched as some of the last holdouts of fall drifted down from the trees and listened as they came to rest next to those leaves that had already fallen. It was then that she realized there wasn't any noise. No, that wasn't true; there was plenty of noises, just not the ones she was used to hearing. There was no steady hum of people, horses clomping in the street, or motorcars. What she was hearing was leaves rustling in the wind. A screech from a group of large black birds watching her from their perch upon the trees. Another bird, larger with brown feathers, screeched as it floated effortlessly overhead. She turned in a circle and realized she could see for miles, and what she saw was more of the same. Except for the house, outhouse, and barn, there were no other structures in sight. The thought both intrigued and terrified her.

She studied the house, a simple white structure with a wide covered porch that stretched the length of it. In the daylight, the house seemed even more welcoming than it had last night. More so, maybe, as she'd slept the whole night without being disturbed. Standing there, she realized she'd not heard anything in the way of screaming or fighting. Was this the way of this part of the country, or were the occupants simply on their best behavior in front of their new guest?

She started for the house, remembered the barn, and

decided to take a closer look, enjoying the sound of the leaves crunching underfoot. She laughed out loud as the chickens ran to greet her. She stood watching as they pecked away at things only they could see. She thought of Tobias and Ezra and wondered what they would make of their cheerful clucking as they scratched in the dirt. She looked up in time to see a flurry of wings headed her way. This chicken was different from the rest, beautifully colored with reds, yellows, and dark greens, its head lowered, and wings spread as it charged angrily in her direction. As it approached, the chicken hopped as if it was going to grab her with its feet. She jumped out of the way, and the colorful chicken came around for another try. She turned, running as fast as she could, making it up the few stairs and inside the back door with seconds to spare. She pulled the screen closed just as the chicken rammed into the bottom of the screen door. The chicken stood, jutted its head, and made a funny noise. She would have laughed if she hadn't been so scared.

"I see you met Jed," Mrs. Sina said when she came back into the room.

"I didn't know chickens are mean. They always seemed so nice and seldom minded when the chicken lady pulled them out of the crate to wring their necks."

Mrs. Sina laughed. "Jed's not a chicken; he's a rooster. He'd just as soon spur you with his claws as to look at you."

"Why do you keep him around if he's so mean?"

"We can't wring his neck until we get another rooster."

"Does he lay good eggs, then?"

Another laugh. "Roosters don't lay eggs; they fertilize them."

She had no idea what that meant. "Do the eggs need to be fertilized before you eat them?"

"Chickens will lay eggs with or without a rooster. If you

have a rooster, you need to collect the eggs right away, so the hens don't go sitting on them."

"Why does she sit on them, and why is that bad?"

"The chicken sits on them to keep them warm so they can hatch into baby chickens. All this talk about chickens is making me hungry. You think you can find your way around the kitchen to make us some breakfast?"

"Yes, ma'am," Anastasia said. "Have you been to the market?"

The smile left Mrs. Sina's face. "I haven't left the house in months. Not to worry, you'll find what you need. If not, write it down and give it to Charles. As long as it's reasonable, he'll see you get it. The kitchen's yours now. I can't get my chair in there, so you best make yourself acquainted with it. While you're at it, start thinking about the evening meal. The men will be hungry when they return."

Anastasia fixed a breakfast of oatmeal with honey and brought two bowlfuls to the table. She then helped Mrs. Sina maneuver the heavy wheelchair to the table, where they sat eating the simple meal.

After a moment, Anastasia asked the question that had been on her mind. "Is that why you wanted me? To cook for you and them?"

Mrs. Sina lowered her spoon and sat back in her chair, and Anastasia mirrored her actions.

"It was a big part of it. Since the accident, I've not been much good around here. Caleb's had to stay home and take care of me. He's been trying to learn his way around the kitchen, but his food's not much good to eat. Poor Charles is mostly skin and bones these days. The boy's trying. But boys should not be made to wash their mother's undergarments and help them onto the chamber chair when they have to go. I heard about the train and how there would be children needing a home. I thought maybe we could find a girl who would not mind helping around the house in exchange for a clean place to sleep. I guess it wasn't right for Charles to bring you here without telling you the reason, but if he had, maybe you wouldn't have agreed to come." Mrs. Sina reached across the table and placed her hand on top of Anastasia's. "Charles told the agent you'd write him a letter when you get settled. There is writing paper and a quill pen in that desk over yonder. Give it a month. If you find we aren't fair, or if you're not happy here, you can write to Mr. Swan and tell him to come fetch you. I'll see to it that Charles posts the letter."

Anastasia considered the woman's words. While a part of her wished she was with a family who wanted her just to be their daughter, nothing had happened thus far to make her want to leave. She thought of the girl she'd met in the asylum in the city. The one who worked at the asylum and didn't get paid. The girl had seemed content enough, and this situation seemed much the same. Only, Anastasia had her own room and was the one doing the cooking. Anastasia knew how to cook, and her food was pleasant enough, and she'd been taking care of her family long enough; it didn't really seem like a chore. She looked at the woman across from her and nodded her agreement. She'd stay. At least until she found a reason not to.

***

"We had two of those," Linda said when Cindy flipped over the last page in the journal she was reading.

"Mom, you're speaking in half sentences again," Cindy said, picking up the next journal.

"Outhouses. I was just sitting here remembering ours."

Cindy handed Linda one of the journals she'd copied. "Really? I guess I never knew you had one."

"Oh no, not one; we were a two-outhouse family," Linda said, running her hand across the journal. "We had one for the guys and one for the gals."

"You're serious?"

"Of course I am. Lots of people had two. Mind you, the girls' outhouse had two holes."

"Two?"

"Yep, it was a double seater. We had a big hole for the adults and a smaller hole for us kids so we didn't fall in. We didn't have any of those fancy seats, but my daddy sanded that wood so fine, we didn't have to worry none about any dang splinters."

Cindy laughed. "You know, just talking about your younger days growing up in Kentucky, and your accent comes flooding back."

"The girls' outhouse had a moon, and the boys had a star. That's how people knew which one to use," Linda said, ignoring her comment. "A lot of people couldn't read, so they just looked for either a star or a moon."

"What about the people who only had one outhouse?"

"If it was a single, it had a half moon."

"Why have anything at all? There's one outhouse, just use it."

"Like Anastasia wrote in her journal, it helped allow the light to shine in. See there; you have something else you can teach those kids of yours at school."

Cindy sighed. "The only things the kids know about outhouses these days is they are used for outhouse races."

Linda chuckled. "Can you imagine traveling back in time and telling that to people?"

Cindy picked up the next journal. "I think there's a lot about today's society that would shock them."

Chapter Twenty-Six

Anastasia woke to the rooster's crow announcing the arrival of a new day. She hurried from her bed with a yawn. Caleb had shown her how to collect the eggs for the morning breakfast, and she was eager to show she was capable of running the kitchen. She struck a match to light her lantern and stepped into the hallway. She could hear Mr. Charles and Mrs. Sina talking quietly behind their bedroom door and saw the soft glow of light beneath the crack in Caleb's door.

Not realizing he'd succeeded in his task, the rooster crowed for a second time. *I'm awake,* he seemed to say, *the day's upon us. Get your lazy bottoms out of bed and join me.* She'd join him alright; only today, she'd come prepared. Lantern in hand, she grabbed the egg basket and kitchen broom, and went to face her nemesis.

The chickens had been moved inside the barn to give them extra protection during the colder temperatures. Anastasia opened the heavy barn door, hung the lantern on the hook, then walked to the winter coop and opened the screen door. The chickens clucked their greeting as she moved through the coop, pulling the eggs from the nesting boxes the way Caleb had shown her, making sure to stay clear of the brooding hen who'd decided she was ready to become a mother. She caught movement out of the corner of her eye and used the broom to shoo the rooster.

"You're not getting me," she said firmly. "I'm onto your shenanigans."

She picked up the egg basket, ready to return to the house, when she heard the contented clucks from the brooding hen. Turning, she watched as the hen pulled the straw closer then settled back onto the nest. *I wish to be a mother too. If I had a baby of my own, no one could take it from me.* She saw the feed bin and smiled. *Maybe I can be a mother to one of the chicks.* She leaned the broom against the wall, walked to the feed bucket, and took out a cup of feed, spreading it onto the ground. As she'd hoped, all the chickens, the brooding hen included, converged upon the feed.

Anastasia looked to make sure she was alone, took one of the eggs the hen had been protecting, and slipped it into her pocket. She'd keep it warm in her pocket until it hatched and then it would think her to be its momma. Feeling pleased with herself, she picked up the basket full of eggs and turned to leave. She'd taken several steps when she remembered the rooster. Too late, the rooster charged towards her, head lowered. She reached for the broom, but she wasn't fast enough; the rooster jabbed her with one of its spurs. She jumped back to avoid another attack, landing on her backside. Thankfully, she was able to avoid spilling the basket full of eggs. She grabbed the broom and thrust it towards the rooster, sending him on his way once more. She remembered the coveted egg, reached into her pocket, and knew in an instant that egg hadn't fared as well. Withdrawing the contents, she saw a half-formed chick. Tears sprang to her eyes as she held the chick, picking away at the bits of broken shell. Devastated, the tears continued to flow. She cradled the chick in her hands, willing it to come to life. As she cried, she thought of her mother and her desperate tears before her milk had started. She thought of Tobias and Ezra and how she'd left them alone at the market, wondering if they'd actually found their way home. She thought of Runt and the way he'd looked at her when she told him she couldn't stay. She was still mourning her loses when a shadow fell over her. She looked up to see Caleb standing over her, blonde hair tousled, milk bucket in hand.

He lowered his bucket and sat on the ground beside her. Once she stopped crying, he spoke. "You okay?"

"No," she sobbed. She opened her hands to show him the chick. "It's my fault. I stole it from the brooding hen. I put it in my pocket, thinking if I could hatch it, the chick would think me to be its mother. I forgot about the rooster. He spurred my leg, and I fell on the egg."

Caleb sighed and pushed his shoulder against hers.

"I found a baby kitten in the haystack a few years ago. It wasn't very old, but it was crying and making an awful ruckus. I figured the mama cat had abandoned it, so I snuck it inside and hid it in my bedroom. I took a small bowl of milk from the cow and fed it by dipping my smallest finger into the bowl and allowing the kitten to suckle," he said, extending his pinky. "I kept that kitten alive for three days, and on the third night, the kitten wouldn't stop crying. I was afraid it would wake the rest of the family. Desperate to keep from being caught, I brought the kitten to my bed, hoping to keep it warm. I woke the next morning to find I'd rolled over during the night, and in doing so, had suffocated the tiny kitten."

Her tears were flowing once more, so she leaned her head against his shoulder. "Thanks for not laughing at me."

"Babies are meant to be with their momma," he said. "You couldn't have hatched that egg no more than I could've kept that kitten alive. Pa's going to be expecting his breakfast. You go on in, and I'll take care of the chick. Make sure to rub some honey on that rooster spur so it doesn't become infected."

***

December, 1914

Anastasia finished drying the last of the morning dishes and looked around the kitchen. In the month since she'd arrived, it had become her kitchen, fully stocked and ready for the next meal. She'd not left the homestead since her arrival, not that she'd had to, as most everything she needed was in the root cellar. Anything else was brought home when Charles and Caleb returned from their jobs at the shoe factory. Charles had even brought her a new pair of boots that both he and Caleb had made just for her. She hadn't gone to school since her arrival, but Mrs. Sina, as she had taken to calling her, was a wealth of information and didn't hesitate to share her knowledge. Still, the woman seemed reserved and only answered the questions Anastasia thought to ask. The woman was sad, and Anastasia often caught her crying when she came upon her unaware.

While no one in the family was overly affectionate, there'd been no screaming or yelling, and Anastasia had taken to sleeping with her bedroom door wide open. She'd opened it on the second night after hearing the clock in the front room chiming in the distance. She found something about the sound comforting and had opened her door to enjoy the tune. She woke the next morning and realized she'd fallen asleep without shutting the door. She'd lain there for several moments remembering the life she'd left behind, further wondering how her momma and brothers were faring. While she thought of them daily, she hadn't given any thought to Albert.

Today was the day she was to write to Mr. Swan and tell him how she was getting along. The day she was to decide whether to stay or ask the man to come and take her away. She hadn't given it a lot of thought, mostly because she'd been too busy. She rose every morning just as the sun breached the far hill. She would have breakfast well underway as Charles wheeled Mrs. Sina from their room. While she helped Mrs. Sina when Charles was away, the moment he returned, he took over tending to her every need.

She pulled on her coat and walked outside to get some air. She no longer had to fear the rooster. Caleb had taken care of the bird the day it attacked her and had brought in another more docile fellow. She'd felt bad at first. But he'd told her it was the way of life on the farm, saying he'd been attacking the hens as well. If a rooster gets out of line, you bring in another. She remembered thinking she wished that were true with humans as well. If her momma had thought that way, maybe she wouldn't have had to leave.

She went to the barn and spread out a bit of feed for the chickens, placing a second pile for the newly hatched chicks.

A horse snorted, and she turned to see Caleb entering the barn.

"You ain't thinking of putting one of those chicks in your pocket, are you?" he asked as he approached.

She felt her face turn red. "No, they're fine right where they are."

"Ma said you were out here thinking," he said when he neared.

"I am." She hadn't realized the woman knew she'd gone.

"You're not planning on leaving here, are you?"

"What's it to you?"

"What's it to me?! Why, everything, of course. I'd have to quit my job again, on account I would have to stay home and take care of Ma. Sometimes I wish…"

"You wish what?" Anastasia asked when he stopped.

"Sometimes, I wish she would've died when Emily did," he blurted, his face turning red.

"Caleb Payne, you don't mean that!"

"But I do."

"I thought you love your ma."

"I do, it's just, well, you didn't know her before. She's different now."

"Different how?"

"She was happy before the accident. She liked to sing and dance. She even played the piano. Pa was happier too."

"He seems happy to me."

He frowned. "He hardly ever smiles and barely eats, even though your food is mighty tasty. What makes you think he's happy?"

"He doesn't yell."

"Why would he yell?"

"I guess I just thought all men yelled," she replied.

He shrugged. "I don't recall ever hearing him yell."

"Well, he's nice to your mother."

"I've heard him cry, you know."

"Who, Mr. Charles? Why?"

"Yes. He doesn't know I heard. He cries in the outhouse or when he doesn't think anyone is around. I think he misses the way Ma used to be too."

Anastasia had only seen Albert cry once. It was the day Sharon had told him she was pregnant with Ezra. Those had been happy tears. Then Momma had gotten sick, and things had never been the same. She suddenly wondered if that was why Albert drank so much; maybe he missed the way Sharon had been.

"I was with them, you know," Caleb said, pulling her from her thoughts. "We were coming home from Sunday service. Papa had ridden in separately, as he was going to ride over to old man Crandle's house. I wanted to go with him, but he told me to see Ma and Emily made it home safe. I didn't know it at the time, but he was picking up a new calf for me and wanted it to be a surprise. Well, on the way home, Emily got stung by a bee. We didn't think anything of it, but all the sudden, she started gasping for air like she couldn't breathe. Ma turned the buggy around, thinking to get her to the doctor. She was running that horse real fast, and I was hanging on to keep from flying out of the buggy. Only now Emily is slumped over like she's dead. Ma started screaming and hitting the horse harder, and the horse is running for all its worth. I see the hole, and I'm hollering for Ma to stop, but she ain't hearing me. The horse saw it and skirts around the hole, but it's going too fast, and the whole wagon starts tipping to its side. I jumped and landed in a blackberry bush, but Ma didn't get out in time. She hit hard when she landed, and that buggy rolled right on top of her. I guess that bee had a sickness or something, 'cause Emily was already dead. But Ma, well, she was bleeding something fierce by the time I was able to climb my way out of that bush. I used my belt and tied it around her leg. I don't know why I thought of it, but it worked, and the doctor later told me I'd done real good. They had to take the leg anyway. It was mangled pretty bad, but he said she'd of died if not for me."

Caleb closed his eyes briefly, and she wondered if he would cry.

He opened his eyes once more. "We have one, you know?"

"One what?"

"A piano. It's over here," Caleb said, leading her to the back area of the barn. He pulled back a blanket to reveal a beautiful upright piano. "Ma made Pop take it out of the house after Emily died. Took four men to bring it out here."

Anastasia pressed on a key and smiled at the sound. "But why? I thought you said your ma liked to play it."

"She did. She and Emily used to play it all the time. After Emily died, Ma couldn't stand to look at it."

"Can you play it?"

"A little, I guess. Not as good as Ma and Emily could."
He shrugged. "Emily was older and could do most things
better'n me."

"Do you miss her? I know I miss my brothers something
fierce."

"Yeah, I guess. I reckon I mostly miss the way things
were when she was here."

Anastasia sat on the bench and scooched to the end.
"Play me a song."

His face wrinkled. "I told you I ain't no good."

"I can't play at all, so that means you're already better
than me," Anastasia reasoned.

He considered that for a moment. "I guess."

She patted the bench beside her and smiled her sweetest
smile. "Please, for me. Just one song?"

His face turned red, and he looked as if he were about
to run. Instead, he sat next to her, making sure to keep his
distance. He stared straight ahead, and his fingers trembled as
he plucked several of the keys.

Anastasia watched his every move, determined to
memorize where he placed his fingers. He was right; he wasn't
very good. When he finished, he sat without looking in her
direction, the tips of his ears a deep shade of red.

Chapter Twenty-Seven

August, 1918

Anastasia finished wiping off the stove and looked around the kitchen. Satisfied, she dried her hands and picked up the brown wicker basket. The blackberries were in full bloom, and she intended to gather some for a pie. If she had any left over, she might even make a cobbler as well.

She started into the living room and saw Mrs. Sina sitting in her wheelchair, embroidering a new tablecloth. Tears were flowing down the woman's face as she sewed. Softly, so as not to be heard, she backed into the kitchen to allow the woman time to collect herself. Try as she might, she couldn't reach through the woman's sadness. "Mrs. Sina?"

"Yes, dear," Mrs. Sina called after a moment's hesitation.

Anastasia plastered a smile on her face and came into the room as if for the first time. "I'm going up on the bluff to pick some blackberries. Do you need me to do anything for you before I go?"

"No, no, I'm fine, just sitting here working on the tablecloth. Idle hands, you know." The woman said, pushing the needle through the cloth. "Mr. Charles is going to be mighty pleased you're making blackberry pie. He was just saying the other day as how he'd like some."

"If the deer haven't gotten to them all, I'll make a cobbler as well." She turned to look out the window when the goose sounded the alarm. She looked out the window, not that she needed to. She'd gotten a letter from the post a week ago letting her know Mr. Swan would be stopping by soon to see how she was faring. With few exceptions, they rarely received visitors.

"Is it that nice man from the Children's Aid Society?" Mrs. Sina asked, craning her neck to see.

"Yes, it's Mr. Swan. Will you be all right for a while?" Anastasia asked, knowing Mr. Swan preferred to speak in private so the kids could speak freely.

"I'll be fine. Make sure to invite Mr. Swan in for lemonade when you are through chatting. If he's agreeable, he's welcome to stay for supper as well."

"Yes, I'll insist upon it," Anastasia promised. She hurried out the door, greeting the man just as he stepped from his buggy. "Good day, Mr. Swan."

"Why, Anastasia, how lovely to see you again," he said, eyeing the goose with a wary eye.

"She won't bother you none," she assured him. "She just likes to let us know when something's amiss."

"I've been chased by far worse," he said, placing his hat on top of his head. "Would it be all right if we take a walk before we go inside?"

She smiled and held up the basket. "There's a blackberry bush on top of the bluff. I was just heading out to pick some. I'll make a pie for supper. You must stay. Mrs. Sina insists."

"Splendid. Blackberry pie just happens to be one of my favorites," he said, falling into step beside her.

She smiled. He'd said the same thing about blueberry the last time he'd stopped by.

"So how is life treating you?" he asked as they started across the field that led to the bluff.

"Real good. I pretty much run the house," she said

proudly.

"Do they work you hard, Anastasia?"

She turned at hearing the concern in his voice. "It's not so bad. I do much less than when I was at home. Mrs. Sina has two good arms and helps whenever she can."

"You've been here, what? Four years? Do you ever regret agreeing to stay?"

"Almost five. I'm nearly fifteen now. And, yes, I'm happy here." It was the truth. Though she still missed her brothers, the pain of leaving them had lessened. She turned towards the path that led towards the top of the bluff.

"How is the family treating you?"

"Mr. Charles and Mrs. Sina treat me just fine," she answered truthfully.

"They never offered to formally adopt you?" There was a sadness in his voice.

"No, it's not like that. They were never looking to replace the daughter that died. I guess I'm more like a helper, but I knew that when I agreed to stay. They promised to treat me fair, and they have. They say they're not rich, but I think they may be. They buy me anything I need. I have a nice room all to myself and a closet full of dresses. Mrs. Sina likes to sew," she said by way of explanation. "Neither she nor Mr. Charles has ever so much as raised their voices to me. I guess that's because I've never given them reason to."

That seemed to please him. "They have a son, if I remember right. He's what? Sixteen now? How do you get along with him?"

She stepped up her pace so he couldn't see the blush spreading over her face. Caleb had been sneaking kisses of late. "Oh, Caleb is nice enough."

They stopped at the top of the hill, and she pretended to be flushed from the climb. She placed the basket over her arm and started pulling berries from the bush. Mr. Swan took off his jacket and proceeded to help, both eating nearly as many as went into the basket.

"If you had it to do over again, would you? Come out on the train, that is," Swan asked, dumping a handful of blackberries into the basket.

She'd often wondered the same thing. "Under the same circumstances as I left? Yes, I would."

"You told me once your mother had kicked you out of the house. What if she'd not done that?"

She looked at him to see if he was serious. "Then I guess I wouldn't have needed a home now, would I, Mr. Swan?"

He laughed. "No, I reckon you wouldn't. I guess I didn't phrase the question correctly. I'm just trying to make sense of the program. Checking to see if it really works."

She moved to a different spot and started clearing the berries. "What about you, Mr. Swan. Do you think it works?"

"Statistically, yes. Most of the children I visit have agreeable homes," he replied.

"But you're worried about the ones who don't."

Swan smiled. "You've always been very astute, Anastasia."

"Mr. Swan, children belong with their mothers and fathers, but sometimes..." She looked at him, willing him to understand. "Sometimes, they're much better off without them."

"Young lady, I believe you may just be the wisest fourteen-year-old I've ever met."

"Almost fifteen," she reminded him.

***

"That was an amazing dinner, Anastasia." Mr. Swan

said, pushing back from the table. Don't tell Mrs. Swan, but that was probably the best blackberry pie I've ever eaten."

"Yes, we're fortunate to have her with us," Mrs. Sina agreed when Anastasia didn't respond right away.

Swan cast a glance out the window. "It looks like a storm is brewing. I guess I'd best be on my way if I'm to make it to Poplar Bluff before it rains."

"Does your train head out tonight, Mr. Swan?" Mrs. Sina asked.

Swan shook his head. "No, I'll be catching the late morning train back to Sedalia."

"Then you'll stay the night here. No sense paying for a room when we have plenty," Charles said, casting a glance at Caleb.

Caleb nodded his agreement. "You can use my room, Mr. Swan. I'll take a bedroll out to the hay."

Mr. Swan looked towards the window once more. "If you're sure it won't be too much trouble. I'd rather not be caught out in the storm with a horse that doesn't know the way."

"We insist," Mrs. Sina agreed.

Charles walked to the window to get a better look. "Better go see to the livestock, Caleb. See to Mr. Swan's horse and buggy while you're at it."

Anastasia stood, collecting the supper dishes as the adults moved to the living area. She placed the dishes in the sink and picked up the water bucket. "I'm going to fetch some water from the well. I'll see if Caleb needs any help getting the chickens in while I'm out."

"Those chickens are smarter than most people; they'll be well into their roosts by now. That cow is another story. If Caleb's not in the barn, check in the back pasture. That dang cow's probably hiding under a tree," Charles said, tilting his head in that direction.

The skies were indeed dark, the wind picking up so that it whipped the screen from her hand the moment she opened the door. She walked to the well and lowered the bucket, waiting for it to fill. She placed her hand on the rope, then placed one hand lower, alternating the sequence and pulling on the rope to bring the bucket to the top. Using both hands, she lifted the bucket, then tilted it and poured the contents into the empty bucket she'd brought from the house. She hung the well bucket back on its hook and went to check on the chickens. Finding them all inside the coop, she closed the door and went in search of Caleb.

She found him in the barn, his back to her. He was spreading hay for Mr. Swan's horse. The horse neighed, and she ducked from view. Staying to the shadows, she went to the piano and sat on the bench. She flipped up the lid, her fingers dancing out one of the few tunes he'd taught her. She wasn't very good, but then again, she hadn't had the best teacher.

"You really should learn to play that thing better," he said, sliding next to her.

"You should've been a better teacher," she replied, and started into a different tune.

"Maybe you should just ask Ma to teach you."

"No, I don't want to upset her." It was the same answer she'd given each time he suggested it; afraid Mrs. Sina would insist Mr. Charles take the piano away if she knew it was being played. It was the piano that had cemented her decision to stay. Even though she wasn't any good, the thought of not being able to play was worse than playing poorly.

"When we marry, I'll see that Pa lets you take it to our home," Caleb said with a grin.

She stopped playing and stared at him. "Why, Caleb Payne, I'm not going to marry you."

"Sure you are."

"Am not."

"Why not? I thought you liked me. Ain't I good enough for you?"

"I like you plenty. I'm just not going to marry you," she said when his lips formed a pout.

He cocked his head to the side. "You didn't seem to mind when I kissed you."

"Of course I didn't mind. You kiss real nice."

"So you'll kiss me, but you won't marry me? You don't make a lick of sense."

He wasn't the only one confused. "What does kissing have to do with marrying?"

He turned his head to stare at her. "Why, it's got everything to do with it."

"I kissed a boy before, and he never said anything about getting married."

His eyes opened wider. "You was no more than a baby before you came. Why'd you go and kiss a boy?"

"I wasn't a baby; I was ten. And now I'm almost fifteen," she said, rising.

He slid off the bench and faced her. "Exactly. You're old enough to be getting married."

"Just because I'm old enough to get married don't mean I have to do it," she said, placing her hands on her hips. "I don't want to get married, and you can't make me."

He turned to leave, and she moved in front of him. "Where're you going?"

"You said you don't want to marry me."

"That's because I don't want to marry anyone."

"So you still like me?" His voice was hopeful.

"Of course I like you. I wouldn't kiss you if I didn't like you."

"I don't understand girls," he said with a sigh.

Mrs. Johnston would be proud. She smiled. She hadn't thought of the woman in years.

"You have a strange look on your face," he said, staring at her.

She closed her eyes, trying to picture the woman. "I was just thinking about an old friend."

"That boy you kissed?"

She opened her eyes. "No, not that boy I kissed."

He lowered his voice and dug at the dirt with his toes. "Anastasia?"

"Yes?"

"Why don't you want to get married?"

She considered her answer for a moment. There were so many reasons, but mostly because she didn't want to end up like her mother. "Because I'm not a mule."

He laughed. "What kind of answer is that?"

She shrugged. "The only answer I have."

***

Anastasia lay in bed listening to the thunder roll in the distance, the lingering remnants of the evening storm. She'd yet to get used to the massive storms that plagued Missouri, especially the ones that brought with them the dark cyclones dipping from the sky. While none had done any significant damage to where she lived, she'd viewed the destruction to nearby farms when delivering meals to families who'd lost everything. She jumped as the thunder clapped once more, closer this time, letting her know danger was still afoot.

She thought of Caleb sleeping alone in the barn and wondered if he was scared. She thought to go collect him and ask if he wanted to sleep on the floor in her room then wondered what Mr. Swan would think if he did. Somehow, she didn't think the man would approve. Still, she didn't like the idea of him alone in the barn, so she pushed from the bed, pulled on her robe, and gathered her lantern. She waited until she was near the back door before striking the match then quietly made her way outside, deciding to make a quick trip to the outhouse before checking on Caleb.

She exited the outhouse and stood staring at the starless sky. The rain had stopped, but lightning raced overhead like dozens of bright blue fingers reaching as far as the eye could see. She was about to turn towards the barn, when she saw a shadow of a man standing on the porch. Thinking it to be Caleb, she lifted the lantern and hurried towards the house.

"I see I'm not the only one who couldn't sleep," Swan said as she approached.

She chided herself for not checking the porch and was glad she'd decided to go to the outhouse before checking on Caleb. She cast a look at the barn then joined Mr. Swan on the porch. "I don't believe I'll ever get used to storms of this size. I don't remember the sky being so angry when I lived in the city."

He moved to the chairs, and she followed, setting the lantern on the rail a few feet away to draw the bugs from them.

"I believe you're right. We can get some bad ones out here. I've seen whole towns destroyed in the blink of an eye. You don't have to worry about that much here with the way the farm is nestled in the bottom of the bluff. Payne was a smart man to place the house and barn where he did. Mr. and Mrs. Payne think rather highly of you, in case you don't already know."

She thought she did, but it was nice hearing it, especially Mr. Charles, who could be rather reserved with his words.

"You could've done a lot worse than those two."

Again, he was telling her something she already knew.

"I don't know about the boy, though."

"Who? Caleb? Why, he's nice as he can be," she replied.

Mr. Swan chuckled. "So you do like him."

He was trying to trick her. "I said he is nice. I didn't say I like him."

"He likes you. I can see it in his eyes when he looks at you. Why, the boy doesn't give a lick about your scar. Not that he should, considering his mother and all. You're an excellent cook, mind your manners, and I think you'll make a fine wife someday."

She blew out a frustrated sigh. "Mr. Swan, why does everyone think girls are supposed to get married?"

"It's what girls do, run the house and have children."

"But why? My momma got married, and I saw where it got her. She had to do everything my papa said, even when she didn't like it. She said it was because she was his property. She's no better than a mule he can beat on anytime he wants."

Swan leaned forward in his chair. "Has that boy been beating on you?"

"What? No, no one's been beating on me. Not since I came here anyway. But men change after they're married. I know that to be true."

Swan leaned back and rocked in his chair. "I'm not going to sit here and tell you that doesn't happen, but I've met a lot of men in my life, and I'd say most of them are good souls."

"That may be, but then again, maybe they don't let you see into their house. Up until Albert started drinking so much, he never let any outsider see how bad he behaved."

"I can speak from experience. Not all men hit. What about Mr. Payne?"

"What about him?"

"You've lived here for nearly five years. Have you ever seen the man hit his wife?"

"No." Actually, she'd never even heard the man raise his voice to the woman or anyone else, now that she thought of it.

"There, you scc. I'm not saying you have to get married right away. Someday you'll want a family of your own. Don't let one dark cloud steal your thunder." He'd no sooner gotten the words out of his mouth, when a large clap of thunder shook the porch beneath their feet. They both laughed at the timing, allowing the moment of seriousness to pass.

Chapter Twenty-Eight

December 18, 1919

Anastasia sat by the edge of the pond, coat pulled tight against the late morning chill. A family of ducks floated merrily at the far side of the pond, dipping their beaks in the water and preening feathers, unaware of her inner turmoil. She cast a glance at the sky and sighed. The sun was high in the trees, which meant she needed to get back to the house to prepare Mrs. Sina's afternoon meal. The mere thought of cooking tugged at her stomach. She stood, took two steps, and retched. It was not the first time the thought of food made her ill, and that frightened her. She'd been with her mother during two pregnancies. She knew the signs. So far, she'd been successful at keeping her condition a secret, her heavy winter dresses hiding the swell of her stomach. She'd also managed to avoid Caleb of late. The mere thought of the boy brought tears to her eyes. He'd wanted to marry her. She'd even given it some thought. But now… Whatever would he think of her?

She kneeled by the pond, closed her eyes, and dipped her hands, bringing the cool water to her face. Opening her eyes, she saw her reflection staring out from the water. She plunged her hands once more, distorting the image, and used the water to wash the acid from her mouth. The chill of the water did little to settle her stomach. She rose from the bank and slowly made her way back to the house. She stopped and pulled a bucket of fresh water from the well, pouring it into the kitchen bucket. She took a breath to settle her nerves and walked towards the house.

Mrs. Sina looked up when she entered. "How was your walk? Not too chilly, I hope?"

"No, it was fine. I went to the pond to see if the ice had taken hold. I don't think it's quite cold enough yet."

"Charles said the temperatures have been mild for this time of year. It might not freeze over this winter." Mrs. Sina looked up and smiled. "It's cold enough to give your face a rosy glow."

Anastasia turned so the woman could not look any closer. She moved into the kitchen and called to Mrs. Sina over her shoulder. "Are you hungry?"

The woman laughed. "I believe I may have a tapeworm. I am always hungry of late."

Anastasia busied herself cutting a slab of ham off last night's hock and placed it between bread. She'd use the rest to flavor bean soup for the evening meal. She added a thin slice of cheese to the sandwich then added a swath of mustard and carried it to the table. She helped Mrs. Sina wheel her chair close and started back towards the kitchen.

"You're not eating today?" the woman asked.

Anastasia turned too fast and fought back the bile that threatened. "I guess I'm still full from breakfast."

The woman's gaze trailed over Anastasia, stopping at her stomach, then lifted her eyes to meet hers. "You've barely eaten a thing in over a week."

"I...I haven't been feeling well," Anastasia stuttered.

Mrs. Sina placed her sandwich on the plate and nodded to the chair. Anastasia sat, keeping her eyes lowered.

"Does Caleb know?"

"No, and you mustn't tell him," Anastasia said and burst into tears.

The woman sighed. "Caleb has a right to know.

Everyone will know before long. Best be sooner than later, so he can make an honest woman of you."

"An honest woman? I don't understand," Anastasia said, wiping the tears from her eyes.

"That's his baby in your stomach. He'll be wanting to marry you."

"It's not his baby; its mine. And he'll not want to marry me. Not now."

Mrs. Sina wheeled her chair to face her. "You mean to tell me that baby isn't Caleb's?"

"Of course not. We aren't married." Anastasia sniffed.

Mrs. Sina bit at her bottom lip. "Girl, do you know how a baby gets in a woman's stomach?"

Another sniff. "Yes, she gets married."

Mrs. Sina raised her eyebrows. "Just how do you think that baby got into your stomach?"

Anastasia stood, knocking her chair back in the process. She righted the chair and paced the floor, wringing her hands. She'd been trying to figure that out for weeks.

"I just don't know. Caleb said he wanted to get married and I keep telling him no. I'm not sure I ever want to get married. Now we can't and I think that makes me sad."

Mrs. Sina frowned. "I'm afraid I don't understand."

"I was in Momma's stomach when she married Albert. He told her it was okay, but it wasn't. He was always mad at Momma because he said I didn't belong to him. I can't marry Caleb. I don't want him to be mad at me because I have a baby in my stomach. I hated Albert. I don't want to hate Caleb."

Mrs. Sina's face softened. "Come," she said, patting the chair, "we need to have ourselves a chat."

***

Anastasia walked through Hecht & Sons looking at the

fabric. It was a rare trip into town for her, one Mrs. Sina had insisted upon, saying she didn't trust the menfolk to pick out suitable fabric to make a wedding dress. Mrs. Sina insisted she be allowed time to make Anastasia a new dress, after which they would call for the reverend to perform a simple ceremony. *Off white,* she'd told her; *we don't want to upset the preacher when he finds you to be impure.* While Mrs. Sina had blamed it on the preacher, Anastasia knew the woman had been worried about Mr. Charles's reaction as well. While she'd been made to tell Caleb about the baby, they'd all agreed to keep the news from Mr. Charles for as long as possible. *We'll tell him right after you and Caleb are hitched*, Mrs. Sina had told her. *Then, when the baby arrives, we'll just let him think the baby's done come early. Menfolk are easy to fool about such things,* she'd said with a wink.

Anastasia decided on the perfect shade of cream, just as Caleb and Charles joined her.

"I'm just finishing up. I like this color," she said when Charles frowned.

"Take your time." Charles sounded agitated. "Buckley has two jobs ahead of us. He said he can fix the wheel, but it will be a few hours."

The wagon wheel had snapped just as they'd arrived in town and they wouldn't be able to get the wagon and supplies home without having it fixed. Anastasia hugged the bolt of fabric to her chest, worried about leaving Mrs. Sina home alone for so long.

"Sina will be fine," Charles said as if reading her mind. "That woman's stronger than the three of us put together. If you're set on that fabric, then get what you need. We may as well have supper while we wait."

***

The sun was low in the sky by the time they started for home. While Anastasia enjoyed having someone else do the cooking, she'd had a nagging worry in her gut throughout the meal. She blamed it on the baby but knew there was more to it than that. If she could've gotten away with it, she would've insisted on walking, but knew Caleb would put up a fuss, and in doing so, would've had to explain his reluctance to allow her to go off on her own. In the end, she stayed put and listened as Charles and Caleb discussed plans to build a small cabin for the two of them in the field near the pond. She would've preferred her house to sit on top of the bluff, but then remembering Mr. Swan's words, decided not to voice her opinion. Not that she was asked for it in the first place. She'd agreed to be Caleb's wife. Wives didn't get to vote on such things.

As the horse made its way along the road, she thought of the fabric they'd purchased and imagined it cut and sewn into a lovely dress. She hadn't thought she'd ever wish to get married, but now the thought of being Caleb's wife made her smile.

He'd told her Charles had agreed to give her the piano as a wedding present. Caleb had kissed her and promised to drive her to town in the buggy on Sundays so she could receive proper lessons from the woman who played piano at the church. She'd laughed, telling him he didn't need to pay for the lessons. She said he just needed to let her get close enough to the piano so she could watch where the fingers go.

"Looks to be a doozy of a sunset," Charles said with a nod toward the sky.

As they neared the rise leading up to the bluff, the horses seemed on edge. As they topped the bluff, their agitation grew. They neared the turnoff leading to the valley, the brilliant sky stretching before them, magnificent in its beauty.

"Looks like the Lord has the whole sky lit up tonight," Charles said. "I hope your ma is looking out the window; she always appreciates a good sunset."

The horses shied and Charles shook the reins to get them to pick up the pace. As they rounded the bend, they each took a collective breath. In the midst of the fiery sunset was another, more unnatural glow.

The house was on fire.

Instantly, Charles snapped the reins and yelled for the horses to go. Against their wishes, he sent them towards the scorching blaze. Caleb leapt from the wagon even before it stopped. Stumbling, he picked himself up and raced towards the burning house. He screamed for his mother. She returned his call and Caleb ran inside, disappearing into the flames. Charles pulled the wagon to a stop, wrapped the reins over the side, and took off towards the house.

Anastasia stood in the wagon bed, voicelessly trying to make sense of the chaos before her. Charles had taken only a few steps when a tremendous crack filled the air. Instantly, the roof of the house let go, sending sparks soaring through the evening sky. Anastasia's screams filled the air, and for a brief moment, it looked as if a thousand fireflies had taken flight, clambering in different directions. Charles fell to his knees, his screams for mercy rising unanswered into the smoke-filled air.

This all proved too much for the horses, who darted forward in a panic sending Anastasia crashing against the buckboard. She scrambled to her knees, crawling forward towards the bench seat, clawing at the reins, which were still loosely draped over the side. Just as she caught hold of the leather, they were stripped from her hands. She debated jumping, but the wagon was going too fast. She remembered what happened to Mrs. Sina and Emily and was rethinking her decision when the wagon started slowing. It was then she realized she wasn't alone in the wagon.

"Whoa there. Easy now fellows," the stranger called to the horses. "That's it, then. Yes, yes, easy does it."

She wasn't sure where the man had come from or how he'd managed to get into the wagon. He wore a fine suit, which didn't seem appropriate for such a wild ride. Still, he obviously knew his way around horses and managed to get them settled in short order. The horses were lathered with sweaty foam when the stranger turned them back towards the house. He didn't ask her any questions, instead, he focused his energy on keeping the team calm as they neared the homestead.

When they arrived, all that remained were a few timbers standing amongst the fiery glow. As they approached, Anastasia cupped a hand over her mouth to keep the screams at bay. The man guided the horses next to the barn and pulled the wagon brake to keep them from running off again. Jumping from the wagon, he lifted his arms to help Anastasia to the ground.

"Are you all right?" the man asked once she was free of the wagon.

"They were in the house." Her words came out on a whisper. "Caleb and Mrs. Sina… they didn't come out."

He closed his eyes in response.

They heard crying and hurried to where Charles still knelt in the same spot she'd seen him fall. He looked up, his eyes wide with disbelief.

"They're gone." He licked his lips and turned his head towards the house. When he spoke, his voice was full of despair. "My family; they're all gone."

***

Anastasia stared out the window of the hotel watching

as people moved through the streets with unhurried ease. Strange how life could end for some and others were allowed to move on with their day oblivious to the sorrows of those around them.

It had been two days since the fire, and she'd yet to see or speak with Charles. The stranger ended up being a neighbor who lived further down the valley. He'd been on his way home from visiting his mother when he'd heard her screams and raced to the rescue, leaping from his horse and into the runaway wagon just to save her. He'd helped her and Charles into the wagon and drove them back to town. Some ladies had visited her the day before gifting her with a basket of food, a new set of clothes, and some ribbons for her hair. She'd thanked them and apologized for having no money with which to pay. They'd told her the church had taken a collection, saying it was the neighborly thing to do.

A knock at the door pulled her attention from the window. She hurried to see who it was and burst into tears upon seeing Charles. She wrapped her arms around his waist and cried. She stood there for several moments before realizing he'd not returned the embrace.

"May I come in?" His voice lacked emotion.

"Of course," she said, stepping out of the way.

"I came to say goodbye," he said without looking at her.

"Goodbye? I don't understand."

"The inspector said the fire was probably started by a lantern. Multiple ones, by the looks of things. I shouldn't have left her alone. She never did like the dark much." He shrugged. "Nothing to be done about it now. I've lost everything. My wife. My son. I reckon they've gone to be with Emily. I'll see them again someday, preferably sooner than later. I've nothing left to offer you."

She felt the fear knotting in her stomach. Where was she

to go? *She'd tell him about the baby. Then he'd have to let her stay.* "Mr. Charles, I…"

"I've sent a telegram to Mr. Swan," he said, cutting her off. "I reckon he'll be coming for you before too long. You'll stay here until he comes to collect you. The good people of the church will see you have what you need until then."

"But I want to stay with you," she pleaded. "Caleb wouldn't wish for me to go."

"Don't you know I can't stand to look at you, girl!" he said and turned away. "You're a reminder of what I've lost. I wouldn't be able to look at you without seeing my wife excitedly telling me we are gaining a new daughter. My son, eagerly planning his home for his new wife. You'd be a constant reminder of all I've lost, and in the end, I'd come to hate you. I'll not do that to you, girl. It's best you go with Mr. Swan and get yourself placed in a new home. It won't be for long. You're nearly grown up."

Tears rolled down her face as she watched him walk to the door. He placed his hand on the doorknob and hesitated. "I hope in time you'll forgive me. But you have to remember, it wasn't my idea to bring you here; it was Sina's, God rest her soul. It is she too who must bear some of the blame."

She wanted to plead with him and beg him to reconsider, but knew in that moment it wouldn't do any good. She'd seen that look before when her own mother cast her aside. It was the second time in her life she'd been evicted from her home. Only this time, she wasn't going alone.

Chapter Twenty-Nine

December 22, 1919

Anastasia sat in the chair, half dozing, when she heard the knock on her hotel door. A second, more insistent knock jarred her into action. She opened the door to find a messenger boy staring up at her. He handed her a slip of paper then hurried down the hall. She unfolded the paper and read the contents.

I'm waiting downstairs. Come join me. J. W. Swan.

Anastasia walked to the mirror to check her reflection and blinked uncaringly at the dried tearstains laced with black soot that trailed the length of her face. Her dress was much of the same, along with several rips and tears from the wayward wagon ride. She pulled her fingers through her hair in an attempt to settle the unruly strands, caught a tangle, and gave up. Except for going down the hall to use the water closet, she hadn't left her hotel room since her arrival four days prior. Not even to use the hotel bath. She realized she'd taken better care of herself when she was living on the street. She considered changing into one of the dresses she'd been given but decided against it, instead reaching for her coat to hide the stains. Dirty and torn, it hadn't fared much better. She made a halfhearted attempt to brush the dirt from the coat, before realizing she just didn't care.

She took her time descending the stairs, though the thought of seeing a friendly face held some appeal. Still, she knew Mr. Swan had come to persuade her to find another home, and she'd already made up her mind about that.

He was standing in the center of the lobby, hat in hand,

when she reached the bottom of the stairs. He smiled, then took in her appearance, and his mouth dropped. Though she promised herself she wouldn't cry, she burst into tears the moment she saw him. Until that moment, she'd thought all her tears had expended. He handed her his kerchief and waited for her to cry herself out.

"I'm sorry," she said, returning it to him.

"There, there, child, I would think something wrong with you if you didn't cry," Swan said, pocketing the soiled cloth. He looked her over but didn't make mention of her appearance. "When is the last time you ate?"

"The ladies from the church brought a few things. I ate a little." She'd forced herself to take a few bites after, amid her despair, she'd felt a tiny flutter from deep inside her belly. She wasn't certain the flutter was the baby, but she'd never felt anything like it before, so she thought maybe.

He looked her over once more and blew out a sigh. "Let's go to dinner, and you can tell me what happened."

They walked down Main Street and ducked into the first restaurant they came to. Swan asked to be seated in the back of the room so they could have a bit more privacy. She wondered if it was also because he was embarrassed to be seen with her. He waited until they'd ordered before asking for the particulars. Anastasia recounted what had happened, leaving out one tiny unborn detail.

"Don't you worry, we'll find you another place to live." He winked. "If we don't, Mrs. Swan and I will take you in ourselves."

"I don't want another home," she sniffed.

His brow creased. "I can't just leave you to your own resources, not that you have any as far as I can see."

She raised her gaze to his. "I want to go home."

"Now, Anastasia, that's impossible. Surely you are

aware that Mr. Payne wired me to come collect you."

"Not that home. I want to go back to New York City," she replied. Payne wasn't the only one who wanted to run from the memories.

Swan leaned forward in his chair. "I spend my days getting children out of that city. Why in heaven's name would you wish to go back?"

She wasn't sure she could answer that. Not to his satisfaction anyway. "I'm not a child."

"Won't you let me see what can be done? I'm sure it won't be difficult to find you another family."

She shook her head. "No. Please, Mr. Swan, I've given it a great deal of thought over the past few days. I cannot do this again. I cannot get my hopes up only to have them crushed again. I wish to go to the asylum. I met a girl there before I left. She said she works there. I wish to do the same."

He considered this for a moment. "You are certain that is your wish?"

"I am." She had her baby to think of, and try as she might, it was the only solution she could think of, knowing no one would welcome her into their home in her condition. She felt some guilt at not telling the man the whole truth, but he would learn of her deceit soon enough. By then, it would be too late.

Swan chatted throughout the meal, telling of things his wife, Hattie, had said or done, and regaling her with stories of the children he'd visited since last seeing her. He seemed to know she wasn't in the mood for talking and didn't wait for a reply. Instead, he would go straight into another story as soon as he finished the first.

"You'd better eat while you have the chance, Anastasia. The meals at the asylum are a bit more institutionalized."

She looked up in surprise. "Does that mean you'll send

me back?"

He pointed his fork at her. "I'll send a telegram to New York. If they are agreeable, which I imagine they'll be, I'll see you there myself."

She sighed, and for the first time in days, actually felt like eating.

***

March 6, 1920

Anastasia woke to the sounds of Corinna, one of the mistresses, turning on the overhead lights and clapping her hands loud enough for all to hear. Anastasia didn't mind rising early; she'd done it every day while living on the farm with the Paynes. What she did mind was the obnoxious screech Corinna used to wake the girls. She much preferred the rooster's crow. Though she wouldn't dare tell that to Corinna, who took her position of authority seriously. Only a few years older than some of the girls, Corinna always made it a point to let the girls know she was in charge. Jobs were hard to come by and even harder to keep with so many eager to work. Corinna, an orphan herself, had worked her way up to the position. She had a wicked temper and had fired girls for much less.

Dressed completely in black with her hair pulled into a tight bun, Corinna looked much older than her eighteen years. She walked through the room, nudging bunks and rousting the girls who lived in the special dorm reserved for the workers. "Time to greet the day, ladies. There are hungry mouths to feed."

Anastasia hurried from the bed, turning to shield the growing size of her stomach. While a few of the girls in the dorm knew of her condition, she'd been able to keep it from any of the mistresses thus far. She pulled her dress over her slip and added the apron, tying it loosely to camouflage the swell. She felt the baby move and smiled.

"What's so funny, Missy?" Corinna called out from the other side of the room.

"Nothing, Miss Corinna. I just remembered that today it is the sixth of March. That makes this my birthday," Anastasia answered in reply. It was true. She'd seen the date on the calendar in the kitchen the previous day. Not only was she surprised to learn the next day to be the day of her birth, but that she would have the birthday without any celebration. Mrs. Sina had made certain birthdays did not go by without ceremony, even though it was Anastasia who baked the cake. This birthday was to be even more special, as she and Caleb were to have been married by now. Her stomach clenched at the thought of both Caleb and Mrs. Sina. For a brief moment, she thought she would vomit. She brought her hand to her mouth, pretending to hide her smile, and held it there until the threat passed.

Corinna clapped her hands once more. "Everyone to the kitchen; the children will be expecting their morning meal."

Anastasia fell into line behind the others. Mr. Swan had seen to her placement in the kitchen, assuring the headmistress of Anastasia's wealth of knowledge when it came to food. He'd sung her praises so highly, the woman had no recourse but to give in. Anastasia liked the work well enough, though it had taken a bit for her to get used to working with others. In the end, she was grateful she wasn't alone in preparing the food when she'd discovered the number of children they were feeding.

Once in the kitchen, the girls went to their stations to begin morning breakfast preparations. While breakfast itself was simple, usually oatmeal and bread, it took a great deal of organization to feed hundreds of children each morning.

Anastasia worked with several other girls at the bread station. Bread-making was an ongoing job, as they offered fresh bread at both morning and evening meals. The dough had been left to rise overnight. They placed those loaves in the oven before starting the bread for the evening meal. She'd been standing at her station for several hours, when a sudden swift kick from the baby caught her off guard. Instinctively, she placed her hand onto her stomach, cupping the area where she'd felt the kick.

"Anastasia!" Corinna shrieked. "Come over here at once."

Anastasia glanced down and realized that she'd unwittingly showcased the bump she'd worked so hard to hide. *Nothing to be done about it now.*

"I'm waiting," The agitation in Corinna's voice was palpable. She turned to one of the younger girls. "Run, get the headmistress."

Not in a hurry to be disciplined, Anastasia took a moment to wipe the flour from her hands. When finished, she casually walked to where Corinna stood.

"Why, you little thief, the asylum gives you a job and a bed to sleep in, and this is how you repay them?" The girl's anger at being ignored was obvious in her tone. "Stealing food will not only get you fired, it will quite possibly get you thrown into prison."

Thief? So she hadn't seen her bulge. It didn't matter now. The girl wouldn't stop until she knew. Anastasia decided to have some fun with her. She'd never seen Corinna so angry. Instead of arguing, she simply smiled.

Corinna's eyes bugged, and some of the other girls laughed, which further infuriated Corinna, who turned a brilliant shade of red.

"Get back to work, all of you!" she said, whirling on the others. She turned back to Anastasia. "Do you think this is funny? Have you not heard a thing I've said? I'll see to it myself that the headmistress makes an example of you."

"Why, no, I don't find it funny at all. I actually find it most frustrating, as my dough will not rise properly if I don't tend to it," Anastasia replied.

For a moment, Corinna just stood there staring. When she failed to offer further comment, Anastasia decided to return to her station. As she turned to go, Corinna grabbed hold of her arm, twisting it as she pulled her back. It had been years since anyone had laid a hand on her. But in that moment, memories of Albert's abuse came bubbling to the surface, and something in her snapped. She yanked her arm free and punched the girl right in the nose. Corinna doubled her fist to retaliate when the headmistress grabbed her arm.

"What in the devil is going on in here?" the woman asked firmly.

"She punched me," Corinna said, hand to her nose, which was beginning to dribble blood. "She's stealing food, and I told her I would see her punished. She got angry and punched me."

The headmistress released Corinna and turned to Anastasia. "Is this true?"

"No, ma'am," Anastasia answered.

"Liar!" Corinna spat.

"That'll be enough from you," the headmistress said, raising her palm. She turned to Anastasia once more. "Which part isn't true?"

"Why, all of it to be sure. I wasn't stealing food. I was making bread. And the only reason I hit her is because she hurt my arm."

"Look under her dress," Corinna pressed.

"Are you hiding anything under your dress?" the headmistress asked.

"Yes, ma'am." Anastasia sighed.

"There, you see. I told you she was stealing food. You should have her locked up," Corinna gloated.

"Enough with the games, girl. Raise your dress," the headmistress ordered.

Anastasia stepped forward and lifted her dress, exposing her swollen belly for all to see. There were a few gasps from the girls who hadn't been privy to her secret. Even Corinna blinked her surprise. While Anastasia wished to gloat, the stern expression on the headmistress's face kept her from doing so.

The headmistress pulled herself taller and adjusted the waist of her skirt. "Corinna, find someone else to take Anastasia's station. She'll be coming with me. And for heaven's sake, clean yourself up before you get blood in the food."

***

Anastasia sat in the hallway outside the headmistress's office, waiting to learn her fate. It wasn't the way she'd envisioned spending the 16th anniversary of her birth, but she'd known the authorities would find out sooner or later. Still, she hadn't counted on there being such an uproar. *Seriously, what was one more child in a place where children were the main commodity?*

The door opened, and the headmistress motioned her into the room and onto a hardback chair. Sour-faced, she stood over Anastasia and delivered her sentence. "You'll be leaving here this afternoon. You'll go to a home for unwed mothers until after the baby is born."

That doesn't sound so bad. "Where will we be going after that?"

"There will be no 'we,'" the woman said unapologetically. "You have no job, no man to provide for you.

You'll not be permitted to keep it. After the birth, the baby will go to an asylum. A different one than you; it will be easier for you that way."

Anastasia felt a punch in her gut just as real as the one she'd delivered to Corinna. "But I do have a job. I work here. What do you mean I can't keep my baby? I am its mother. The baby will stay with me."

"You had a job. The job is no more. The law does not allow for a pregnant woman, or child, as in your case, to work. It just isn't done."

That's not fair. "Then I'll leave and take my baby with me."

The woman's face remained stoic. "Just where do you think you'll go? Onto the streets?"

"If I have to, then yes," Anastasia said, jutting her chin.

"And do what, then?" the woman asked. "Get a job? Who's going to hire a girl? Even if you get a job, you'll never be able to make enough money to provide for both yourself and a child. A moot point, as you'll not have anyone to watch after the baby while you are working."

"Then I'll find another way." Anastasia was on her feet now, pacing the room in search of answers.

"You can always do what the others do and sell your body for money. Is that what you want for your baby? A mother who's a harlot? You do that, and it won't be long until you have another baby to tend. And just what do you plan on doing with the children while you are lying there with your legs spread?" The woman's expression softened. "I wish I could tell you that is not the way of things, but I've seen it all too often."

"I won't allow it," Anastasia said, crossing her arms. "I won't let anyone take my baby."

The woman smiled a sympathetic smile. "I'm afraid it is not up to you."

Chapter Thirty

June 1920

It was near dawn when Anastasia decided to leave. The labor pains had started the evening prior, but, having lived on the streets for a time, she'd been afraid to leave. She'd wanted to leave days ago, but her friend Barbara had begged her to stay, as she was in the midst of giving birth to her own child. Anastasia had stayed, been witness to the birth, and cried along with the others after Barbara had failed to survive giving birth. One of the midwives said Barbara was too young. Anastasia tried not to let that worry her any, reminding herself she was two years older than the girl.

She tiptoed down the hallway, shoes in hand, careful not to make a sound. The pain was getting worse. It wouldn't be long before the baby pushed its way into the world. She snuck out the door and breathed a sigh of relief.

One step closer.

She'd tried to escape before but hadn't gotten very far before fear had her turning back. It was dark, and she didn't know the neighborhood, so she'd had some trouble finding her way back. All the houses looked the same. Then she'd seen the wrought-iron fence that set the house apart from the others.

This time was different, as it was her last chance at escape before the baby arrived. The tall iron gates were unlocked, same as before. They weren't really made to keep anyone inside, but more of a warning to those who passed by. Cold and shielding, as if saying *you do not wish to come in here;*

this is a place of sin. The only sin she and the others were guilty of was lying with a man, or as in her case, a boy old enough to do a man's deed.

The thought of Caleb made her blood run cold. No longer did she mourn the boy who'd left her to fight a winless battle. She was angry at him for leaving her. Angry at him for giving her something she'd always wanted and not living long enough to see that she was able to keep it. If they'd been married, things would be different. Society would've looked upon her as a widow with a child. Instead, she was now just another soiled child fixing to deliver yet another bastard into the world.

She placed a hand to her back as she made her way down the tree-lined street. It was getting harder to walk; she'd waited much too long. She paused to wait for the pain to pass, wondering in her mind where she thought she was going. She'd been so intent on escaping when the pains began that she hadn't considered where she'd go once she did. She turned and looked over her shoulder. The iron fence was still in view. Tears streamed down her face as she realized she had no recourse but to return.

By the time she reached the gates, the pain was unbearable. It wouldn't be long before her baby arrived.

Her baby. Not for long.

As another pain shot through her body, she grabbed on to the unbending steel and screamed her sorrow for all to hear.

***

Anastasia lay in bed looking up at the ceiling, wishing it would fall and crush the breath from her body. The door opened, and Miss Rebecca, one of the house mothers, entered, bringing with her a tray of food. A much too cheerful woman with dull brown hair, she smiled as she sat the tray across Anastasia's lap. There was a small glass vase on the edge of the tray, which held a single flower, a round black circle lined with brilliant yellow petals. For a moment, it looked as if the flower was smiling at her, taunting her, as if saying, *here's your prize for a job well done.*

Anastasia slapped the vase from the tray, sending it to the floor in a crushing blow. She looked over the side, narrowing her eyes at the flower, which had survived unscathed.

Miss Rebecca reached into her pocket, pulled out a small metal bell, and clanged it from side to side. A second later, the door opened, and a young girl poked her head inside. Anastasia recognized the girl as Trudy, one of several housemaids that worked in the home. Miss Rebecca pointed to the mess, and the girl left without a word.

"I believe you scared the neighbors this morning. We had the police come to see that nothing was amiss," the woman said, ignoring her actions. She moved to the window, pulling back the curtains.

"Leave them shut!" Anastasia ordered when the sunlight poured in. She reached for the tray, intending to send it to the floor, when the woman spoke.

"You get one free pass. Any more outbursts, and I'll call for the doctor to give you a shot to calm you down."

Trudy returned broom in hand and busied herself cleaning the mess. She kept her eyes lowered, making sure not to make eye contact with Anastasia.

"I want to see my baby," Anastasia said.

"I'm afraid that isn't possible," Miss Rebecca said softly.

"I want to see my son," Anastasia said more firmly. She watched as the woman cast an accusing glance towards the girl, who shook her head, leaving Anastasia no doubt she'd guessed correctly.

"You agreed to the conditions of your stay when you first arrived," the woman replied.

"I was told the rules. I never agreed to abide by them."

"You're making this much more difficult than it needs to be. Things went well with your delivery. Someday, when you are duly married, you shall have another child."

"I shall never get married. I want the boy I birthed today."

"Not possible. The boy has already been removed from the building." The woman must have realized she'd confirmed Anastasia's deduction as she turned a bright shade of red. "I mean, child. I was just saying that as you seem to have made up your mind. Regardless, it is our custom to remove the child as soon as possible. It does no good for the girls to hear a baby's cry."

Miss Rebecca turned toward the dresser and opened a drawer. As soon as she turned away, Trudy looked up and mouthed the word "boy."

"Hurry up there, girl. I need your help with the binding," Miss Rebecca fussed. Stepping beside the bed, she moved the tray to the table.

Trudy finished, collecting the glass, and dumped it into the wastebasket. She then hurried to wipe the water with a towel. Trudy offered the flower to Anastasia then shoved it into her pocket when she declined, and moved to the other side of the bed.

"We're going to bind your breasts. It will prevent your milk from coming in. You won't need it," Miss Rebecca said when Anastasia opened her mouth to object. "You'll do best to leave the sheets in place. It'll be much less painful for you."

With that, the two went to work wrapping what looked

to be long strips of bedsheet tightly around Anastasia's breasts. When they were finished, the woman used safety pins to hold the wrap in place.

"That will be all for now, Trudy," Miss Rebecca said, dismissing the girl. She waited for Trudy to leave before returning the tray to the bed and addressing Anastasia once more. "You'll stay in this room until tomorrow, and then we'll decide what's to be done with you. I'll leave your tray for now. Do try to eat something. I'll have Trudy come collect it later."

Anastasia pushed the tray away the moment she closed the door, her mind a jumble of inner turmoil. How could she even think of eating when she couldn't even feed her baby? She thought back to the anguish in Sharon's cries when she'd been unable to feed Tobias at first. For the first time, she could truly identify with her mother. She pictured Sharon standing there wailing her anguish, and her anger boiled. At least, in the end, the woman had been able to nurse her son. She pushed her mother's image away, refusing to identify with the woman who'd sent her away. It was all her fault. If she hadn't sent her out into the streets in the first place, she wouldn't be sitting here mourning the loss of her son. Rage boiled inside, and she threw the tray across the room.

Anastasia was still seething when the door opened. Trudy's gaze settled on the new mess as she stepped inside. She closed the door and once again cleared the remnants of Anastasia's anger.

"I'm sorry," Anastasia said when the girl turned to leave.

Trudy turned her eyes wide. "You needn't apologize."

"Well, why not?"

"I'm just doing my job, miss."

"No, your job was to take the tray to the kitchen, not pick it up from the floor."

"It happens a lot," Trudy said with a shrug.

It was Anastasia's turn to be surprised. "It does?"

"Oh, yes. Not for all; some are pleased to be rid of their dirty secret. But for some, like yourself, it becomes too much to handle. I would think I'd do the same if my boy were taken from me," Trudy said and opened the door to leave.

Anastasia leaned forward. "So it was a boy? Did you see him? Tell me what he looked like."

Trudy took a step back, "Oh no, miss. I've already said too much. If Miss Rebecca finds I talked to you, she'll send me into the streets myself."

Anastasia smiled and patted the bed beside her, hoping to gain the girl's trust. "I won't tell. Please, won't you sit for a moment?"

Trudy wavered for a moment as if considering it. Then she turned and bolted from the room.

Anastasia pulled up her gown, unfastened the pins, and pulled the binding from her breasts, stuffing the evidence in the bottom of her clothes bin. She'd find a way to get to Trudy, and when she did, she would find her son.

***

Anastasia was dressed and standing by the window when she heard voices outside her room. She tiptoed to the door and pressed her ear to the wood.

"Trudy, run fetch a tray for Anastasia. She'll be leaving us today, and we cannot send her away hungry."

Frustrated, Anastasia hurried back to the window and waited for the door to open. She'd wanted to get Trudy alone in hopes of forcing the girl to tell all she knew.

"You're up," Miss Rebecca said, sounding surprised. "How are you feeling?"

"You mean besides angry?" Anastasia asked.

The woman blew out a sigh. "Yes, besides that?"

"A little sore, but I'll get by."

"I know you're upset. We see it sometimes."

"Only sometimes?"

There was a knock on the door, and Trudy entered. She stepped up beside Anastasia and placed the tray on the side table. Anastasia stepped aside as she left the room.

"Anastasia, most girls who come to us come on their own looking for a place to hide out and birth their baby without anyone knowing. It's a way for them to save their reputation so they can go on and marry without being scorned. Occasionally, we have someone like yourself who has formed an attachment to the thought of being a mother. Most of the time, it is because the girl's mother didn't give her the love she deserved and she wants to do better for her own child. Is that the way it is with you?"

Anastasia hadn't considered why she wanted her baby, but that sounded as good of a reason as any, so she shook her head.

"Then you have to believe me when I tell you that your baby is in a position to get the life you want for it. He—yes, your child is a boy—has been placed in a good home, where he is well-loved. He'll grow up happy, and he'll get an education. Don't you like that? Doesn't it please you that your child will learn to read?"

"My baby belongs with me. I'll teach him how to read. Just like my mother taught me," Anastasia spat.

"Your mother," the woman said softly. "Would that be the same mother that sent you away when she couldn't afford to put food in your belly? The walls in this place are thin; I heard you telling Barbara how you'd come to live on the streets. What is your mother's name, Anastasia?"

Anastasia gritted her teeth, refusing to answer.

"Tell me about your mother, child. What was she like?"

Anastasia turned away. She didn't want to talk about her mother.

"Did she sing to you when you were little? I bet she used to brush your hair and tell you stories about when she was young. You loved her, didn't you, Anastasia?"

Tears rolled down Anastasia's cheeks as she thought of how nice Sharon used to be.

"Then something happened that changed all of that. Didn't it?" Miss Rebecca pressed.

Yes. It was true, all of it.

"She was different, and you began to wonder if she still loved you. And one day, she did the unimaginable; she said you weren't welcome there and that you'd have to go. Think about that day, Anastasia. Remember it as if she were standing here now. Did you see her face when she told you those words or was she turned away like you are now? Turned so you wouldn't see the tears that burned like hot coals when she knew that to save any of her children, she would have to sacrifice one. Your mother loved you, Anastasia, but she knew she had to release you in order to give any of you a chance at life. She had to make a hard choice. The same choice you yourself have to make now. The choice to let your child go so he can have the life you're not able to provide for him. It's either that or to try to hang on to him while you figure it out. If you do that, you will ensure he grows up hating you. Is that what you want, Anastasia? For your son to hate you?"

Tears streamed down Anastasia's face. Her silent turmoil turned into uncontrolled sobs as she crumpled to the floor and pulled her knees to her chest. It was at that moment she knew she had no choice but to let her son go.

Chapter Thirty-One

Anastasia was taken to an asylum across town via motorcar. The trip should have excited her, as it was her first ride in one. Instead, she merely placed her head against the windowpane and watched the streets go by without caring. It reminded her of the time she stood in the hotel watching out the window after Caleb and Mrs. Sina died. Once again, everyone was oblivious to her sorrow.

Like the home she just came from, the asylum was situated within a residential neighborhood, but unlike the Home for Wayward Angels, which blended into its surroundings, this building stood five stories high and took up nearly half a city block. The car pulled to the curb, and the driver waited for Anastasia to exit before leaving. Her arrival was unceremonial. There was no one to ensure she went inside. No one to hold her hand as she walked the concrete path to uncertainty. She had with her the clothes on her back, a letter of introduction, and a small cloth sack with what little belongings she owned. The decision was hers whether to go inside or simply turn and keep walking. In the end, she walked the path, pushed open the massive door, and breathed a sigh of relief when the door slammed shut behind her. Like it or not, she was home, and something about the cold stone walls felt welcoming.

Her shoes echoed in the empty hallway as she followed the signs to the office. Reaching her destination, she knocked on the door. She was just about to knock for a second time when the door opened, and a stern-looking woman with her hair pulled tight against her head motioned her in.

Anastasia handed the woman the introduction letter and watched her long black skirt whisk along the floor as she took a seat behind the desk. She tested the wax with the nail of her thumb, then gave up and used a thin knife to break the seal. The woman frowned as she read, making Anastasia wish she'd read the letter herself before arriving. Uncomfortable with the woman's glances, she turned and took in the room's décor. Not that there was much to take in, as the room was dark and unadorned. Yet, somehow, the room with its richly polished wood walls and tall windows flanked by heavy brown curtains fit the woman seated before her. Both seemed to say, *don't mess with me, for if you do, you will not win*. If not for the breeze that floated in through the open windows, the room would have proved absolutely stifling.

"I am Headmistress LaRue. You will address me simply as Headmistress. I see you were sent to us by the Home of Wayward Angels."

Anastasia nodded.

"Your introduction letter says you wish to work here. I'm afraid I do not have any paying jobs at this time. You're old enough to help oversee some of the younger children if you'd like. There will be no pay, mind you, but if you wish to stay, something will come up eventually. In return for helping out, you'll have a clean bed and food. You'll get a few more privileges. See that you do not abuse our kindness. If you agree to that arrangement, I will call Clara to help get you settled."

Not having any other choices, Anastasia nodded her agreement.

"Very well, then," the woman said, rising from her desk. She opened the door and rang a bell hanging on the wall outside the door. A moment later, a girl hurried into the room.

Anastasia wondered where the girl had come from, as

she hadn't seen anyone in the hallway.

The girl seemed to be about the same age as she and wore a blue gingham dress. She cast a quick glance at Anastasia when she entered then stood ramrod straight in front of the desk. "Yes, Headmistress?"

"This is Anastasia. She just arrived here from the Home of Wayward Angels. They've seen to her hygiene there, so she will not need to get dipped. Like yourself, she'll be helping with some of the younger children. See that she gets a change of clothes and a bed and take her to Mistress Flora to get assigned. Tell her anything but the fourth floor."

"I have a change of clothes," Anastasia said, holding up the small bag.

"Do as I said, Clara, and dispose of the rest. That will be all. Close the door behind you," the woman said with a wave of the hand.

"You'll do best not to talk back to any of the mistresses, especially Headmistress," Clara said once they'd taken several steps.

Anastasia followed the girl down the hallway, watching her ponytail sway with each step. She moved up beside the girl. "What's on the fourth floor?"

"You'll find it best not to ask too many questions," Clara replied. "The matrons don't like it when we do."

"I didn't think you are a matron," Anastasia replied.

"I'm not, nor do I wish to be, but I know to keep my questions to myself."

"Why don't you wish to be?" Anastasia asked, ignoring her.

"Because I'm going to get married someday, and when I do, I'll be leaving here."

"Why would you want to get married?"

Clara stopped walking and looked at her as if she'd said

something wrong. "I'm a girl; it's what we do."

"I'm not ever going to get married."

"You will if you ever wish to have a child." The girl realized what she'd said and started walking once more. "I'm sorry."

"It's nothing," Anastasia lied.

Clara pushed open a door marked "washroom" and stepped inside. Anastasia followed her into the room, jumping when the door slammed behind her. Even though the bank of windows along the far wall were open, the room was stifling hot. Anastasia looked around for the source of the heat and saw a large black stove with steaming kettles sitting on top. Several children were bathing in large metal tubs with a healthy-sized woman hovering over them. Clara ignored their stares and approached another woman on the far side of the room.

"She's come from the Home of Wayward Angels. Headmistress said she doesn't need a dip."

The woman pushed past Clara and reached for Anastasia, twining her fingers in her long locks. Anastasia made an attempt to wiggle free, but the woman's grip held fast, pulling her towards one of the large windows. Anastasia dropped the bag she'd been carrying and grabbed the woman's wrist.

"Be still," the woman commanded. "I'll have no bugs in my building."

Anastasia did as told, quelling her anger as the woman rooted through her hair.

"You'll do," the woman said, releasing her hair.

Anastasia pressed her fingertips to her scalp to relieve the pain and glared at the woman. Ignoring her, the woman picked up the bag Anastasia had dropped. She looked inside and wrinkled her nose. Without as much as a word of apology, she walked across the room, opened the belly of the stove, and tossed the bag and its contents inside.

Seething, Anastasia took a step forward, stopping when Clara grabbed her by the arm and warned her off.

The woman returned and appraised Anastasia wordlessly. Stepping around her, she walked to the shelf and removed several items before returning and handing them to Anastasia. "Put these on and leave the ones you are wearing on the floor."

"I don't have bugs," Anastasia whispered when the woman was out of earshot.

"No, because if you did, you'd be in there," Clara said, nodding towards the tubs.

"I wouldn't mind a bath," Anastasia said, then swallowed in disbelief as the woman approached one of the tubs, lifted the child's hair, and snipped it at the base of her head. She then moved to the stove and tossed the locks inside, totally oblivious to the child's tears. Anastasia hurried to change before the woman returned, turning to hide her engorged breasts. It was not the first time she'd regretted not leaving the binding in place. When she was finished, she raised her arms and pulled up her hair, squinting against the pain. She tied it with an identical bow as what Clara wore. Not surprising, as the rest of her outfit was also the same.

Clara picked up a set of linens from the counter and motioned for Anastasia to follow. "If you want to work here, you'll do best not to cross the matrons."

"She didn't have to pull my hair. I would have walked to the window if she'd only asked."

"A lot of the children who come in here do not speak English," Clara said by way of explanation.

"Well, I do. She didn't even ask."

"Here are your sheets," Clara said, ignoring the comment. "I'll show you where we sleep and then take you to meet Mistress Flora."

The room ended up being a dorm room on the second floor, much like the one she'd slept in at the Children's Aid Society. Only this room was somewhat smaller, with half the amount of beds.

"The girls have a separate dorm down the hall, but since we are helpers, we sleep in here. There are others you shall meet them in time. The water closet and rain shower are through that door," Clara said and pointed.

"What's a rain shower?"

"I guess you haven't used a rain shower before. It's easy; you stand under it while the water rains down on you." Clara laughed. "I don't have to explain how to use the water closet, do I?"

"No, I've used them before. Although I must admit, I missed them when I lived in the valley."

"I've never heard of that place."

"It's not a place, not like a town anyway. It's what they called the place where our farm was."

Clara's eyes grew wide, and she sank onto the bed. "You've lived on a farm?"

"Yes," Anastasia said, joining her on the bed.

"Did you have chickens?"

"They weren't really mine, but we had them. We even had a goose and a rooster." Anastasia smiled, remembering how scared she'd been of Jed.

"I don't understand. If you were happy there, why are you here?"

The memory subsided as she told Clara about going out on the train and gave her an abbreviated story of what happened to bring her back.

"Is that how you got your scar? Being tossed about in the wagon?"

Anastasia touched her hand to her face. She hadn't thought about her scar in ages. "No, I fell on a broken jar when I was young."

"Oh, no, that story will never do," Clara said, waving her hands. "You want the kids in here to be afraid of you. We must think of something better."

"Why do I want the kids to be afraid of me?"

"Why, so they'll do what you tell them, of course." Clara placed a finger alongside her head as in thought. A moment later, she shook the finger in the air. "I've got it. We shall tell everyone you were in a knife fight. We'll tell them that all you got was this small scar."

"It's not so little," Anastasia said, tracing the scar once again.

"Ah, but it is compared to the one you gave the person you were fighting."

"Who shall I tell them I was fighting?"

"That's the brilliant part; you won't have to. They'll be so scared of you, they'll be too afraid to ask."

Anastasia still wasn't sure why she needed the story but agreed to go along to appease her new friend.

"We must go," Clara said, scooting from the bed. "I've got to take you to Mistress Flora. As long as you do as she says, you won't have any trouble with her. Same with Mrs. Gretchen. She sounds like she's yelling all the time, but I think it's mostly because she speaks in German."

"I don't speak German. How will I know what she's saying?"

"Just nod your head a lot and do what everyone else does," Clara replied.

"Clara," Anastasia said as they reached the stairwell, "What's upstairs?"

"The boy's dorm is on the third floor," Clara said with

a smile.

"What about the fourth floor?" Anastasia asked, remembering Headmistress' words.

"Nothing to concern yourself about right now," Clara said, dismissing her question.

Clara paused in front of a door, knocked once, then opened the door. Two women turned and stared at them. Neither looked pleased with being interrupted.

"What is it, girl?" an older woman with white hair asked.

"I'm sorry. I didn't mean to interrupt. We have a new girl. Headmistress told me to bring her to you."

The woman looked at Anastasia then cast a glance to the woman with whom she'd been speaking. "It's late. Show her around, and I'll deal with her tomorrow."

"Something's amiss," Clara said as soon as she closed the door. "It's not like her to send the new girls away without assigning them a duty."

Anastasia didn't mind being told to wait. Her milk was in, and her breasts were beginning to feel sore.

***

Anastasia rolled over in bed and was instantly awake. Her breasts were full and uncomfortable to the touch. She placed her hands on them to ensure they weren't hard or hot to the touch. They weren't, and she breathed a sigh of relief, as Mrs. Johnston had told Sharon that was something to watch for. At the moment, they were just full of milk with no way to empty them. She lay there for a moment, wondering who was feeding her son and hoping it was someone who held him close and spoke to him as he ate. *This is not helping.* Her thoughts drifted to Della, the milk cow they'd had in the barn, and she remembered one of the few times she'd had to milk her. Caleb had shown her how to place her hand on the cow's teat just so and squeeze to release the milk. She'd laughed when it worked, and he'd stolen a kiss. It was the first time he'd done so. His image came to mind and she quickly pushed it away. She closed her eyes and concentrated on how she'd used her hands to express the milk, mimicking the motion on her own breast. After several tries, it worked, leaking out onto the covers. She got out of bed thinking to go to the water closet to express some of the milk. She saw the light was on and realized someone else was awake. Not wishing to be caught, she took a towel and went into the stairwell instead. Just as she sat on one of the steps, she heard a door open, followed by footsteps in the stairwell above. A young girl hurried down the stairs, stopping when she came upon Anastasia unaware.

"You gave me a fright," the girl said, clutching her chest. Blonde hair pulled high, she was fully dressed in the same gingham dress and apron that seemed to be the standard dress code for all the girls. Anastasia hadn't met the girl yet, and she wondered what she was doing up so late.

"I couldn't sleep," Anastasia said by way of excuse.

"Aye, I wish I had time to sleep," the girl replied.

"Why are you up so late?"

"I work on the fourth floor," the girl said as if that explained everything. "I must go; one of the babes won't take to the nipple and is having a devil of a time."

The girl rushed off without another word. Anastasia listened as her footsteps grew further away. A door opened, slammed shut again, and the stairwell was silent once more. Anastasia pulled herself up, her task forgotten. With trembling legs, she climbed the forbidden stairs.

Chapter Thirty-Two

Anastasia opened the heavy door and peeked inside the vacant hallway. No surprises; it was the same as the corridors on the first and second floors. While she hadn't seen the third floor, she was fairly certain it was also the same. White walls that flowed seamlessly to the matching tile floor, the only hint of color came from the occasional framed picture and large red crocks spaced evenly along the hallway.

She'd asked one of the mistresses at the Children's Aid Society about the crocks and was told they were water crocks only to be used in case of a fire. The mistress seemed agitated at being asked such a simple question, but Anastasia had found them fascinating. Especially when the woman had told her that every building in the city had them. She'd thought to argue with the woman and tell her they hadn't had them in the Triangle Shirtwaist Factory but decided against it. She didn't like talking about that, as she still had dreams of being locked inside with the flames dancing around her. Still, the crocks fascinated her, and she'd wondered at the time if something so simple could have made a difference at the Shirtwaist Factory, thinking perhaps maybe they would. The papers had said the fire might have started in a wastebasket; sad to think that all those deaths might have been prevented if only for a crock of water. She wondered if Mrs. Sina had tried to put out the flames in the house.

She shook off the memory, eased the door shut, and stepped inside the hallway, taking care to be quiet. She walked down the corridor, tried the first door she came to, and found it locked. She repeated the process several times before finding a doorknob that turned when she tested it. She opened the door a hair and peeked into the room, which was lit with a soft glow. As her eyes adjusted to the light, she sucked in her breath. Inside the room in five single rows stood lace-trimmed bassinets. Stepping closer, she discovered each bassinet filled with a sleeping infant. She moved further inside the room and stood over one of the bassinets, eyes misting, as she watched the tiny baby suckle in its sleep. Though it was fast asleep, the baby smiled as if sensing she were near. It was almost too much. Instantly, she felt the need to gather the child in her arms and flee with her new prize. There were so many; surely they wouldn't miss just one. *Where would I go?*

She was just reaching for the infant when she heard the angry wails of another. She frantically searched the bassinets, trying to find the source of the cries, but all the babies in the room were sleeping peacefully. She walked to the back of the room, pushed open the door, and saw yet another bassinet inside. Just one, inside a room without light. She flipped on the light and hurried to the bassinet. The infant was small and looked not to be more than a day or two old. Although its cries were insistent, the infant seemed weak. W*hy are you here all alone? Are you scared or hungry? Or, perhaps a bit of both.* For an instant, the cries reminded her of another baby, young Tobias when his mother's milk was not yet able to satisfy him. The memory caught her short. She hadn't thought of her brother in some time.

Lying next to the infant was a glass bottle with a brown rubber nipple attached to the top. She paused, staring at the impersonal device. She'd thought that maybe they would've found a wet nurse to feed her own son; now, she wasn't so sure. Tears welled in her eyes, and she pushed them away. *No, Miss*

Sherry A. Burton

Rebecca said he is with a family who will love him. She'd not think of him this way.

"You're hungry, aren't you little one?" she said, hovering over the bassinet. *Why is no one here to care for you?* She thought about the girl she'd met in the stairwell and wondered if perhaps she'd gone to get help. *But he needs help now.*

Anastasia reached inside the bassinet and picked up the bottle. Instantly, her nipples tingled, as if reminding her they were there. *Could I? My breasts are so full, it would be such a shame to waste the milk.* She thought of the woman across the hall in their tenement building and how she'd used her milk to feed Tobias before her mother's milk came in. *Caroline didn't even want to feed him; Mrs. Johnston made her come. I really don't mind. Surely it wouldn't be wrong to give the baby some of my milk.* She looked around to make sure she was alone, then unbuttoned her nightdress and lifted the baby to her breast. It took a moment for the infant to latch on, but when it did, it suckled with eager gulps. She eased onto the rocking chair, taking care the baby didn't lose its grip. The baby closed its eyes in satisfied bliss, drinking for several moments before slowing. She shifted the child to her other breast, both of them sighing their content.

She closed her eyes, and for a moment, it was her son feeding at her breast. If she dared to imagine further, she could almost envision Caleb standing over her, smiling his pride. *Almost.* The infant stopped suckling, and she realized it had fallen asleep. She opened her eyes, revealing the concrete walls, a stark reminder that this wasn't her son, and Caleb was dead. She wouldn't be taking the child home with her, as this place was now her home.

She placed the infant in her lap, covered her empty breasts, and buttoned the buttons to her nightdress. She reached and pulled up the lace, exposing the basket under the bassinet, pleased to see a fresh stack of white cloths. She pulled a cloth free from the stack, lifted the infant's sleeping dress, unfastened the pins, and smiled. *So you are a boy after all.* Placing the pins in her mouth as Sharon had shown, she carefully changed the boy's diaper, swaddled him in a light blanket, and returned him to the bassinet. She picked up the bottle, thinking to rinse it. She'd just turned as the girl she'd met in the hall returned.

"What are you doing here?" the girl asked, blinking her surprise.

Anastasia hid the still full bottle behind her back. "You said there was a problem. I used to help my mother with my brothers, and I wanted to see if I could help."

"You got him to eat?" The girl sounded surprised.

Anastasia looked toward the boy. "Oh yes. It took him a moment to figure it out, but he drank just fine. He soiled his diaper, so I changed that as well."

"Oh good; we thought we'd lose him. He's so small. He's been refusing to take to the nipple and hasn't eaten anything since he arrived yesterday."

Yesterday? Could it be? She already knew the answer, but she had to ask. "He came in yesterday? Do you know from where?"

The girl shook her head. "No, they don't tell us that. I only know that he arrived with his sister. It's not often we get twins. Mostly the parents will keep one and give the other away."

"A sister," Anastasia repeated, the disappointment showing in her voice. Though Miss Rebecca had said her son had been adopted, she'd thought that just maybe, like her, he'd been brought here instead. It would've explained why the headmistress had told Clara to keep her from the fourth floor.

"Oh, not to worry, his sister is a healthy one. She

must've been born first, as she's a bit larger and is not afraid to drink from the rubber nipple."

A baby's cries rang out from the other room. "Oh, I have to go; it's going to have the lot of them screaming if I don't hurry."

"Go. I'll rinse out the bottle." Anastasia moved to the sink and emptied the contents of the bottle. While she hated to waste the milk, she didn't feel guilty, having fed the baby. She rinsed the nipple and tube, setting them on their side to dry.

The girl returned with the crying infant and handed the baby to Anastasia without asking. Anastasia gently bounced the infant in her arms as she followed the girl into the small kitchen area. The girl pulled a bottle from the icebox and placed it in a pan on the stove. "Have you ever heated baby milk before?" she asked, turning to Anastasia.

"No," Anastasia said softly.

"You don't want to let it get too hot." She waited a moment, then pulled the bottle from the pan and tested it on the crook of her arm. "You test it here, or on your wrist. If it doesn't burn, then it's okay to give. Do you want to feed her?"

Anastasia looked at the bottle and shook her head. Nonplussed, the girl took the infant and settled into the rocking chair and placed the rubber nipple into the infant's mouth.

"We bring them in here when they're fussy. It keeps them from waking the whole room. If the boy there does well, we'll move him in with the others tomorrow."

Anastasia sank onto a low stool. "How do you tell them apart?"

"They have names sewn in their gowns. He," she pointed to the bassinet of the infant Anastasia just nursed, "doesn't have his name sewn in his clothes, mostly because he wouldn't eat and the mistresses didn't think he'd survive."

Anastasia felt bad for the boy; he'd only eaten because

she'd offered him her breast. *What would happen to him tomorrow, or the day after that?*

"Sometimes, it's their real name. Sometimes, they arrive without names, and we get to name them. Funny, he came with a name, but his sister didn't. I still ain't figured that one out."

Anastasia started to ask the baby's name, but the girl continued talking, and she didn't wish to interrupt her.

"During the day, there are others who help, but at night, I'm mostly alone. I needed a break from all the crying, so I popped downstairs to have a smoke. Don't tell anyone. They wouldn't be happy to hear I left the babies alone. Speaking of names, mine's Ella. What's yours?"

"Anastasia. You smoke?"

Ella laughed. "Don't look so surprised. A lot of us girls smoke."

"Where do you get your cigarettes?"

This produced another laugh. "We've got our ways. You ask a lot of questions. You're not going to squeal on me, are you?"

"Of course not. I just thought maybe I might want a smoke is all."

The girl raised her eyebrows. "Do you smoke?"

It was Anastasia's turn to laugh. "No, but I might if I had a cigarette."

Ella held the bottle with her chin, reached into her blouse, pulled out a pack of cigarettes, and tossed them to Anastasia. "There's only two left; keep em. I've got more. Don't let the mistresses catch you with 'em. They'll take them away and keep 'em for themselves. You want to smoke, you go out the back door. There's a rock on the corner of the porch; make sure to use it to prop open the door or you'll get locked outside."

Anastasia put the cigarettes in her pocket and stifled a yawn. It had been a long day made longer by the fact that she'd recently given birth. "I should be going."

Ella pulled the bottle from the baby's mouth, placed the baby on her shoulder, and patted her back. "Thanks for the help with the kid. If you ever have trouble sleeping, you know where to find me."

Anastasia stood, stretched her arms overhead, and turned to leave. Her fingers lingered on the doorknob, and she cast one last look over her shoulder to the baby boy she'd nursed, hoping come daylight, they could get him to eat.

"Don't you worry about him," Ella said as if reading her mind. "You did a great job. Now that you got him eating, little Franky will be just fine."

Chapter Thirty-Three

Anastasia stared at the ceiling willing herself to go to sleep. While she'd been sleepy when she left the baby ward, she still hadn't managed to fall asleep. She kept thinking about the babies and wondering what would become of the little boy who'd tugged at her heartstrings. That in itself caused her grief, as she felt in worrying about the child, she was being unfaithful to the child she'd birthed. *He's with his new mother now and doesn't need me anymore. The child upstairs needs me.* Her inner turmoil continued until at last she drifted off to sleep.

"Anastasia, it's time to wake. You sleep like the dead. I've called for you three times," Clara said once she opened her eyes. "Hurry and dress so I can take you to Mistress Flora. Hopefully, she'll be assigning you a job today."

"What is your assignment?" Anastasia asked, sitting up.

"I'm a runner."

Anastasia pulled her dress over her head. "I don't think I would like that much. I don't like to run."

"I don't actually run, not very much anyway. I do errands for Headmistress and some of the other mistresses. And I watch for the new kids to come in. Most of the time, they can't read the signs, so I take them to meet Headmistress. After she meets with them, I show them where to go."

"Where do the kids come from?" While she knew how she'd gotten there, she wasn't sure about the rest. There were so many.

"Everywhere," Clara said with a shrug. "Some are

picked up on the street. Some are dropped off by their mothers or fathers. Some come as babies and never know who their mothers are. Some, like you, come when they are much older."

"What about you? How did you come to be here?"

"I've lived here all my life," Clara said with a shrug. "That's why I don't want to stay after I get older. I've read so many books that talk about beautiful places, and I want to see those places for myself."

"I haven't read in forever," Anastasia said longingly.

"You went to school?" Clara sounded surprised.

"For a while."

"We have classrooms here, but not a real school. What was it like?"

"It was okay. The teacher was always busy with the other kids."

"So you can only read a little?" Clara sounded disappointed.

"No, I'm a good reader. My mother was a teacher. She taught me how to read."

Clara smiled. "We need to go see Mistress Flora."

"What kind of work do you think she will give me?"

Another smile. "Maybe she'll have you work in the washroom."

"You mean with the lady that pulls hair?" Anastasia didn't like the sound of that.

"Don't worry. I was poking fun at you. Mistress Eleanora and Mistress Alma prefer to work alone. Just remember, if they put you anywhere around the children, you mustn't let them see how nice you truly are. If you do, they'll never listen to you. I've seen mistresses fired because the children didn't do as they say."

They pushed open the door to the stairwell, and it was all Anastasia could do to walk down the stairs. Her body ached to return to the baby ward to see how the little boy was faring. It didn't help that her breasts were once again full of milk.

They heard a door open from above, followed by a loud murmur. Anastasia stopped to see what the commotion was. The murmur grew louder until she realized it was whispers of excited children.

"Quick, before we get stuck in the stairwell with the lot of them." Clara started running down the stairs without waiting for Anastasia to answer.

Anastasia tried to keep pace, but the quick steps proved too much. She was still tender from giving birth, and her engorged breasts did not welcome the added movement. The whispers came louder, and she knew the children were nearly upon her. She pressed against the wall, catching her breath as the children filed past three deep. The boys wore white button-up shirts, dark pants that stopped at the knee, black socks, and shoes. With the exception of when they were eating and sleeping, the boys wore black slouchy caps. It was the same thing with the girls, who all wore the same blue gingham dresses, white aprons, white stockings, and large blue bows in their hair. Several of the children turned away the second she made eye contact; others stared as if she was a total anomaly. A little boy pointed and said something in a language she didn't understand. His words were met with laughter from the boys around him. It was then she realized they were laughing at her scar. She raised her hand towards her face, thinking to shield it from further scrutiny. Just before touching her face, she remembered Clara's words. Something came over her, and instead of hiding her scar, she bent her fingers as if they were claws and made the ugliest face she could summon. The children shrieked, their laughter forgotten as they pushed into the children ahead of them in an effort to get away from her. Feeling emboldened, she met every stare with a solemn glare of her own.

"You should've run when you had the chance," Clara said when she finally reached the first floor. "I heard some of the kids whispering about you. That's good. I'll make sure to tell some of the older children about your fight. It won't take long before the children know to stay clear of you. We'll get some mush, and then we'll go see Mistress Flora."

"Won't she be upset I'm taking my time?"

"Not if she sees you are with me," Clara replied.

***

Mush ended up being another term for plain oatmeal served with warm bread. While edible, it considerably lacked flavor. Anastasia wished she could sprinkle it with sugar or maybe a dab of honey. Then she remembered her time on the streets, the hunger she'd felt, and felt guilty for her greed. Instantly, she thought of Runt, the boy she'd been friends with so long ago, and wondered how he was getting along. What would he think if he knew what she'd been through since leaving him? She thought of Caleb, and all they'd shared, and instantly knew Runt would not be happy that she'd graduated from the simple kiss she'd shared with him. Her thoughts drifted back to Caleb and she realized her anger had eased.

"This mush is nothing to smile about," Clara said, pulling her from her thoughts. "You must be thinking impure thoughts."

Anastasia blushed deeper at getting caught. Before she could respond, she watched as an older girl snatched a roll from the tray of a much younger child. "She stole that girl's food."

Clara looked to see where she was looking. "It keeps the children quiet during their meals."

"I don't understand."

"It's one of the requirements for working in the dining room."

"Stealing food?"

"No," Clara said, lowering her voice. "Keeping the children quiet. Look how many children are in the room."

The large room was filled with tables, each one nearly full. "There are too many to count."

"Yes, but what do you hear?" Clara asked.

It was so quiet in the room, Anastasia wasn't sure what Clara wanted her to hear. "I don't really hear anything."

"That's the point. With this many children, you'd expect it to be loud, but the children are quiet because they are busy eating. They're eating because they're afraid we'll steal their food. After they finish eating, there'll be more noise, but by then, it'll nearly be time for them to begin their day. It's harsh, but it works, and the mistresses don't yell at us for not doing our job."

Several of the girls sitting around them nodded their agreement.

"I'm not sure…"

"This is not the farm," Clara snapped. "Most of these kids come from the streets. They're used to lying, stealing, and going to bed hungry. If we didn't steal their bread, one of the other kids would. By having us older kids be the bad guys, it causes the younger kids to stick together to avoid the bullies, which is what they call us. Sure, some of the girls take things too far, but if not for us, the kids would be rallying against each other instead of joining forces against us."

Put that way, it didn't sound half bad. She'd often wondered if Sharon had stood up to Albert if he would have stopped doing all the bad things he did.

"Anastasia, did you spill your milk?"

"What?"

"Your milk, did you spill it?" Clara repeated.

Anastasia looked down and to find the front of her apron wet. Baffled at first, she realized her breasts were leaking. She looked up, embarrassed. "Yes, but not the milk you think."

Several of the girls gasped, and Clara shushed them. "Did they not bind you before you left?"

"They did. I took the sheets off. I'm glad I did, because if not for that, I would not have been able to feed the baby," Anastasia admitted. It felt good to have her secret out in the open. She went on to tell the girls about her adventure the night before.

Clara stared at her in disbelief, and a couple of the girls placed their hands in front of their mouth and whispered to each other. Anastasia pulled herself taller. She was not ashamed of the fact that she'd given birth, nor was she sorry she'd used her milk to feed the baby boy who surely would not have lived through the night if not for her. It would have been well past time for him to eat by now, and she wondered for the hundredth time how the boy was. *Franky,* she reminded herself. *Not "boy." The baby has a name, if he's still alive.*

***

Anastasia was sitting in the Headmistress' office once again awaiting her fate. Clara had not spoken to her while walking her down the hall, insisting she wait outside while she spoke to Headmistress alone. The door had opened; Clara had come out and raced down the hall without a word as the Headmistress summoned her inside the room, telling her to be seated. That had been nearly fifteen minutes ago. The door opened once more, and Clara entered with Ella in tow, looking as if she'd been rousted from sleep. While the girl was fully dressed, her hair was a shambles. Ella saw her sitting there, and her eyes grew wide.

"What..."

Silence!" Headmistress interrupted. "I'll not have the two of you collaborating your stories. You'll each remain silent until spoken to."

Clara turned to leave, and the Headmistress stopped her. "You'll stay."

"But—"

"Sit," the Headmistress said firmly and waited for Clara to be seated in the last vacant chair. She turned to Ella. "I'll start with you. Are you of the mind to allow strangers to just come onto the floor uninvited?"

"No, Headmistress," Ella said, lowering her gaze.

"And yet you allowed this girl to walk into the nursery and wet nurse a sick infant?"

Ella's eyes grew wide. "Wet nurse? She told me she'd used the bottle."

No I didn't. You just heard what you wanted to hear.

"You're telling me you didn't know?"

"No, Headmistress."

"And just what was it you were doing that had you so preoccupied?"

Anastasia knew if the girl told where she'd been, she'd get in trouble. While she didn't agree with the babies being left alone, Ella shouldn't be punished for something she'd done.

"I...I was..."

Anastasia rose from her chair. "She knew. It's not her fault for not telling the truth. I told her I would beat her up should she tell my secret."

Headmistress tilted her head and looked down her nose. "And why would she be scared of a girl who is smaller than herself?"

Anastasia moved her head so the scar would be

prominent. "Because I told her I would beat her like I did the girl who gave me this scar."

From beside her, she heard Clara suck in a breath of air. She hurried to finish her story before anyone questioned it. "I saved Franky, and I'd do it again."

Headmistress' eyes grew wide. She walked to her desk and sat. When she looked up, she seemed a bit more composed. "Of all the babies to be suckled, why'd you choose the one you call Franky?"

That was a silly question. "Why because he was crying, of course."

"Of course," Headmistress repeated. "You say you saved him?"

I hope so. "He ate."

"Ella, how was the infant when you left him this morning?"

"I'm afraid he still refuses to take the bottle. I thought I was doing something wrong. It turns out it wasn't me at all."

Headmistress sat back in her chair. "It appears I find myself at an impasse. If I punish you, the baby will die. If I allow you to go upstairs, then you're rewarded for defying me."

Anastasia thought about that for a moment. "Headmistress…I didn't defy you."

Headmistress placed her fingertips together. "Please explain."

"You told Clara to tell Mistress Flora not to place me on the fourth floor, but you never actually told me not to go to the fourth floor." Anastasia was stunned when Headmistresses' lips formed the slightest smile.

Chapter Thirty-Four

Late November, 1920

Anastasia traced her thumb across Franky's cheek, and the baby smiled. The boy had made great strides in the last few months and had been moved to the second tier nursery with real cribs. She made a clicking sound, and the smile transformed into a full-blown giggle. She smiled and made the noise again, delighted when Franky tried to imitate her. She heard someone clear their throat and looked up to see Mistress Irene staring at her.

Long past her childbearing years, the woman placed the infant she was holding in its crib and slowly walked to where Anastasia sat. "I'll take him now."

Anastasia hesitated. Mistress Irene frowned, stepped closer, and took the boy from her hands. It had been the condition of her being allowed to help nurse the child. She could hold Franky long enough to feed him, but no more. Headmistress explained that Anastasia would become too attached to him otherwise. The so-called job had dovetailed to her acting as wet nurse to several other infants who'd come in since. Even though she enjoyed holding and feeding all the babies, she'd developed a soft spot for Franky. Maybe it was because she'd been responsible for keeping him alive. Maybe it was because he was the same age as her son, and she found it easy to imagine what the boy would look and act like as he grew. The only thing she didn't know was what name they'd given to her son.

"That'll be all," Mistress Irene said and shifted Franky to her shoulder.

Anastasia hesitated. "Do you not wish for me to nurse any of the others?"

"No," Mistress Irene said briskly. "Go downstairs and see to the other children."

As Anastasia descended the stairs she wondered what she'd done wrong. Mistress Irene had never been short with her before. She was still pondering this as she entered the meeting room. Distracted, she tripped over a chair, and several children standing near laughed. She righted herself and glared at them. When that didn't produce the fear she'd been after, she swatted at them, and they hurried away.

"Don't let them get to you," Clara said, coming up behind her.

"They don't bother me none," Anastasia lied. In reality, it truly hurt when the kids laughed at her. She didn't let their taunts go unpunished, as she made sure to target those kids when the opportunity arose.

"You know Dorthia?" Clara said with a nod to the girl in question.

While Anastasia didn't know a lot about Dorthia, she knew her to be one of Mary's girls. Mary fascinated her, and she'd often watch the girl, who seemed to be in charge of a small group of children. Though there were some children in the mix, such as Dorthia, who were obviously older, it was mild-mannered Mary the group looked to for direction. Mary reminded her of Penny, one of the hens on the farm. Penny would only have to cluck once, and all the other hens would come running. Caleb had told her it was because Penny was a mother hen. He explained that he didn't mean she was their actual mother, but she had mothering ways that made the other hens listen to her. It was the same way with Mary. She had a small group of children, both girls and boys that she'd taken under her wing. In many ways Anastasia envied Mary and those under her care.

"She's one of Mary's girls, right?"

"That's right. Dorthia's the oldest girl in the group. She's been helping out on the baby ward lately. Word is she's been asking about you."

"What's she want to know?"

"Everything. It sounds like someone put her up to it, but I haven't figured out who."

Anastasia was still burning from the mockery. "Maybe I should have a chat with her."

Clara shook her head. "You'll not get anything from her if she's around her friends. Let me know when you are going to step outside tonight. I'll send her out to see you."

***

Anastasia leaned against the building, smoking a cigarette and waiting for Dorthia. She'd positioned herself so she could see the back door and yet wouldn't be seen unless she stepped into the light. A northerly breeze skirted around the building, and she pulled her coat tight against the chill. Winter was setting in; it wouldn't be long before the streets were covered with snow. As if on cue, a few soft flakes flittered through the air. She sucked in one last breath from her cigarette, tossing it aside as the door pushed open.

Dorthia stepped cautiously onto the stoop, glanced from side to side, then reached for the door handle as if to go back inside.

"I'm here," Anastasia said, making her presence known. "Come on over."

"I'd rather you come over here," Dorthia replied.

"I'm not going to hurt you. I just want to talk. Come over here so no one sees us."

"What if someone moves the rock, and we can't get in?"

"They won't. Everyone knows if the rock is in the door, someone's outside."

Dorthia considered this for a moment before finally joining her. "Clara said you wanted to see me?"

"I figured if you wanted to know something about me, then maybe you should ask me instead of others." Anastasia moved so that the girl's back was facing the wall.

Dorthia looked from left to right as if planning her escape. "I was just curious about you is all."

Anastasia didn't waver. "If you got questions about me, you ask me."

"Is it true you got in a fight and almost killed the girl who cut your face?" Her words came out fast, showing she was nervous.

Anastasia was glad it was dark in the shadows so Dorthia couldn't see her smile. "Who'd you hear that from?"

"Chalkie." Dorthia's voice trembled.

"The boy who stands by the blackboard so he can steal chalk?" She'd seen Chalkie eating chalk but had never had a conversation with the kid. "You sweet on that boy? Surely you could find someone better to spend your time with. Heck, the boy is a good head shorter than you."

"I ain't got no use for him in that way. I've got my sights set on Percival," Dorthia replied.

Percival? Though she knew most of the children, that name didn't sound familiar. She thought about it for a moment then realized the girl was distracting her from the reason she'd called her out. She took a step closer, hoping to further intimidate the girl. "So just why were you and Chalkie talking about me?"

Dorthia stepped back to put more space between them and found herself pressed against the wall. "It wasn't my doing. Chalkie found me. He said a couple of the new boys were asking about you. Said they had a friend outside who was looking to pay for information about you."

Who on the outside would want information on me? No one knows I'm here. Mr. Swan? Unlikely; he only has to visit to find out how I'm doing. Maybe Albert found me after all. The thought sent chills racing up her spine. Anastasia pinned the girl against the building. If Dorthia thought her capable of hurting someone, she'd use it to her advantage. Besides, she had to know if Albert had found her. "I ain't got no friends on the outside. You better start spilling your guts now before I spill them for you."

"I didn't say it was your friend. I said it was Percival's friend." Instantly, Dorthia put her hand to her mouth, realizing she'd outed her friend.

"Percival? I don't know any Percival."

"He's the tall good-looking boy in Mary's gang."

Mary's gang is it? "You mean Slim? The boy that can't keep still?"

"Yes, I thought maybe if I told him what he wanted…"

Now she understood. Obviously, Dorthia had her sights set on the boy. From what she'd heard, Dorthia had her sights set on a lot of boys. She released the girl and took a step back.

"Do you want me to talk to Slim and find out why he wants to know?"

Anastasia thought about that for a moment. She had her doubts if she could trust the girl. In the end, she decided it would be best to get her information directly. "No. And I'd better not hear that you've mentioned our little chat to anyone. Now go before I tell the mistresses I caught you trying to sneak out."

Dorthia took off as if eager to be finished with the

conversation. When she got to the stoop, she hesitated.

Anastasia didn't have to guess what the girl was thinking. She already knew. It was the same thing she'd be thinking in her place. She took several steps closer to make her voice heard. When she spoke, her voice was as cold as the November wind. "Dorthia, touch that rock, and I'll use it on your pretty little face while you sleep."

***

Anastasia stopped on the second floor long enough to tell Clara about her conversation with Dorthia, and the two devised a plan. Anastasia would nurse Franky his evening feed and make her excuses about nursing the others. That would give her enough time to be waiting in the hall when Slim arrived. Clara would roust the boy, telling him Dorthia wanted to meet with him to share what she'd found out. She'd pretend not to know anything else, just say that Dorthia had promised her something if she delivered the simple message. Clara had offered to be there as a backup, but Anastasia insisted she knew how to deal with boys such as this. *At least she hoped she did.*

She pushed open the door to the second-tier nursery and hurried over to Franky's crib, only to find the boy sound asleep. While she hated to wake him, she'd have to hurry if she was going to be in the stairwell when Slim arrived. Just as she was reaching into the crib, Ella came into the room.

"Isn't it wonderful?" Ella whispered. "Mistress Irene worked with him all afternoon and finally got him to accept the bottle."

The bottle? That meant she'd no longer be required to feed him.

"But why?" Anastasia questioned, trying to keep the panic from her voice. "I didn't mind nursing him."

"I'm not supposed to tell you why, but it is because Mistress Irene feels you are becoming too attached to Franky, and more so, he is becoming too attached to you. She's agreed to allow you to continue to nurse some of the others for now. But since Franky is drinking from the bottle, he doesn't need you anymore."

He doesn't need me anymore. Ella's words felt like a dagger to the heart.

"That's not true. Franky does need me and I him," Anastasia said, turning towards the crib.

"Anastasia!" The firm voice of Mistress Irene stopped her in her tracks. "You'll leave that boy be."

"But why, Mistress? He was getting along just fine. He needs me." Anastasia tried to keep the tears from falling, but the thought of losing another baby was too much.

"He did, and you did right by him, but you're growing too attached to him. I saw it this morning when you refused to allow me to take him."

"I gave him to you," Anastasia argued.

"No, you hesitated. That's when I knew. You'll still be allowed to nurse the younger infants, but Franky will be left to the others."

"You can't do that."

"I can, and I did. If this is going to be too much for you, we can discontinue the nursings altogether. Take the night and let me know what you decide in the morning."

"But—"

"That's an order," Mistress Irene said firmly. "I'll be on the ward all night, so don't bother sneaking back in."

It was all she could do to put one foot in front of the other, as her legs felt as if they would give way. She held on to the rail as she descended the stairs, hot tears stinging her eyes. She struggled to catch her breath through her sobs. *Why can't I be happy? What have I done to deserve so much pain in my life? To have everything and everyone I've ever cared for ripped away whenever I get too close?*

Anastasia let go of the rail to wipe her eyes, missed a step, and tumbled down half a flight of stairs, rolling to a stop at the base of the third-floor landing. Pulling her legs into her chest, she continued to weep.

Chapter Thirty-Five

She wasn't sure how long she lay there sobbing before she finally cried herself out. Sore and scraped, she gingerly started peeling herself from the floor. It wasn't until she'd sat upright and wiped the tears from her eyes that she realized she wasn't alone. On the stairs just a few feet away was the boy she'd sent for. *Slim.* Slumped and staring, his face a mixture of fear and concern. His long arms wrapped securely around long legs, which bounced furiously as if saying, *set me free so I can run away from this sorrowful sight.*

In her grief, she'd forgotten all about meeting him. She sniffed, wondering how long he'd been there watching her wallow in her pity. She wanted to scream at him to go and tell his friends how the evil Anastasia had fallen and shed her tears of shame. She was afraid if she did, he would indeed leave, and truthfully, she wasn't quite ready to be alone. He'd seen her at her most vulnerable state. There was no need to pretend any longer.

"It was I who sent for you. Though I didn't expect you to see me this way."

"You hurt?"

"Just a few scrapes."

"That was a mighty lot of tears for just a few scrapes."

"Sometimes, when you cry, it's hard to stop the tears." She shrugged. "I guess that's a stupid thing to say."

He shook his head. "Nah, I get it."

She tried to stand and winced at a pain in her ankle. He

came to her, lifted her as if she were weightless, and sat her on the stairs. He sat next to her and took her ankle in his hands, rubbing away the pain.

"Where'd you learn to do that?" she asked, closing her eyes.

"My ma was a dancer. She'd come home and have me rub her feet."

"What happened to your ma?"

He hesitated a moment then started rubbing her foot once more. "She went to work one night and didn't come home."

"And your dad?"

"Ma never told me who my pa was. I don't think she really knew."

"They weren't married?"

He pushed her foot from his lap and stood. "No, they weren't married. Go ahead and call me names. I've heard them all before. Don't make no difference to me."

"Ow," she said, rubbing her ankle. "I wasn't going to call you anything."

"No? Then why'd you make a big deal about it?"

"I didn't know women could keep their baby if they weren't married is all."

"Sure they can. They do it all the time."

She closed her eyes to staunch the tears that threatened. She opened them once more. "Your momma was lucky to have you."

His agitation lessened. "What makes you think so?"

"Sometimes mothers aren't given a choice," she said softly.

He sat next to her once more. "You seem nicer than I thought."

"Yeah, well, you'd better not tell anyone," she said

firmly. She remembered why she'd wanted to meet with him. "Why were you asking questions about me?"

"Maybe I liked you and wanted to know more."

That's not what Dorthia said. "What do you want to know?"

"The scar? How'd you get it?"

"I was in a knife fight. Some girl cut me, and I beat the snot out of her. Haven't you heard?"

"Sure, I've heard. We've all heard. We've heard lots of things. I'm just trying to find out if they're true."

"What's it to you if the things you've heard about me are true or not?"

His legs were shaking worse now. "Maybe I just don't like seeing people get a bum rap."

She pressed a hand on his knees to calm him. "What kind of things have you heard?"

"I've heard you hit some of the kids."

"I have. Come to think of it, I've heard the same about you," she said.

He bristled at that. "I ain't never hit anyone that didn't deserve to be hit."

"Neither have I."

"I saw you hit a boy the other day. He was minding his own business and you clobbered him. You saying he deserved to have you smack on him?"

She knew the boy of which he was speaking. Earlier in the day, he'd passed her in the hallway, ran a finger alongside his face to mimic her scar, and mouthed the word "ugly." Yes, he deserved it. "He did."

"What did he do to you?"

"Why does it matter?"

"It matters a lot. You say he deserved to be smacked. What'd he do to deserve it?"

"He told me I was ugly."

"Well, are you?"

"What?"

"Just because someone calls you a name doesn't make it true. Are you ugly?"

She really hadn't given it any thought before. People always looked at her differently because of the scar. Because they stared, she figured she must look pretty hideous. The only one that hadn't paid any mind to it had been Caleb, and she figured that was because he'd grown used to his mother's scars. Still, most people she'd come into contact with had made it a point to comment on it. "I guess if you get told it enough, you start believing it to be true."

Slim took hold of her hand and placed it on the side of his head, pressing her fingers so she could feel a long, raised scar that ran from above his ear to the back of his head. "You're not the only one with scars."

She wanted to remind him that his was well hidden but decided against it. "What happened?"

"Ma would bring men home, and sometimes those men didn't like the thought of having a kid around while Ma conducted business."

"I thought you said your ma was a dancer?"

"Ma had a lot of jobs." Though his face turned red, the words were said without emotion. "Anyway, one time, one of those guys was drunk and hit me upside the head with a bottle. Split my head open in the process."

Instantly, she was reminded of her life before being sent out on the streets, and a silent sob worked its way to the surface.

Slim bumped her with his shoulder. "Now don't go crying on me again. The pain's long gone from that. Besides, something good came out of it. One of Ma's regulars was a boxer, a pretty good one at that. He showed me how to duck and move so that no one could hit me no more. He said I was a natural. Can you imagine that? Someone like him telling me I was good? It was almost worth being clubbed upside the head. He came around a lot there for a while and even taught me how to throw a punch."

"Is that why your legs move all the time?"

"Nah, that started after I got hit in the head. The doctor said the bottle must have broken something more than my head."

"My papa used to hit me. He beat my momma mostly, but he beat me too. He just used his belt and fists. I'm glad he never used anything else." She thought about telling him that Albert wasn't really her papa but didn't want to explain about the apple man.

"Is that why you ran away?"

"I didn't run away. My momma told me to leave. I guess she decided she loved my brothers Ezra and Tobias more than she did me." She'd learned that wasn't the case, but her new hurts were opening old wounds. She felt his shoulders stiffen. When she looked at him, his face was white. She wondered if what she'd said reminded him of his own mother disappearing. "Are you all right?"

"Yes…I guess what you said surprised me. It must have been hard leaving your brothers. Wouldn't you like to see them again? Either of them?"

She thought of the events of the day and how everyone that ever mattered to her had been ripped from her life. No, she didn't wish to see them again. Ever. If only to protect them from the evil that lurked around her. Look what happened to Caleb and Mrs. Sina and ultimately to her son. *No, my son is safe. Mistress Rebecca told me he's in a loving home. At least my child didn't fall victim to the curse.* She looked at Slim, her eyes telling of her sincerity. "No, I wish never to see or hear of my family again."

His brow was creased, and he seemed to be struggling with her answer. "Are you sure?"

"I am. I couldn't bear it. I'm thinking you have more questions. You best be getting on with them."

His knees drummed a rapid beat. "They say you came here to have a baby. Is that true?"

Instantly, her heartbeat increased, and for a moment, she was unable to breathe. Why the question came as a surprise she didn't know. Maybe it was because she'd thought she'd kept her secret hidden. She remembered what Clara had said about Dorthia helping out in the baby ward and knew who'd relayed the news. Everyone knew a girl couldn't possibly wet nurse a baby unless she'd first had one of her own. There was no sense denying the rumor. Doing so would mean disowning the child she'd birthed.

She turned to him so he could see the truth in her eyes. "No, I did not come here to have a child. I had my son before I arrived."

"So you gave him away?" There was no mistaking the accusation in his voice.

"I did not," she said heatedly. "I was sent to a home where they send girls like me. I wanted to keep my baby, but they wouldn't allow it. The mistress told me I would have to spread my legs in order to keep him and told me all the bad things that would happen to him if I did."

"Maybe you shouldn't have spread them in the first place." His tone was as vile as his words.

She slapped him before she realized what she'd done. The look on his face was one of shock and disbelief. She closed her eyes, bracing for the punch she was sure would follow. When she opened her eyes once more, he was gone. Seconds later, she heard the door to the stairwell above close. A pity, as up until that moment, she'd enjoyed speaking with the boy.

She stood and tested the strength of her ankle. Deciding it was too painful to walk on, she sat, replaying the conversation they'd just had and wondering how long it would take for everyone to know of her secrets.

A few moments passed until she heard the unmistakable click, letting her know a door had opened. She thought maybe it was Clara coming to see what was taking her so long. Instead, she was shocked to see that Slim had returned. His face seemed somewhat calmer now.

He descended the stairs without a word and sat next to her as he'd done previously. She wondered if she should speak to him and apologize for what she'd done. Pride kept her from doing so. While he hadn't lifted a hand to her, he'd hurt her with his words.

"Did you know the baby's father?" he asked after several moments of silence.

"I did."

"Did you love him?"

"I think so. We were to be married. It hurt me very badly to watch him die." Why she was telling Slim this, she did not know. Once she started the telling, she couldn't seem to stop, so she told him everything.

When she'd finished, his eyes were as wet as hers.

He sighed a heavy sigh. "You're not what I thought you to be."

"Is that a bad thing?" she asked, batting away the tears.

"It's not a good thing or a bad thing."

"I know someone put you up to the questions. Dorthia told me you have a friend on the outside that wants to know. Is it my papa?"

"No," he said with a shake of his head. "It's no one who knows you. The only reason my friend was asking about you was that he'd heard you made trouble for some of the kids inside. He has a girl he's been protecting, and her mother is very ill. He knows the only way he can keep her safe is to place her inside a home. He paid me to come in so I can help protect her."

"You must love your friend very much to come into a place such as this for him. I hope he appreciates your loyalty."

"He does. Can I tell my friend you'll help watch over this girl?"

Anastasia considered this. She'd just made a promise to herself not to get close to anyone and yet she liked the boy. She knew not to get too close to the children, but if she promised to protect the girl, she'd have to do just that. *I can't.* Maybe there was another way. "Talk to Mary. If she agrees to watch over the girl, I will see that no one bothers her."

"Mary will agree."

"Slim…" She hesitated. "I'd prefer you not tell anyone what I've said to you."

He laughed. "And sully your evil reputation? Why, I wouldn't think of it."

Chapter Thirty-Six

December 24, 1920

Anastasia moved through her day without caring. While she still nursed some of the newborns that arrived on a daily basis, her arms ached to hold Franky once more. She put on a bright face whenever on the fourth floor, knowing if Mistress Irene suspected her depression, she'd ban Anastasia from the floor. While not being able to hold Franky caused her pain, at least she was still able to see him. If only from a distance.

Aside from her daily glimpses of Franky, the only real bright spot in her life was the fact that the asylum had acquired a second-hand piano, which they placed in the common room for anyone to use. Everyone knew Anastasia enjoyed banging at the keys and had quickly come to steer clear whenever she was in the room. On occasion, such as today, she'd sneak into the room well after hours and play some of the songs Caleb had shown her, mostly simple lullabies or hymns he'd learned at church.

She was playing one such song when a shadow fell over her. She continued to play, knowing the shadow to be Slim. Though the boy fidgeted something fierce, he had a way of sneaking up on her and usually was able to catch her unaware. Exactly how he was able to sneak around the halls without getting caught was still a mystery to her. She didn't mind his watching her or seeking her out just to say hello. In fact, she welcomed it. They'd become close after he'd witnessed her vulnerability, and in a way, it seemed as if he looked out for her. At first, she thought it was because of her vulnerability, but then she'd seen a look in his eye that told her there was more. She'd seen that same look in Caleb's eye. While she enjoyed his company and the talks they often shared, she'd refused to allow him into her heart. Not only did it protect her from being hurt again, it was the only way she knew of keeping him safe.

She finished her song and turned to face him. The first thing she noticed was his increased fidgeting. She took a breath to steady herself, as she'd learned his agitation increased when he was upset. "What is it?"

A smile passed over his lips. "Am I that easy to read?"

"Your legs are a dead giveaway."

"I need to tell you something," he said.

"I'm ready." *No, I'm not. Anything that has him this upset can't be good.*

"I lied to you. I didn't do it to hurt you. I guess I thought to protect you from further pain."

She swallowed, quickly thinking through their conversations and wondering which could have been a lie. They'd had so many, she couldn't venture a guess.

"That day in the stairwell. The first time, when you'd hurt your ankle. I told you that you do not know my friend on the outside. That was a lie. You know him, and he wishes to meet with you."

Him? It must be Albert. She jumped to her feet. "You told me it wasn't my papa."

"It isn't. As far as I know, your father's dead." There was no apology in his voice, as he knew she wouldn't care.

Albert is dead! That means I can go home. She was just about to say the words aloud, when his words stopped her.

"Tobias said his brother killed the man," Slim said, nodding his head.

As his words sank in, her body started to tremble. She

didn't mind the man was gone but wondered what had caused Ezra to kill him. "Ezra killed Papa? Why?"

Slim's legs were moving so fast for a moment, she thought they were going to take off on their own, dragging the boy with him.

"Mouse said it was because your papa killed your momma." This time, his voice showed their sympathy.

Anastasia couldn't breathe. She had a sudden desire to run but had nowhere to go and knew her legs wouldn't hold her if she tried. In the end, she sank onto the piano bench, trying to process all she'd heard.

"I guess I should have let Mouse tell you himself," Slim said after a time.

Mouse? It was the second time he'd used the moniker to refer to Tobias. "He asked you to call him Mouse?"

"Sure, it's what everyone calls him. I'm not sure how he came by the name. Maybe it's because he's so quiet. He can sneak up on a person, and you don't know he's there until it's too late. He taught me a little, but I'm not nearly as good as he is. That boy is like a ghost sometimes." The admiration in Slim's voice was unmistakable.

She knew exactly where he'd gotten the name. She'd given it to him. Though at the time, she hadn't realized he'd use it so freely. Why'd he need a street name anyway? *Unless he was living on the streets.* "Where is Tobias now?"

"He wants to meet with you."

Tobias knew she was there and had come for her. "He wants to meet with me?"

"Sure, I told him you've agreed to look after his girl, but he wants to make sure. He said he needs to talk to you and see the look on your face when you agree."

It took a moment for his words to sink in. Tobias knew she was in the asylum, but the only reason he cared was because he needed her help. Wanted her to look after his girl. Yet he'd not sent anyone to look after her. Oh, he'd sent them, alright. Sent them to spy on her. She wondered for a moment if Slim's friendship was real then decided it was. He'd had plenty of time to tell all he knew and hadn't. Tobias was another story. He knew she was his sister and clearly didn't care. The coldness of the situation cut through clear to her heart. *I won't do it. I won't meet with him or look after the girl.*

She'd spent years worrying about him and trying to find a way to take him away with her. Yet the moment she'd left, he'd forgotten all about her. Obviously, he was doing fine without her as he had loyal friends willing to give up their freedom for him. He'd done fine without her. That was the key. She hadn't been there to destroy him. It all made sense. In her grief, it did not dawn on her to question why things continued to fall apart, even though she hadn't been there.

"Who takes care of Tobias now?" Even she heard the hollow tone in her voice.

"Why, he's Mouse. Mouse doesn't need anyone to take care of him. It's he who takes care of everyone else," Slim replied.

Not everyone. "He's doing all right for himself, then?"

Slim grinned. "He's doing better than okay."

"What have you told him about me?"

"Not a lot. We haven't really talked about you since you and I became friends. You told me not to tell anyone how nice you are. I figured that meant Mouse too."

"Thank you, Slim," she said calmly. "When does he wish to meet?"

"Tonight. He's probably out there now," Slim replied.

Tobias must have been confident in Slim's power of persuasion. That or he was just used to having his way. Slim hadn't told Tobias of their friendship, which meant all Tobias knew was the rumors he'd heard. If he expected to see the mean Anastasia, all the better. She could play that part well. What she couldn't play was the poor sister whose heart was being torn to shreds, again. That part was much too painful to show.

***

Anastasia pulled on her cloak and stepped outside. She held the door with her foot as she reached for the rock to wedge in the opening. The wind caught her cape and sent an icy chill up her spine, fitting, since her heart had already turned to ice. She moved into the light. If he was out there, she wanted to make sure he could see her.

She saw him cross the street and almost smiled. She'd recognize him anywhere. Though his approach was one of a man who'd seen a lifetime of struggles, not of the boy she knew him to be. She pulled back her hood, exposing her scar. If he had any doubt it was her, this should convince him of her identity. She stared at him, wishing to memorize his every feature. The wind caught a strand of her hair, and she pushed it behind her ear to lock it into place. He seemed to waver for a moment, and she remembered the child she'd left at the apple cart that day. She had the sudden urge to call to him and beg him to love her once again. She held out her arms and smiled, aching to hold him near.

He stopped as if saying, *you had your chance. I don't need you anymore.*

She pulled herself taller and took a cigarette from her pocket to quell her trembling fingers. Tobias had made his choice. She would not let him see how deeply his rejection cut. She lit the cigarette, inhaled, and blew the smoke out slowly to further calm her nerves. She offered him a draw, retracting her arm when he rejected her yet again. Though she didn't want to contaminate him with the darkness that seemed to follow her, a part of her wished he needed her as much as she'd needed him. He was clean and healthy-looking, leaving no doubt he was better off without her. She took another puff and blew the smoke directly in his face. It was time to play the part.

"Look at you. Little Tobias nearly all grown up. What are you now, ten? Slim told me you're a pretty tough guy these days. If I had known what you'd become, I would've given you a better name than Mouse."

"I do okay." His words came out in a smoky haze. It was freezing out. She'd have to hurry so he could find someplace to get warm.

"I'd say you do more than okay if you can convince guys to come into a place like this for you." His eyes grew wide. Slim hadn't lied about keeping their conversation private. She laughed. "Don't worry; your little secret is safe with me."

That wasn't the point. "Slim wasn't supposed to tell anyone."

"He didn't tell everyone; he just told me," she said, taking another pull from the cigarette.

He looked past her as if expecting to see his friend. "Why would he tell you?"

"Because I asked nicely."

"Is it true you are a mother?"

She hadn't expected this. Then again, it was the same question Slim had asked in the beginning. She narrowed her eyes, took one last puff from the cigarette, and flicked it aside. Seeing the hurt in his eyes was too much. It was time to send him on his way. "There is a baby, but I'm not its mother. Mothers love their children, and I don't have any love left to give. That's why I left when I did."

"I don't understand."

Anastasia drew in the chilled air and blew out a smoky

breath of steam. She shivered and pulled her coat tighter. "It doesn't matter. I'm glad you are out of the house, Tobias. How is Ezra?"

"I don't know," he replied and told her what happened the night he left.

She was glad Slim had told her the news earlier. It was easier to take it all in without emotion. "You've been on the streets all this time?"

"Most of it."

She'd barely survived a week on the streets. Still, she wanted to be sure she had nothing to worry about. "How do you get by?"

He shrugged. "My sister taught me how to steal apples."

You needed me for a little while. She smiled. "Well, it's good to know I did something good in this world."

A motorcar approached, slowed, and continued on its way.

"I need to get back inside," she said, looking toward the door. "I don't know how you found me, but it was good seeing you again."

"Wait," Tobias said as she turned. "I need you to do something for me."

"I figured as much. You want me to be nice to your friend?"

"I do. Her name is Mileta, and if I have my way, she'll be coming here soon. I need you to look out for her until I can find another place for her."

She bit at the corner of her mouth. She'd been thinking of Slim. "I thought you wanted me to be nice to Slim."

Tobias laughed. "Slim don't need me to look out for him. The boy can throw a punch like no one I've ever seen."

"Oh, little Mouse, you still have so much to learn."

Anastasia shook her head and reached for the door. "This girl, are you sweet on her?"

Tobias wrinkled his nose. "Of course not; she's just a kid."

And so are you, even though you pretend so hard to appear all grown up. "Then why go to all the trouble for her?"

He pulled himself straight and yanked his hat low. "You just take care of the girl when she comes, and I'll see to it you have smokes and a bit of dough as well. You're not to tell her about me or even mention my name. You don't hold up your end of the bargain, and I'll make sure the headmistress knows you sneak out at night."

Sneak out at night. I've never gone further than the side of the building. Oh well, if that's what he thinks, so be it.

"You would too, wouldn't you? You're not a mouse; you're a little rat."

"I'm your brother. The least I can do is help you uphold your reputation."

She could tell by the look on his face that she'd played her part well. She only needed to say one last thing before she sent him on his way. She had to convince him she didn't love him anymore, for if not, he would be lost. She knew this to be true because she'd never gotten over the pain of being separated from her son. She knew she couldn't look into his face and say the words she had to say, so she closed her eyes briefly and conjured up an image of Albert, the man who was the root of all her pain. Opening her eyes, she spoke to the image in her mind. "I'm glad I left you. I hate you. I've always hated you all."

He stood there for so long, she almost wavered. She clenched her jaw to stave the tears that threatened. Just as she'd made up her mind to confess everything, he spoke.

"You have yourself a Merry Christmas, Anastasia," he

said, then tipped his hat and walked away without another word.

She watched him go until he was out of sight, then slowly turned and made her way inside. To her surprise, Slim was waiting for her. From the look on his face, it was obvious he'd heard everything.

"Why?" His voice was barely a whisper as he gathered her into his arms.

"Because I love him," she sobbed. "It's the only way I know to keep him safe."

Chapter Thirty-Seven

January 1921

It was still dark when Anastasia woke to the sound of rain pelting against the tall windows of the older girl's dorm. Though a few girls were stirring, most remained asleep. She stretched and pulled herself from the bed. She liked waking before the others. She didn't have to wait her turn in the water closet and could take a little more time standing under the rain shower. She pulled the brush through her wet hair and added the bow, securing her hair into place. She looked to the ceiling, wondering if Franky was awake. He liked to rise early, maybe for the same reason as her. Rising early meant a little less competition. Especially on the baby ward, where the one with the strongest lungs usually got fed first. Franky didn't have much in the way of competition there. Once he'd started eating, he'd grown into a chubby, bright-eyed mass of giggles and smiles. Watching him continued to fill the void left by the loss of her son. It didn't hurt that she felt personally responsible for giving him his start in life. The problem was she rarely got to see the boy, and when she did, it was sometimes no more than the few seconds it took to pass through the second-level ward, a trip that was not necessary, as she had to pass the nursery to get to the room.

While she used to look forward to climbing the stairs, doing so had become just another job, one she no longer enjoyed. She'd taken to placing a blanket over the infant she was nursing so she could not see into their eyes as they suckled.

In the past, she would offer her thumb for the infant to grab on to, something she no longer did. At the end of the day, she was nothing more than a living bottle — a way for an abandoned newborn to acquire nourishment and no more.

She left the cuddling and mothering to those not in danger of becoming too attached. She'd lost too much and pushed the rest away, in the process becoming an empty shell of her former self.

She peeked inside the second-tier ward, hoping to get a glimpse of Franky. Finding his crib empty, she walked to the back of the room and opened the door to the feeding station. Several infants, Franky included, sat strapped to chairs drinking from nipples that were attached to glass bottles by a long brown rubber tube. Franky looked up and smiled at her when she entered, a mistake because the nipple dropped from his mouth, landing in his lap. His face scrunched and his lips quivered uncontrollably before finally settling in to unhappy wails. His cries caused a chain reaction from several of the other infants, who joined in on his sorrowful chorus.

Anastasia hurried to where Franky sat, found the nipple, and plugged his mouth just as Mistress Irene came into the small room.

"What are you doing in here?" she asked upon entering.

"I was just checking on Franky on my way to the nursery," Anastasia said above the cries.

"And in the process disrupted the morning feeding of the whole room," the woman chastised.

The door pushed open once more and several of the women who helped on the floor rushed in to tend to the screaming infants.

"I'll help settle them," Anastasia said, moving towards the small group.

"You've done quite enough," Mistress Irene said firmly.

"But…"

"Leave," Mistress Irene said, pointing toward the door.

Anastasia left, not realizing Mistress Irene had followed her from the room. "This is to be your last feeding."

Anastasia turned to face the woman. "You don't wish for me to come back tonight?"

"You're not understanding me, child. Your services are no longer needed on this floor. Go to the nurse's office and tell them you need to have your breasts bound. You'll be more comfortable that way."

Not trusting herself to answer, Anastasia merely nodded.

"Anastasia," Mistress Irene said when she turned away. "I know you think of this as a punishment, but it's not. You may be doing the duties of a woman, but really you're still a child. I pray someday you find some happiness to feed your soul."

"So do I," Anastasia said as she entered the nursery. *So do I.*

***

She'd just left the infirmary, when Clara found her. Unaware of Anastasia's anguish, her friend's eyes were bright with excitement.

"She's here!" Clara said the second she saw her.

"She who?"

"Mileta. She just arrived this morning. Barefoot and soaked to the bone. She's in the washroom now. You might want to clear a seat at your table so Mary can bring the girl into her fold. Do you want me to have one of the other girls initiate her?" Clara asked, falling into step beside Anastasia.

Why did she have to come today of all days? "No, I'll take care of it."

"She should be finishing up if you want to head to the dining hall. I'll go collect her and the others and bring them down. I'll see she's the last in line so you know who she is."

Anastasia took her time getting to the dining hall. She'd wondered how she would react to the girl that had stolen her brother's heart. She further wondered why Tobias had been so insistent the girl not be made aware of his existence. At the moment, she had no interest in such childish games. Heartbroken that she'd no longer be able to make daily trips to visit Franky, she shouldn't have any problem pushing Mileta under Mary's wing. Best get her in there from the beginning than to see her pulled into another, less friendly group. Slim told her he'd enlisted several others to help look after the girl. She hadn't asked for details; the boy was loyal to Tobias. He'd do everything in his power to keep from letting him down.

The dining hall was full when she entered. She took her tray and set it on the end of the table. There was no need to protect it. No one would dare touch her tray. To her surprise, there was an empty seat next to Mary. She searched the boy's table for Slim, who smiled a knowing smile when he saw her puzzlement. *Of course the seat was empty; they'd known the girl was coming. Tobias had gotten word to his friends.* Slim nodded toward the door, and Anastasia turned to see Clara entering with three young girls in tow. The girls' hair was freshly chopped clear to the base of their heads; the two girls in front were still weeping at their ordeal. To her credit, Tobias' girl, though scared, held her head high and unashamed. Anastasia stood at the head of the dining hall and directed the first two girls away from Mary's table. She stepped aside just as Mileta exited the food line with her tray. Mary's table was the first in the center of the room, a direct route for a person looking for a place to sit. Mileta hesitated, as if looking for the girls she'd arrived with. Dorthia whispered something to Mary, who smiled the slightest smile of welcome. It was all the encouragement the girl needed as she hurried to claim the empty spot.

Anastasia almost wavered when she saw Mileta lift her hands in prayer then, remembering the events of the day, hurried to where the girl sat with her eyes tightly closed. In that instant, she knew with clear certainty the lesson the girl had to learn. Who better to teach it than a girl whose own prayers had never been answered? She lifted the bread from the tray and returned to her place just as Mileta opened her eyes. The girl's tears didn't bother her; this place was full of them. She lifted the bread to her mouth as Mileta's tears turned to burning anger. Anastasia took a bite and smiled. The lesson had been successful.

***

Anastasia normally went to the fourth floor to nurse the infants after the evening meal. The binding that held her breasts tight was a constant reminder that that service was no longer needed. Displaced, she followed the children into the common room and watched as they gravitated into their own tightknit groups. Except for the meeting room, this was the only place where the boys and girls were allowed to coexist. She positioned herself so she could see Mary's group, watching to ensure Mileta was welcomed. As she watched the children laughing, she realized the girl already fit in better than she. With the exception of Clara and the occasional chat with Slim, Anastasia was an outcast.

She sighed and walked to the piano, sitting on the bench. She pushed back the cover and banged aimlessly on the keys. She played one of the tunes Caleb had taught her, not caring when she missed a note. The piano normally brought her comfort. After today, she didn't think she'd ever find a reason to smile again.

Some of the younger children came to watch her play. It didn't surprise her; music, even when played badly, always held an allure. Anastasia was still sitting there taking out her frustration on the keys, when, to her surprise, Mileta approached. She wondered how long it would be before one of her tight little group pulled the girl away. To her surprise, no one did.

"Please? May I try?" Mileta asked softly.

Anastasia stared at her for a long moment before finally nodding her agreement. Why she agreed, she didn't know. Maybe it was because when Mileta had asked, she'd looked at the piano and not her. She recognized that look and knew it was the same one she'd given the first time she sat down to play. What she hadn't expected was the way Mileta's fingers danced across the ivory keys, playing a song so intense, it felt as if she was pouring out all her sorrows. In turn, it felt as if the sorrow inside her own body was leaving. Tears flowed onto her cheeks, but she didn't care. The room grew silent, and Anastasia realized she was not the only one affected by Mileta's playing. She closed her eyes, sighing as the music extinguished her anger.

The song lasted for several moments until it finally came to an end, to the gasps and exclamations of everyone in the room.

"How did you learn to play so well?" Anastasia asked on a sob.

"My mother taught me. She taught many."

"Will you teach me to play as you do?"

Mileta studied her for a moment then looked to her new friends for approval. "I will, but in return, we will need something from you."

Anastasia glanced to where Mileta was looking. Seeing Mary, she understood what Mileta was asking. The girl was quick, she'd give her that. What she didn't realize was that it was she who'd placed Mileta in the group she was now looking to protect. It worked out well; she was tired of playing the bully, and she wouldn't have to work as hard to keep up the charade.

***

Cindy finished the journal she was reading and held it to her chest, breathing against the emotions she felt. She glanced at Linda, waiting for her to finish before she spoke. "You're usually finished before I am."

"I had to take a few breaks along the way," Linda admitted. "It's about time that girl found a bit of sunshine in her life, even if it's short-lived."

Cindy frowned. "You think so?"

"Look at what we've read so far. I'm telling you that girl was born under a dark cloud," Linda said with a sigh.

"Do you really believe in such things?"

"Of course I do. I've seen it too many times to count. It's like some people just aren't meant to find happiness."

"I guess you're right. Are you up to reading some more, or do you need a break?"

"I'm okay. I need to find out what happens to Franky."

"He lives a long life and ends up at the medical care facility," Cindy reminded her.

Linda looked over her bifocals at her. "You know what I mean."

"I do," Cindy agreed, and handed Linda another stack of papers.

Chapter Thirty-Eight

October 1924

Anastasia knocked on the door to Headmistress' office and stuck her head inside.

The woman sat hunkered over a piece of paper, chewing on the end of a pencil, and appeared to be deep in thought. Anastasia cleared her throat, and Headmistress looked up. To Anastasia's surprise, the woman smiled.

"Clara said you wanted to see me?"

"Anastasia, yes, please come in," the woman said, waving her in. "Please be seated."

Anastasia entered the room, sat, and waited for the woman to speak.

"Our asylum has been accepted in the Placing Out Program," the woman said, diving into the reason she'd requested Anastasia to come. "I'm aware you were once a part of that very program. While things did not work out so well for you, I think you will agree it's a rare opportunity for children in this asylum. As you know, we have many children in here that have lived within these walls all their lives and others who haven't been here all that long but would welcome the opportunity to have a chance at leaving. Lord knows what they expect to find."

Anastasia felt her pulse increase. She hadn't realized Headmistress was aware she'd been sent out on the trains. Surely the woman wasn't suggesting she be sent out again. This was her home, the only place she'd ever really felt safe. Besides, she wasn't a child. Not anymore. "Mr. Swan, he was my placing agent, offered to have me placed elsewhere. My return was of my own accord."

"You did not think anyone else would take you in?"

"Not in my condition at the time," Anastasia said, meeting her stare.

"Oh, that's right you were...you came to us from The Home of Wayward Angels. My apologies; it's difficult to keep track of so many."

"And yet, you remembered the trains," Anastasia reminded her. The woman was after something; she just wasn't sure what it was.

"Yes, well, perhaps some things are best left forgotten," Headmistress said, removing her glasses and massaging the bridge of her nose.

"I'm sure forgetting is easier for some than others," Anastasia said, matching her tone.

Ignoring Anastasia's sarcasm, the Headmistress handed her the paper she'd been reviewing when Anastasia arrived. "Those at the Children's Aid Society have graciously allocated funds for us to send out fifty-three children to find new homes. I've put together a list of the children to be included in the trip. If this works out well, we may see about sending more. Since you're somewhat familiar with the process, I thought perhaps you would look over the names. It always helps to have a second set of eyes, you know."

Anastasia took the paper and scanned the list. Most of the names were children she knew but had little dealings with. She turned the paper over and continued to read. Halfway down the page, her fingers started to tremble. Most of Mary's little gang had been chosen, including Mileta and Slim. Though she'd promised herself she wouldn't become attached to the boy, their friendship had grown over the years. As they both matured, their slight age difference didn't seem to matter. Slim always acted older than his years, at least when the boy wasn't with his friends. It didn't help that things had become physical on numerous occasions. She blinked back the shock of seeing his name and continued perusing the list. Her mouth went dry as she read the last name. There was no need to question if it was he, as he was the only boy in the asylum with the name. *Franky.*

She'd had to wait a heart-wrenching two and a half years to see him again, but now seeing the boy was one of the highlights of her day. Four months ago, Franky and a group of other children were brought downstairs to mingle with the older children each day. Each evening, they were taken back to a supervised dorm. It was a way to slowly integrate the younger children before finally transitioning them to the main group. Once integrated, the children would remain in the main dorm until they were either adopted or grew old enough to leave.

Though she hadn't seen him since he was six months old, she'd known him the instant she saw him. He'd walked up to the piano while she was playing and smiled at her. There was something familiar in that smile. She'd missed a key, then had recovered enough to finish the song. Her suspicions were confirmed when she'd heard one of the other children call him by name. The days that followed proved to be the happiest she'd been since leaving the farm.

Now the boy's chance at happiness threatened to destroy her own. She looked up from the paper to find Headmistress watching her.

"You don't approve?" she asked.

Anastasia struggled to keep all emotion from her voice. "One of the children is far too young to be sent out."

A frown creased the woman's forehead. "I'm sure I followed the criteria the Children's Aid Society sent over."

"The little one near the bottom. He's only three, and much too young to be going out. He'd never be able to tell the agents if his home life is pleasant or not," Anastasia said, making her case.

"What's the number beside the child's name?" Headmistress put on her glasses and jotted the numbers down on a piece of paper as Anastasia related it to her. She pushed from her chair and opened the tall door behind her desk, disappearing inside the room. The door blended into the wood so well that, until that moment, Anastasia hadn't realized it was there. She rose and quietly maneuvered to where she could see inside. Large cabinets lined the perimeter of the room. She watched as Headmistress trailed a finger along the outside of the cabinets until she found the one she was searching for. Then she slid her fingers into the notched groove and pulled out a long drawer. She thumbed through the files, pulled one out, and skimmed it with her finger. Headmistress gasped at something she'd read then hurriedly returned the file to the cabinet. Anastasia hurried to her seat as Headmistress slid the drawer shut and looked up when the woman returned to the room.

"This child you are concerned about, what does he mean to you?" she said as she returned to her seat.

"To me?" Anastasia asked as casually as possible. The last thing she wanted to do was to tell the woman the truth. That the boy filled the void her son had left. "Why, nothing. I'm just concerned for his safety. Him being so young and all."

"I see. Tell me, Anastasia, isn't that the same boy you nursed when you first arrived?"

So she did know. "Why, yes, now that you mention it, I think I did nurse him. I've nursed so many. I guess you're right; it is rather easy to forget such things."

The woman looked over her glasses at her. "And you're telling me the only objection you have to the child being sent out is his age?"

"Yes, ma'am," Anastasia lied.

"If I remove the boy, that will leave a vacant seat. It's a rare opportunity to help these children find homes. I'd so hate not to use all the spaces allowed. Perhaps you would like to go in the child's place?"

"No!" Anastasia realized she'd yelled and lowered her tone. "No, I'm much too old. I turned twenty just this year. I'm only here because I'm helping out until a mistress position opens up. Do you not recall?"

"Yes. Yes, of course I do. Whatever was I thinking? That works out quite well, as I happen to have an opening coming up if you are still interested. I'd thought that Clara would change her mind about leaving us, but the girl is determined she's going to set off to see the world." There was a hint of sadness in the woman's words. Anastasia guessed it was simply because the girl had been at the asylum for so long.

"Yes, becoming a mistress is the only reason I've stayed." *That, and I've nowhere else to go.*

"Very well. I will let Mistress Flora know to assign you a room in the Mistress Quarters. Still, if I were to hold the boy back, that would leave us one child short. You know the children; who would you recommend we send?"

Anastasia looked over the list once more. Flipping the paper over, she realized there was one name missing from Mary's little gang. Maybe this was her chance to have Slim removed as well. "I would suggest Dorthia."

"Really?" Headmistress said, tapping her fingers together. "I would think her to be too old."

"She's no older than Slim, and he's on the list. They are both close to being adults. I guess it would get them out of the city before they come of age. Or maybe you should keep Slim here," Anastasia replied, wondering if it was enough. If not, it would at least get Dorthia onto the trains so she could help keep an eye on Mileta. *At least until she is placed.*

Headmistress sighed her acceptance. "I suppose she'll do. Okay, you've gotten your way, for now."

Though her heart ached at the thought of not seeing Slim, Anastasia breathed a sigh of relief that she wouldn't have to say goodbye to Franky again.

She wondered how her brother would react when he found out his little plan hadn't worked as well as he'd thought. At least with both Slim and Dorthia gone, she didn't have to worry about Tobias finding out she'd used up her one request on the boy that reminded her of her son and not the girl he'd asked her to protect. While she'd always be grateful to Mileta for teaching her how to play the piano properly, she wasn't ready to let Franky go. Not yet anyway.

***

Anastasia sat at the piano, letting the stress of the day float out through her fingers and onto the ivory keys. It was as if the music drifting through the room could heal her heart in ways nothing before ever could. Music healed her soul. Whenever she played, nothing else mattered.

Well, almost nothing.

She thought about her conversation with Headmistress and how the woman had agreed to allow Franky to remain in the asylum. Anastasia tried to tell herself she'd pulled him from the train for his own good, but whenever she stopped to think about it, she knew her reasons were purely selfish. She prayed Franky never discovered it was she who had kept him there. She who'd kept him from a chance at a normal life. Maybe she would be able to let him go the next time an opportunity arose. *Maybe.*

***

"Sometimes, I think you play better than Mileta," Slim said as she pulled the cover over the keys.

"I didn't know you were here." Anastasia could tell the boy was upset by the way he moved. He, along with the rest of those chosen, had been given the news shortly after supper. Obviously, Slim had some reservations. Normally, his eyes were full of smiles and mischief; tonight, they held a mixture of sorrow and fear. Unable to face him, she turned away, pretending to wipe dust from the piano. "I couldn't sleep, so I came down to play."

"I'm not sure I want to go."

She knew if she said the wrong thing, he would take it as a sign she wanted him to stay. Asking him to stay wouldn't be fair to him, as Headmistress was not likely to change her mind about not sending him out. Sure, he could do something to get himself removed, but she'd made Headmistress aware of his age. If the woman sensed trouble, she wouldn't hesitate to have him removed from the asylum altogether.

Anastasia turned to him and smiled her encouragement. "Of course you want to go. Why wouldn't you?"

"Why wouldn't I? Why because of you. I like you."

She forced a laugh. "You like what we do together."

"And you don't?"

"I didn't say that. But you can't stay just on account of that. You have a chance at a whole new life. Mileta is leaving. She's the reason you agreed to come here in the first place. If she's gone, there's no reason for you to stay."

"You're saying you ain't a good enough reason for me to stay?"

She closed her eyes briefly. "That's exactly what I'm

saying. They're making me a mistress. I'll have a lot more responsibilities and won't have much time to see you. Why, I'm even getting my own room. I probably won't be able to see you at all."

The hurt in his eyes was instant. "You don't sound all that broken up about it."

"I had my share of fun. But you didn't give me nothing I can't find anywhere else." She'd said the words with so much conviction, even she believed them.

"Yeah, well you weren't nothing special either. I just come onto you because I told Mouse I'd keep an eye on you," he said, turning away.

If she'd hadn't seen the tears before he turned, she might have believed his words. She wanted to call him back so they could both take back the hurt. In the end, she remained stoic until he'd left the room. Then she melted into a pool of tears.

Chapter Thirty-Nine

September 1926

Anastasia led the group of children into the dining room. She'd traded her previous gingham uniform for her new all-black wardrobe that let everyone know she was one of the mistresses and not just another helper. As she stood waiting for her group to get their trays, she looked around the room for Franky. He wasn't in his usual spot, so she walked through the room thinking maybe he'd switched tables. As she walked, she realized he was not the only child missing. *Don't panic; maybe his classroom has been delayed.* She looked for Clara, hoping to ask the girl what she knew, only to find the girl missing as well.

"Is there a problem, Mistress Anna?" one of the older girls asked.

She'd taken to using the abbreviated version of her name, as many of the younger children, Franky included, had trouble pronouncing Anastasia. "Some of the children seem to be missing, I was just looking for them. Have you seen Clara?"

"Miss Clara came in a little while ago and collected some of the children. She had a list and called them all by name," the girl said.

"Was Franky one of them?" Anastasia asked.

The girl shook her head. "I'm sorry, there are so many children. I don't know them all by name."

"Thank you, Molly." Anastasia said, knowing she was one of the few who did know everyone by name. It was a gift of hers; she only had to be told the child's name once and was able to commit both child and name to memory. She'd done the same with the tunes Mileta had shown her how to play, though admittedly, she sometimes had to hear them several times before being able to play without missing a key. Mileta had told her that her mother would have liked her very much, a comment that had made Anastasia smile.

"If you tell me what the boy looks like, I can tell you if maybe he was one of the ones that Clara took."

Clara took? Something about the way the girl phrased her comment made Anastasia uneasy. She thought about describing Franky but knew it to be a wasted effort. There were dark-haired boys, light-haired boys, and a few redheads. The problem was, unless they had something that made them stand out, they all pretty much looked alike, mostly because they were all dressed the same. She looked at the girl and smiled. "No, that's all right. I'll find her after lunch."

***

Much to her chagrin, she'd hadn't found Clara after lunch. Clara and the children, twenty-three by her calculation, did not eat their evening meal in the dining room, and Clara did not sleep in her room during the night. Anastasia knew this for a fact because, after checking multiple times, she'd finally sat in front of the girl's door waiting for her to arrive. Now she waited at the base of the stairs watching for any sign of Clara or the children as everyone made their way downstairs for their morning meal. She continued waiting long past when the children stopped trickling down the stairs.

Something's wrong.

Anastasia hurried to Headmistress's office. Finding the door closed, she rapped on the door then reached for the doorknob, surprised to find it locked. *It's never locked.*

Headmistress insisted on greeting each new child as they arrived and in turn had an open-door policy. Her stomach gurgled as she continued to search for someone who could tell her where they'd taken the children. Someone who could alleviate the fear that was bubbling within. She raced down the hallway and turned the corner, nearly running directly into Mistress Flora.

The woman clutched her chest. "Goodness, Anna, you nearly scared me to death. Where are you off to in such a hurry?"

"I'm sorry, Mistress Flora. I didn't mean to startle you. I'm looking for Clara. She and some of the children seem to be missing. I tried to ask Headmistress, but she's not in her office. Her door's locked. It's all very peculiar."

"There, there, it's nothing to be upset about," the woman said, patting Anastasia's arm. "Clara went with Headmistress to see the children to the train. I'm sure they'll be back by late afternoon."

Franky's gone?! The panic that had been bubbling rushed to the surface. There had to be another reason. Headmistress hadn't even asked her to look over the list. "What do you mean, to the train?"

"I'm sorry, I thought you knew. The Children's Aid Society contacted Headmistress just last week and asked if she'd like to send some children out. The placements worked out so well last time, so she was eager to compile a list. She and Clara have been working on it all week." Her brow furrowed. "I'm surprised they didn't tell you. I thought everyone knew. Surely you're happy for the children, are you not?"

"Yes, of course," Anastasia said, turning so the woman couldn't see the worry on her face. She took her time walking towards the dining room. Just as had happened with Caleb and her son, Franky was gone and she hadn't even gotten the chance to tell the boy goodbye. *It's for the best*; at least that was what she tried to tell herself. *He's not my son. It's not fair to keep the boy here when I have nothing to offer him.* While she'd managed to save the money she'd earned, it wasn't enough to raise a child. Even if it was, how could she think of raising another child when she had no clue what had become of her own son? She knew the answer. Because with the absence of her own child, Franky had become hers. Seeing him every day secured the boy's place in her heart, and sadly, she rarely thought of her son anymore. When she tried, all she could see was the face of Franky, the boy who'd filled the void. Now that he was gone, she wondered how long it would be before she forgot him as well.

***

Anastasia had just reached her dorm room when she heard footsteps running down the hall.

"Anastasia!"

She recognized the voice and turned to see Clara coming towards her.

"Mistress Flora told me you were looking for me. Here, this letter came for you today."

Anastasia took the letter and placed it in her pocket. She didn't have to look at the return post to know who it was from. Slim had written to apologize shortly after leaving. In the time since, he'd written several more. "I've nothing to say to you."

Clara grabbed her arm to stop her. "What's gotten into you?"

"How could you do that to me?" Anastasia asked, squaring her shoulders.

"Anastasia, I don't know what you're talking about. I

didn't do anything to you."

"The devil you didn't. Why didn't you tell me about the kids going out on the trains?"

"Is that what's got you upset? Headmistress didn't want anyone to know. She said it would upset the others if they knew they weren't selected."

"That's not true, Mistress Flora told me everyone knew. She was surprised when I told her I didn't."

"She said that? I promise Anastasia, Headmistress told me it was a secret."

Anastasia studied Clara's face to see if she was telling the truth. "She lied to you."

"Why would she do that?"

"She didn't want me to know."

"I don't understand," Clara said with a sigh.

"She didn't want me to know she was sending Franky out."

"I know you like the kid, but you should be happy that he gets a chance for a good home."

"I should be."

Clara's eyes grew wide. "But you're not?"

It was Anastasia's turn to sigh. "Remember the baby I got caught nursing right after I arrived?"

"Yes."

"That was Franky. He was born the same day as my son, and when I was nursing him, I could close my eyes and pretend it was my son. The problem was the more I nursed him, the more I wanted it to be true. I became attached to the boy. That's why I got banned from the floor."

"Oh, Anastasia. You must've been heartbroken. We're friends; why didn't you tell me?"

"It hurt too bad to talk about it. Then one day, I was playing the piano and he smiled at me. I knew it was Franky. I also knew if I wanted to see him and be a part of his life, I couldn't let anyone know how I felt. Headmistress tried to send him out on the trains the last time and I was able to convince her he was too young. She pulled his file and something she read bothered her. I didn't see what it was, but I saw how upset it made her when she read it."

"What do you think it was?"

"If I had to guess, it was a note from Mistress Irene telling of my fondness for the boy."

A sly smile crossed Clara's face. Reaching in her pocket, she pulled out a set of keys. "We could find out."

"You have the keys to Headmistress' office?"

"I have keys to all the rooms," Clara said, leading the way. "I've helped Headmistress for as long as I can remember. I guess she trusts me."

"She said you were leaving. But you're still here."

"I'll go someday. I was going to go a couple years ago, but Headmistress agreed to pay me."

"So you became a mistress."

"I'm not. I told her no. So she offered to pay me to keep doing the job I'm doing. She said I would have to wear the mistress uniform and sleep in the dorm. I guess technically I'm a mistress, but I'm doing the same thing I've always done."

"She must really like you."

Clara stopped in front of Headmistress' office and found the key to the door. "I guess."

Anastasia followed her inside and locked the door behind them.

"Where are the files?"

"Behind that door. I thought you'd already know."

The door was unlocked as Clara opened it and turned on the light. "No, I guess this is probably the only room in the building I've never been inside. There are so many cabinets, how will we find the file she was reading?"

Anastasia closed her eyes, picturing where the woman had stood. After a few seconds, she opened her eyes and frowned. "It was on this wall, but I don't remember exactly where."

"With your memory? Try harder." Clara pulled the drawer from the wall. "These are all alphabetized. What's Franky's last name?"

Anastasia felt a moment of panic. "I don't know. I've only heard him called Franky."

"Well, if you're sure this is the right side, I guess we'll have to go through them all. Some of these only have first names. Let's try F for Franky," Clara said, pulling out the drawer marked F.

"You look. I'm going to see if I can find my file." Anastasia walked to the cabinet marked C, pulled the drawer open, and flipped through the files until she found the one with her name. She pulled it from the drawer and began to read.

Anastasia Castiglione, sent over from the Home of Wayward Angels. The file went on to state she'd been sent out of the trains and had arrived back in New York heavy with child. She'd given birth June 17, 1920 to a son. Anastasia arrived at the asylum two days later. On the bottom of the paper was a number. As she read the number, her hands began to shake. *I've seen the number before.* She turned to Clara, who was staring at her eyes wide. In her hand was a file.

Clara handed it to her without a word, and as Anastasia read, everything made sense. The way her heart swelled from the moment she held Franky in her arms. The aching to be near him. The reason she'd known his smile, though she hadn't seen him in over two years. The reason his absence now was tearing her in two. Benjamin Franklin Castiglione, also known as child number 587823, was her son.

Chapter Forty

Anastasia sat in the dark waiting for Headmistresses to arrive. Clara had wished to join her, but she'd convinced her to return to her room. This was not Clara's fight. She, on the other hand, had already lost everything she cared about. She intended to have Headmistress contact the Children's Aid Society and have them send a wire asking to have Franky returned. She heard the doorknob jiggle and felt her heartbeat increase.

The light switched on, and Anastasia watched as Headmistress walked unaware to her desk. The woman saw Anastasia just as her bottom touched the chair. Clutching her chest, she let out the smallest of screams.

"Good Heavens, Anastasia, you gave me an awful fright." Headmistress looked toward the door. "How'd you get in?"

Anastasia held up the keys.

The color drained from her face. "Clara gave you the keys?"

"Of course not," Anastasia said with a shake of her head. "That girl is as loyal as the day is long. No, I lifted them from her pocket."

"But why?"

"I think you already know the answer to that."

Now recovered from the initial shock, Headmistress pulled herself taller. "No, I'm afraid I do not. I could have you arrested you know. As a matter of fact, I think I'll phone the authorities."

Anastasia glared at the woman. "And just what do you

think the authorities will say when I tell them you stole my child?"

The woman lowered the receiver. "I did not steal your child. He was sent here before you even joined us."

"You knew, and yet you told them not to allow me onto the fourth floor."

"Of course I did; you'd just given birth. Your motherly instincts were heightened. The fourth floor was the last place you needed to be."

"I needed to be with my son," Anastasia said firmly.

"That's not how things work in this place." To her credit, the woman actually looked sympathetic. "This is not a home for mothers. Children are sent to us for care. Sometimes those children are fortunate to find a new home. But there are so many. You've seen them. In here, on the streets, in one of the many other institutions. Why, it's an epidemic. You should be pleased your son was chosen. Can you imagine his life if he were to remain behind these walls until he comes of age? Surely that is not what you want."

"He'd have a good life. I'd see to it."

Headmistress leaned back in her chair. "And how do you propose to do that?"

"I've got a job now and my own room. Franky could stay with me."

"First, there are no children permitted in the Mistress Quarters. Secondly, you would not be able to tell the child you're his mother. Think about how the others in the institution would treat the boy if they were to find out. He'd become an outcast, fighting to survive."

"I'd protect him."

"You cannot watch over him night and day. He will get out of your sight at some point. Children can be cruel, Anastasia. You've been there. Why do you think Clara told you to be firm with the children? If not for you striking first, your life would have been miserable. I've seen it all before. I knew the second I saw your scar how the children would treat you. That's why I instructed Clara to befriend you."

Clara was ordered to be nice to me?

"That's right," Headmistress said, watching her face. "Clara was your friend because I told her to be. Before you go all pouty, she needed you as much as you needed her. I told her to be nice to you, but I never told her to keep being nice. She is your true friend. She's disobeyed me more than I care to remember because she's loyal to you. Though I've asked, she's refused to keep me updated on you. Until you were in my office a few years ago, I didn't know you even knew your son was here."

"I didn't know. Not until last night."

This seemed to surprise the woman. "But you came in here and convinced me to remove him from the list."

"I didn't know he was my son. I never knew his name. I only knew he was born on my son's birthday. At first, I hoped it to be him, then I was told he had a twin sister. I only gave birth to one child. I couldn't explain it. I just knew I needed him near me."

"The girl was abandoned the same day as your son arrived. It was convenient and provided a great cover for the truth. As you said, you knew you only had one, so it would go to reason the child was not yours."

"But he is mine, and I want him back."

"I'm afraid that's not possible. The child has already been placed by now."

"So send the family another child."

Headmistress stood and walked to the front of her desk. "Anastasia, please try to think about this with your head and not your heart. If we were to bring the child back, he'd always wonder what he did to get removed from the home. As I've stated, you would not be able to tell the boy you're his mother, so he would continue to wonder. It would eat at his mind and continue to cause self-doubt. He would act out, rebel, and find himself in constant trouble."

"Then I will leave here and take him with me."

"You have no husband to provide for you. What kind of life would he have? You too, for that matter?"

Doubt was starting to creep in. "I'll get a job."

"Working where? In a sweatshop? From what I've heard, you tried that before and nearly died in the process."

Clara must have told.

"Clara may not have told me everything. But she's told me a great deal about you," Headmistress said, reading her thoughts. "What if things would have been different? What if you were working in that shop, putting in all those hours to make what, a few dollars a week? Who's watching your son while you work those twelve-hour days, Anastasia? If he'd been with someone else and you perished in the fire, who'd care for your son?"

"I don't know."

"I do; he'd come here or at least to an asylum such as this." Headmistress closed her eyes for a moment. "We gained so many that day and the days that followed. So many lives lost. So many children left without mothers to tuck them in at night. And that was just the ones we know about. I'm sure many of the children ended up on the street. You were on the streets for a while. Is that what you want for your child?"

While she doubted the likelihood of a fire, she remembered Slim telling of how he'd ended up on the streets. *One day, my mother didn't come home.* Could she, in good conscience, bring Franky back here just to have him end up back on the streets? *He would grow to hate me.*

"I just want my son to find some happiness."

"Then let him go."

Her anger was subsiding, sorrow taking its place. "You just don't understand what it's like."

Headmistress looked towards the door once more. "I'm going to tell you something, and it must stay within these walls. If you breathe a word of it, I'll deny it and have you thrown out onto the streets with nothing but the clothes on your back. Do you understand?"

Anastasia gave a simple nod.

"I understand more than you think. My family name got me this job. To be sure, I was highly qualified, but the name helped. Shortly before coming to work here, I got pregnant. I was an educated woman in a well-to-do family whose fine name would've been tarnished if word got out that their unmarried daughter was taken in by the smooth words of her college professor. He was married and ran back to his wife to avoid the scandal. I worked until I could no longer hide my situation. Then I lied to both my family and the foundation and said I was taking an extended trip abroad. London has had institutions for years, and I told everyone I'd found a brief course that could further my education and help to streamline things here at the asylum. I used a fake name and went to a home for unwed mothers."

This caught Anastasia's attention. "And the home forced you to give your child away?"

"No, my situation was different," the woman said softly. "You see, my family had money — lots of it. I bribed the home I was in to send my daughter to this institution. While I knew I'd never be able to tell the girl who I was, I knew I'd be able to keep a watch over her. In turn, while it ate me up inside, I got to watch her grow up."

"Your situation was nothing like mine," Anastasia said

heatedly. "You made a choice. I had no money. The law said I was a child, so the choice was made for me."

"I didn't keep you from your child to punish you. I did it to protect both of you. Had I told my family, they would've taken her away from me. If I would've let my daughter in on my secret, not only would the children have treated her differently, but the staff would've as well. I didn't even get the privilege of nursing my daughter. I had to watch as wet nurses placed her to their breasts and mistresses wiped away her tears. In the end, I'm not the girl's mother. I am only the one responsible for bringing her into this world. Though she is grown, telling her now would only make her hate me for all the untruths I've told. As it is, we have a civil relationship."

Stop trying to justify your wrongs. "You had money. You could have left here and taken her with you."

"My parents had money. I make good money here, but I've never married. I guess in some ways, I consider myself married to this asylum. I live in a room on the upper floor. What life could I give her on the outside? A life with nannies who she'd think of as her mother? At least in here, I can be near her."

Anastasia realized the woman was talking in the present tense. *The girl is still here.* She did a quick rundown of all the girls old enough to be her daughter. The answer was so obvious, she was surprised she hadn't realized it before. Now that she knew, the resemblance was unmistakable. *Clara.*

There was a knock on the door, and Mistress Flora stuck her head inside. "I'm sorry to interrupt. There's an issue in the washroom."

Headmistress pushed off the edge of her desk with a sigh. "As you can see, there's always something needing my attention. Take some time to think about what I've said. We'll talk again later."

Anastasia followed the women out and turned in the

opposite direction. She walked several steps before chancing a look over her shoulder. Seeing she was alone in the hall, she returned to Headmistress' office and slipped inside. Closing the door behind her, she hurried to the file room, pulled open the drawer, found the file, and removed Franky's birth record. She was getting ready to close the file when she had another thought. She searched through the C's, looking for Clara's name. She found three children by that name, none the one she was looking for. She was just getting ready to leave, when she had another thought. If Clara was Headmistress' daughter, maybe they'd share the same last name. She walked to the drawer marked L and pulled it from the wall. With the proper name, it didn't take long to find the file. *Clara LaRue.*

***

October 1926

"Anastasia, wait up."

Anastasia turned to see Clara hurrying towards her. The girl waved an envelope and smiled.

Chills raced down her arms as she took the envelope. "Did Headmistress see this yet?"

"No, it came with the daily mail. I slipped it in my pocket before she saw it. It's what you've been waiting for, is it not?"

Anastasia looked at the return address on the envelope, showing it had come from the Children's Aid Society. It had been nearly a month since Franky and the others left on the train. She'd bided her time, waiting for the placement report, which would show where Franky had been sent. "I think so. We'll need to be careful breaking the seal."

"We can use Mistress Flora's office; she's in the meeting room and is not due back for some time."

Anastasia slipped the envelope into her pocket as both girls hurried to the unused office. Once inside, Anastasia watched in awe as Clara opened the envelope without disturbing the wax seal. "You've done this before."

"I get curious sometimes," Clara said with a shrug.

Anastasia wondered if Clara had ever seen anything that would give the girl a hint as to her heritage. If she had, she'd never mentioned it. For that reason, she didn't think the girl knew the Headmistress to be her mother.

Anastasia unfolded the letter and skimmed the list of names until she found the paragraph regarding Franky. A sadness crept over her as she read of her son's placement. *Franky Castiglione has found a home with a nice couple in Illinois. The couple are well off and have a lovely home in Chicago.* Tears rolled down her face as she finished. *They have a large yard and a dog, which has taken to the boy and boy to the dog. I expect they will have a grand time, and the boy will have fine stories to tell when I next visit.* She wiped the tears and jotted the address on a slip of paper, which she placed in her pocket.

"Didn't he find a nice home?" Clara asked.

"Actually, it sounds as if he found a lovely home. He even has a dog," Anastasia said, handing her the letter.

She watched as Clara took a matchbox from her pocket. She pulled a matchstick from the box and struck it along the side. She waited for the flame to take hold and held it close to the wax. As the wax began to soften, she blew out the flame and carefully pressed the wax to the envelope.

"Good as new." Clara beamed when she'd finished. "I'll slip this in with tomorrow's mail."

"Will you go for him, then?" Clara asked once they were out of the office.

"I don't know," she said with a sigh.

Chapter Forty-One

Anastasia stayed in her room well into the morning after spending a nearly sleepless night debating what to do. Up until she'd read the note from the placing agent, she'd been determined to find Franky and bring him home. Where that home would be, she hadn't cared, as long as she and her son were together. Now, she wasn't so sure. Her son barely knew her; how could she compete with the home he'd been given? On her own, she'd never be able to give him a home with a yard and a dog to look after him. She remembered Runt, the boy she'd known years ago, and the dog that was never far from his side. She then remembered the excitement on Tobias' face when the dog had licked his face and how he'd giggled while running his fingers through the dog's fur. *Every boy should have a dog.*

Sighing, she went to her dresser and pulled out the pile of letters she'd received from Slim since his departure. She opened the last letter and reread it for the hundredth time. As he'd always done, he told her about her brother and the fact that he'd gone to Chicago to take care of some business. Though Slim didn't go so far as to say what kind of business her brother was into, it seemed as if Slim was living vicariously through his friend.

If he's gone to Chicago once, maybe he'll go again. I can ask him to check on Franky and see that he's getting on well. According to Slim, Tobias likes to take care of people. If Franky is not okay... No, he's doing fine; the agent said so.

Leaving him there would be best for him. I'll ask Tobias to look in on him. Just to be sure. Though it broke her heart, she knew leaving her son there was the right thing to do.

Anastasia gathered her writing supplies and thought about what she wanted to say. She'd have to be careful how to word the letter so that Tobias would be willing to check on her son after the way she'd treated him. *Best to do a simple letter and structure it so it's just a sister requesting something from her loving brother. I'll write as though nothing happened. Yes, that would be best.* She picked up the pen and began to write.

My Dearest Tobias,

I hope this letter finds you well. I'm writing to tell you of your nephew, Franky. You asked about him before, but I was filled with hate at that time and could not speak of him. The mistresses told me it would be best if I did not tell him I was his mother. While he doesn't know me, I've watched him grow and made sure he was well taken care of. That is until now. He was sent away on the trains without my knowledge. Maybe it was for the best, as if not for the trains, the boy would spend his whole childhood behind these walls. I guess I have some goodness left inside as I do so worry about him.

Slim wrote and told me you have been to Chicago. That is where Franky is now. Please, dear brother, if you ever find yourself there again, could you find it in your heart to go to him and see to it he is well?

With all my love,
A.

When she'd finished, she started a second letter.

My Dearest Slim,

Much has changed since I received your last letter. I've finally found my son. Franky has been here all along. While I know the boy, I did not know him to be my son until after they'd sent him on the trains. While my heart aches to go to the boy, his placement sounds better than what I could offer. In your letter, you mentioned that Tobias has traveled to Chicago. I've written him a letter asking him to look in on my son should he get the chance. As I do not know how to contact my brother, I'm sending the letter to your address in hopes that you will give it to Tobias.

With everything that has happened of late, I find I am no longer happy in this place. I will be leaving soon. I'll send you my address whenever I get settled.

Until then, know that I miss you.

With warmest regards,

Anna

Anastasia reread the letter, still surprised at what she'd written. Was she really planning to leave? She hadn't even considered doing so until the words flowed out through her pen. *There's nothing left for me here.* While the thought of leaving frightened her, the thought of staying scared her worse. She couldn't trust Headmistress and she'd never be able to walk into any of the common rooms without expecting to see Franky. An image of the little boy running through a grass-filled yard with a dog by his side came to mind. While she didn't know what color of dog he had, she imagined him running with the dog that had accompanied Runt. He was a good dog, and her son deserved a good dog. She committed the image to memory. Whenever she thought of her son, that was the image she wanted to see. She folded the two letters, placed them in envelopes, and laid them on the desk. Next she took the papers from Clara's file, folded them, and placed them in an envelope with the girl's name on it.

She walked to her closet, pulled out her clean black dress, and placed it in her pillowcase, opting to wear yesterday's dress instead. She ran the brush through her hair, pulling the length into a tight bun. Moving to the dresser, she opened the top drawer and retrieved the few spare undergarments she owned. She placed them in the pillowcase with her dress. She removed the money from her money sock. Though she knew how much she'd saved, she re-counted it just to be sure. Between the money she'd gotten from Tobias and the wages she'd earned since becoming a mistress, less the price of her room and meals, she had one hundred ninety-seven dollars and fifteen cents. *Please let it be enough.* She kept out one dollar and fifteen cents and returned the rest to the sock, stuffing it in the inside pocket of her cloak.

Anastasia took a final glance around the small room. Sparse as it was, she would miss the space. Heaving a sigh, she draped the cloak over her arm, picked up the envelopes, and left.

She met Clara as she reached the first floor.

"Headmistress sent me to find you. She's not pleased you missed the morning meal."

Anastasia laughed. "She won't be pleased tomorrow or the days after that either."

Clara's gaze landed on the cloak. "You're leaving?"

"I am."

"But where will you go?"

"I guess I don't rightly know."

Clara smiled. "I wish I had your courage."

Anastasia hugged the girl. Stepping back, she handed her all three envelopes. "Can you post these without

Headmistress seeing you?"

"Absolutely." Clara sifted through the envelopes and held up the one with her name on it. What's this?"

Anastasia smiled. "Open it when you're alone. It may just give you the courage you're looking for."

***

If she'd taken time to think things through, she might have stayed. She'd even wavered the moment she stepped outside the iron fence that enclosed the asylum. She didn't have a destination in mind, which was good, because having never ventured from the asylum, she had no clue where she was. She simply chose a direction and walked until the tree-lined street gave way to tall buildings.

Anastasia heard a noise, looked up, and saw a man standing on a board attached by two long ropes. She stood transfixed for a moment, watching as the man cleaned the window then used the rope to lower himself to the next. Her stomach growled, reminding her she'd left without eating breakfast, and started walking once more.

A man bumped into her, tipped his hat, and apologized. She reached into her pocket and only felt the coins she'd saved. *The money sock's gone.* After the initial panic, she remembered placing the money sock in her inner pocket. Still, the bump was a stark reminder of the dangers that lurked on the street. Not only did she need something to eat, but she'd need to find a place to spend the night. The money she had seemed like a lot, but she wasn't sure how long it would last. *I need a job.*

She walked faster now, skirting around people as if she actually knew where she was going. She turned down a street, and another, and kept walking. Suddenly, she'd arrived. She hadn't been there in nearly twelve years, but the building still looked the same. She climbed the five steps, opened the door, and stepped inside. Again, nothing had changed. She looked to the long hallway, remembering all the times she'd traveled those halls to visit Mrs. Johnston. A pang of sadness clutched her heart. *Why'd you have to die?*

She opened the stairwell door and climbed the steps, trying her best to ignore the stench. She opened the door, walked through the hallway, and stopped at the door to the apartment she'd once called home. Unlike when she'd lived there, the door was open. She stood staring at the threshold she'd crossed through too many times to count.

For a moment, she was a girl again, bringing home the items Sharon had sent her to purchase. She half expected to hear her mother's voice calling to her welcoming her home. She saw movement out of the corner of her eye and watched as a rat ran across the room. A moment later, a woman she didn't recognize appeared, shooing the varmint with a broom. The lady's eyes narrowed as she noticed Anastasia standing in the doorway.

"I don't know what you're selling, lady, but we'll have none of it," the woman said, forgetting the rat and wielding the broom as if it were a weapon.

Anastasia took a step back. "I must have the wrong apartment."

"You do. You'd best be moving along if you know what's good for you," the woman said, holding the broom higher.

She took the stairs slower this time. A part of her had hoped the stories she'd heard weren't true and that her mother was still alive.

Anastasia made her way to the market and found it bustling with activity. A dog barked and she spun around, half expecting to see Runt, but the boy was nowhere to be seen. *He's not a boy anymore.*

She walked to where the apple cart had sat every day for as long as she could remember. It wasn't there. *So many things have changed.* In its place sat a different cart selling mincemeat pasties. She smiled a weak smile at the lady and held up a single finger. She reached into her pocket and retrieved a coin, handing it to the woman in exchange for the pie.

The meat pie didn't do much to help her mood. The day was half done. Except for a full belly, she was no better off than before. She walked through the streets with a renewed sense of desperation. She was wallowing in her self-pity when she saw the sign — stuck in the window of a ticket booth of a theater. It was small with just three written words that made her heart leap.

Piano player wanted.

A man with slicked-back hair sat looking out the window. He had a mustache, and for a moment, she thought him to be rather fearsome-looking. He smiled when she approached, and his eyes lit up. Suddenly, he appeared more handsome than fearsome.

Anastasia pointed to the sign. "I want the job."

The man in the booth looked her over, his gaze coming to rest on her scar. "Can't have it."

She'd seen that look before, and it angered her. She narrowed her eyes at the man. "Why not?"

"Job's been filled. Guess I forgot to remove the sign." He pulled it from the window and set it aside.

"What kind of job was it?"

Another laugh. "Playing the piano, of course."

"Here?"

"Of course here. The pianist plays while the movie's showing."

"What song do they play?"

"They don't play a song. They play the piano to match the movie."

"How do they know what keys to play?"

"Haven't you ever seen a movie before?"

She shook her head.

The man looked around to see if anyone was watching then slipped a ticket under the opening in the glass. "This one's on me. It's an old one from last year called *Wizard of Oz*, but since you haven't seen it, it's okay. Don't go blabbing it to everyone I let you in, or I'll lose my job. You want popcorn, you'll have to pay for it on your own."

"Thank you," she said, taking the ticket.

Anastasia sat through the film with a mixture of awe and horror. While she'd never seen a film before, she'd read the book, *The Wonderful Wizard of Oz*, so she thought she knew what was going to happen. As it turned out, the silent film was nothing like the book. It was a story of the queen of a town who'd been kidnapped. Some of the scenes were absolutely frightening. Still, seeing the scenes come to life filled her with excitement she'd never felt before. What she didn't care for was the piano music the man played to go along with the film. He'd played it all wrong. She followed the piano man out, planning on speaking with the guy to explain what he'd done wrong. He was standing out front talking with others, so she paused, waiting for him to finish his conversation.

"Well, what'd ya think?" the ticket guy asked as she was waiting.

"I liked the movie well enough," Anastasia replied.

"Sheesh, try not to sound so excited," the guy said with a chuckle.

"I just wished the piano man would've played better. It's such a great story, but it's hard to stay in the story when the music doesn't match. I was just waiting for him. I thought maybe I could give him some suggestions."

"I thought you said you've never seen the movie."

"I hadn't until now, but it's not hard now that I know what's supposed to happen."

The guy rocked back on his heels. "Do you have someplace you need to be right now?"

Every place and no place. "No."

He took her by the arm. "Good. Come with me."

Anastasia rushed after the guy, who walked as if he was in a great hurry. He led her back into the theater and motioned her to sit at the piano. "Give me a moment to restart the film. I want to hear what you'd do differently."

Anastasia waited for the film to begin and began playing a soft melody as the words rolled onto the screen. The scene opened with a sad-looking old man. He looked to be a doll maker, so she thought maybe he was just tired. She played to convey this. She increased the tone as a little girl came down the stairs asking the man to read her a story. Anastasia weaved the music throughout the movie, adding just the right tone and dramatic flair to bring the film to life until the very end, when the writing on the screen let the viewers know that Queen Dorothy and her prince lived happily ever after. To her surprise, the man from the ticket box rose from his seat, clapping his hands together.

"I cannot tell you how many times I've seen that movie. Never have I enjoyed it as much as now. Your playing is beyond amazing. Why, with playing like this, we'll have the seats full every night. Maybe we can even bring in some first-run movies. Honey, if you want the job, it's yours. You'll play three shows a day and I'll pay you three dollars a week. What do you say?"

She thought about it for a moment. As much as she wanted the job, she knew that three dollars wouldn't be enough to pay for a place to stay. She shook her head.

"No? Why not? I just told you how great you play."

"I still have to find a place to stay. Three dollars just

isn't enough."

The man rubbed his chin. "Honey, you sure do drive a hard bargain. I'll make it five dollars a week, and you can stay here rent-free for as long as you work here."

She looked around the room. "Where will I sleep?"

"Not here, Silly." He looked toward the ceiling. "There are some apartments upstairs. I had one come empty just a few moments ago."

"A few moments ago. How could you possibly know? You've been down here all along."

"Why, that's when I fired my last piano player," he said with a grin.

Anastasia felt her eyes grow wide. "You can do that?"

He leaned in and whispered in her ear, "Doll, I can do anything I want. I own the place. By the way, the name's Logan, and I think I love you."

Chapter Forty-Two

Monday, May 21, 1928

Anastasia sat on her windowsill enjoying the fresh air. She placed the cigarette in her mouth and inhaled, blowing the smoke out in a lengthy stream. She took another draw as someone rapped on her door. "Enter, it's open."

Logan entered carrying a huge vase of red roses. Impeccably dressed in a black pinstripe suit, the man was insanely handsome. "Would you please be so kind as to climb down from that windowsill before I have to come over there and rescue you?"

She pulled another drag, flicking the butt out the window with a smile. "Good to know chivalry can overcome a man's fear of heights."

"It can, but I'd rather it not," he said, placing the vase on the table.

"Another one of my admirers?" she asked, walking towards him. Since she'd begun playing, someone was always sending her flowers professing their love for her, her music, or in many cases, both.

"More like a lovesick puppy." His voice sounded agitated.

She plucked the card from the bouquet and smiled. *Thinking of you. Love, Slim.*

"You might as well marry the boy," Logan said, watching her face.

"You're just mad that I haven't said yes to any of your

proposals." She kissed Logan on the cheek. "I've told you, I am not the marrying type."

He grabbed her by the arm and pulled her in for a full kiss. She drank in his cologne as she'd done so many times before knowing she could feel safe here—if she'd only allow herself the chance.

"We've no time for this," he said, pulling away. "Get dressed and meet me downstairs in twenty minutes."

"What's the hurry? There's no evening show tonight."

"Do you have to argue about everything? Just get dressed and meet me downstairs. Can't you do that for me, please?" he asked, then walked to the door. "Twenty minutes. Don't be late."

"I wasn't arguing," she said to the back of the door.

***

"I'm two minutes early," she said when she met him in the lobby eighteen minutes later.

"I'd hoped you'd be wearing something nice."

Puzzled, she looked down at her dress to make sure there were no rips or tears. She knew it didn't smell, as she'd washed it and hung it to dry the day before. "What's wrong with my dress?"

"It's the same one you always wear."

"It's not the same one. I changed. My other dress is soaking in the sink."

His brow furrowed. "You're telling me you only have two dresses?"

"I work in the dark, I rarely go anywhere, and I'm perfectly capable of washing my dress at the end of each day. Why do I need more than two dresses?" He'd seen her every day for the last seven months and had never complained about the way she dressed.

"What do you do with the money I give you?"

"You mean the money I earn from working for you?" she corrected. "I save it."

"Are you happy working here, Anastasia?"

I've never been happier. "I like it here just fine."

"Good, because I don't want to lose you. Ticket sales have never been better, and each show is sold out. I've been meaning to talk to you about that, as I plan on giving you a raise."

That piqued her interest. "How much?"

"Perhaps I'll give you ten dollars a week. You'll be happy with double the money, right? Good," he said, not waiting for a reply. "We'll work out the details later. We're going to be late."

"Late for what? We don't have an evening show on Mondays."

"There you go arguing again." He looked her over once again and shook his head. "This will never do."

She crossed her arms and narrowed her eyes. "I'm starting to not like you."

He laughed. "Turn around."

"Why?"

"For heaven's sake, can you just do what you're told for once?"

"Gladly." She kept her arms crossed and turned so she wouldn't have to look at him. The next thing she knew, his hands were in her hair, pulling the strands free of the tight bun she wore. She closed her eyes as he ran his fingers through the locks several times.

"Now turn," he ordered. She did as he said and he smiled. "Not perfect, but it'll do."

"And you wonder why I do not wish to marry you."

He looked out the front window. "Time to go. Our cab has arrived."

"Cab? Where are we going?"

He took her by the shoulders and turned her towards the door. "Just once. Please, for me."

***

"We could've walked," she said when the cab stopped on Broadway a few moments later.

He pointed to the Royal Theatre. "We could have, but this way, we can get in early and find our seats."

She looked up at the theatre's marquee, blinking her surprise. Surrounded by dazzling lights, it read *Mae West in Diamond LIL*. She'd never been to the theatre before. "Oh Logan, are you serious? You've gotten us tickets to the theatre?"

"What, no arguments?"

"None," she said, shaking her head.

Anastasia's joy was short-lived. The second they walked into the theatre, she knew why Logan had balked at her outfit. Standing in the lobby were groups of people. While the men wore suits, the women all wore sparkling dresses, some so long, they skimmed the floor—others dripping in beads so short, one could see their stockinged legs. Most of the women wore hats or headbands with feathers. Almost all wore pearls and gloves of various lengths, which covered their hands. Several women engaged in conversation stopped to stare at her then erupted in giggling whispers. Anastasia hesitated, then remembering Mrs. Johnston's words, tucked her hair behind her ears, straightened her shoulders, set her jaw, and walked through the crowd and stood next to the theatre steps.

"You are the most fascinating woman I've ever met,"

Logan said, coming up beside her.

"You'll get no argument from me," she said in return.

***

Anastasia stood inside the department store, taking in the racks of dresses. Too many to count, the choices were overwhelming. She hadn't stepped inside a department store since leaving Popular Bluff over nine years ago. Even then, the colors and styles had been more subdued.

A young woman wearing heeled shoes approached. "Is anyone helping you?"

"No," she answered meekly. She'd used all her bravado the evening prior. The situation was made worse when Mae West sauntered onto the stage with a personality larger than life and oozing sex appeal. For nearly two hours, she'd watched the sultry actress sass around the stage, causing her fellow actors to drool. Even Logan had been totally enamored with the woman. Of course, that might have been because her breasts were in danger of popping out of her dress. West's brazenness reminded her of Mrs. Johnston. Anastasia had taken an instant liking to the actress and found herself wondering if Mrs. Johnston and Miss West had ever met, knowing if they did, each would have found a kinship with the other.

Anastasia had walked into the ladies' room during intermission and watched as women painted their lips and powdered their noses. She'd reached into her pocket for a cigarette, only to leave it there when she saw several ladies smoking cigarettes that sat in long dainty tubes. Even their cigarettes looked sexy. It was at that moment she'd decided to open her money sock and purchase some things that would make her smile.

The store clerk gave her a once over. To Anastasia's

delight, there was no judgment in the woman's eyes. "Is there something I can help you find?"

"I went to the theatre last night," Anastasia replied.

"Oh, how delightful. What did you see?"

"I saw *Diamond LIL*." She twisted her hand to bring attention to her attire. "This is what I wore."

The woman gulped her understanding as her eyes traced Anastasia once more. "Oh, you poor dear."

Anastasia nodded.

"Is that the only dress you have?"

"Oh no," Anastasia said, shaking her head. "I have one at home just like it."

***

Anastasia stood in front of the department store, waiting for her cab. While the walk home wasn't a long one, she felt a bit unsteady in her new heeled shoes. She held her bags tight, wondering what her mother would think of the fact that she now had a different dress for each day of the week. Not only that, she'd even purchased a long red sequined gown just in case she decided to make another trip to the theatre. She doubted she would wear it any other time, as the beads made the dress incredibly heavy. The store clerk assured her that was the latest fashion and that the looks it would garner would be well worth a little headache.

A breeze touched her legs, and she sucked in a breath. Never had she been on a public street with so little clothes. Even the dresses she'd wore while living on the farm covered her ankles.

The cab pulled to the curb. Anastasia stepped forward as the driver opened the door and hurried to relieve her of her bags. She smiled, wondering what he'd think had he known he was carrying bags with silk undergarments, satin nightdresses, and matching robes trimmed with fur.

"Right this way, ma'am," he said, opening the door.

She slid across the seat and gave him the address, feeling silly since the ride would be so short. Pulling away from the curb, the driver angled the mirror where he could see her.

Though her hair was now cut short, exposing her face, she didn't feel the least self-conscious. She knew he couldn't see her scar. The woman at the makeup counter had seen to that, applying the makeup slowly, showing her how to recreate the look to camouflage her flaw. When the woman had finished, Anastasia had nearly cried. Not only had the scar disappeared, but she'd instantly seen her mother looking back at her through the mirror. Not the sickly shell of the woman she'd become, but the beautiful lady who'd once walked through the market turning heads as she went. *I'm beautiful*, Anastasia had said, making no excuses for her words.

"That's a lot of packages to take to a movie," the driver said as he maneuvered the motorcar to the curb. "I could keep them and come to pick you up after it's finished if you'd prefer."

"That won't be necessary. I live upstairs," Anastasia replied.

Disappointment crossed over the man's face. "Just my luck."

She waited for him to come around to open the door and handed him the change for the fare, then walked to the back of the car and waited for him to lift her packages from the trunk.

"Want me to carry them inside?" His voice sounded hopeful.

"I can manage from here," she said, gathering the bags from him.

"Just my luck," he said once more. He slipped a piece

of paper into one of her bags. "You need a ride, you give me a call."

She walked to the entrance and realized she'd left the key in her old dress, which was now at the bottom of one of the bags. Sitting the bags down, Anastasia kneeled and began searching the bags. She heard the door click open.

"Is there something I can help you with, ma'am?"

She straightened and turned to face Logan, waiting for recognition to set in.

His eyes took in her transformation. He brought his hand to her face, his fingers tracing her hidden scar. "You never cease to amaze me."

She looked past him to see her reflection in the glass and saw the ghost of her mother once more. She smiled, knowing the woman would have loved the soft pink chiffon tea dress. She removed her hat. "I've cut my hair."

He lifted the soft curl that framed her jaw. "You look stunning."

"I should get these things upstairs," she said, gathering her purchases once more.

He took the packages and led the way to her apartment. "You'll have just enough time to put everything away and change into your black dress before the show."

He doesn't like my new dress. Anastasia followed after him, slowly navigating the stairs with her new elevated shoes.

He opened the door to her apartment and placed the packages on the table. "I've got to go check on ticket sales."

***

Anastasia stared into her floor-length mirror and cringed. Though she'd worn the black uniform of the asylum for years without hesitation, the frumpy dress now reminded her of everything she'd lost. It had felt as if she'd been transformed and now she was back to a life she no longer wished to be a part of. She'd thought Logan liked the dress.

Had the expression on his face been a lie? What's it matter what he thinks; you know you'll never marry the man. She switched off the light and pulled the door closed behind her as she started for the theatre room. She got to the base of the stairs, and for the first time since she'd arrived, was not looking forward to playing. *I'll show him. I'm not even going to play tonight. Then we'll see what he thinks of that.*

"Anastasia!" Logan called as she started back up the stairs. "Where are you going? The show's about to start."

"I'm not playing tonight. You don't like me in this dress, and you can't stand to see me in the new ones. If that's the way you feel, you could've just said so. I wouldn't have wasted all that money on the new wardrobe."

"I don't know what you're talking about. You'd look beautiful in a sack."

"Then why tell me to change into this old thing?" she said, grabbing at the faded fabric.

"Because the dress was pink. It would be too distracting." His eyes grew dangerously alluring. "If you'd worn that dress, not one person in the theatre would be watching the show."

Chapter Forty-Three

Tuesday, November 5, 1929

Anastasia finished playing to scattered applause. The lights came up, and she watched as a handful of people trickled from the theatre. She followed the last person out and saw Logan standing by the exit, presenting a frozen smile as he thanked each person for coming. The smile disappeared when the last person exited. He locked the door, saw her watching, and his face turned grim. He hadn't been sleeping, and heavy bags sat under his eyes in dark weighted circles.

"It's bad, isn't it?" she asked when he neared. It had been a week to the day of the stock market crash, and ticket sales had been dwindling.

"Today's sales were dismal. I've already canceled the evening show. People are afraid, and when they're afraid, they don't like to spend money," he said solemnly.

"But the papers said this would be short-lived," she said, trying to alleviate his fears.

"That was the banks trying to avoid a panic. I'm telling you, this is just the beginning. People have only been without pay for a week. Most still have some form of food in their cupboards. You let the food run out and no money to get more, and it's going to get worse. A lot worse." Worry lines tugged at his mouth.

Anastasia thought of her family and how bad things got when Albert began handing over less money. That had been bad enough. What would Sharon have done if he hadn't had any to give her? *There's no need to worry about that now. The family is gone. No, Tobias had made it out okay. But what about Ezra?* She sighed, realizing she might never know the answer to that question.

"There's something I need to discuss with you." His voice was solemn as his eyes begged her to understand. "I can't afford your wages anymore."

"You're firing me?" Though she'd been expecting this, it still came as a shock.

"No, not firing you. I just need to cut your wages. Would you be agreeable to working for half wages? Better still, marry me." Desperation filled his voice.

Though he'd asked many times, she knew this time to be different. It sounded more like a business deal than an actual proposal. "Because if I marry you, you won't have to pay me."

He cocked his head to the side. "Of course not; you'd be my wife."

She laughed. "Nice try."

"What?"

"I've told you, I'm never getting married." What she didn't tell him was she cared for him too much to take that chance. Every time she got too close to someone, they were taken away. "I'll work for half wages until things get better. Five dollars a week is better than nothing."

He brought her hand to his lips. "Are you sure I can't convince you to marry me?"

It touched her that she meant so much to him. "I'm sure."

"Darn. I was hoping to be able to rent your apartment." He laughed when she pulled her hand away. "Can't blame a man for trying."

"Yeah, well, you can't blame a woman for saying no either. I expect to eat dinner at your place tonight," she said.

"You want me to pick you up or should I send a cab?" Logan asked.

Logan's apartment was directly across the hallway from hers. It was a running joke, as she'd fallen in the hall once while still trying to adjust to wearing heels. "I believe I'll walk. I wouldn't want you spending money on a cab. You might decide to cut my wages again."

"First, you reject my proposal, and then you kick me when I'm down. Remind me again why I put up with you," he said, pulling her into his arms.

"I can think of a few things," she said, placing her lips on his.

***

March 1931

Wearing a tattered coat and scuffed shoes, she'd long learned to keep her eyes lowered so she didn't draw attention to herself. It also helped her guilt when she was able to move through the crowd unnoticed. Someone sneezed and she looked in the man's direction. A mistake, as they'd made eye contact.

The man stepped free of the crowd and pressed his face close to hers, stale alcohol leaching from his skin. "Hey, lady, can I borrow a dime?"

She weaved away from the man without answering, keeping the pace until she finally broke free from the crowd. Only then did she allow herself a glance over her shoulder, grimacing at the sight. *The breadlines are getting longer each day.*

She was still looking behind her when she ran smack into someone. "I'm sorry."

She'd no sooner said the words when the man grabbed hold of her arm and began dragging her to the alley. She had her purse on her arm, but it was useless since she couldn't get her arms free. The man pushed her against the building. Her purse slipped from her arm as the wind left her lungs. The man ignored the purse, showing money was not his quest. He took hold of her coat, ripping it open to expose her sequined dress and pearls. Obviously, the man didn't expect to claim such a prize, as his mouth dropped open in stunned surprise. She managed a scream. He released her arm, raised his hand, striking the side of her face. Her cheek stung where he'd hit her, but she'd suffered far worse. Anger seared through her veins. She'd promised herself she'd never fall victim to another man's wrath.

For a moment, it was Albert standing over her, and her rage intensified as she remembered Mrs. Johnston's words. Kicking out with all the strength she could muster, she connected with such force that the man's eyes bulged. He released his grip and fell to his knees, clutching the place she'd just kicked. She plucked her weighted purse from the ground, catching him in the jaw on the upswing. If she were still alive, Mrs. Johnston would be pleased to know she'd remembered the story about the brick.

***

Anastasia sat on the sofa, holding a thin steak to her cheek, when she heard a door shut across the hall. She willed him to keep going and sighed when a knock showed it wasn't to be. "It's open."

Logan opened the door, entered the room, and stopped. He'd seen her bags sitting on the floor and the beef against her cheek and couldn't seem to decide which to address first. "You're leaving?"

Of course he'd begin with that. "I am."

"I assume you're going to run off with the man who did that to your face." His voice was as cold as the beef.

"Hardly," she said on a laugh. They'd had many spats of late over Logan's suspicion of her seeing other men. The accusations started when she'd gotten a job playing piano at a rooftop nightclub on 42nd Street. The secret nightclub offered loose booze and even looser women, both things men couldn't get enough of with Prohibition in full swing.

"Where will you go?" His tone was more civil.

"I've found an apartment on West 43rd Street."

"What's wrong with this apartment?"

Nothing and everything. Keeping with the times, Logan had been forced to begin showing the new talkies on the theatre's screen. No one wanted to see a silent movie when they could pay the same price to watch a film without having to read subtitles. Both silent movies and the piano that accompanied them were considered ancient technology. "Logan, we've had this talk before. I can't keep staying here rent-free. It's not right."

"Then marry me."

"No." Her face hurt, and she didn't feel like arguing a moot point. While she cared for the man, something had changed. She was pretty sure he felt the same way.

"Shall I call someone to help you move your things?"

"I've already made arrangements. The cab company is sending the driver up," she added when his eyebrow arched.

"Will I see you again?"

"You know where I work."

"We had a good run, you know," he said, using the theatre term for when a show goes well.

She smiled. "I like to think so."

There was another knock and Logan opened the door.

The cabbie stuck his head in and nodded towards the

bags. "Want me to take those down for you?"

"Yes, please. I'll only be a moment." She placed the raw steak on a plate and wiped her face with a cloth.

"You'd better take that beef with you. There are men on the streets that would hurt a person for less."

You're not telling me anything I don't already know. Rising from the sofa, Anastasia looked around the room, making sure she hadn't forgotten anything. "Maybe you should leave it in the icebox as an incentive to rent out the room."

"You always did like to argue."

She laid her hand on his cheek. *Why is saying goodbye always so hard?* "Nah, you just never liked the fact I wasn't like all the other dames."

He brushed a tear from her cheek. "Doll, that's what I liked the most about you."

Chapter Forty-Four

"Mom? Are you sure you copied every page?" Cindy said, rifling through the remaining pages.

Linda finished the page she was reading before she answered. "Sure I did. I may be old, but I'm not senile. Not that I'd know it if I was. Come to think of it, I might be. Have we had this conversation before?"

Cindy stared at Linda open-mouthed. "Mom, it wasn't a trick question. It seems like some of the pages are missing."

Linda got up, looked over Cindy's shoulder, and read the first sentence. "She had the baby?"

"Yes, it says she just gave birth to Dad."

"The date's right. What's the problem?"

"Are you serious? I've been waiting all this time to find out about my grandfather, and she's like, okay, so after the baby was born?"

"You mean she doesn't say who the father is?"

Cindy took a breath to calm herself before she answered. "That's what I've been trying to tell you. You must have missed some pages."

Linda shook her head. "No, I'm sure I copied everything."

Cindy sat the pages aside. "Where's the original journal?"

"It's in the box. Hold on; I'll get it." Linda walked to the pile of wooden boxes and found the one with Anastasia's name. She unlocked the box and handed it to Cindy. "It should be the last journal."

Cindy flipped through the pages until she got to the correct page. "Were there any loose pages in the box?"

"Nope. Just what you see here."

"Look here," Cindy said, pulling the pages back to show what she'd discovered. "Someone tore some of the pages out."

"You mean the journals have been censored?"

"Of course they have; you've seen how some of them have been re-written or crossed out to remove foul words."

Linda considered this for a moment. "She did just give birth. Maybe she did a lot of swearing when she had Paul. He did have a big head. I always had to buy him large hats."

Cindy placed a finger between her eyebrows and pressed to alleviate the tension that was building. "Mom, she was not writing the journals while she was giving birth. I'm telling you, someone ripped out an entire section."

"Who'd do something like that?"

"Obviously someone with something to hide."

"Is there anything else missing?"

Cindy stared at Linda.

"What?"

"If there is, I'm sure I wouldn't know."

"Oh, well, I guess we'd better keep reading so we can see if the rest is still there."

Cindy watched as Linda settled back onto the couch and picked up the final stack of papers. While the woman wasn't senile, she thought she might be slipping just a bit. She gathered the papers she'd set aside, starting from the beginning of the page.

***

March 13, 1933

Anastasia held her breath until she heard the baby cry. "Is it okay?"

"Ten fingers. Ten toes. So I think he's about as perfect as a mother could hope for."

A boy. "Bring him to me.*"*

"Just as soon as I get him cleaned up. Babies are slippery when they first come out. I wouldn't want you to drop him."

Anastasia bided her time until the midwife finally placed the squalling infant in her arms. She brought him to her chest, willing herself not to hold him too tight. He rooted for a moment before finding what he'd been searching for.

"You don't have to show that one what to do. He's going to grow big and strong," the midwife said, watching the baby suckle. "He's not the only one that knew what to do. He's not your first, is he?"

"No," Anastasia said, closing her eyes.

The woman took her simple answer to heart and didn't ask any follow-up questions, something Anastasia was grateful for. She wasn't in the mood to answer. She'd thought a great deal of Franky over the past few months, comparing the two pregnancies and struggling with the guilt of not having insisted Franky be brought back to her. No amount of wishing would correct that wrong.

"Have you thought of a name for the child?" the midwife asked, interrupting her thoughts.

"Paul Michael Castiglione," Anastasia replied. "I'll call him Paulie."

"You didn't take any time with that. Is he named after his father?"

"No, I named him that because I like the name. I'm his mother, and I get to choose," Anastasia said, omitting the fact that she hadn't told the father about her pregnancy. It wasn't as if there'd been anything between them. He'd given her something she'd needed at the time. Arms that held her while she cried, an innocent gesture that turned into a single night of passion. It wasn't until a few months later that she realized he'd given her so much more.

***

March 18, 1933

Anastasia knocked on the door of her neighbor, Mrs. Clayton, a round woman with a motherly touch. Anastasia had liked the woman from the moment they'd met. As soon as Anastasia had discovered her pregnancy, she'd asked the woman if she would care for her child after she gave birth. A mother of five, the woman had agreed without hesitation. The woman's husband had objected at first, saying he already had enough mouths to feed. She understood, he being one of the few men in the building with a job. He'd changed his tune when Anastasia assured him she'd pay the woman for her troubles.

Mrs. Clayton opened the door and smiled as Anastasia handed Paulie to her. "You're feeling well enough to go to work, then?"

"I sit at a piano. Besides, if I don't return today, they'll give my job to someone else."

"As if anyone could take your place."

"That would mean more if you'd actually heard me play." Anastasia reached into the blanket and slid a finger along Paulie's cheek. "You'll take good care of him, won't you?"

"I'll look after him as if he were my own son."

"Only until I return home," Anastasia reminded her.

The woman chuckled. "Don't you go worrying about me stealing your son. I've got plenty of my own to tend to."

It was a few blocks to where she worked. As she approached the building, she was grateful the building had an elevator. Though she'd sworn she'd never enter another, she'd relented when she realized she'd have to walk to the top floor nightclub in heels. She braced for the elevator to stop and readied herself for the barrage of questions that would follow. Sure enough, the second the doors opened, the manager made a beeline towards her.

"Anastasia, where've you been? I thought something had happened to you," Jimmy said in excited tones.

"I've been ill. Didn't you get my message?" It was a lie. She hadn't sent one. What was she to say? *I know I hid my pregnancy from you, but now that I had my kid I'm ready to come back to work.* If they'd have found out she was pregnant, she would've been fired on the spot. It didn't matter that the nightclub sold illegal liquor. Pregnant women were not allowed to work. Some rules were not meant to be broken. Hiding the pregnancy wasn't all that difficult. She hadn't gained all that much weight. She'd bound her stomach while at work and wore dresses that didn't cling. It also helped that she sat behind a large baby grand piano.

"That must have been some illness. You look as if you've lost weight."

"Yes, but I'm healthy now. Do you think Marven will let me come back to work?" Marven was the owner of the club and hadn't been happy when she'd refused to do more than play the piano. He was triple her age, had a temper that reminded her too much of Albert, and was not happy that she'd repeatedly spurned his advances.

"Of course he will. The guy's a jerk, but he's smart enough to know a lot of the regulars come here just to hear you play. I'll smooth it over with Marv, don't you worry."

"Thanks, Jimmy. You're the best."

"Good, you tell my wife that. On second thought, don't," he said with a wink. "She might think we've got a thing going on."

***

September, 1933

Anastasia sat in the doctor's office waiting for the results of her X-rays. She'd developed a cough shortly after Paulie was born and couldn't seem to get rid of it. She'd met the doctor in the nightclub where she worked. He'd commented on her cough and told her she should come see him.

The door opened, and the doctor came in, films in hand. He sat and intertwined his fingers. "Anastasia, there is no easy way to say this. You have a growth on your right lung."

Anastasia took out a cigarette and placed it in the slender holder. Her fingers trembled so much, she dropped the match. The doctor retrieved it, striking it against the box for her.

"I wish I had better news," the doctor said, holding the match to the end.

Instantly, she thought of Paulie. "What can you do for it, Doc?"

He shook his head and struck another match to light a cigarette of his own. "There's nothing that can be done."

"No, that's not good enough," she said, exhaling the smoke. "My son needs me."

He sat back in his chair. "There have been some surgeries of late, but they're quite invasive. It would mean cutting through your chest and removing part of your lung. You think the scar on you cheek is bad, I assure you, this one would be much worse. "

Worse than dying? "These surgeries, do they work?"

"It's still early, but the ones that have been done thus far are deemed successful."

"Then I want it done."

"Hold on, missy. I don't even know if I can find a surgeon who'll agree to do it."

"You'll find one, or I'll tell your wife you're refusing because you're the father of my child."

"Excuse me," he said, choking on the smoke. "Why, she'd never believe you!"

"Wouldn't she? I can find witnesses that will back my story."

"But it's not true."

Anastasia pulled on her cigarette and blew the smoke out slowly. "I know that, and you know that, but I've never told anyone the true identity of my child's father. It makes sense that I'm keeping things secret, so I don't tarnish your good reputation."

"You'd blackmail me when I was only trying to help you?"

"Doc, I'd do just about anything to have my son grow up knowing his mother."

***

December 6, 1933

Anastasia struggled to get up, fighting against the pain.

"You shouldn't be up," the nurse said, coming into the room. She eased Anastasia back onto the pillow.

"Did they get it all?"

"The doctor will be in shortly to speak with you."

Anastasia closed her eyes. "That doesn't sound promising."

"It's standard procedure," the nurse assured her.

"Miss. Castiglione?"

Anastasia opened her eyes to see the surgeon standing over her. It took her a moment to focus enough to speak. "Yes."

"How are you feeling?"

"You tell me."

He pulled a chair to the side of the bed, his face full of concern. For a moment, he looked older than his years. "When we got inside, your lung was in worse shape than we thought. We ended up removing the entire lung."

That can't be good.

"It's not the optimal circumstance, but you are cancer-free. For now," he said, emphasizing the latter part of his statement.

"So you're saying it could come back in the other lung?" He'd already told her the risks, but she wanted to hear them again.

"It could. Or you could get pneumonia. Either way, it would likely be a death sentence.

"I appreciate your honesty."

"I wouldn't want my wife to be the recipient of any unscrupulous phone calls now, would I?"

She laughed then clutched her chest to ease the pain. "Doc told you about that, did he?"

"He did."

"And yet you agreed to perform the surgery."

"It's not often the hospital gets a patient who volunteers to undergo a radical new surgery by a newly licensed surgeon." His smiled and the childish face she remembered returned.

"Is that why you took the entire lung?"

"No, I assure you that was the only way to be sure."

"At least for now," she reminded him.

"At least for now," he agreed.

"Anastasia?"

Anastasia opened her eyes, surprised to see Doc standing over her. "How'd you get in here?"

He plucked at his jacket. "I've got a white coat. They

see me walking through the halls and presume me to be a doctor."

"I'm surprised you didn't smother me in my sleep. It would be easy. I've only got one lung."

"You're alive, that's the important thing."

"You're a lot nicer than I'd be under the same circumstances," she said, wincing at the pain.

"I was upset. Then I went home, saw my daughters, and realized if I were in your shoes, I too would do just about anything to be with them. Speaking of which, do you have any plans when you get out?"

"Plans?"

"I'm afraid Marven isn't as understanding as I am."

"You told him?"

"Not on purpose. I assumed you had told. It really doesn't matter; they repealed Prohibition last night. Speakeasies will soon be a thing of the past. What do you know about the almshouse upstate?" he asked, changing the subject.

"Only that they've been visiting of late and seem pretty adamant they're going to take my son away."

"Yes, well, what if I offer you a different solution?"

"I'm listening."

"My brother-in-law has connections. I've told him about your situation, and he wants to offer you a job."

"Go on."

"He's agreed to hire you on at the almshouse and give you and your son your own room. You'll work at whatever job you both decide and he'll pay you a wage. You can stay there as long as you like. Call it a safety net. Your child will not end up on the streets if…"

She nodded her understanding. "What happens to my son if I die?"

"If he has any relatives, he could go to them. If not, he

would more than likely go into an asylum. We do not even know if this will come back. You have time to think about that and make the necessary arrangements. Don't worry about things you cannot control. You've got a second chance to go and spend time with your son. Isn't that enough?"

She'd been writing to Tobias for months, and his return letters seemed amenable. She knew if things took a turn for the worse, she'd be able to reach out to him and ask him to care for her son. She nodded her agreement. "It's enough for now."

"For now," he repeated.

***

"I sure hope Paul knew how much his mother loved him," Linda said closing her journal.

"So do I." Cindy agreed. "Did you notice the date?"

Linda thumbed back through the pages. "December 6, 1933, the day after they repealed prohibition."

"Do you remember what else happened that day?"

"Pearl Harbor?"

Cindy sighed. "Pearl Harbor was December 7, 1941. Mom, that was the same day Tobias died."

"Holy smoke, you're right. Anastasia must have found out that Franky was with Howard and Mildred. That's why she decided to contact them to adopt Paul."

"That's what I'm thinking," Cindy said, nodding her agreement. She stood and placed her journal on the previously read pile. "At least Anastasia seems to have found some happiness."

"She sure deserved it."

"I need to run an errand. It won't take long; want to come?"

"No, I think I'll stay here and tidy up a bit."

"Okay, want me to bring back something to eat, or do you want to cook?"

"How about a kid's meal from DQ?"

Cindy smiled. "Since when does a kid's meal fill you up?"

A sly smile crossed over Linda's face. "When you trade in the kiddy cone for a large Oreo Blizzard."

***

Cindy sat in the rocker, watching Frank sleep. She'd hoped that by some miracle she would arrive and find him lucid and ready to answer all her questions. She had so much she wanted to know, but mostly, she wanted to know if he'd ever taken the time to read his mother's journals. Surely if he had, he would've known how much the woman agonized over losing him.

Sitting there watching him sleep, she pictured the baby tied to the chair, smiling as his mother entered the room. *Could he have known who she was? Probably not.* He probably only wanted her for her breasts. *Just like a man.* She laughed out loud, and his eyes fluttered open. He blinked several times before bringing her into focus.

"Hello, Franky," she said, using the name he'd used when young.

For the briefest moment, she thought he was going to answer back.

"I came by to give you a message from your mother. She wants you to know that she loves you and is proud of the man you became."

This time, her words evoked a smile. A moment later, he'd fallen back to sleep. Brief as the smile was, it warmed her heart, and for a moment, she thought that must be what it felt like to be a mother.

***

"Ha! The apple doesn't fall far from the tree," Linda said when she returned with two kids' meals and two large Blizzards.

"Mom, I decided there's enough sadness in the world, and if I have the chance to smile, I'm going to do what makes me happy."

Linda lowered her spoon and tapped the cup against Cindy's. "Atta girl, Cindy, you sure know how to make a mother proud."

Cindy looked towards the stack of wooden boxes. "So who's next in line?"

"Franky."

Cindy thought of the shell of a man she'd just left. "Hopefully, his journals will be able to answer some questions."

"Agreed. I'm itching to know if he ever learned Anastasia was his mother. If he did, maybe he'll tell us what happened to her. What's with the frown?"

"It's just the more we read, the more we don't know. How many conversations have you had with Uncle Frank over the years?""

Linda laughed. "Too many to count."

"Exactly, and not once was any of this mentioned. I just don't understand what the big secret was. It's like they were all hiding something that they all knew. I just don't know who they were hiding it from."

Linda got up, walked to the other side of the room, and retrieved two large stacks of journals. "We can sit here debating this all day or we can start reading; which will it be?"

Cindy held out her hands and waited as Linda filled

them. As she pulled the papers close, it occurred to her they represented nearly a hundred years of memories. Memories the man who'd lived them no longer remembered. She slid a glance at her mother and wondered how many memories she'd forgotten over the years. If the revelations over the course of reading the journals were any indication, there was plenty of history soon to be lost and no one left to fill in the gaps. The realization hit her hard. Uncle Frank was already gone; his body had just failed to get the memo. And, as hard as it was to admit, her mother would not always be there. *When she passes, I'll be all alone.*

Maybe I should start a journal. And who's going to read them?

"You keep frowning like that and you're going to have more wrinkles than I do."

"I was just thinking that maybe we should start journaling."

"You mean writing stuff down and leaving out the important parts to keep people guessing?"

Cindy shook her head. "No, let's start a new tradition and write down everything we can recall."

Linda's eyes took on a faraway look. "That could be fun."

"Mom, I think it would be best to leave out the juicy parts."

Linda sighed. "I thought you said no secrets."

"It's no secret you and Dad loved each other. Since we don't know who'll be reading the journals, it is probably best to skim the specific details of that love."

"You're probably right. I wouldn't want my future grandchild to read about such things."

"No, we wouldn't," Cindy agreed.

Linda's eyes grew wide. "This is the part where you

normally tell me you're never going to have children."

"Never is a long time, Mom," Cindy said, meeting her stare.

A Brief Note from the Author

In *Treachery*, I introduce two placing agents: Anna Laura Hill (the woman Anastasia meets in the market), and Mr. Swan, who rode with Anastasia and visited the farm after her placement. While the encounters in this book are fictional, both Miss Hill and Mr. and Mrs. Swan were in fact placing agents employed by The Children's Aid Society.

Over seventy placing agents, both men and women, were involved with, and employed by, the Children's Aid Society during the seventy-five-year run of the orphan trains. Those agents arranged the placing out meetings and traveled with the children to their destination. The agents took great pride in their work, picked the committees, and many remained in touch with the children far into adulthood.

A special thanks to:

My editor, Beth, for allowing me to keep my voice.
My, my cover artist and media design guru, Laura Prevost, thanks for keeping me current.
My daughter-assistant, Brandy for helping with all the extras.
To my amazing team of beta readers, thank you for helping take a final look.

Reviews are greatly appreciated. The more reviews the book receives, the more Amazon will show the book to others. You may leave your review on Amazon, Barnes & Noble, Goodreads, and Bookbub. If you wish to leave a review on Amazon and did not purchase the book(s) through Amazon, please begin the review staying how you found the book. (i.e. at a private signing, borrowed from a friend, library etc.)

Keep up to date with all my new releases by following me on:
Facebook page:
https://www.facebook.com/SherryABurtonauthor
Bookbub: https://www.bookbub.com/profile/sherry-a-burton
Instagram: https://www.instagram.com/authorsherryaburton

About the Author

Born in Kentucky, Sherry married a Navy man at the age of eighteen. She and her now-retired Navy husband have three children and nine grandchildren.

After moving around the country and living in nine different states, Sherry and her husband now live in Michigan's thumb, with their three rescue cats and a standard poodle named Murdoc.

Sherry writes full time and is currently hard at work on the next novel in her Orphan Train Saga, an eighteen-book historical fiction series that revolves around the orphan trains.

When Sherry is not writing, she enjoys traveling to lectures and signing events, where she shares her books and speaks about the history of the Orphan Trains.

Made in the USA
Middletown, DE
22 December 2023

46708724R00225